D0196711

DEMO...

"An excellent entry in a great series . . . Another winner as the multifaceted Guardian saga continues to expand in complexity while remaining entertaining . . . Complex and beautifully done as always."   —*Book Binge*

"Be prepared for more surprises and more revelations . . . Brook continues to deliver surprising characters, relationships, paranormal elements, and plot twists—the only thing that won't surprise you is your *total* inability to put this book down."
—*Alpha Heroes*

"Readers will be blown away by the fascinating and unique heroine."   —*Romantic Times*

"Raises the bar on paranormal romance for sheer thrills, drama, and world-building, and hands-down cements Brook's place at the top of her field."   —*Romance Junkies*

DEMON NIGHT

"Meljean is now officially one of my favorite authors. And this book's hero? . . . I just went weak at the knees. And the love scenes—wow, just wow."
—Nalini Singh, *New York Times* bestselling author of *Slave to Sensation* and *Visions of Heat*

"This is the book for paranormal lovers. It is a phenomenal book by an author who knows how to give her readers exactly what they want. What Brook's readers want is a story that is dangerous, sexy, scary, and smart. *Demon Night* delivers all that and more! . . . [It] is the epitome of what a paranormal romance should be! I didn't want to put it down."   —*Romance Reader at Heart*

continued . . .

"Poignant and compelling with lots of action, and it's very sensual. You'll fall in love with Charlie, and Ethan will cause your thermometer to blow its top. An excellent plot, wonderful dialogue . . . Don't miss reading it or any of Meljean Brook's other novels in this series." —*Fresh Fiction*

"An intense romance that will leave you breathless . . . I was drawn in from the first page." —*Romance Junkies*

DEMON MOON

"The fourth book in Meljean Brook's Guardian series turns up the heat without losing any of the danger." —*Entertainment Weekly*

"A read that goes down hot and sweet—utterly unique—and one hell of a ride."—*New York Times* bestselling author Marjorie M. Liu

"Sensual and intriguing, *Demon Moon* is a simply wonderful book. I was enthralled from the first page!" —Nalini Singh

"Action-packed, with a fascinating, one-of-a-kind vampire hero and a heroine with some very unique qualities."

—*Romantic Times*

"Brings a unique freshness to the romantic fantasy realm . . . Action-packed from the onset." —*Midwest Book Review*

"I loved every moment of it." —*All About Romance*

"Fantastically drawn characters . . . and their passion for each other is palpable in each scene they share. It stews beneath the surface, and when it finally reaches a boiling point, . . . OH WOW!" —*Vampire Romance Books*

DEMON ANGEL

"I've never read anything like this book. *Demon Angel* is brilliant, heartbreaking, genre-bending—even, I dare say, epic. Simply put, I love it." —Marjorie M. Liu

"Brook has crafted a complex, interesting world that goes far beyond your usual . . . paranormal romance. *Demon Angel* truly soars." —Jennifer Estep, author of *Jinx*

"I can honestly say I haven't read many books lately that have kept me guessing and wondering 'what's next,' but this is one of them. [Brook has] created a unique and different world . . . Gritty and realistic . . . Incredibly inventive . . . This is a book which makes me think and think about it even days after finishing it."   —*Dear Author*

"Enthralling . . . [A] delightful saga."   —*The Best Reviews*

"Extremely engaging . . . A fiendishly good book. *Demon Angel* is outstanding."   —*The Romance Reader*

"A surefire winner. This book will captivate you and leave you yearning for more. Don't miss *Demon Angel*."
                                                                —*Romance Reviews Today*

"A fascinating romantic fantasy with . . . a delightful pairing of star-crossed lovers."   —*Midwest Book Review*

"Complex and compelling . . . A fabulous story."
                                                                —*Joyfully Reviewed*

FURTHER PRAISE FOR MELJEAN BROOK
AND FOR "FALLING FOR ANTHONY"
FROM *HOT SPELL*

"An emotional roller coaster for both the characters and the reader. Brook has penned a story I am sure readers won't soon forget . . . Extraordinary work."   —*Romance Junkies*

"In-depth and intriguing. I loved the obvious thought and ideas put into writing this tale. The characters are deep, as is the world that is set up."   —*The Romance Readers Connection*

"Brook . . . creates fantastic death-defying love . . . Extremely erotic . . . With a paranormal twist."   —*Fresh Fiction*

"Intriguing . . . The sex is piping hot."   —*Romance Reviews Today*

"I look forward to many more tales from Ms. Brook."
                                                                —*Joyfully Reviewed*

DEMON FORGED

meljean Brook

BERKLEY SENSATION, NEW YORK

THE BERKLEY PUBLISHING GROUP
Published by the Penguin Group
Penguin Group (USA) Inc.
375 Hudson Street, New York, New York 10014, USA
Penguin Group (Canada), 90 Eglinton Avenue East, Suite 700, Toronto, Ontario M4P 2Y3, Canada
(a division of Pearson Penguin Canada Inc.)
Penguin Books Ltd., 80 Strand, London WC2R 0RL, England
Penguin Group Ireland, 25 St. Stephen's Green, Dublin 2, Ireland (a division of Penguin Books Ltd.)
Penguin Group (Australia), 250 Camberwell Road, Camberwell, Victoria 3124, Australia
(a division of Pearson Australia Group Pty. Ltd.)
Penguin Books India Pvt. Ltd., 11 Community Centre, Panchsheel Park, New Delhi—110 017, India
Penguin Group (NZ), 67 Apollo Drive, Rosedale, North Shore 0632, New Zealand
(a division of Pearson New Zealand Ltd.)
Penguin Books (South Africa) (Pty.) Ltd., 24 Sturdee Avenue, Rosebank, Johannesburg 2196,
South Africa

Penguin Books Ltd., Registered Offices: 80 Strand, London WC2R 0RL, England

This is a work of fiction. Names, characters, places, and incidents either are the product of the author's imagination or are used fictitiously, and any resemblance to actual persons, living or dead, business establishments, events, or locales is entirely coincidental. The publisher does not have any control over and does not assume any responsibility for author or third-party websites or their content.

DEMON FORGED

A Berkley Sensation Book / published by arrangement with the author

PRINTING HISTORY
Berkley Sensation mass-market edition / October 2009

Copyright © 2009 by Melissa Khan.
Cover art by Cliff Nielsen.
Cover design by George Long.
Interior text design by Laura K. Corless.

ISBN: 978-0-425-23041-1

BERKLEY® SENSATION
Berkley Sensation Books are published by The Berkley Publishing Group,
a division of Penguin Group (USA) Inc.,
375 Hudson Street, New York, New York 10014.
BERKLEY® SENSATION and the "B" design are trademarks of Penguin Group (USA) Inc.

PRINTED IN THE UNITED STATES OF AMERICA

10 9 8 7 6 5 4 3 2 1

ACKNOWLEDGMENTS

Writing is solitary work, but a book can't be produced alone. Thank you to my editor, Cindy Hwang, who is patient and brilliant, and I thank God every day that she's mine. To her assistant, Leis Pederson, who gets me everything I need. To the art department at Berkley, and the cover artist, Cliff Nielsen, who blew my socks off with this spectacular design, and an image that is everything I write my heroines to be: strong, strong, strong . . . and sexy. And to everyone else at Berkley whose work has touched the books in this series—I can't thank you enough.

Also, my undying gratitude goes to Nathalie Nguyen, who helped me out with the French that my Spanish classes in high school and college never covered. To Michelle Dominguez, who checked my Italian. Everything correct is theirs, every error is, of course, mine. To Ilona Andrews, Jill Myles, Jennifer Lampe, Holly Mercer, and Kate Garrabrant, who always manage to send me e-mails at exactly the right time, whether they know it or not. And to all of the readers who stop by my blog, drive to a signing, or send me e-mails and cookies to share with my daughter, and whose lives touch my strange little one—thank you.

To the city of San Francisco: I'm sorry. I couldn't pick up City Hall and move it, so I took liberties.

Excerpts from an unprepared speech by Rep. Thomas Stafford, delivered during a closed-door meeting in Washington, D.C., to five members of the Senate, the Secretary of Defense, and the Secretary of Homeland Security, May 2009:

Two years ago, the senators and I met in this room to discuss the formation of Special Investigations, which now operates under the Homeland Security umbrella. Madam Secretary, Mr. Secretary, in that meeting, your counterparts in the former administration heard the story of the First Battle, during which rebel angels, led by Lucifer, were defeated and transformed into demons. These demons were tossed into Hell, but were able to travel to Earth through the Gates until the events two years ago that brought the Guardians to the attention of your government.

In addition to the demons, nosferatu—angels who refused to take a side in the First Battle, and who were cursed with bloodlust—were banished here to Earth. Although the nosferatu have been hunted almost to extinction, those who come out of hiding still pose a terrible danger to humans.

Initially, warrior angels loyal to Heaven protected humans from both demons and nosferatu. When humans began worshipping them as gods, however, Lucifer became jealous. He summoned a dragon from the Chaos realm, and used it to wage another war upon the angels—but this battle took place on Earth, instead of Heaven.

Mankind joined the side of the angels, and one man, Michael, struck down the dragon by severing its heart. With Lucifer's most dangerous weapon slain, the angels prevailed.

After the Second Battle, the angels bestowed upon Michael the powers of a Guardian, and gave to him the power to change any other men or women who sacrificed themselves to save another with the same power. The Guardians' only duty is to protect human free will and life from the threat of the nosferatu and demons. . . .

In the past two years, however, new threats have arisen. The nephilim, created by an alliance between Lucifer and one of the grigori—a half-demon, half-human offspring born before the Second Battle—now intend to take the throne in Hell, and suppress human free will. That grigori, Anaria, was imprisoned by the Guardians more than two thousand years ago; she has recently escaped, and now leads the nephilim. . . .

Despite our recent losses, the Guardian corps is strong, and Special Investigations remains committed to protecting mankind against those who threaten human lives and free will. Defending human life and liberty is our purpose, our duty. We will persevere with or without your support, with the utmost faith and confidence that we will prevail against our enemies. I trust, however, that we have your support and that recent events have clearly demonstrated the necessity of our continued operation.

We are all that stands between you and Hell, gentlemen.

CHAPTER I

Three months earlier . . .

Once upon a time, all roads had led to Rome. As a human girl, Irena had been marched into Rome on the Via Salaria, as frightened by the imposing city walls as she had been of the shackles binding her mother's wrists. Frightened—and forbidden the comfort of remembering the home that had lain at the beginning of their journey. They hadn't been allowed to look back; all that lay ahead of a conquered people was service to the Empire.

Twelve years later, the Visigoths had sacked the city, and Irena had escaped by the same road. She'd looked back then, but only because she'd hoped to see Rome burning behind her.

It hadn't. To Irena's bitter disappointment, the barbarians had shown restraint. Although fires had lit the nighttime sky, the city hadn't been consumed by flames.

Time consumed it, instead. Over sixteen hundred years, all that Irena had known of Rome slowly crumbled. In another sixteen centuries, the celebrated remnants of the empire might collapse into nothing. Humans labored to preserve and restore the ruins, but Irena wouldn't be sorry when they were gone. She preferred what had risen in their place.

Now, as she jogged across the Via Salaria, she relished the feel of smooth concrete beneath her leather soles rather than paving stones under bare feet. Automobiles with their blinding headlights and blaring horns swerved to avoid her. One driver shouted obscenities, and Irena grinned at him through the windshield. One of the few things she'd liked about Rome had survived—and Italians were still inventive.

Irena suspected she'd soon be coming up with a few curses of her own.

The vampire she was scheduled to meet at the nearby Piazza Fiume shouldn't have been here. Not in Rome. Less than a year ago, the nephilim had slaughtered every vampire within the city. The demons might still be here, hidden within the bodies of their human hosts and shielding their psychic scents.

The nephilim still might be here . . . but they weren't just demons, Irena reminded herself, and her amusement leached from her thoughts, leaving them sour and dark. The nephilim had come from Hell, but they hadn't been created when Lucifer and his angel comrades had rebelled against Heaven and been transformed into demons. No, the nephilim were the offspring of Anaria and Zakril, two demon-spawned grigori who'd once called themselves Guardians.

There were *still* other grigori who called themselves Guardians. Until a few weeks ago, Irena would have fought to the death for one of them: Michael—the first Guardian, and their leader.

She would not die for him now.

Michael hadn't explained why he'd lied about his parentage for millennia, or why he'd written in the Scrolls that he'd been human before slaying the Chaos dragon. Not that an explanation was necessary. As the son of Belial and a human woman, Michael was half demon—and lies were as natural to demons as their scales and horns.

Since she'd learned the truth, Irena couldn't make herself

trust or believe in him. Not while Belial's blood ran through his veins.

But although she'd lost faith in the Doyen, she was still a Guardian. Still believed that every demon and nosferatu needed killing, that humans—and some vampires—needed protecting. And she would have met with Deacon even if the vampire hadn't been a friend.

A friend, but not close enough to know what this part of Rome had meant to her. She'd never told Deacon that she remembered the walls when they hadn't been ruins, and the gate that had opened Rome to the Via Salaria. This meeting and location had nothing to do with her past. And she could have avoided this road and the memories associated with it by flying directly to the piazza, but she'd wanted to be reminded of the changes in the city. She wanted the stink of exhaust burning her nostrils, rather than the stink of bodies, animals, and waste.

And she'd wanted to see the metal. So much metal.

Yes, she liked what had risen—and *who* had risen. Whether they lived here or were tourists fascinated by the past, humans experienced the same emotions they always had, but they governed those emotions differently. There were still too few with too much power, but despite the corruption at its foundation, the civilization that humanity had built was impressive.

Impressive, but not perfect. There were always exceptions, large and small.

On the sidewalk ahead of her, beside the entrance to a wine bar, a small exception slouched at a wrought iron table. His jacket and shirt were unbuttoned despite the crisp autumn evening, and a medallion winked from a bed of dark hair. Empty wine bottles stood next to an overflowing ashtray.

His bleary eyes sharpened as they fixed on Irena. *"Mi sento come un buon pompino. Quanto, puttana?"*

How much? She studied his face as she drew nearer, and dug into his emotions—arrogance, overblown machismo, a need to humiliate, a sharp loneliness—but she was unable to summon either pity or disgust.

And she felt no surprise at his suggestion. No matter the century, there were always men like this. Men who would see the brief top she wore, the cling of the soft suede from her hips to her upper thighs beneath the belt and straps of her leather stockings, the face that had aroused a Roman senator before she'd reached her ninth summer and assume rights they didn't have.

At least this one offered to pay—and she'd known too many whores to be insulted when mistaken for one. She dismissed him, and her gaze moved on. Ahead, a fenced monument marked the Piazza Fiume.

The human's derisive command returned her attention to him.

"Venite a succhiare il mio cazzo." He cupped his crotch, jiggling his hand as if Irena were a horse and his balls a bag of oats. His mouth slid into a leer. *"E si inghiottire troppo."*

At that, Irena smiled. She would swallow—but only if she bit off a chunk first.

She didn't need to tell him so; her expression served as a reply. He dropped his gaze to his table.

Cowed, but not quieted. Even if she hadn't heard the word he muttered as she reached him, its shape was unmistakable on his lips. *"Stronza."*

Bitch.

Irena's breath hissed from between her teeth in a thin stream. This one, he did not know when to quit. She halted in front of him and bent over to grip the arms of his chair. Her smile was still vicious, but he didn't glance at her face. Unease slithered through his psychic scent as he took in the winding blue serpents tattooed from her wrists to her shoulders.

"You are a handsome man," she told him, and didn't attempt to suppress the accent that chopped at her Italian, "but you use your tongue in the wrong way." Irena crooked her index finger beneath his necklace. Gold. Such a worthless metal. Far too soft, even when blended with stronger materials. Irena favored steel, iron, or platinum. She tugged lightly on the chain. "Stand, and I will show you what your mouth is good for."

Like a dog, he obeyed. Her fingers drifted down over his chest as he rose from his seat, and she shape-shifted subtly, increasing her height so that his tobacco-scented breath gusted heavily over her lips. His breathing stopped when she reached the waistband of his tight jeans, and she paused to test his emotions. Fear trembled in him, but also lust.

And this one had no resistance to lust. Even as his flesh hardened beneath her hand, his arousal left him as malleable as gold. Left him easily manipulated. Demons loved humans such as these.

Irena did not. She dragged her fingertip up his brass zipper, and her Gift melded the teeth together.

The human wouldn't sense the psychic touch. If Deacon had already reached their meeting spot, however, he would know she was near.

And if she'd revealed herself to any other creatures who might be in Rome, she looked forward to meeting them. Killing them.

Excitement fermented within her, and she imagined rending a demon's crimson skin when she placed her mouth to the male's. The flesh behind his zipper swelled as her tongue slid over his, pulling, sucking.

He reached for her chest and she stepped back. He panted, his eyes glazed.

She wiped his taste from her lips with the back of her hand, leaving a sneer. "Not good for much, after all."

His face reddened. Rage choked him; she'd turned away and walked half a block before he managed to roar *"Stronza!"* after her.

She continued on. The insult did not anger her so much now that a plea lay beneath it. A small-minded man, frustrated by such a small thing.

He would know true frustration as soon as he sought release for his bladder or his arousal.

Her good mood was restored and her steps were lively as they carried her to the piazza. The evening was cold and clear; on the tundra, this was the kind of night when only the sharp, freezing air separated the earth from the heavens. A night for hunting. All that this moment lacked was the use of her blades. But if a nephilim or demon had felt her Gift, perhaps bloodshed wasn't far off. She couldn't detect any nearby, but they could block their minds and hide from her psychic probes.

She had expected to find Deacon—a vampire's mind wasn't as powerful as a Guardian's, and his shields weaker—but she didn't sense him, either. Only humans.

She rounded the stone blocks at the corner of the monument, her gaze sweeping the piazza. It froze near the monument entrance. A tall male stood in front of the iron gate. His dark eyes met hers.

Olek. Her step didn't falter. She didn't betray her surprise with movement or breath, but her heart became a sledgehammer against her ribs. Did it pound with anger, shame, or need?

It did not matter. With Olek, they were all the same.

He was Alejandro to every other Guardian, but always Olek to her. Try as she might—and she *had* tried—she couldn't think of him as anything else.

Olek, the silk-tongued swordsman whose idea of honor was to die for nothing.

Like Irena, he dressed not in modern clothing, but clothing comfortable to him. A black long-sleeved shirt hugged his torso, loose enough to allow movement but leaving little for an enemy to grab. His fitted trousers were tucked into knee-high boots. She knew their soles were as soft as hers—and as sure-footed. Both she and Alejandro would sacrifice a hardened boot and the damage a heel could inflict in order to feel every aspect of the ground beneath their feet.

Old-fashioned garb, but it hardly drew a second glance from the humans milling near the monument with cameras in hand. There had been centuries when Guardians had been careful to blend; these days, almost anything was acceptable, if unconventional. For all Irena knew, her leather leggings and the ragged cut of her auburn hair might have even been fashionable.

Alejandro's haircut was severe. Gone were the overlong, thick curls that he'd worn when she'd met him. Now his dark hair was short, with edges as sharp as his face. It was not a style that invited a touch.

And she hated her desire to comb her fingers through it. She refused to clench her fists against the urge.

Alejandro was as controlled as she was. He held his lean body still and his mouth in a firm, immobile line.

Her gaze rested on the sharp point of his beard. She had seen his facial hair diminish over time, according to human custom, until it was short and tight. The beard no longer extended past his chin; the mustache curved just past the corners of his wide mouth. A devil goatee, her young friend Charlie had once called it.

The description was more accurate than Charlie knew.

Irena pushed away the memory of a silken brush against her inner thigh, of heated lips. Pushed away the anger, shame, need.

"Alejandro," she said deliberately.

Dark and unwavering, his gaze lifted from her mouth. He spoke in French, lightly accented with Spanish. "You tread near a line that cannot be uncrossed, Irena."

With the human whose zipper she'd ruined. Any Guardian who broke the Rules by killing a human or denying his free will had to Fall or Ascend. But kissing a man without his consent didn't interfere with his free will—only kissing one who resisted did.

"Did he refuse my touch? Attempt to escape?" With his Guardian senses, Alejandro would have heard everything that had transpired between her and the male.

Alejandro didn't reply, with words or a change of expression.

"Obviously he did not," she continued with a shrug as light as the French on her tongue. There was no reason to feel defensive. Yet she did, and she resented it. She wanted to strike him for it. She turned and examined the piazza again. "Has Deacon already come and gone?"

"No."

Irena frowned. Deacon hadn't known how to contact her; she hadn't met with him since she'd begun using the satellite phone that allowed other Guardians to reach her no matter where she traveled. But the American law enforcement agency, Special Investigations, had made itself known to vampire communities worldwide, offering them the Guardians' protection against the nephilim, demons, and nosferatu. Deacon had called SI and asked for Irena specifically. The text message had come through her phone—sent by Lilith, the hellspawn who headed the agency . . . and who often directed Alejandro, as well.

And if Alejandro had come, he must have thought *she* wouldn't.

"I would never shirk my duty," Irena said.

"You shirked it when you didn't respond."

He left the rest unspoken: that, because this was Rome, whatever Deacon had to tell them might be critical in the Guardians' fight against the nephilim. SI couldn't assume she'd received Deacon's request. They had to be certain.

She met his gaze again. "I don't answer to hellspawn. Send the message yourself, or have another Guardian or vampire do so. Then I'll respond."

Alejandro's dark eyes glinted with emotion before he concealed it. Did she anger him? She wanted to, but wasn't sure if she had. Reading his face was impossible. His only reply was a short nod.

"Have you sensed Deacon?" she asked.

"No."

"Any other vampires?"

"None."

The flash of a tourist's camera whitened the right side of Alejandro's face. Even in shadow Irena could clearly see his features, but the burst of light made her realize how her gaze had been tracing the angular lines of his cheekbones, his jaw.

She looked away, scanning the square. Their reflection in a passing vehicle window revealed that Alejandro still watched her.

Always, he watched her. She didn't know what he searched for.

Even pinched by the French, Alejandro's voice tugged over her nerves like fine kid gloves, tight and supple. "You will recognize this vampire?"

"Yes."

"You know him well?"

"Well enough," she answered simply, though Alejandro would want more than that. After a moment of silence, she gave it to him. "Forty years ago, I tracked a rogue vampire near

Prague. He'd already murdered several humans. I caught him and returned him to his community."

"You didn't slay the rogue yourself?"

She'd wanted to see what sort of community it was. "I let them decide the proper punishment. Deacon leads them, and he carried it out." Once Deacon learned of the murders, he hadn't hesitated to execute the rogue. It was one of the reasons Irena liked the vampire so well. "I return now and again to see that all is well with him."

And the last time she'd visited, all *had* been well. Why, then, had Deacon come to Rome? Had he brought the entire community?

She couldn't believe he'd be so foolish.

The nephilim, led by the demon-spawn Anaria—one of the grigori and Michael's sister—intended to overthrow Lucifer's throne in Hell and enslave human free will in the name of Good. And, because of a prophecy that predicted the nephilim's destruction by vampire blood, the nephilim had been killing vampires, one city at a time. Just because the nephilim had already slaughtered the vampires in Rome didn't mean the city was safe for others to move in.

Not remotely safe. And Irena was beginning to worry now.

Relief replaced her concern when a man with a farrier's shoulders came out of a hotel several blocks down the road. "There he is," she told Alejandro. "Black hair, dark gray suit."

A wrinkled suit, as if he'd spent his daysleep in it. His white shirt was untucked and half unbuttoned. Peach lipstick stained the collar. Deacon pushed his fingers through his shoulder-length hair, tying it into a queue as he walked.

"Are those your swords that he wears?" Alejandro asked quietly.

"Yes." Vampires had no mental cache to store their weapons, so Irena had designed Deacon's short swords to be concealed beneath his clothing, yet still easily accessible. Deacon carried the swords in sheaths that crossed between his shoulder blades; he only had to reach behind his waist for the handles. When he lifted his arms, as he was doing now, the grips disturbed the line of his jacket over his hips.

His hair and clothing were rumpled—who had he been with? The vampire was upwind. Irena tested the air, and caught the odor of alcohol, sex, and blood mixed with Deacon's individual scent.

Human blood.

He'd fed from a *human* woman? Irena did not like this. She had not expected this. What had forced him to use a human?

Vampires were slaves of a different sort: to bloodlust. The accidental offshoot of the nosferatu, their existence was the result of an attempt—a failed attempt—to honor a proud and strong girl. Though nosferatu and vampires both burned in the sun, the similarities ended there. Vampires, though stronger than humans, were much weaker than nosferatu. And although nosferatu suffered from bloodlust, they didn't need to feed to survive; vampires had to regularly consume living blood. Drinking it from humans threatened exposure, however, and so vampire communities required their members to find a vampire partner—or partners—to feed them.

Where were Deacon's partners? He wouldn't have left them behind. Eva and Petra didn't just share blood with him; the two vampires were his friends and lovers, as well.

Yet they must not be with him if he'd used alcohol. Vampires weren't affected by the drink. But after a human drank enough, she'd probably forget that a vampire had fed from her. Even if she did remember, a few drops of vampire blood would heal the bite and erase evidence of it.

From behind her, Alejandro said, "I trust that, despite the drink, she was willing."

Irena clenched her teeth. Though Alejandro employed polite words and phrases, he was lying; he didn't trust it.

She slid her right hand behind her back, and used the Guardian's sign language to reply. *Of course she was willing. Deacon knows the Rules.*

Although vampires weren't bound to follow the Rules as Guardians and demons were, Irena had made it clear to Deacon that if he didn't, she would slay him. Feeding wasn't the same as hurting or killing humans, however. Guardians would tolerate his drinking from human women if he had no other option.

On silent feet, Alejandro came to stand beside her. *Willing to invite him into her bed* and *to take her blood?*

Irena gave him a disbelieving look. When a woman invited a man into her body, what did it matter if, in addition to her mouth and her sex, he also tasted her blood? "You split too many hairs, Olek."

"You clump them all together."

And that, Irena thought, was the difference between them: details. She refused to focus on them.

There was a saying in English that the devil lay in the details—the little flaws brought down the whole. And that was exactly how the demons worked: focusing on the details, boring at tiny weaknesses until the entire structure was so brittle it collapsed. They talked in dizzying circles until nothing was left of meaning, and only their purpose remained. They smoothed everything with slick words, until nothing was left to grasp.

Irena preferred rough edges, even though they scraped and tore. But Alejandro, he was all sleek speed and elegance, from his words to his body. The leopard to her bear, the fox to her wolverine. Solitary predators who avoided one another, respecting too well the teeth and claws of the other—and when they couldn't keep apart, they ripped pieces from one another in passing.

Wounded predators, she admitted . . . and wounds were weaknesses. Irena had been trying to excise hers for centuries. But this one wouldn't heal, so she tried to ignore the pain.

And Alejandro was correct: She did lump many things together. But wounded predators were also dangerously short-tempered, so she gave him no response but a sneer before heading across the piazza to meet Deacon.

Olek did not follow her.

She had not expected him to.

❧

The first time Alejandro had seen Irena, she'd been standing with a group of her friends on the opposite side of a courtyard in Caelum—the Guardian realm. It had been almost one hundred years after his transformation; although his training neared completion and he would soon return to Earth as a full-fledged Guardian, Alejandro had still been a novice.

And he'd known *of* Irena, who—at the time more than twelve hundred years of age—was one of the oldest Guardians. He'd known of her Gift to shape metal. He'd known she had created the exquisite swords he practiced with, and that Michael had assigned her to oversee Alejandro's final weapons specialization and his transition to Earth.

He'd known all of that, but he'd not yet met her.

And so he hadn't known who had mesmerized him with a single toss of her head, her long braids bright auburn beneath Caelum's sun. Hadn't known who had hardened his body with one shout of her loud, brash laughter. It had fallen silent when his gaze had caught hers. Without hesitation, she'd stridden toward him across the white marble square—just as she was walking toward Deacon now.

He'd been arrogant enough to think that she'd be impressed when he introduced himself. His talent with the swords had been praised by Guardians centuries older than he was, and there were already predictions that, given another century, his skill would surpass Michael's. And when she'd said her name, he'd been bold enough to challenge her, to suggest there was nothing she could teach him.

She'd accepted his challenge. When she'd offered up a single dagger against his swords, he'd been foolish enough to imagine that she wanted to lose—that she wanted to be under him as badly as he wanted to sheathe himself within her.

Before ten seconds had passed, she'd had him laid out on the marble pavers with blood filling his mouth and his vision floating in and out of focus.

Until she'd straddled his waist and kissed him—then everything had become sharp and pointed, and devastatingly clear.

He'd still been reeling when she lifted her head and said, "When I am satisfied that your training is complete, I will take your body as I have just taken your mouth. Until that time, young Olek, there is only this. Only the fight."

Then she'd driven her dagger into his side, and chided him for letting his guard down.

It was fitting, Alejandro thought, that their only kiss had been flavored by blood and followed by pain.

Too much pain, because she'd been wrong: There hadn't just been the fight. There had been her laugh and her temper. Her unrelenting schedule, her unexpected moments of tenderness.

And there had been the days spent in her forge, where he discovered his Gift of fire complemented her affinity with metal. Where they'd created weapons, where firelight had danced across her pale skin. Where he'd pretended to study manuscripts, but watched over the pages as Irena shaped her intricate sculptures—where he'd posed for her more than once. And he'd trained tirelessly, waiting for the moment she was satisfied.

For months, there had only been swords and Irena—his heart, his life.

And with a single misstep and a demon's monstrous bargain, it had ended. Ended with the destruction of Alejandro's honor as she traded her body for his life. Ended with Irena holding the demon's head, his face a mirror image of Alejandro's. Ended with Alejandro walking into a bedroom whose iron walls had been decorated by blood, seeing what she'd done to the demon's body—and knowing how the demon must have used hers.

And he'd known that he'd failed her. Utterly failed her.

She'd cut off her braids one by one, tossed her hair and the demon's head onto the bed, and asked him to burn it all. Then she'd walked away without looking back.

Two centuries had passed before he'd seen her again.

In the two hundred years since, every infrequent encounter had been accompanied by his wish that he'd never laid eyes upon her. And with every encounter, it was an effort to tear his gaze away.

He made the effort now, turning to examine the memorial statue for a boy poet that stood beside a remnant of the ancient wall. Alejandro well remembered the gate that had once led into the city. It had already been falling to ruins in the late fifteenth century when, still a human, he'd journeyed to Rome. Now only a plaque marked the gate's former location, and it described how Roman slaves had opened the gate to the invaders who'd sacked the city. Irena, he knew, had been one of the slaves, serving in a senator's household.

In his human life, Alejandro hadn't been a senator, but almost the equivalent in the Spanish courts. Born into the position rather than elected—but still responsible for his people and his lands, even if it meant trying to protect them from the fanaticism of his king and queen. A politician, always maneuvering, staying a step ahead, making alliances with men he'd hated just to keep the long, dangerous fingers of the Inquisition from touching his people.

For years, he'd performed that subtle dance. Every movement was calculated. He'd married as one step, made alliances as another. And when a demon had outmaneuvered him, he'd died for it.

Irena's hatred for politicians almost burned as hot as her hatred for demons. Alejandro thought she had forgiven him for being one only because he'd died protecting his wife and children.

At the time, Alejandro's youngest son had almost been the same age as the poet memorialized here. All of his sons had all grown into men, he prayed, but he only remembered them as boys. He had small statues of them in his cache—statues that Irena had made for him after he'd projected the image of his sons into her mind. She'd captured them perfectly, giving each figure details that were heartbreakingly realistic.

Even after five hundred years, he found it too painful to pull the statues out of his cache to look at them, but he took comfort knowing they were there.

Irena called out a loud greeting in Italian, and Alejandro's gaze returned to her as she threw her arms around the vampire's waist.

When in Rome, they all did as Romans do. Among the public, Guardians almost always spoke the local language. Unlike her French, Irena's Italian carried a Slavic accent, as it had when he'd heard her speak to the wastrel on the street.

And his body reacted in the same way as the wastrel's had.

In those months Alejandro had spent with Irena, she'd spoken Russian—but even then, her voice held the flavor of something older. And just as it was Guardian custom to speak the local tongue, so it was for a novice to speak the language of his mentor. Alejandro had defied custom, and answered her blunt commands in Spanish to signal that he'd had as much to show her, that he was her equal.

But after the demon's bargain, when they'd finally met again in Paris, she'd greeted him in French. But for his name, she'd spoken nothing but French to him since, and Alejandro had replied in no other language.

Four centuries had passed, yet he still responded to her husky accent. He listened for her every word and wished himself deaf. It was madness.

The vampire smiled as he returned Irena's embrace, but not enough to show his fangs. His broad hands splayed over the long muscles of her back, her pale skin bare but for the two leather ties that fastened her apron-like shirt. Over her head, Deacon's flat gaze targeted Alejandro.

The vampire didn't appear apprehensive. Perhaps Deacon didn't know Irena well enough to guess what was coming. Alejandro did, and he returned the vampire's stare until Deacon pulled back to look at Irena.

With a swift punch to Deacon's jaw, she laid the vampire out flat.

Yes. There was more than one reason Alejandro didn't often take his eyes off her.

CHAPTER 2

"What the *hell* was that for?"

Deacon's new lisp prevented Irena from taking his anger seriously. She picked up his fang from the sidewalk and wiped the long, pointed tooth against her leather stockings. Deacon sat up and snatched it from her fingers.

"That was for coming to Rome." Before he could resume snarling at her, she added, "Put your tooth back before your mouth heals."

Deacon pushed the fang into the bloodied gap between his upper teeth as he got to his feet. "Is Rome forbidden now? Fucking make up your mind, Irena. You Guardians talk about free will, but—"

"You idiot. The nephilim might still be here, and they are out for vampire blood."

"Ah." The fingers holding his tooth in place ruined his sudden grin. "So you were worried about me?"

"You are too stupid for me to care." She hooked her thumbs into her belt, took a casual glance over her shoulder. Around the piazza, humans lost interest when no more punches were thrown. She'd heard exclamations of surprise and a few whispers when she'd slugged him, but little other response. Irena wondered whether they'd have interfered if she'd been a man and Deacon a woman. She turned back to him. "And I wouldn't have hit you if you couldn't take it."

"Thanks, Irena. That makes it hurt less." Deacon managed sarcasm even with his hand stuffed in his mouth. He nodded over her shoulder at Alejandro. "Would you hit him?"

No. That meant touching him. "I would never have to, for he is never stupid." If only Olek *had* been a fool. Then she would not admire him so much. "He is Alejandro Sandoval de Córdoba y Hacén. A Guardian and a friend."

"Does your Guardian friend ever change his expression?"

"No."

"He doesn't look like your usual type. Too many brains, not enough muscles."

Irena smirked. "And so *you* are my type?" Not that the vampire lacked brains. She continued over his muffled laugh, "Why are you in Rome, Deacon? Has your community been threatened?"

"No. They're fine." His gaze shifted from hers. "And it's not *my* community anymore."

Irena stared at him in disbelief. He'd been leading the Prague community for more than sixty years. "What happened?"

"Another vampire moved in. Strong. Nosferatu-born, maybe."

Vampires transformed by nosferatu blood were stronger than those who transformed with vampire blood. And in most communities, leadership was determined by deadly combat—so the most powerful vampires led.

Cleverness and skill could overcome strength, however; it surprised her that Deacon had been outmatched physically *and* mentally. And where had this new vampire come from? The nosferatu-born were uncommon. Unless a Guardian interfered, the nosferatu would kill its human prey.

Had any Guardians recently created a nosferatu-born vampire? She would have to find out.

Alejandro came up beside her, and regarded Deacon with a

flat, unwavering stare. "The one who defeated you allowed you to walk away?"

Yes, Irena also found that strange. Only a foolish vampire would leave a rival alive—unless he thought slaying Deacon might cultivate resentment instead of inspiring loyalty. Deacon was beloved by his community; mercy might win his successor more support than ruthlessness could.

"He claimed he didn't want to kill me. Only to take over—and he didn't need to finish me off to do that." Deacon looked to Irena, bitterness in his psychic scent. "Let's just say that yours wasn't the first hit I've taken in the last month. And that this healing was nothing in comparison."

Irena met Alejandro's gaze and saw the same question that she knew was in hers. In the past two years, since the Gates to Hell had been closed, several demons had tried to pass as vampires. If a demon insinuated himself into a community and assumed leadership, he could force the vampires to kill humans or deny their free will. As long as the vampires carried out his orders, the demon didn't break the Rules.

"He hit you?" Irena asked Deacon. "With his hands?"

"You know any other ways to hit?"

"Yes. Were his fists cold?" A demon's skin was hot.

A demon's skin—and, at times, Alejandro's.

"As cold as mine." Deacon flexed his jaw and released his tooth. "So, I came to Rome because there aren't any of us here. If I'd gone to another community, the heads there would be looking to kill me, sure I'd be gunning for their spot."

That was probably true, but Irena suspected that he avoided other vampires chiefly out of pride. Vampires throughout Europe respected Deacon; those who didn't feared him enough that he'd rarely been challenged. His defeat would have destroyed the reputation he'd spent decades building.

"Why aren't Eva and Petra with you?"

Another snarl twisted his mouth. "I was *beaten* in front of them, Irena. Beaten to a fucking pulp. Would you have come with me?"

She'd have thought Eva and Petra would. She didn't like being wrong. "You should have come to me."

"To your forge, out in the middle of Siberia? Who would I feed from? Would you make me your whore and pay me in blood?"

Irena sucked in a breath, clenched her hands. Violence came easily to her; it always had. But although she might hit her friends out of fear or worry, never would she do so in anger. She backed away.

Alejandro stepped in, patrician disdain stiffening his tone and posture. "I presume you did not contact Irena over a community squabble."

Deacon looked past him to Irena, but the flicker of regret in his psychic scent didn't soothe her temper. "No. I called her because there's a nosferatu setting up house beneath a church." He smiled with brittle humor. "And if I can't take down one of the nosferatu-born, I'm sure as hell not going to try slaying one of their daddies."

❧

Irena set a rapid pace through Rome's streets, leaving Alejandro and Deacon to walk in silence behind her. It was not just fury that quickened her stride, Alejandro knew—she was anticipating the hunt. Alejandro looked forward to it, as well; slaying a nosferatu would repair her mood . . . and by doing so, repair his.

Irena's temper always ignited his own. And even if he hadn't been the one to infuriate her, inevitably they turned on each other.

Alejandro was not proud of the man he became in response to her anger.

Yet they were friends—or so they told anyone who asked. Alejandro didn't think anyone who spent more than a few minutes with them believed it.

Deacon hadn't yet caught on. If he had, Alejandro doubted the vampire would look to him as an ally.

Beside him, Deacon asked, "You've been friends with Irena awhile, then?"

For an eternity, it seemed. "I have."

"You know her well?"

Alejandro's gaze caressed the bare skin from her shoulders to the wide leather belt circling her hips. Her figure was sturdy, but she wasn't tall—her head didn't reach his shoulder. Her imposing personality took up more space than she did, giving the impression of a much larger woman.

Yes, Alejandro knew her. Long enough to memorize every inch he would never touch.

"I do," he finally said.

"So when I've pissed her off like this, how do I keep her from chopping off my head?"

That was simple. "Toss another nosferatu in her path."

"And I will throw you both in line after it," Irena bit out over her shoulder, and Alejandro's rigid tension began to ebb. That she'd answered meant her temper had cooled. She stopped and waited for them, her gaze fixed on Deacon. "How did you come by the nosferatu?"

The vampire must have realized her anger had passed. He relaxed, sliding his hands into his pockets. "I've been looking for a location on this side of Rome to hole up in if I was caught out near sunrise—mostly tombs and catacombs that aren't open to tourists during the day. I scoped out the one we're heading to last night, and just missed being seen on my way back up. That's when I called you."

Irena nodded, but the explanation didn't settle well with Alejandro. For a nosferatu to be seen without the creature detecting a vampire in return stretched his belief. Nosferatu did not *just* see. Like Guardians and demons, each had sharply attuned senses.

For that reason, they made no attempt at silence as they walked. Any nosferatu would hear their approaching footsteps, their heartbeats. As long as Irena and he did not use their psychic senses or Gifts, they might be mistaken for human, and the nosferatu taken by surprise—not because of their presence, but their strength.

At the edge of a small, deserted square, two modern apartment buildings flanked a narrow church. Scaffolding climbed its ornate façade, the stone used for the repairs darker than the weathered original. Aluminum fencing separated the square from the broken plaster and limestone rubble piled just inside the chained and padlocked gate. Despite the Renaissance-era façade, the church was nearer to Irena's age than Alejandro's. Like many other churches in Rome, this one had been rebuilt on an ancient site.

A plastic sign wired to the chain-link fence said the church would reopen to visitors by the next season. Alejandro's gaze searched the upper levels of the building for light; he heard no movement from within.

Irena cocked her head as she listened, then turned to him. A question joined the glitter of anticipation in her green eyes.

Her Gift could slice through the metal locks. It'd give them away, but Irena wouldn't want to take the nosferatu by surprise. No, she wanted it to run, so that they could hunt it down.

Alejandro didn't want to give it the opportunity to escape. He shook his head.

"We climb," he said for Deacon's benefit. Flying or jumping over the gate would also reveal them to the nosferatu—and would risk them being seen by humans.

Irena narrowed her eyes, but a smile curved her lips as she clambered over the fence. They traversed it more quickly than humans would—but lingering would risk exposure, too, and the authorities being notified. Although Alejandro had developed connections within the Roman police force when he'd led the Guardian team that had covered up the vampire massacre, they'd be smarter to avoid police involvement from the outset.

Deacon produced a set of lock picks and made quick work of the front doors. Alejandro dipped his fingers into the stoup of holy water as he entered.

Irena's mouth flattened when he made the sign of the cross, and she followed Deacon down the nave's bare aisle. Carpets had been rolled up and tucked beneath benches; paint-dotted plastic draped the altar and the pews. "You will give Deacon the wrong impression of Guardians by performing such an empty ritual."

His eyebrows drawn, Deacon glanced over his shoulder at Irena. "Don't drag me into this."

Ah, it hadn't taken much time for the vampire to catch on. Alejandro allowed himself a smile. At least his Latin invocation had not invited comment. The first time Irena had heard him recite a prayer, she'd laughed tears into her eyes. Then she'd taught him the language as she'd once known it, bringing life to a tongue that had grown stale over the centuries.

Her laughter would have been a welcome interruption to many a boyhood mass.

"It has meaning to me, and therefore it is not an empty ritual," he countered, walking beside the altar rails surrounding the sanctuary. "When you hunt, Irena, you eat a piece of the animal's heart—*that* is meaningless. It does not sustain you. You receive no strength from it."

"It is respect. I honor the life that was given."

"So do I. Self-sacrifice is the one thing all Guardians can appreciate." Every Guardian had sacrificed his life to save another, earning him the right to transformation.

Irena looked to the plastic-wrapped figure hanging behind the altar. Her brief smile kicked at his stomach. "As you like," she said. "I'll be grateful my sacrifice didn't take that form—or yours—and leave it at that."

On the left side of the sanctuary, Deacon pushed aside a heavy curtain, revealing a hallway. He turned to frown at Alejandro. "I know Irena jumped over a cliff with a nosferatu. What happened to you?"

She hadn't just jumped over a cliff—she'd saved the tribe of slaves she'd led after escaping Rome. And he . . .

"I was named a heretic and burned at the stake." He could not suppress the irony in his tone.

Alejandro's mother had been a Moor and a convert. With the words whispered into the right ears, that had been enough to cast suspicion on him and his family.

Alejandro had seen the inquiry coming, though he hadn't known the man behind the whispers was a demon. He'd secreted his family away, but remained behind, believing—arrogantly, perhaps—that he would be acquitted. Despite the torture, he hadn't confessed, and he hadn't revealed his family's location. If the demon hadn't been so greedy, had just gone after Alejandro, he'd never have become a Guardian. But he'd saved them by refusing to give them up—and upon his death, Michael had come to offer him the transformation.

But he'd burned first.

Deacon shook his head before stepping behind the curtain. "And that is why—except for when I'm hiding—I stay clear of churches."

But he hadn't always, Alejandro wagered. A man did not come by a name like Deacon while avoiding the church.

"It was not the religion," Irena said, "but the politicians in Rome and in Spain."

"There were also priests." Alejandro followed them into the hall. "And, of course, the demon."

Irena snorted. "In those years, there was no difference between any of them."

Irena had once told him that she'd been in Russia while the Inquisition had spread its deadly fingers through Spain, but she hadn't been unaware of events in the rest of the world. The Guardians had done what they could to curb demonic influence in the courts and the church—but, aside from Alejandro's trial, the accusations had been brought by humans vying for power and position, not demons.

Guardians could do little to help humans when humans were the cause of their own misery.

Deacon led them to a small chamber. A wooden door had been set into the center of the slate floor. On the walls, signs forbidding flash photography and souvenir collection hung over velvet upholstered benches. Alejandro eyed the stick figure clutching its head beneath a warning about low ceilings, and debated the merits of shape-shifting to Irena's petite height versus stooping his way through the corridors.

"I was transformed by a beautiful vampire on a bed of silk," Deacon said as Irena circled the chamber, peering out the small, barred window and testing the lock on a closed door. "All things considered, it makes me glad I'm not a Guardian."

Without a word, Irena formed her wings. White feathers arched over her head and swept down to elegant wingtips.

Seeing her wear them always stole Alejandro's breath.

The awe faded from Deacon's expression, and he sighed. "And now you've made me a liar."

"I'm sure I am not the first to do so," she said, kneeling on the floor and pressing her ear to the wooden door. Suede pulled tight across a bottom framed by the straps of her leather stockings and arcs of white feathers.

"We are none of us saints," Alejandro murmured, grateful that they had long since passed the altar. His thoughts were far too impure to cross himself now.

With both relief and regret, he watched Irena stand and vanish her wings.

"I hear nothing," she said, calling in her kukri knives from her cache. The angled blades were sharp and sturdy, but at only sixteen inches, their length forced her into closer proximity with an enemy than a sword would.

Alejandro tightened his jaw against his protest. Using the knives demanded that she was nearer to the kill—and, for that reason, it was also more satisfying to her.

He understood her; how could he not, when he took so much pleasure in his own weapons? When he anticipated the feel of their grips against his palms and treasured the memory of their creation?

Irena stilled when his swords appeared in his hands, and he immediately wanted to vanish them again.

She didn't lift her gaze from the swords. "Did you repair the blade yourself?"

He gave a short nod. She studied the fracture, her expression impenetrable. He'd mended the break with his Gift by heating the steel and hammering it back into shape—and no one but Irena would have noticed the faint discoloration of the blade, the slightly uneven balance.

Oh, he was a fool. He wished he'd brought out any blades but these—the last of the weapons they'd made together in her forge. But he hadn't considered it; he used no other swords.

"Why did you not come to me? We could have—" She caught herself with an indrawn breath. Her gaze hardened and snapped up to his. "You thick-brained ass. I should let you be killed when it shatters."

"Yes," he agreed, to punish her for saying it so casually now. When it had mattered, she had not let him die.

The punishment became his when pain slashed across her features, and she looked away. But he could not unspeak his response.

Her voice was flat. "Rid yourself of them, Olek. Then open your hands."

As soon as he did, a pair of swords appeared in his palms. He examined the intricate hand guards, hefted the deceptive delicacy of the blades, and fought the ache building in his chest. They had perfect length and balance—had been created specifically for him.

Had she made them recently, or carried them in her cache for the past four hundred years? He didn't know which he hoped it was.

"These are satisfactory," he finally said.

Deacon cleared his throat, and reached back for his short swords. "So, Irena—do you have anything nosferatu-sized in there for me?"

Irena tossed him a semiautomatic pistol before swinging the door open. Deacon caught the gun and raised his brows in query.

Alejandro explained as Irena dropped into the catacombs. "The bullets have been coated with hellhound venom. A shot will slow the nosferatu down."

"Good to hear. Thank—"

"*Barely* slows it. If the nosferatu comes close enough for you to use your swords," Alejandro said, moving to the hole in the floor, "then you are already dead."

Two steps beyond the narrow, spiraling stairwell that brought them to the third level beneath the church, Irena froze.

Not just one nosferatu. A *nest* of them.

Her heart pounded. She stared down the gray stone corridor, praying that she'd been mistaken. An unlit string of electric lights ran along the ceiling, but she had no difficulty seeing through the darkness. None of the pale, hairless creatures lurked in the corridor, but she detected three distinct heartbeats in a chamber ahead and to the left.

The nosferatu were lying in wait for them.

She clamped her lips, swallowing the invectives that leapt to her tongue. They had no time for that.

Turning, she signed, *Three. Is that your count?*

Alejandro nodded, his gaze never leaving the corridor ahead of them. She bit back another curse when she realized how cramped he was in this space. His shoulders were hunched, his knees bent.

Nosferatu, however, usually neared seven feet tall—and they couldn't shift their shape. She and Alejandro would have the advantage under the low ceilings.

We flank the chamber entrance and wait, she decided. If the creatures remained inside the chamber, she and Alejandro would slay them at dawn, after the creatures fell into their daysleep—but the nosferatu were not that stupid. *They will abandon their position before sunrise. We'll take them in the corridor as they leave.*

Deacon looked around Alejandro's shoulder. "Why did we stop?"

"It is a nest," Irena told him.

"A nest? But I was—" Uncertainty flashed through his psychic scent. He shook his head. "I only saw one. And they are usually solitary."

"Usually." Irena turned away from the vampire before he saw her revulsion. Never had she seen him so disgustingly timid. Dread clutched her stomach at the thought of facing three nosferatu, but she'd never let fear prevent her from doing what needed to be done. "Yet it isn't unheard of to find two or more together."

Not unheard of, but incredibly rare. The only other nest Irena could recall was a group of nosferatu who'd made a bargain with Lucifer two years before.

She moved silently down the corridor, stopping a few feet from the entrance to the chamber. Had these nosferatu made a bargain with another demon? Or had they been here for years, waiting to carry out one of Lucifer's plans? Or did they nest together for a different reason?

Alejandro took the other side of the doorway. *We will slay two,* he signed. *The last, we shall bring back to SI and question him—* His hand fisted. Irena's lips parted. She could hear it now: another heartbeat, rapid and weak. The heartbeat of someone who'd lost too much blood.

Deacon scented the air and grimaced. "Too much rot. Is it human?"

Human, vampire—it wouldn't matter. She and Alejandro couldn't wait now. The nosferatu would kill whoever it was before they abandoned the chamber.

She turned to Deacon. "Stay at the door. There may be more nosferatu that haven't yet returned. Give a shout the moment you see one." An important task, but it wouldn't require him to fight. A vampire couldn't stand his ground against a nosferatu.

"Christ, Irena." Deacon smoothly chambered a bullet. Not as nervous now, she noted. "Can two Guardians handle three nosferatu?"

What a stupid question. She'd just told him nests were rare—how would she know what chance Alejandro and she had?

But someone needed rescuing, and so she would soon find out. Her blades would taste nosferatu flesh; their blood would run.

She let her anticipation rise, washing away the fear, the dread, and turned to grin at Alejandro. He returned her gaze beneath half-lowered lids.

Ah, yes. His furious expression.

He wasn't like her. She loved killing the nosferatu. For Alejandro, it was a duty he willingly performed—until moments such as these, when a life was at stake. When the nosferatu's inherent evil was clear to see, and not just words.

In moments such as these, he was as impatient as she was to rend them limb by limb and burn the remains.

What did you see? she asked. Alejandro had passed the chamber entrance in a fraction of a second—more than enough time to memorize the layout and the location of any nosferatu.

An ossuary, he signed. At the touch of his psyche against hers, she lowered her shields, and he projected the image into her mind. Crude block columns, wide enough to conceal a nosferatu, stood at regular intervals throughout the large room. Bones were piled against the walls, skulls arranged in pyramids. *Square, twenty meters deep. The ceiling is twice the height of the corridor.*

She and Alejandro would have to watch their heads. The nosferatu could cling to the ceiling like bats. *The nosferatu?*

I did not see any of them.

Irena exhaled slowly through her teeth, nodding. Most likely, the nosferatu were in the same positions as she and Alejandro: against the entrance wall, waiting for her to rush through. As soon as she did, the nosferatu would attack from behind.

You find the human, he signed. *I'll cover your back.*

Irena flicked a small mirror past the door. The spinning disk caught the reflection of a nosferatu clinging above the entrance; she had a glimpse of one against the wall to the right. She didn't see the other one.

She signed their locations to Alejandro and charged through.

The nosferatu waiting above the door dropped. She heard the thud of flesh as Alejandro intercepted it. Irena spun to the right. The nosferatu against the wall lifted his arms, preparing to strike.

She struck faster. Her knife impaled the creature's exposed chest, the tip of her blade digging into the wall behind him.

Too low. She'd missed the heart. Stupid, stupid.

Already triumphant, the nosferatu's thin lips pulled back over his deadly fangs, sword raised high.

Irena let him swing it.

She flared her Gift the instant the blade touched her skin, forcing the metal to soften. Steel flowed like mercury over her neck. She hardened it again, grabbed his ruined blade, and yanked.

Unbalanced, the nosferatu staggered. Irena scythed her second knife toward his thickly muscled throat, cutting through the spine. She didn't wait for his head to topple from his shoulders before yanking her first knife from his chest and turning.

The third nosferatu skittered across the ceiling like an enormous white spider.

From behind her, she felt the drawing in of Alejandro's Gift as if he pulled in a psychic breath. Orange light burst through the chamber, followed by the sizzle of flesh and a terrible shriek. A burning body rocketed over her head, toward the nosferatu scrabbling across the ceiling.

Startled, the creature lost his grip, came tumbling down. Instantly, he was up on his feet and sprinting for the rear corner of the chamber—after the human? To kill, or take a hostage.

Irena went after him.

Catching up was impossible, but by the gods, she *would not fail*. She pushed her speed to the limit, her teeth clenched with effort. Still not fast enough. Without missing a step, she whipped her arms forward and released her knives.

They pierced the back of his knees like arrows. The nosferatu stumbled—and that was enough time.

Irena called in her saber and swung as she sped past him. The blade sliced through his torso, ripping bone and flesh and tearing free in a spray of cold blood. She pivoted, and separated his head from his shoulders.

And it was done. Alejandro pulled his sword from the chest of the still-burning nosferatu. The flames cast a flickering light against the stacks of bones.

Her gaze fell to Alejandro's hands. The flesh of his palms and fingers had split open, his skin blistered and charred. His blood trickled over the hilts of his swords, mingled with the nosferatu's.

Alejandro's Gift did not come without a price.

Irena met his eyes. His lips had flattened, his nostrils flaring as he breathed through the pain. Nosferatu blood streaked his jaw, splattered his neck. His own ran the length of his arm, soaked his sleeve. She wanted to lick it off. Wanted to take him now, with the heat of battle pounding through their veins.

A long breath steadied her. From near the chamber entrance she heard the tinkle of glass—the mirror she'd tossed shattering as it finally landed on the stone floor.

She looked away from Alejandro, her gaze searching for the human. The faint heartbeat was closer now, and the fetid scent of decaying blood hung heavily in the air.

Irena retrieved her kukri knives, and stepped around a column. Horror froze her lungs.

Dried blood crusted the woman's face, her nude torso, her legs. Her long brown hair was clumped with it.

A woman, but not a human as they'd assumed. No human would still be alive, not with a spike through her forehead, pinning her upright against the stone column.

A Guardian.

A Guardian—and an endless font of blood for the nosferatu. They could drain the body to the point of death, and because a Guardian healed quickly, drink their fill again the next evening. With that much brain damage, she couldn't have projected her emotions, called for help. Even if another Guardian had looked for her, they couldn't have detected her psychic scent. The woman's mind was as empty as her ruined face.

How long had she been here?

"Help me, Olek." Irena's throat was raw. Her final steps to the Guardian's side were a blur. She rose up on her toes, cupped the flat end of the spike in her palm.

She felt the heat from Alejandro's body, heard his sharply indrawn breath as he came up beside her. He slipped his gloved hands under the woman's slack, blood-encrusted arms.

"We have you, Rosalia," he murmured in Italian. "You are with friends."

"You know her?"

Slowly, Irena used her Gift to draw out the metal. She pulled her hand back; the iron followed. Rosalia's brain would immediately begin healing, but unless they brought her to a Guardian with a healing Gift, it might be hours before she regained consciousness.

"She specialized with me," Alejandro said.

So he'd honed her fencing skills. Irena vanished the spike, produced a thin blanket. "When? Who are her friends?"

Rosalia would need them when she realized what had been done to her.

"Two centuries ago. Who her friends are, I could not say."

"Who was her primary mentor?"

His gaze never left Irena's face as she tucked the covering

around Rosalia's motionless form. "Her early studies were with Hugh."

Irena gritted her teeth. Hugh Castleford, after eight hundred years as one of Caelum's best warriors, had voluntarily Fallen and become human again . . . and had since taken up with the hellspawn, Lilith.

But despite his choice of bed-partner, Hugh was still a brilliant mentor to the novice Guardians. And he was still, Irena hated to admit, a man that she would trust with her life.

More importantly, she would trust him with anyone else's life.

"Then we will take her to Special Investigations," Irena said, lifting Rosalia and cradling the woman against her chest. "Call Selah, have her teleport us there."

Selah's Gift would take them to San Francisco faster than using the Gates—the portals that were scattered around the world, linking Earth to Caelum.

Alejandro called in his phone from his cache and glanced at its face. "No signal."

Irena sighed and strode toward the corridor, vanishing the nosferatu's bodies and their blood into her cache. Humans would find little evidence of the battle—only a few dings in the walls, and the lingering reek of roasted nosferatu.

Irena stopped in front of Deacon. "Take her."

The vampire did, gently, his breath skimming between his teeth. The puncture in Rosalia's forehead gaped open, exposing brain tissue shredded by shards of her skull.

"Will you be coming with us?" Irena asked, calling in her knives again. To phone Selah they had to get aboveground, and might encounter any nosferatu who were returning late.

Deacon stared at Rosalia, his face paler than usual. "With you, where?" he finally asked.

"San Francisco. But if you stay, you will have to fight with us."

Pained indecision contorted Deacon's features before determination smoothed and hardened them. "I'll come."

She glanced at Alejandro. His lean hands were bare again, his skin healed. "Will you take the front or the rear?"

Asking was unnecessary. Irena's greater speed and skill made her the obvious choice for the lead position, and Olek would know she wanted it . . . but she also wanted him to offer it to her.

He took his time. His thumb and forefinger stroked from the corners of his mouth to the point of his goatee. His dark gaze ran her length, settled on her hips.

"Rear," he decided.

Pig. Irena threw her knife at his head, and didn't wait to see him catch the blade before it split his skull. She struck out for the stairs, smiling.

It had been a good fight.

CHAPTER 3

Her fine temper lasted until Olek said, "Special Investigations has no use for a weak man, Irena."

As if she would befriend a milksop. Irena snarled at Alejandro over Deacon's body before hauling the sleeping vampire off the floor and tossing him onto a narrow bunk. The sun shone over San Francisco, and he'd dropped into his daysleep—and onto the wooden floor of the windowless dormitory room that Selah had teleported them into—the moment they'd arrived.

Anticipating Deacon's collapse, Selah had held Rosalia when she'd teleported them. Then she'd jumped again, taking Rosalia to a Guardian healer and leaving Irena and Alejandro alone with Deacon.

And, most likely, Deacon would be alone when he woke at sunset.

"You are blind, Olek," Irena said as she turned to search the small desk for a pencil and paper. If she didn't leave a message for the vampire, he might venture out into the city, seeking blood. "He is not weak. He is broken."

"You believe losing his community destroyed his confidence?"

"Yes. Never have I seen him like this."

Irena painstakingly composed a short note in English, instructing Deacon to wait for her return. She slipped the folded paper into the vampire's mouth and stabbed the note onto his right fang. If she'd made the effort to write the message, then she wouldn't risk him overlooking it—or mistaking her penmanship for a six-year-old's.

Alejandro stood at the foot of the bed, his eyes shadowed as he looked over the vampire. "And so you brought him to SI for repairs?"

She strode into the narrow hallway that led to the warehouse's common room. "Yes."

Irena felt his surprise. No, she'd made no secret of her hatred for Lilith and Special Investigations. Irena could barely tolerate knowing a halfling demon was SI's director, giving Guardians their assignments; more than that, Irena despised the idea that Congressman Thomas Stafford—a demon known as Rael—had been instrumental in SI's creation. Now, SI depended on Rael's support in Washington for its continued operation. Despite the demon's involvement, however, Irena couldn't deny that the novices and vampires received the best possible training from Hugh and the Guardians who worked for SI. It was the best place for Deacon.

"He only needs to be given a task. To be made useful. Perhaps"—she tossed over her shoulder—"he will kill Lilith for me."

Irena couldn't slay the halfling demon without breaking the Rules—not since Lilith had become human again.

"If you believed she was evil, you would kill her yourself. Even if it meant you had to Fall."

"You know nothing, Olek. She continues to live not because I think she is good, but because she poses no threat to anyone."

"Lilith, no threat? You either lie or have become a spitting fool."

Irena swung around, and found him closer than she'd expected. Too close. She planted her feet. It would not be she who backed away. "*I* am a fool and a liar? If *you* truly believed her a threat, you'd have finished her."

"No threat to us." Alejandro stared down at her over his aristocratic nose. He'd vanished the nosferatu's blood from his skin and clothes; hers were still streaked and splattered with crimson.

She bared her teeth in a smile. "Us? Perhaps not to me."

"Us, the Guardians." He lowered his mouth to her ear, and added softly, "There has been no *us* for four hundred years. You know that, yet observe how easily you twisted my meaning. You say in one moment that Lilith is no threat, then say she is a threat to me. Your tongue might as well be a demon's."

Irena stood motionless when he straightened. Her blood pounded in her ears; fury blurred her vision.

But never would she strike in anger. Instead, she audibly inhaled as he moved past her, and let the pleasure she took in his subtly smoky scent slip through her psychic shields.

Pleasure *and* arousal—but this time, shame did not accompany them. Olek's scent was one of the few things the demon hadn't been able to replicate.

She saw the hesitation in his step, the slight turn of his head before he tightened his jaw and continued on.

He took her fury with him.

Her sigh was silent. She turned to watch him, the fluid sword fighter's stride that only hinted at the explosive power coiled within. By the loose set of his shoulders, she judged that the anger driving him to compare her to a demon had faded.

But their argument hadn't gone unnoticed. Beyond the mouth of the hallway, Becca sat curled on one of the common room sofas, pretending to read. Though the novice's nose was buried in the book, her eyes were too wide and her body too still. Listening, then. And if she'd understood their French—which was likely—perhaps she was wondering if Irena intended to kill Lilith.

But Irena doubted Becca would ask. Although the novice possessed a bold mouth with anyone aged less than one or two centuries, she became a mouse around the older Guardians.

At the end of the hall, Alejandro paused in front of one of the closed doors, turning his head as if he'd caught a scent. Irena caught up to him just as the door opened.

Dru's brows rose when she saw them. Her body blocked Irena's view of the room.

How is she? Alejandro signed.

The healer sighed. She squeezed out of the room, followed by her novice apprentice, Pim. They carried the odors of a human and dried blood with them—Hugh, Irena recognized, and Rosalia.

Physically, she's fine. Mentally, we will have to wait and see. Dru rocked back and forth from the toes to the heels of her red sneakers. Usually, she bobbed; Rosalia's condition must have been worrying her. *Hugh is speaking with her now—telling her how you found her.*

Soundproofing shielded the room; with the door closed, Irena couldn't hear anything of Hugh's and Rosalia's conversation. *Should we give her a personal account?* Irena asked.

Dru shook her head. *What you can give her is ten minutes with Hugh.*

Irena narrowed her eyes; Dru's never lost their friendly expression, but her voice dared Irena to argue when she shoved her hands into the pockets of her lab coat and repeated, "Ten minutes."

The healer would fight her if she didn't comply, Irena knew. Dru only appeared bubbly and soft, as if she was composed of smiles and laughter. But when she'd specialized with Irena almost twenty years earlier, the healer had revealed a stubborn streak comparable to a deaf ox. Every time Irena had severed one of the healer's limbs—teaching Dru to fight through that shocking loss—Dru had simply reattached it, despite Irena's commands to the contrary.

Dru had been one of Irena's favorite assignments.

"Ten minutes," she agreed.

Dru nodded. "I'll be downstairs if I'm needed. Pim?"

The novice hurried after the healer, the expression on her round face open and awed before she caught up to Dru and began gesturing wildly, questioning Dru's method of removing the bone shards from Rosalia's brain and rebuilding her skull. The novice's awe went far beyond appreciation for the healer's skill, and Irena wondered if Dru had realized yet that Pim was in love with her.

And she wondered if she and Olek were the only two Guardians who looked outside Caelum and the vampire communities for their bed-partners. They had that in common. . . although Olek's arrangements typically lasted much longer than hers. Years, rather than a single night.

She knew the name of his most recent lover by accident; four months ago, while visiting Drifter in Seattle, she'd overheard Jake telling young Charlie that he'd teleported into a bedroom while searching for Alejandro—and found a human in with him.

Emilia.

Irena had known a few Emilias. They'd all had long, curling dark hair, ripe-cherry lips, and passionate spirits.

And she'd liked each of them. His Emilia probably wouldn't be any different—and Irena wanted to hate her for that.

She felt Olek watching her, but didn't look up as she walked past him into the common room. The floor shivered beneath her feet. The novices practiced in the gymnasium on the first level, and the soundproofing between the floors and the thick rugs spread around the sofas didn't completely absorb the impact vibrations. The clattering of keyboards and the murmurs of phone conversations floated up the stairs from the main offices.

Though plenty of seats were available, Irena plopped down next to Becca. The microfiber upholstery was cool and soft against her back; she put her feet up on the low table, made herself comfortable. The novice lifted her dark head and gave Irena a tight, quick smile before returning to her book.

Ah, so she tried to cover her unease with polite disinterest. Irena couldn't allow that. She called in a billet of steel, and began working the metal with her fingers and her Gift.

Alejandro moved around the room, stopped behind the facing sofa. He rested his hands on the curving back. His gaze fell to the regal stag forming between Irena's hands, its body caught in a mighty leap.

Becca glanced over. Then looked again, brown eyes lighting with curiosity.

Snared as easily as a hare.

Beneath Irena's fingertips, her Gift molded the steel antlers into a wide forehead, a powerful jaw. A running wolf quickly took shape, its fur ruffled by the speed of its passing.

"You are not training with the others, Becca?" Irena asked in English, smoothing away most of her accent.

Despite that effort, the mouse almost went back into her hole. Then Becca tilted her book, showing Irena the spine. "I'm supposedly training my mind."

Irena worked through the Chinese characters of the book's title. She could read symbols more easily than alphabets, but she was hardly well-read. And so when she made out the name, she was surprised to recognize Lao Tzu's work.

She hadn't read it, but she'd heard it recited—in Caelum and on Earth—many times.

She didn't follow any part of it.

"The *Tao Te Ching*?" Alejandro said. His fingers flexed against the back of the sofa with each pulse of her Gift. Irena's breath moved to the same deep rhythm.

"Lilith recommended it. To help me find inner peace and balance."

The wolf in Irena's hands became a razor-edged dagger. "And has it trained your mind to obey like a dog or sharpened it?"

"I don't know yet. I'm still trying to figure out the 'being like water' part." The novice hesitated, her gaze on the spear rising out of the knife. "Do you have any suggestions?"

To be like water? "Submerge yourself in a lake with a sword, and practice with it."

As if finally noting his response to her Gift, Alejandro straightened and clasped his hands behind his back. "Perhaps Sun Tzu's *The Art of War*. It is somewhat similar to Irena's philosophy."

Her lip curled, and she said to him in French, "Sun Tzu too often ignores his gut in favor of his head. That is the best way to get a sword stabbed through it."

Becca looked at Alejandro, a hint of mischief in her smile. "So it'll teach me to fight without arms and legs? Eat hearts?" She glanced back at Irena and her shoulders hunched. "Or so I've heard."

She'd never forced anyone to eat hearts. "I suppose you will find out when you specialize with me in a few decades."

Becca's eyes widened. "God, I hope not."

There it was—that spark Irena had wanted to see. She grinned and reshaped the spear to resemble Mackenzie, the novice's vampire lover. She tossed the statue to Becca.

"Oh, wow. Thanks. Holy crap, it's just like him." Her fingers ran over the chest, the face. She jerked her hand away, sucking in a breath. Blood welled on her thumb, and the novice stuck it between her lips.

Irena frowned. "You put blood into your mouth but balk at eating a heart?"

Becca yanked her thumb out. "Was that a lesson? Was I supposed to learn something useful?"

Learn something useful—from a statue of a skinny vampire? Yet Becca was in earnest. Irena closed her eyes and fought to remain silent. The sort of laughter she was prone to might destroy the small progress she'd made in drawing out the novice.

"Yes," she heard Alejandro say with dry amusement. "A simple lesson: Fangs are sharp."

"Oh. I already know that."

"Good," Irena said, rocking up to her feet. She didn't know if ten minutes had passed, but it felt as if they had. "And if you do specialize with me, bring Lao Tzu's book with you."

She sensed they were both going to need it.

Rosalia sat on the edge of a narrow bunk with her arms crossed, running her hands up and down the sleeves of a soft red sweater. She'd showered, Irena saw, and left her dark hair to dry into damp curls.

Guardians could clean themselves by vanishing dirt into their cache, but sometimes there was no replacement for water.

And even water couldn't always clean deep enough.

Hugh had pulled a chair to the bedside. He'd leaned toward Rosalia, his elbows resting on his knees, his gaze steady on hers.

It was, Irena noted with relief, a few moments after she and

Alejandro entered the room before Hugh and Rosalia broke eye contact.

Trust still existed between them, despite the changes in Hugh after his Fall. He'd aged in the eighteen years since he'd become human again, growing from the boy he'd appeared to be as a Guardian into a man. He wore glasses to correct his vision; he had to eat, sleep, and breathe again.

But his psychic scent was the same, as was his core of strength. Rosalia would be able to take comfort in that—would *need* to take comfort in that. Because everything else had changed.

Little of it was for the better.

Rosalia glanced at Irena, then looked to Alejandro. A sad smile touched her mouth. "Hugh has just told me of the Ascension."

Lead balled in Irena's stomach. Had Rosalia been in the catacombs that long? More than a decade had passed since the Ascension—when thousands of Guardians had given up the fight, their duty, and moved on to their afterlives.

After the Ascension, less than a hundred Guardians remained—and half of those had been lost in battle with Lucifer's nest of nosferatu two years before. Though she'd once counted many Guardians among her friends, Irena despised those who had Ascended. Those who had died fighting—those she still grieved.

But whether they'd Ascended or been slain, Rosalia had likely just learned that most—if not all—of her friends were gone.

"Is there anyone?" Alejandro asked.

Rosalia nodded. "Mariko and Radha," she said, then looked to Hugh.

"Radha is on assignment in Calcutta, and Mariko has taken over most of eastern Asia as her territory," Hugh said. "If you wish, Jake or Selah can teleport them here, or bring you to either of them."

Rosalia nodded, and her eyes filled. "I cannot remember anything you say has happened to me. I shouldn't need to see them, but I do. It is so stupid."

In her distress, Rosalia had spoken in Italian, and so Irena's quiet reply was in the same language. "It is not stupid."

"If you say." Rosalia firmed her jaw. "I left Caelum not long after you Fell," she said to Hugh, then sliced her hand across the air in front of her when his brows rose in question. "My reason had nothing to do with your Fall. I told Michael I would watch Rome and destroy any threats I saw, but I wanted nothing to do with anyone in Caelum for some time."

Irena understood that—she'd left Caelum behind several times. Leaving didn't mean she wouldn't hunt nosferatu or protect humans from demons; she just didn't seek out other Guardians.

The last time had been after she'd made a bargain with a demon who had copied Alejandro's face.

She met his eyes. They'd darkened to black. Yes, he was remembering, as well.

Shame burned; she looked away before he saw it, and forced her thoughts back to Rosalia.

If Rosalia had told her friends she was leaving, that explained why no one had been looking for her. And so she hadn't necessarily been in the catacombs for as long as she'd been missing from Caelum.

"What date is your last memory of Rome?" Irena asked.

"It was July of 2007."

A year and a half ago. "And after the Gates were closed," Irena said, frowning. *After* Lucifer's nest of nosferatu had been sent to Chaos realm, and Lucifer had been locked in Hell. So Lucifer couldn't have captured Rosalia for the nosferatu.

Rosalia stopped rubbing her arms. "The Gates are closed? The Gates to *Caelum*?"

Hugh shook his head. "The Gates to Hell. Lucifer made a bargain with a group of nosferatu. They were slaying humans. Performing rituals."

Rosalia studied his face. "Humans close to you," she guessed.

"Students of mine," Hugh confirmed. "Michael made a wager with Lucifer—and Michael won. Lucifer is bound to keep Hell's Gates closed for the next five hundred years. That was in May of 2007."

"But there were demons who escaped Hell before the Gates closed," Alejandro said. "Several hundred."

"There were some in Rome." Rosalia swallowed. "That is the last I remember—coming across a group of demons in the catacombs."

Hugh frowned. "Are you certain? A group of demons—not nosferatu?"

"Yes."

"Lucifer's demons or Belial's?"

"I don't know. Does it matter?"

"No," Irena said.

"Yes." Alejandro's reply smoothed over hers.

Hugh leaned back in his chair. "In August of last year, Michael and Selah killed seven demons in Rome. Michael told me that he couldn't find you then, but we thought you must have been shielding."

Even Michael couldn't teleport to someone if they completely shielded their psyche. With the iron spike through her head, Rosalia hadn't been shielded—she'd simply not been there.

"The demons are dead?" Rosalia's voice was even, but wrath burned through her psychic scent. Wrath—and disappointment.

Was she hoping to avenge herself? Irena approved. "Yes," she said. "But only those ones. There are others to kill, and demons are all the same."

"That isn't true," Alejandro said. "There are those who follow Lucifer, and those who support Belial in his rebellion against Lucifer—"

"You split hairs again. Demons, nosferatu—the Guardians' only purpose is to slay them. You create a meaningless difference so that you do not feel dishonored by being here. Here, where you are *supported*"—Irena let the full force of her anger turn the word into an accusation—"by one of Belial's demons."

Alejandro's profile was a rigid mask. "Our *purpose* is to protect humans."

"By killing demons."

"Even those demons who can be useful to our purpose?"

"Yes."

On the bed, Rosalia tore her wide-eyed gaze from them and looked to Hugh. "Dru said Michael created Special Investigations so that we'd have a human avenue when we need one. That you are training the novices here . . . with Lilith."

Hugh smiled slightly. "Lilith has Fallen—or rather, the demon equivalent of Falling. She'd only been a halfling demon: A human changed by a ritual," he added when Rosalia's brow creased.

"A *willing* ritual," Irena said.

It wasn't as if Lilith had been forced to become a demon; she'd had a choice. And given the options of serving Lucifer or death, Irena would've chosen much differently than Lilith had.

Hugh inclined his head, acknowledging Irena's clarification. "Michael asked Lilith to head the agency. She spent almost two decades working for the FBI, and so she was most qualified for the position here." He pulled off his spectacles and began to clean them against his shirt before adding, "And I'm *with* her, Rosalia. Not just here at SI."

Rosalia's brows rose in surprise before she smiled. "You always had a soft spot for her."

Irena curled her lip. "And do we also love Rael?"

Alejandro sighed. "We could not do this without the access we are afforded by the American government."

"Yes, we could—"

"Could not do it *as easily*." His fingers clenched at his sides.

"You don't know Rael's motive."

"No, we don't," Alejandro admitted.

"Do you believe it's in our interest?"

"Do you believe we're blind to his nature?"

"So you get in bed with a demon because it's easier." Irena sneered up at him. "It is sickening."

Alejandro faced her, his silken voice deceptively mild. A muscle ticked in his jaw. "I thought you'd understand this, Irena. The Ascension has put a knife to our throat."

Irena's breath left her in a rush. She took a step back, then another.

But it lay unspoken between them: Olek wasn't the one who had chosen to get into bed with a demon.

And she could still see the blade that had been against his throat.

The only way to stop the pain and anger crushing her chest would be to cut out her heart—and so she did now the same thing she'd done then.

She left. She didn't look back.

CHAPTER 4

Always, everything went back to his misstep. Back to that blood-spattered room.

With regret digging a hole in his chest, Alejandro listened to the door close behind Irena. Only his will prevented him from succumbing to his need to follow her.

His will versus his need. For centuries, they'd battled each other. One day, he knew, either his will or his need would crumble into nothing. He didn't know which it would be.

And he didn't know which he *wanted* it to be.

But even if he went after her, nothing more could be said. On the matter of demons, Irena was as capable of compromising as an armless man was capable of holding a sword. The only outcome would be more anger, and sharp words, and another return to the room he'd burned four hundred years ago.

And he still wouldn't be certain if it was her stubbornness that infuriated him, or the knowledge that she was right: It *was* sickening that the Guardians collaborated with a demon.

But the Ascension *had* put a knife to their throats. Though the Gates to Hell were closed, hundreds of demons remained on Earth—far more than there were Guardians. Given a few decades, the Guardians could gather resources, technology, and the human and vampire staff that would bolster the Guardians' small numbers, forming an organization that served the same function as Special Investigations. Given a few decades, Michael could find and transform more humans into Guardians. Given a few *more* decades, those Guardians could be trained and ready to fight demons.

They didn't have decades, however. And so they'd revealed themselves to a select few within the American government, and been forced to pick their battles with demons—Rael in particular. Irena would have the Guardians slay every demon openly, if necessary—but if the demons felt threatened and presented a united front, it'd likely be a Pyrrhic victory for the Guardians . . . assuming it *was* a victory.

Alejandro wasn't ready to make that assumption.

The anger drained from him, as did the heat from his skin. Fortunately, his Gift didn't manifest as color in his face—and although Castleford and Rosalia watched, they likely didn't know how much Irena's leaving bothered him.

Or so he preferred to believe. Maybe they would believe it, too. "I apologize. Irena and I have been friends long enough that we no longer spare our tongues."

Perhaps Castleford, with his ability to read lies, detected Alejandro's. For although it was true that he and Irena didn't spare their tongues, it was more accurate to say they could not control their tongues.

Or *he* could not. He didn't think Irena tried to.

But Castleford only looked to Rosalia again. "Obviously, not everyone is pleased with the arrangement."

"Yes."

She rose from the bed and approached Alejandro, her arms crossed beneath her breasts and her hands tucked into the crooks of her elbows.

She fussed, he suddenly remembered. During her specialization with him, she'd had a habit of absentmindedly—almost maternally—straightening his clothing or his hair. Not just his, but anyone of her acquaintance.

And he hadn't shown her his discomfort then, just as he didn't step back now.

Of course, *then* he'd been waiting for Irena to return. Rosalia had specialized with him during the second century Irena had been away from Caelum, when any other woman's touch had still been unwelcome. Only after she'd come back, after she'd spoken to him in French as she would a stranger, after he'd realized that too much damage had been done and no amount of time could heal it . . . only then had he looked at another woman.

And now . . . now was no different.

Except that although Rosalia's gaze ran over his hair and his shirt, her hands remained tucked. She turned her face as if studying the windowless walls and walked slowly past him, her bare feet pale against the dark wood floor.

She'd never have any memory of how the nosferatu had used her. Alejandro couldn't decide if that was better than knowing. Perhaps the details that her imagination filled in weren't as bad as the unknown reality.

Perhaps they were worse.

"How are the demons different?" She glanced over her shoulder at him. "Some follow Lucifer and some follow Belial, but they have never been *different* in any significant way. Has that changed, as well?"

If her tone had been harsh and fueled by frustration, her question might have come from Irena. And even though Rosalia was obviously more willing to listen, Alejandro didn't have the energy to go through it one more time.

"Their natures haven't changed, no," Alejandro said quietly, and inclined his head toward her former mentor. Castleford had infinite patience. As both mentor to the youngest novices and Lilith's partner, he needed it. "But I'll let Hugh explain how their interests have. I am glad to see you well again, Rosalia."

She nodded. "And you."

The moment he opened the door he regretted leaving the soundproofed room. From somewhere downstairs, Irena's laughter hit him, swept through him. His body tightened with need, but he forced himself to walk smoothly out of the room.

Will and need. He let them wage their war.

Finding Rosalia as they had brought too much too close to the surface. The Guardians often fought demons and nosferatu. Battles were quick and fierce and bloody. It wasn't unusual that Guardians were injured or killed. But it wasn't common that Guardians were *violated* in the way that Rosalia had been . . . as Irena had been.

No, the demons' natures hadn't changed. They just rarely got the opportunity to have a Guardian helpless and unable to fight back.

Or bound by a bargain that prevented her from fighting back.

Pim had joined Becca in the common room. When they saw him, discomfort squirmed through their psychic scents. Alejandro had little doubt they'd been discussing the argument Becca had witnessed. But did they truly think Irena would kill Lilith?

Biting back his irritated sigh, he nodded at both of them, then looked toward the corridor that led to the southwest corner of the building. At the end of the corridor was a room full of mirrors, and a quiet observation area. It would be empty; the room was only visited by the two vampires who suffered from a curse that transformed mirrors into a visual link to the Chaos realm.

But Alejandro didn't want quiet. Didn't want to be left to his thoughts. Not when they were filled with Irena. It would have been easier if only anger and lust existed between them. They'd have fucked. They'd have fought. And it would have been done with.

But it never would be done. And there was just this endless . . . nothing. A nothing punctured by brief moments of fighting and their so-called friendship.

Dear God, how he wanted to be done with both.

Silently, he crossed the common room, heading for the stairs leading to the first level. The metal stairs ended in a large open room that served as the warehouse's central hub. A painted zodiac circled the ceiling. Hallways radiated in four directions: the main corridor leading to security and the front offices, beyond which most humans and visitors never saw; the tech room, more offices, and conference rooms to the right and left; and toward the practice gymnasium and locker rooms at the back of the warehouse.

Irena stood in the hall leading to the gymnasium, talking to a Guardian in a long brown coat who dwarfed Irena's smaller height. If she'd run into Drifter, that explained her laughter—and why she hadn't already left the building. Drifter could put anyone at ease, pull anyone from their temper. It wasn't a Gift, but it was a talent—particularly with Irena.

The tall Guardian tipped his head at Alejandro. Irena remained facing Drifter, her shoulder propped against the wall, her hip cocked and her weight resting on her right foot.

Alejandro fought the urge to walk up behind her, to see how long she'd pretend he wasn't there. Of course, that she hadn't looked around told him exactly how attuned she was to his position. Irena never let anyone else approach her from behind unwatched.

From the offices on the left, a woman lifted her voice and called Alejandro's name.

Lilith.

Irena looked around then, her eyes glittering. Alejandro took a small measure of satisfaction turning his back to her and heading toward Lilith's office.

No, Irena might not understand Alejandro's willingness to take assignments from the former demon, but they'd been doing good work here at SI, no matter who directed it—and no matter how difficult Lilith could be.

She'd been one of Lucifer's demons, though she probably couldn't have been called loyal to him—only desperate to survive. If she hadn't become human again, hadn't fallen for Castleford, she still wouldn't have been like Lucifer's other demons. Those who'd escaped Hell before the Gates had closed now grabbed whatever power they could before Lucifer returned to Earth.

Those were the demons that the Guardians hunted most often through SI. Belial's demons posed a different problem.

He stepped into Lilith's office. She was sitting behind Castleford's desk, the phone receiver at her ear, her expression trapped between impatience and affection. She began to speak in Hindi and was cut off midsentence. Her fingers dragged through her black hair, then she caught his gaze and waved at the chairs facing her desk.

Alejandro walked toward the oil painting of Caelum filling the wall, instead. It'd been painted by Colin Ames-Beaumont, one of the two cursed vampires—and the only vampire who could resist the daysleep and walk in the sun, which had allowed him to visit Caelum. Alejandro thought he'd done a fine job of capturing the realm's beauty, its cerulean skies and white marble towers, the temples and arches and minarets. Incredible . . . and yet still nothing compared to the reality of Caelum.

He studied the painting until, after a few more stuttered attempts and interruptions, Lilith disconnected the phone.

"Fuck me," she said quietly.

Alejandro faced her, lifting his brows.

She walked by the door to kick it closed with the toe of her boot. The soundproofing silenced the noise from outside the office, though the psychic scents of the Guardians in the building were still present. Lilith removed her black suit jacket as she stalked to her desk, and tossed it over the back of one of the chairs she'd offered him.

"Auntie," she said with a slight glare, as if daring him to laugh.

Ah. After Hugh Castleford had become human again, he'd been taken in by an Indian woman and her granddaughter. Auntie had become Lilith's grandmother by association—a seventy-year-old woman who'd apparently just ridden roughshod over the two-thousand-year-old Lilith, who'd once stared down and out-lied Lucifer.

Practice and diplomacy kept Alejandro's lips from twitching. He gestured at the closed door.

"Is this regarding something you don't want the others to hear?"

"No." Lilith dropped into her chair and began swiveling back and forth. "I just know it'll piss Irena off if you're in here with me, and she can't hear what we're saying."

This time, practice and diplomacy prevented his anger from showing. "You don't need to use me to piss her off."

She grinned. "No, that's true. It's just the quickest way to do it." Her dark eyes regarded him closely before she said, "There's a vampire upstairs. Tell me about him."

"Irena knows Deacon. I do not."

"All right, I'll ask her. And she'll tell me to fuck myself, I'll tell her the same, and at the end of it I still won't know anything. So I'm asking you."

No, she wasn't. Not asking about Deacon, at any rate. The vampire had been the leader of a large community for decades; even if Lilith had never met Deacon, she'd have heard enough to take his measure. This was about Irena.

Stiffly, Alejandro said, "She's never made a secret of her dislike for you, or the way in which SI was created. But she would never bring in anyone she thought might endanger the novices and vampires training here."

"Just one who will endanger me?"

His hands were heating. "No. If she comes for you, she'll come from the front." But Irena wouldn't go for Lilith, because she knew how much those same Guardians and vampires depended on SI. Despite her anger, Irena wasn't blind to SI's value. Alejandro wouldn't tell Lilith that, however. "She doesn't think like you."

"Or like you?"

"No." He had to admit that truth. He preferred subtlety. Preferred to undermine his target, discover their weaknesses, so that their fall came as an almost gentle collapse . . . but by that time, an inevitable one.

It'd been centuries since he'd worked that way. The battles a Guardian fought were better suited to Irena's methods. Irena smashed and hit her enemies until they toppled.

Did Lilith think he was one of those enemies? Was her concern not because of Irena's hatred toward her, but because Lilith hadn't expected antagonism between Guardians?

Lilith knew demons well; she wasn't as familiar with Guardians.

He pushed the heat back and said evenly, "Despite my . . .

friendship with her, I wouldn't hesitate to put my life in Irena's hands. There's no one I'd rather have at my back, no one I trust more."

"No one?" A wry smile curved her mouth. "Was that true before you learned that Michael is the son of a demon?"

"Yes."

Her gaze thoughtful, Lilith continued to swivel back and forth in a short arc, tapping her fingers on the arms of her chair. Finally, she looked up at him. "I had to be sure. Finding out that Michael is Belial's son has created enough tension, even among the novices. We can't afford to lose anyone."

She didn't need to tell Alejandro that. "What have you heard of Deacon?"

"That he's a scary motherfucker."

She looked amused by the description. But then, "scary" had a different meaning for Guardians than it did for vampires—and for Lilith.

"That was not my impression. Irena, however, thinks Deacon only needs to regain confidence, and then he'll be an asset to our cause. I trust her judgment."

Apparently, so did Lilith. She nodded. "All right. And Rosalia? Dru gave me an account of her injuries. I want your take on the situation she was in."

He thought of the ossuary, the spike. The memory of Rosalia's condition hardened in his stomach . . . but that wasn't what Lilith was asking.

"I can't make sense of it," he said. "The church was being restored, but inside, the smell of paint was faint." And if the painting had been completed months ago, the pews and altar had been sitting, covered, for at least that long. "But it hadn't been abandoned. There was no dust. And the water in the stoup was fresh."

"A caretaker?"

Alejandro had his doubts. "One who, in more than a year, did not come across Rosalia or the nosferatu in the catacombs?"

"That is a question. I'll ask Jake and Alice to dig around the church. And the nest?"

"The nosferatu weren't the ones who caught her. The last she recalls is fighting demons."

Lilith stopped swiveling. "Lucifer's or Belial's?"

"She doesn't know. But if they were the same demons Michael and Selah killed in Rome last year . . ."

"They didn't take the time to find out." She stared at him. Though her psyche was tightly shielded, he could almost feel her mind racing behind that flat gaze.

Trying to figure out how alliances might be shifting, he thought. Just as he had been since he'd realized there was a nest beneath the church.

Lucifer had once allied with the nosferatu, but only because he'd promised the cursed creatures a new home: Caelum. Each of those nosferatu was now in the Chaos realm, from which there was no escape.

It was possible that, before he'd closed the Gates, Lucifer had formed another alliance with the nosferatu—or instructed demons loyal to him to carry out his instructions after they'd left Hell. He'd done that once before, ordering a demon to sacrifice vampires in an attempt to change the resonance of one of Caelum's Gates to create another Gate to Hell.

That had been around the same time that Selah and Michael had slain the demons in Rome.

But if the demons Michael and Selah had slain were loyal to Belial, that was something new. What would it mean if Belial's demons had been courting the nosferatu, with a Guardian food source as an incentive?

Unlike Lucifer's demons, Belial's worked together—many of them under the cover of Legion, a multinational corporation. Until the past spring, their only common goal had seemed to be replacing Lucifer on Hell's throne with Belial, who had promised to return them to Grace. Only recently had the Guardians learned of a prophecy that predicted Belial taking the throne after the nephilim had been destroyed. Legion had begun courting vampire communities and trying to replicate vampire blood—which had been proven to weaken the powerful nephilim.

In that, Belial's demons and the Guardians shared a common goal: destroying the nephilim. Their reasons, however, couldn't have been more different.

If the nephilim only carried out the task for which they'd been created—executing those demons who broke the Rules—the Guardians wouldn't have fought them. But once they'd begun eradicating the vampire communities, the Guardians had to stand against them.

And the nephilim had their own leader to put on Hell's throne: Anaria, their mother—and Michael's sister.

Alejandro had thought Anaria—a former Guardian—would be a better choice to take Hell's throne than Belial or Lucifer, until he'd learned that Anaria had once led other Guardians to slaughter a human army. She'd believed that without the terror of war, humans wouldn't be driven to the hatred and murder that landed their souls in Hell, and the slaughter had been the first step of a comprehensive plan to save mankind from themselves and to weaken Lucifer.

No matter how good her intentions, she'd broken the Rules when she'd killed humans and had to Fall, her Guardian abilities stripped. Yet as one of the ten grigori who'd been born after demons consumed the flesh of a dragon and mated with humans, she was still too powerful—and, after Falling, she no longer had to follow the Rules.

Michael had ordered her execution, but Anaria's husband, Zakril, had hidden her away in a sarcophagus, instead. But when Zakril had been killed, she'd been trapped—for more than two thousand years. The nephilim had only recently freed her from that prison.

The Guardians hadn't encountered Anaria since her escape, but Alejandro knew they all dreaded the inevitable meeting. Though Anaria might harbor no ill will toward the Guardians, they *had* to fight the nephilim—and Anaria, as their leader, was a powerful, deadly opponent.

Through the prophecy, had Belial's demons anticipated Anaria's return and allied with the nosferatu to strengthen their numbers against the nephilim? Or had there been another purpose?

With a low sound of frustration, Lilith shook her head. "I don't know what the fuck it means. When Michael gets in again, and Jake reports back on the church, we'll work out how we'll go forward with this info. Until then—" She lifted two folders from her desk, and Alejandro vanished them into his cache. "Rumors of human sacrifice outside London, and a bloodsucker community in Buenos Aires that we need to talk to, because their heads have just been killed."

Which might be just the usual vampire politics, similar to what had ousted Deacon. Or it might be a sign that the nephilim were planning another massacre—and might lead the Guardians to Anaria.

Alejandro looked up as the lights in the room flickered, which meant that Jake had just teleported into the warehouse. Good. After Lilith gave the young Guardian his assignment in Rome, Jake could take Alejandro to his. It was still midday in Argentina, so Alejandro wouldn't find any vampires awake for several more hours. He'd go to London first.

Lilith frowned, picked up her cell phone, and sighed. When she began typing a message on the keypad, Alejandro took that as a dismissal.

She caught him at the door. "Alejandro, hold on." When he turned, she said, "We've got a potential problem: Jake's here with Alice, and Khavi's following them."

Khavi was a Guardian and one of the grigori. She was also Zakril's sister and had hidden with her brother after Michael had sentenced Anaria to death. With her Gift of foresight, she'd been the source of the prophecy, but even that powerful Gift hadn't helped her avoid being trapped in Hell by Belial, or prevented her husband, Aaron, from being killed by the demon. She'd lived a solitary existence in Hell for almost as long as Anaria had been in her sarcophagus. Though Alejandro would never make the mistake of thinking Khavi was harmless, she'd returned to Caelum with a gratitude that was genuine after Michael had brought her back from Hell.

Khavi had visited SI a few times without incident, so Alejandro didn't see the problem. "And?"

"Can you run interference?"

Interference . . . between Khavi and Irena? Christ. Had nothing he said made a difference? Irena hated demons, and everything they'd created—and had openly declared her distrust of the grigori. But that didn't mean she'd kill Khavi without a good reason.

Lilith held up her hand, as if to head off his anger. "Honestly, I'm with Irena on this one—I'm not sure we can trust that Khavi's on our side. But like I said: We can't lose anyone, and I'd rather have Irena's temper directed at you. Michael can take it without hitting back. We don't know enough about Khavi yet."

He couldn't argue that. "You must be thankful that neither one is often here."

She looked surprised. "You're wrong. I prefer it when people are as direct as Irena is. You know where you stand. And in her place, I'd question Michael's decision to put me in charge, too." Lilith shrugged. "But Michael's an idiot, so what can you do?"

"You could, perhaps, refrain from calling the Doyen an idiot," he pointed out. And with a slight bow, he left.

❧

Irena knew she was making the others nervous. Alice's mouth had taken on a thin, pinched look; her eyes were sharp and wary. Drifter had aimed for casual by hooking his thumbs into his suspenders, but the only reason he'd ever strive to look at ease was when he needed to cover up his tension. Jake chewed on a toothpick and held onto a smile, but he'd edged closer to Alice—to teleport her away, if he needed to.

And Khavi knew it, too. The grigori sometimes appeared confused, but her eyes were always clear. She pushed, just to see reactions, to find weaknesses. Irena knew this. Knew she was being tested.

It didn't matter if she failed. Demons played games; Irena did not.

But she should have realized that when Jake and Alice teleported into the warehouse's central hub, it meant that Alice's language lesson with Khavi was over and that the grigori, her time free, might also teleport to SI. And while Jake and Alice had remained in the middle of the hub, Jake holding Alice against him until the disorientation of teleporting faded, Irena should have stayed in the gymnasium hallway—where she had a solid wall at her back—instead of walking out with Drifter to meet them in that wide, open space.

But she'd been distracted by the flickering lights, and Drifter's explanation that the electrical fluctuation was an effect of Jake's new Gift.

Then Khavi had arrived—and although Drifter continued to talk, Irena hadn't been able to concentrate on anything he said. The demon spawn slowly circled their small group, her head tilted back as she examined each sign of the zodiac painted on the ceiling. She'd made it to the Gemini, behind Alice. Only the top of Khavi's braided black hair was visible over the taller woman's shoulder. Irena stepped to the side, trying to keep the grigori in full view between Alice and Drifter.

Alice met her eyes, then moved toward Jake, allowing Irena a better angle. The long, black, silk column of Alice's dress and her braid were just as severe as ever, and she still moved with the disjointed strangeness that she'd picked up from her spiders. But she'd softened, Irena thought, when instead of crossing her arms over her narrow chest, Alice slipped her hand into the crook of Jake's elbow.

Alice caught her gaze again. "Do you want to go to the Archives now?"

Alice had been teaching Irena the demonic symbols she'd been learning from Khavi. Each week, they met in the Archive building in Caelum. They weren't scheduled for another session until tomorrow.

"No. I want you to go to Rome with Jake," she began, but broke off as Khavi moved to the stand beneath the crab. A few more signs, and Khavi would be at Irena's side.

Then behind her.

The hub suddenly felt closed in, shrinking.

"What do we need to do?"

Irena made herself focus on Jake. He'd grown up quickly, this young Guardian. A trip through Hell had forced him to, as had his relationship with Alice. He'd fought, sacrificed—and thanks to a second transformation, was stronger than Guardians several times his age. And now he was developing a second Gift . . . though he'd barely just learned to control the first one.

In the hallway behind Jake, Alejandro slipped out of Lilith's office like smoke. He caught her gaze. She looked away.

"Search the church for evidence that more than three nosferatu lived there—but do not spend *all* of your time in the catacombs." Irena couldn't understand Jake and Alice's fascination with ancient ruins, but she'd give them an opportunity to indulge it. "Find out who is restoring the building, and who looks after it. The condition in which we found it doesn't make sense; I want to make sense of it."

Alejandro took a place between Alice and Drifter. Even if Khavi moved behind Irena, he'd be able to watch the grigori.

The room stopped squeezing in on her.

Though Alejandro spoke to Jake, he looked at Irena. "And when you see Lilith, she'll have the same assignment for you." He rarely smiled in the usual way; his mouth remained flat, though it seemed to deepen at the corners and his cheeks hollowed slightly. His amusement showed in his eyes, instead. "It seems Lilith's and Irena's plans aren't so dissimilar."

Was he trying to bait her? Irena glared at him. "And you'd have given them the same task, as well."

"I reckon it's only sensible to check it out," Drifter cut in, running his thumbs up and down his leather straps. Irena wondered what made him more nervous: standing between her and Khavi, or between her and Alejandro. "And Rosalia—she's doing all right?"

Irena had just told him that Rosalia was fine. She gave him a look. "Yes."

Drifter's face reddened, but as he'd no doubt intended, the topic had moved on from Lilith and her supposed similarity to Irena.

"I met Rosalia a couple of times while I was training with Mariko," Jake said. He cupped his hands in front of his chest, bounced them up and down. "She had the most amazing—"

A poke of Alice's bony elbow cut off the rest. Irena noted that Alice's irritation was false, however—Irena hadn't seen Jake even look at another woman in months. Most likely, he'd just wanted to produce that exasperated look in Alice's eyes, and the faint smile on her lips.

And thanks to Jake's ridiculous comment, Irena was smiling now, too. Even with Khavi circling closer, she let herself relax, and watch the subtle play of irritation and attraction between Alice and Jake.

They made a strange couple, but Irena had to admit they were a good match. Relationships between Guardians were difficult, even at the best of times. Violence filled their lives, and some took on long assignments where they had to adopt identities that had no resemblance to their role in Caelum. Over time, many lovers burned out or grew bored. Guardians had no institution like marriage, although some followed human traditions. They couldn't reproduce. And, in Guardian society, a separating couple didn't face disapproval or disgrace—or the stigma that a divorcing human couple might.

So when Guardians made a commitment to stay together, it wasn't for children or cultural expectations, but just because they loved each other that much. Some relationships were hotter than others, but in those Irena had seen endure, there'd always been deep respect and true friendship between the partners.

Irena hadn't been sure whether Alice's strangeness had been a challenge for Jake or if Alice had just been desperate when she'd met him. But they'd settled into Alice's quarters on Caelum, shared their free time and many of their assignments— and frequently disappeared together, returning with Alice's hair unbound. Disappeared, often after Alice gave Jake the slight smile that she was giving him now.

Which, in Irena's opinion, was worth praising the gods for. Alice had been in severe need of a good bedding for more than a century.

But Alice didn't just appear well fucked; she looked well kissed, too. She and Jake had obviously found that deep respect and intimacy that would carry them through the centuries—or millennia.

Irena suppressed the urge to rub away the soft little ache forming behind her breast. She was happy for her friend; this wasn't envy. But maybe it was . . . a wish.

But she wouldn't look at Olek. And she wouldn't dwell on what she didn't have.

Beside her, Khavi pointed at the ceiling. Irena couldn't stop her reaction; she tensed, shifted her weight, and prepared to defend her space.

She didn't need to. Khavi only asked, "Who painted this? It is not the same person who has painted Caelum."

Like Michael's voice, Khavi's seemed to come from several tongues at once, melded into a harmonious one. Beautiful, soothing. Not unlike a Scitalis serpent that mesmerizes its prey before striking, Irena thought.

And like that mythical serpent, Khavi was physically stunning, with the fine bone structure and bearing of an ancient queen. But she wasn't elegant. She moved with the bold purpose of a warrior—if sometimes a quiet one. Her hair was the same as when she'd come back from Hell, a black cloud held in check by tiny braids. *Bronze Age cornrows,* Irena had once heard Becca call them. Khavi's clothes were no longer ancient, however. She didn't bother with the toga that Michael sometimes still wore; she'd traded them in for jeans and sandals. She looked no older than a teenager—except for her eyes.

Those were old. And although at this moment she had dark brown irises instead of pure black orbs, nothing human lay behind them.

That was what Michael was. He'd fooled them. He'd given them the appearance of a being who'd once been a man, but he was really this. The grigori, unlike other Guardians and vampires, had never been human.

Appearances are almost always deceiving. It was the first lesson taught to Guardians. Irena should have known that meant Michael's appearance, too.

"No, those were painted by Ames-Beaumont." Drifter glanced up. "This one, Dru did."

"Drusilla, the healer," Alice clarified.

"Drusilla," Khavi repeated slowly, as if tasting the name. Like her clothes, she'd updated her language, but her speech was a jumble of styles. Jake had said Khavi had learned English by looking into both his and Alice's futures; Irena thought that, since then, she'd glimpsed more than just that.

"I haven't seen much of her," Khavi said.

No. Many of the Guardians kept away from Khavi. Her psychic scent was unreadable—except that it was dark, and it lay heavily across the mind unless they kept their psychic blocks high.

And Irena knew very few Guardians who appreciated the grigori seeing parts of their futures—knowing when they would die, how they would die. Especially as Khavi chose which information to reveal. To what purpose, Irena did not want to imagine.

So they kept away. If that disappointed or grieved Khavi, Irena did not pity her.

"And that is the goddess Astraea, I think? The figure with the scales?"

Drifter shook his head. "I sure don't know."

"Yes," Irena said. She met the grigori's eyes. "The one who sat in judgment of humans until she decided they were too evil for her to bother with anymore."

Khavi's brows arched. Like the rest of her, they were thin and delicate. *Appearances are almost always deceiving.* "You believe she was weak?"

To set herself up as a judge, but run when the task became too difficult? Her wisdom could not have been worth much.

"Yes," Irena said.

Alejandro stepped closer, close enough for Irena to touch, and looked up at the Virgo. "She did her duty. She judged them all when she said they were evil. Perhaps humans should be grateful she didn't also carry out a punishment."

"Perhaps people would've been more grateful if she *had* killed the evil humans among them." Irena gave him a wry look. "You argue with the devil's tongue, Olek."

"No." Khavi's smile had an edge that was sharper than amusement. "He sounds like an angel."

"*Angels?* You've met—" Jake's phone buzzed. He looked at it and grimaced. He caught Drifter's eyes, then jerked his head toward Lilith's office. "I'm heading in. You want a ride back to Seattle?"

"I do."

"Okay." With his hand in Alice's, Jake backed away, pointed at Khavi. "I'm going to ask you more about that."

Irena held Alejandro's gaze as Jake and Alice took their leave. Jake wanted to ask more about Khavi's claim to have seen angels, but Irena did not care about that. There were no angels here. Only Guardians. Guardians and grigori.

Though when she looked at Olek, Khavi seemed very far away. "Did you think I would pull my knives out?"

"No. If it came to that, I think you would use your teeth." His gaze settled on her mouth as if he expected her to snap her teeth at him—or to laugh. "If you will join me in the gymnasium, we will spar."

She laughed now, in surprise. "Slaying the nosferatu didn't satisfy you? You've had a victory today; do you now look forward to a defeat?"

"When did you last use your sword rather than your knives?" His smile came into his eyes. "You'll find that I've improved."

She knew he had. "I've beaten you with only a knife before."

"That was before," he said. "And you were not satisfied then. Now you will be."

Her heart pounded. When had he last challenged her? Before the bargain with the demon, before she'd created an iron room to keep Olek out, before she'd left him to burn it all. Now, finally, he challenged her again.

The centuries fell away, and she was breathless, her world filled with him. Needing movement, she circled his lean form, her gaze measuring his length. Physically, he had barely changed. He still moved like smoke and flame.

Except for now, when he was a statue beneath her gaze.

"You *are* older. Which means that you use swords that are not matched to your speed or your strength. If we do this, I will measure you for new weapons." She stopped behind him. His muscles were taut. Her fingers remembered gliding up smooth metal that was a match to his aroused form. "Or I will try to. It will be difficult to take your measure when you are begging for mercy upon the gymnasium floor."

"Did you wear braids then?" Khavi's harmonious voice smothered Irena's good spirits. "Or is that something you *will* do?"

Irena held herself still. She wouldn't anger just because the grigori had spoken to her. "Unless you have lied about being unable to see the past, then it must be the future, demon spawn."

And it couldn't be Irena's future. She would *never* wear braids again.

"I saw it long ago, and it was not *your* future. I do not know when it happens. Perhaps it has, or it will." Khavi drew her fingers down the sides of her jaw and brought them to a point a few inches from the end of her chin. "His beard was longer."

Alejandro remained still, but he was like smoke again, dark and gathering. "Mine?"

"No. The demon's whose future I saw. Though the rest of him was like you, the beard was not." She drew the end of a braid to her mouth, ran the tip over her lips like a paintbrush. Her eyes met Irena's. "The demon will say that he loves your—"

"*Nyet!*" The denial burst from her. Her knives were in her hands, and she was already springing forward.

She would silence the demon spawn herself.

Alejandro brought her up short. His arms wrapped around her waist, a steel band that she couldn't bend to her will and wouldn't break. He yanked her back against him.

"I suggest you leave, madam." His voice and his psychic scent were sharp with icy disdain, but Irena felt the blasting heat of anger through his clothes.

"It was your past, then. And Michael has already slain that particular demon." The grigori's eyes flooded with black from edge to edge. Her Gift pushed out and swept back, scraping across Irena's psyche like crushed shells caught in a tide. "Your future holds just as much death. You should be pleased; a demon's spawn will fall beneath your spear. And soon, I think. I must see—"

She vanished silently. Irena stood, her chest a heaving bellows. Alejandro's hands tightened, and she ripped out of his grasp, whirled on him.

"*Never again.*" She held her knife out, pointed at his throat. "I will tear your arms off."

His skin stretched over his cheekbones so that they stood out like blades. He pushed her knife aside. His hands trapped her face, held her tight.

"What did he love?" he demanded.

"Nothing. A demon cannot lo—"

"They can." His gaze searched hers. Looking, always looking. As if he never had before, as if he never would again. "It was your braids. I thought he'd—"

He broke off. Was that relief in his expression?

She hated him in that instant. Wanted to hurt him. "Tied me with them? Whipped me? Strung me up? No, he did none of those things," she said bitterly.

Alejandro's eyes told her that he'd thought all of that and more, and each imagining had been agony for him. That the truth relieved him tortured her more than a demon could have.

And not even the whole truth. Would that be a relief, too? It choked her to think so—and infuriated her.

If she told him what had happened in that iron room, Alejandro would understand her shame. He was not a fool, and he knew her well. But if relief accompanied that understanding, Irena feared her response. Her fury now was pale in comparison to what it could be—to what it had been with the demon when he'd finished with her.

She would not risk losing her head to anger with Olek.

"What did he say, Irena?"

"That they were like ropes of fire." And like flames, the demon made them lick and dance. A brush across her lips, a flick against her skin. And she'd burned. "Let me go, Olek, or I will break each of your fingers."

"They will heal." His thumbs stroked her temples in heated streaks.

There was nowhere she didn't feel that hot touch. She hadn't felt it in four centuries, but her body remembered. Need carried it over her skin, pooled like heavy liquid fire in her core. She wanted that touch. Needed that touch. And resented that it made her so weak.

But she didn't need to break his bones to make him let her go. "You hold me against my will?"

Instantly, his hands dropped away. He took a step back, his face pale. "Forgive me."

She wanted to turn, to go, but she'd already run once today with a crushing weight in her chest. "Do you still wish to spar?"

Stupid to ask. Stupid to try to recapture what they had for a few seconds here, for a few months centuries ago. It could not be done, and nothing good would come from digging up the ruins of what they'd shared.

"No." He bowed slightly. "I have assignments to complete—and I do not want to fight with you anymore."

Not fight? She watched him walk away, her stomach in a knot. Then what would they do?

The answer was too obvious: nothing.

CHAPTER 5

Jake teleported him to London. Thanks to Special Investigations and a plethora of falsified documentation in his cache, Alejandro had credentials that would stand up under scrutiny, but it was too late in the evening to pretend a police interview. Instead, he followed one of the men who'd reported the human sacrifices to a pub.

He'd planned to buy the man—Walters—a pint, but didn't have to make even that small effort. As soon as Walters entered the pub, a group of men hailed him. They set ale in front of him and began their questions. Alejandro sat in a nearby booth, read through the newspaper clippings and police reports from the file, and listened. The men were clearly having Walters on—and clearly disbelieved every word he said. And Walters said more than enough. The more he drank, the more his tongue loosened, and the more Alejandro was persuaded that the Guardians had nothing to be concerned about here. He'd yet to meet a demon who skulked around in a cloak beneath a full moon—and a demon couldn't kill a human unless that person willingly offered his life.

Most of these reports ended up being unrelated to demons. Some were vampires who'd been trying to cover up their nature. When Alejandro encountered them, he offered assistance.

That wasn't the case here.

An hour later, he left the pub with nothing more substantial than a renewed dislike for the scent of vinegar. He'd visit the site of the alleged sacrifice to make certain—though he suspected that if he found any blood, it would be chicken or pig.

Alejandro formed a long coat and turned up his collar as he stepped out onto the street. The cold didn't affect him, but he didn't like the rain on the back of his neck any more than when he'd been human.

At this hour, the streets were mostly empty, and the night quiet. Alejandro walked, and tried to occupy his mind with anything but Irena, and the way he'd left her earlier. He'd even have welcomed Jake's endless—and entertaining—chatter, but the young Guardian no longer trained with him daily. Alejandro hadn't yet taken on another student.

The urge for sex drove hard through him, as it always did after a fight with Irena. He had no one to go to, however. And even if Emilia had still lived in his house, he wouldn't use her as a substitute.

God, what a laughable idea.

There wasn't a substitute for Irena. No woman could be. Every one of his companions had been friends with him first. He hadn't often fought with them, and he didn't provoke them. Until the inevitable end, his relationships were comfortable.

Even when he and Irena hadn't fought, life with her hadn't been comfortable.

The street opened into a square. From a pedestal, a bronze statue overlooked a fenced garden. The male figure strode purposefully to nowhere, a sober expression fixed to his dark face. Alejandro drew closer, but he no longer saw this statue.

And, yes—life with Irena had been torture, sometimes.

He'd stood for nearly an hour in the forge, his clothes vanished. Irena could have recreated his form within seconds, but she took her time with the statue. Long enough that Alejandro's initial arousal, the half-hardness of knowing that she looked at him so intimately, had faded. Long enough that his focus had expanded from her and he'd begun to enjoy the quiet, the soft heat trapped by the thick wooden walls of the lodge, the pattering of rain on the metal roof. And so at ease that an ember popping in the hearth startled him; he cocked his head, to hear better.

Irena's soft growl came from in front of the statue. "Do not move your head if you wish to keep it."

"Perdóneme, maestra." *He gave a mock bow and regained the pose she'd instructed him to take: standing, his weight on his left foot, his arms hanging at his sides. They felt useless there; his hands were meant to hold a sword. But she'd wanted to sculpt a man at rest.*

It seemed a lie. He was at rest, but no semblance of life existed in this pose, or in the statue she created.

She looked around the statue's shoulder, the firelight glinting off her braids. The color of the flames was not half as deep or as varied as the oranges and reds of her hair. "Do you tire of waiting?"

Was that what this exercise was about—his patience? "Sí."

He tired of waiting, but only for her to be satisfied with his training. He didn't tire of standing here, with Irena's gaze running over him, her Gift pouring from her hands.

Laughter rippled through her psychic scent, like a smooth pebble tumbling down a mountain stream. But her voice was even as she replied,

"But that is what a Guardian does: wait. Endless hours, until you finally detect a demon, finally track down a nosferatu. And a few brutal moments later, you will either be victorious or you will be dead."

He watched her fingers sweep down the arm of the bronze figure. "I will be victorious."

"You cannot even defeat me yet."

A flush started up his neck. It was true. In the two weeks since their meeting in Caelum, he had disarmed her, had bloodied her, had ambushed her—but she'd always recovered and prevailed.

Her brows crashed together, and her fury surprised him out of his embarrassment. Despite her anger, her words were as flat and barren as the tundra outside the forge.

"There is no shame in being overpowered by one who is stronger or more skilled. No shame in a battle well fought, even if it ends in defeat."

Her lips compressed, and she moved back in front of the statue.

She was . . . hiding, he realized. That outburst had not been for him. He thought of what he'd already learned of her history. Thought of how she might have been overpowered. She hadn't been overpowered by a demon or nosferatu; if she had been, she'd be dead.

So it had been a man—or men. She'd been a slave, and he had no doubt she'd been a vibrant, strong woman. Who wouldn't have wanted her? What man wouldn't have wanted to prove his strength by overpowering her?

His hands fisted, as if to hold his own rage within them.

"Then what shame would you accept?"

"If you stopped fighting." Her gaze swept over him, and with the next pulse of her Gift, the statue's fists closed. "Even if you cannot physically struggle, if you stop fighting you should feel shame."

She honored defiance, then. He knew well how she appreciated his—not thoughtless defiance, but resistance to anything that went against his core. In the first days of training, her eyes had gleamed when he'd told her how he'd burned, tied to a wooden post. The gleam hadn't been pleasure, and he'd been surprised that he'd understood it: The pain of his execution had faded a hundred years ago, but he would always have his moment of defiance, his refusal to betray his family to save his life. That was something a man could take pride in. Something she'd admired.

But he'd not done much worth admiration in the hundred years since. Only study and train.

Why, then, had she promised more after his training was completed? She was twelve hundred years old. One of the strongest in Caelum, with stories, battles, and victories attached to her name. She'd had lovers and feuds with Guard-

*ians, humans, and vampires all. But she did not carry her age
like Michael did, in quiet and grace. No, she was rough, in a
sleeveless, backless tunic that could barely be called a covering, and a man's leather breeches, her bare feet on the dirt
floor. She was barbaric. A pagan, who could not read or write
despite the library open to her in Caelum and the thousands
of Guardians who'd have been willing to teach her. He did not
understand his fascination for her, and couldn't see why she
might be tempted by him.*

*Did she toy with him? That first day in the courtyard, had
she recognized his desire and used it to keep him in line while
he trained with her? She did not even look at him, naked, with
interest in her eyes.*

And her hands only touched a limp replica of a man.

*Her fingers traced the statue's biceps. Her nails were short,
her hands square. A snake's thin tail wound around her wrist,
increasing in size as it wrapped the length of her arm, joined
by other serpents, all intertwined around each other. He often
thought they changed and shifted with her mood, but he'd never
been certain. He could not see any difference in them now, only
felt that the serpents winding her arms were at rest.*

*The statue was not. She stood at its side, and her hand
slipped down its bronze back, over the sculpted hip. The posture hadn't changed, yet the muscles beneath the metal skin
weren't at ease now, but taut. A man, with his hands clenched
at his sides and poised to fight.*

*She stepped back and raised her arm. The light from the
fire flickered over the blue scales on her arm. "You look at
these?"*

"Are they a warning?" Do not touch.

*"They were, once. An incomplete one." Half the tattoo sud-
denly disappeared from her skin, as if she'd vanished the upper
part of a sleeve. There was no softness in those arms, in her
limbs. He'd never seen any woman built as hard as Irena was.
"We were only to my elbow when the nosferatu came to kill
us."*

*To kill the tribe of slaves that had escaped Rome . . . and
Irena had died saving them.*

"To what purpose?"

The upper half of the tattoo slowly appeared again, winding around the sleek, pale skin until one of the heads rested on her shoulder. The others tucked their heads beneath her underarm. *"As a group, we were weak. It did not matter how well I fought, how strong I was; I was a woman, and with such a leader we would be seen as prey. And so we thought to make me a Gorgon instead."*

A monster—a woman with hair of poisonous serpents and a gaze that could turn men to stone.

"For hours every night, a friend used her awl and her dyes. The image was to eventually cover my arms, my face. Fear would be our defense until we built stronger defenses." She laughed to herself—a low, throaty sound. *"It did not scare the nosferatu."*

And it wouldn't scare demons now. *"Why keep them?"* She could easily shift her skin and conceal them, but instead she had used her Guardian abilities to complete the decoration on her arms.

"I cannot remember her name." She ran her hand from her elbow to her shoulder. *"But these remind me of her, and so she is not lost. None of those who fled Rome with me are."*

So they were her own defiance, her pride. And a link to her human past. Most Guardians maintained some connection. Habits, thoughts—they reflected their human history, as did their Gifts.

She'd said that hers had come because she'd sworn never to be chained. With such a Gift, she couldn't be. But Alejandro thought now that some part of her was cold, hard, like the metal she manipulated.

"Do you do this with all of your novices?"

"Sculpt them? No." She returned to the statue, rising up on her toes and flicking at its hair. Tiny metal strands wisped beneath her touch. Her Gift pulsed, deep and strong, and the statue changed in a single, fluid movement—standing in profile to Alejandro, arms crossed over its chest, jaw set.

"Allow them to bed you afterward." Make them love you.

Her hand stilled. The serpents on her arms seemed to coil. *"I said nothing of a bed."*

If no bed, then what? Was he waiting for a quick fuck? All of this frustration for . . . what? Nothing but a barbaric tumble.

Anger knotted in his gut, his throat. "Then the floor will do."

"It often does." Her smile was sharpened steel. "And this is what matters to you? This is why you have followed my direction—so that when it is over and you are a full-fledged Guardian, you can fuck me on the floor?"

He wanted to say yes. He couldn't. The silence stretched between them. She turned back to the statue, but didn't touch it.

And she didn't use her Gift.

The knots in his throat frayed when he realized why. No matter how strong a Guardian's shields were, the use of a Gift carried emotions. She'd never hidden her anger from him. Only her vulnerability.

And he was suddenly certain he'd hurt her. He hadn't known he could do that.

He never wanted to again.

"Forgive me," he said, and though he'd said it to her before, this was the first time he'd meant it. He struggled to relax, to find the pose that she'd put him in. "I have been fighting to understand you. I am ashamed that I almost let myself be beaten."

"By what?"

"My desire for you." It was difficult to admit when he had no declaration that she desired him in return. "It overpowers me."

He did not expect her laughter, but it rang out then. He stiffened.

She shook her head. "I laugh at myself, not at you. I forget that you are young. You do not always seem so to me. Your silences are deeper than Michael's, and you smile less, too."

Her brow creased as she spoke, her voice full of a question. Perhaps she could not fathom a quiet man, any more than he could his fascination for a brash woman.

He returned her gaze, unsmiling.

Her eyes grew bright, glowing brilliantly green. "If you wish to understand me, you must understand this: I am old.

I fight the same battle against my need for you; I've just had more practice."

She touched the statue. Her Gift was a gentle pulse, but this time he felt the heat beneath it. Heat that seemed to wrap around his shaft and encourage the flesh to swell.

"And I will not . . . bed . . . a Guardian who is not properly trained. I cannot lie quiet with a man I must always protect. Perhaps I will worry that his life will be taken, for nothing is certain—but if he does not have a chance of walking away from an encounter with a demon, I will not give him my heart."

His own thudded painfully against his ribs.

"And I must fight my hunger now," she continued, her hand running down the bronze chest, "because if I took you on the floor, I would not be able to cut your legs off tomorrow. I could not train you as you need to be trained. And so I bury it, and I wait." Her fingers explored a metal flank. "Some days it is not buried as deeply as others."

Her Gift stroked over his flesh. His cock responded, rising like a burning brand against his lower abdomen. Irena moved aside, revealing the front of the statue. With shock, he saw the thick erection she'd formed from its flaccid member.

Her fingers slipped up the cleft of the statue's buttocks; her Gift lifted its erection to match his.

Holy Mother of God. He almost protested when she ran the tip of her forefinger up the length of straining flesh.

But its flesh did not strain; his did. The statue was only his reflection. He clenched his jaw and bore the exquisite ache of another pulse of her Gift, ripe with her need.

Why did she do this now? So that he would learn to fight his need and the effect of her Gift? To bury it as she did?

Never.

He gripped the base of his shaft. His cock felt as heavy as heated iron. On the next pulse of her Gift, he stroked his way up.

Irena froze, her gaze locked on his hand. After a long moment, she looked at his face.

He knew his challenge was written there. He would not allow her to teach him this lesson. He refused to learn to bury his need. If she used her Gift, he would move his hand. If she stopped, he would not.

Her lips curved. "You will regret it."

"So be it."

She turned her back to him, and for a second he was light-headed with the rush of anticipation—then discomfort brought him crashing down.

Dear God, he hadn't thought this through. Rarely had he touched himself this way. Not since he'd been young, and never in front of someone. Now he was utterly aware that he stood on flagrant display, and that when he spent, she would witness the crude emission of seed.

But Irena did not appear uncomfortable. No, she walked toward him, a small pot in her hand. When she lifted the lid, the scent of almond filled the air.

"Oil," she told him. "To make it easier."

He'd only just fathomed her meaning when she tipped the pot, spilling the silky liquid over his shaft and his fist. Alejandro sucked in a breath; his hips jerked toward her. Dear God, the sensation was incredible. He slid up through his fingers and had to clench his teeth against a shout.

"Better, yes?"

He gave a harsh laugh. "Better."

He did not recognize his voice, the low growl of pained pleasure it had become. And when he stroked his cock again, unprompted by surprise or her Gift, he did not recognize any of himself.

She gave him a wry smile. "I have learned the difficult way. Some of my bed-partners were more eager than skilled."

Her bed-partners? As if she'd struck him, he recoiled and stared at her in disbelief. She would mention them now? Good God. He knew she wasn't a virgin, as his wife had been. He'd taken other lovers during his century in Caelum, and hadn't been the first for any of them. But none of them had flung their former bed-partners in his face, either.

Irena's smile vanished. Without a word, she returned to the statue and poured the remaining oil over the bronze penis.

Her expression was hard when she looked at Alejandro

again. Holding his gaze, she backed up against the statue's thighs and bent over, her braids swinging forward. Her hands went to the waist of her breeches. She nodded at his fist, motionless around his cock.

"Will you begin this? And we will have fucking today, after all."

His disbelief swelled. She would not do that.

But she would, he realized. She would. And with every stroke of his hand, she'd make the statue penetrate her.

His disbelief was shattered, replaced by desperation. "You cannot, Irena."

"I said you will regret it."

But this had not been her meaning then. He'd altered the game between them when he'd rejected her frank words—and rejected so much of her life. And he knew she would not back down. But he could not, either. If he did, whatever admiration she'd felt for him, whatever desire she'd buried . . . it would all be destroyed.

If he hadn't already destroyed it.

His heart constricted painfully. Her bed-partners did not matter so much. And the only thing he should have taken from her words was the knowledge that they hadn't all prepared her properly. That she'd used oil with other lovers didn't matter— only that she'd had *to use it.*

"No," *he said hoarsely.* "That statue is my reflection—and a fucking is not what I would give you."

Her expression didn't change, but he sensed the battle within her. Finally, Irena straightened and rested her back against the statue's chest.

"What would you do, Olek?"

Relief rushed through him. He could barely speak, but he managed, "If I stood where it does now, I would first kiss your neck."

She raised her arms, linking her hands behind the statue's neck. "Then I wait for you."

His heart kicked up into his throat. He hadn't given a thought to his awkward display since she'd poured the oil over him, but now the discomfort hit again. He'd left himself no choice, however.

He tentatively moved his hand, and Irena's Gift swept over him, carrying the faint taste of her lingering anger and hurt. His gaze snapped to her face as the statue lowered its head. Her lips parted. Pleasure rose through her psychic scent, but not from the touch of that bronze mouth—she'd focused on his hand. Her tongue moistened her lips when he pumped his fist again.

Dear God. Watching him aroused her. He had to pause and realign his thoughts, and realization broke over him: He could please her this way.

His discomfort receded. His next stroke was bold, and he rolled his hips into it.

"Your breasts, Irena. I would fill my hands with them." *And discover whether they were soft or as firm as the rest of her.*

He envied the bronze fingers sliding beneath her tunic. The linen rucked up at her waist, exposing the pale skin of her stomach. Covered by her tunic, the hands moved higher.

Irena arched her back. "They are cold."

Alejandro bit off his frustrated groan. He'd directed the statue, but it was Irena who made its fingers circle her nipples and tug softly. Was that what she liked—would she want him to do the same? His palm heated the slippery oil, and he lightened his grip, trying to hold back the need lancing through him in hot streaks—trying to learn everything he could from the little he could see.

And he vowed that she would find her release before he did.

"I would kneel behind you. And I would taste every inch of your skin."

Irena dragged in a breath, and her Gift pulsed a deep, heavy beat. The statue sank to its knees, its lips tracing the long, lean muscles of her back.

Alejandro swallowed his jealousy. He would do the same, one day. For now, he watched its hands. Irena kept them on her breasts, kneading, pinching. Her eyelids had half lowered, and her eyes shone in a brilliant green crescent.

"I would suck your nipples into my mouth," *he said.* "Or I would turn you as I knelt, and lick between your thighs."

Her soft moan had him stroking faster, then easing back.

"But not now." No, he did not want that metal tongue on her. Only his. "Now, I would stand and slide my hand between your thighs."

Anticipation pounded through her Gift like a heartbeat. Bronze fingers splayed across her stomach, then slipped beneath the waistband of her breeches.

"Irena."

The hand stopped. She met his gaze.

"Do you need the oil?"

Her lips curved. "No. I have not since my mouth took yours in Caelum."

God. Her words stoked his need, and he fought the urge to thrust hard into his fist.

A spark of anger flickered through her psychic scent. "That pleases you?"

"Yes." He would not apologize for taking satisfaction in her arousal. "I have accepted your lovers, but by all that is holy, I will be the best of them."

He waited, but although the spark of anger smoldered, it didn't ignite. A brief struggle between admiration and resistance rumbled through her psyche. Then her desire burned hot again, as if she'd thrown those emotions into the flame and let them feed it.

He breathed a prayer of gratitude before continuing, "And if you do not need the oil, I would know that you were ready to take my fingers. Are you?"

In answer, she made the hand slide deeper beneath her breeches. And it was torture. He heard the brush of metal against her soft curls, then the liquid slide of aroused flesh. Irena tensed. Her psychic scent filled with aching pleasure. She clenched her fingers around the bronze forearm pressed against her stomach, her breath coming in gasps.

His legs trembled with the need to sink to his knees and taste her. He made himself watch, to see her rhythm—when she went faster, when she slowed. His hand burned the length of his cock. The warm fragrance of almond infused his every inhalation.

Irena's breath hitched. She rose up on her toes, poised and shaking. Her orgasm slammed through her psychic scent like the strike of a hammer against glass, shattering into bright, sharp slices.

With heaving chest, she sagged back against the statue.

"Again," Alejandro demanded.

She shook her head. "You. Now. Both hands."

He cupped his sac, pulled at his shaft. This pleased her, so he intended to draw it out—but he imagined the clasp of her slick heat, her strong thighs wrapping around his waist. He pushed the image away, too late. Tension twisted through his spine, into his cock. His hips jerked as he erupted into his hand.

He felt the color in his face as she strode toward him. He vanished his seed, unsettled by his loss of control—and by the need that still raged through him. The challenge he'd issued and the release he'd found had not been enough. It would never, he feared, be enough.

She reached for his hand. Her fingers pressed into his palm, the oil rolling against the tips of her fingernails. Without her Gift, he no longer sensed her emotions, but he could see his release pleased her, too. She looked up at him, her mouth in a faint curve.

"We have not learned today what we should have, Olek."

Perhaps not. But he found he could not regret it. "I thought the lesson was satisfactory." Even if it had not taken them as far as he wished.

"I could not tell." She let go of his hand. "Next time, you will be as open to me as I was to you."

His shields down and his emotions bare? Uncertainty crawled through his stomach. He did not know if he could. Stroking himself in front of the entire Guardian corps seemed less daunting a challenge.

Yet if Irena needed it . . .

"I will try." He lifted his hand to the narrow braids dancing beside her cheek. He'd used them to his advantage while they'd sparred, grabbing handfuls to hold her or throw her—but he'd never touched them like this. Despite their coarse appearance, they were silken ropes beneath his fingers.

With a frustrated sigh, Irena pulled away. Her white mantle appeared on her shoulders.

"We are leaving?" With some relief, he formed his clothes.

"I am. I go hunting." She put the hood up. "I am a woman of deep hungers, Olek—but my hunger for you is too close to the surface, and a metal hand will not satisfy it."

"You will be satisfied. One day." He was hungry, too. And if she was leaving to bury her need, he did no harm to say, "Next time, it will not be my hands, but my mouth. I will push your legs apart and taste you, and I will not stop even if you beg."

Her eyes glowed before she looked to the door. "I will be gone three or four days. You may return to Caelum during my absence, or find a city to visit. With your shields up," she stressed.

Now he did feel regret, for that would be three or four days away from her. Perhaps it showed; she stopped in front of him and raised a palm to his cheek.

"When you win your fight to understand me, perhaps you will tell me why, after all of these years, it is you." Her face hardened. Her hand slid from his cheek to his hair and fisted. She yanked him closer, until his eyes were level with hers, and he saw the pain she caused was deliberate. "You, with your way of looking down upon me, and with your raw pride. A part of me would like to destroy you. Rip you apart, so that I never imagine how you see me from your great height. Each time you wonder how it is possible that you feel anything for me, I pray I never regret the day I did not fight my own feelings for a man such as you."

It was not his pride scraped raw, but his heart. He had not fought his feelings for her, but he had questioned them. And in doing so, gave insult. Hoarsely, he said, "Why do you not destroy me?"

Her expression opened, softened. "Because I can hardly think of anything without wondering what your opinion is, and I take as much pleasure in your agreements as your arguments. Every weapon and sculpture I create, I want to show you. I look forward to our quiet moments and our battles. And there is the hunger, which even now I fight. There is no part of you I *do not want, no part I will leave untouched."* Her fingers loosened and slid down to cup the back of his neck. *"And, because I am old, I know this feeling is rare—so there is no part of you I do not fear losing."*

She never had to fear that. *"You could not lose me now. And I will never give you cause to regret."*

Irena nodded, but he saw her vulnerability in the way she turned her face away from him. And despite his questions, he was not so oblivious to the answers.

As both human and Guardian, he had only lived in spurts. Parts of his childhood. The initial dance with lovers. His first weeks of marriage. The intrigues of the court. The birth of his children, and the short time he'd had with them. But here, with Irena, he did not exist more in one moment than in another. Every moment, he lived.

He left the forge with her, watched her wings form. Watched her rise into the dark clouds spitting their icy rain.

Watched until he couldn't see her anymore.

♣

"You are boiling."

At the sound of Khavi's voice, Alejandro shook off memory's hold, and glanced up. Steam rose in a column over his head.

"The statue excites you?" She gave him a look that he might have given a ten-eyed dancing goat.

"I was thinking of another statue."

Her expression cleared. "A good memory?"

"Yes." What did it say of a man that his best memories were more than four hundred years old?

He'd felt so much then. Even moments of calm, of contentment, had been deep—his emotions had never remained on the surface. Their strength had surprised him, and he'd fought them, fought *her*. He despised fighting with Irena now, even though it dredged the depths he'd felt then, and for a moment . . . being with her was good. But then he remembered the bargain with the demon, and his failure. And how empty he was when the fight was done.

He could not do it any more. He vowed not to fight with her again—and hoped his will would be stronger than his need.

He'd made that vow before; he'd never honored it. He broke his promises, even to himself. When he fought with her, he left nothing of himself to be proud of.

Headlights swept across the square. Khavi lifted her hand against the glare, watched the car disappear down the street.

She looked back at him. "For more than two thousand years, I waited to leave Hell. Yet sometimes, when I see all that has changed, I want to return and hide."

Rain slid down the back of his neck. Alejandro vanished the drop. "Why not remain in Caelum, then?"

"It is too quiet there. And there is too much to do here." The whites of her eyes turned completely black. "I need to find Irena."

So she'd come to him? "Why?"

"A woman needs protection."

"A human?" At her nod, he said, "I can—"

"No." Khavi shook her head. "No, I have seen. It cannot be that way."

Not seen, but *foreseen*, Alejandro realized uneasily. What had she seen that involved Irena?

Irena . . . and a human who needed protection.

He pushed away his unease and focused on duty. Irena had argued with him. Where would she go afterward?

"You've tried her quarters in Caelum?"

"Yes."

"She is probably at her forge in Siberia, then."

"Give me a picture of where that is."

"I'll go with you. If you show up alone, she will—"

"All right." Khavi took his hand. Her Gift drew in a sharp draft, and she nodded. "Yes, this is much better. Your presence there will convince her to come."

Alejandro pictured Irena's forge and projected the image. The world spun in a dizzying whirl. But there was sunlight, when the frozen Nenetsia region in northern Russia still lay under cover of night.

He looked up, forcing himself to focus past the disorientation. He stood in the shadow of a brick building, partially hidden by the wall. Ahead of him, a crowd of humans gathered at the foot of a columned courthouse. On the wide steps in front of them stood a demon.

Alejandro turned and searched for Khavi—but the grigori had already gone.

CHAPTER 6

Irena didn't need to spar with Olek to take his measure. She didn't even need to see him fight to know how his strength and speed had increased over the past four hundred years. It was in every graceful movement he made.

And she didn't need the furnace or the hammer to shape his swords. Her Gift could have created the blades in seconds. But she needed the work of it, the heat and the precision of each hammer strike. She didn't ask herself why she wanted to linger over them. They would not be better for her effort, and she would finish them with her Gift, removing every imperfection, refolding and strengthening the metal.

Her Gift gave her pleasure, but so did working the metal in this way. Perhaps that was reason enough.

The steel glowed orange when she removed it from the furnace, radiating heat that she could feel through her leather apron and gloves. His blades had always been long and thin, but now she made them longer, heavier.

Sparks flew as her hammer struck the blade. Her Guardian

strength was no help here; if she used any more than a human's, the sword would be ruined.

Olek had learned that quickly. He'd had a delicate artist's touch when he worked with metal. Just firm enough. And so it hadn't surprised her that his mouth had been just as—

That hadn't been Olek.

Her hand slipped. The hammer struck on the edge of its face. Too hard. Much too hard.

Steam boiled up as she plunged the sword into a vat of water, but the damage was done. The blade was a hair's-breadth thick where she'd smashed it flat. A touch would shatter it.

She could repair the blade with her Gift. She wouldn't. This sword was ruined. Perhaps she would reuse the metal, but it would never be a worthy weapon.

Irena tossed the sword onto the pile of damaged weapons heaped near the wall—and frowned as another sound intruded over the clatter. She tilted her head, listened. Someone outside the forge sang her name. A psychic probe met with nothing. She called in her knives.

Outside, swirling white snow filled the air. Khavi knelt in a drift, brushing the fine powder from side to side. She looked up, her black eyelashes dusted with flakes.

Her gaze rested on Irena's weapons. "I do not need foresight to know that jumping into your forge, unannounced, would not end well."

"For you."

"For either of us." Khavi stood, held out her hand. "You will come with me."

"Where?"

Exasperation crossed her face. "You *will* come with me. I have seen it. Do not make me explain. There isn't enough time."

"Until what?"

The image that exploded past Irena's shields stayed a brief second, but she saw enough: Alejandro with blood on his hands, crouching beside a still body. A woman with pale hair kneeled next to him, her white shirt soaked with crimson.

"He is already there," Khavi said. "And so is a demon. He will need help."

Irena extended her hand. This time, Khavi's foresight had tested true. Irena *did* go with her.

❧

Khavi teleported her next to a brick wall. The grigori immediately disappeared again, while Irena fought the spinning effect of teleporting.

The wall belonged to a building. The distant noise and psyches were human. Their English sounded American. Straightening, Irena vanished her knives and traded her apron for her rabbit fur mantle.

She quickly found Alejandro at the edge of the crowd. The protesters were mostly young, she thought, but with a good mix of middle-aged and older humans. Some were holding signs. Others stood, blowing into their cupped hands to warm their fingers.

Alejandro didn't look at her when she stepped up next to him, but kept his gaze fixed on the speaker, a tall, handsome man with blond hair sprinkled by gray.

Irena's lip curled. Rael—the demon who supported SI. He spoke into a microphone about rights and love and marriage. What would a demon know or care of them? Yet the psyches of the humans around her said *they* cared very much. Rael deceived them with every word.

"What game does Khavi play?" Irena asked. Alejandro understood these sorts of games better than she did.

"I don't know." He paused briefly as shouts and applause broke over the crowd. "Did she tell you who we need to protect?"

Protect? Anger ripped through her. They were to protect a human, and Khavi hadn't told them *who?*

Irena scanned the crowd. "She showed me a woman. Pale blond hair."

She projected the image—not tight enough. Though Rael's mind was blocked and he probably hadn't seen the image, he'd felt her. His speech faltered.

He met her eyes, smiled, and continued.

Would it be such a terrible thing if this crowd of humans witnessed her ripping his heart out?

"Did she show you whose blood it was?"

Irena shook her head. There were many women here, but none were familiar, none but—

She met a pair of cool blue eyes. The flat expression in them wasn't dislike, but there was nothing warm in them, either. A human, who shielded her mind as well as a Guardian did.

"Detective Taylor is here," Irena said. She hadn't seen the woman since the night Lucifer had lost his wager with Michael, when Taylor and her partner had stood with the Guardians against Lucifer and the nest of nosferatu.

What she remembered of the woman had been sleek and collected. There was little of that on display now. She looked fragile, her skin drawn tightly over her bones. Her hair color wasn't much different from Irena's, but appeared dull and brittle. Her clothes were creased.

It happened like that, sometimes. Discovering that demons, vampires, and Guardians walked the Earth didn't always sit easy.

"Her partner, Preston, is at a post on the other side of the crowd," Alejandro said. "He has not yet spotted us."

Their presence here meant she and Alejandro were back in San Francisco. Irena looked at the courthouse steps again. "Who is up there with Rael?"

"The mayor of the city stands on his left. Behind and to the right is Rael's wife, Julia Stafford."

It didn't matter what era or country—a woman like Rael's wife was unmistakable. Her highlighted hair swept back into an elegant chignon. Pearls circled her neck. Perhaps they didn't have titles in America, but the woman was undoubtedly an aristocrat.

"Does she know what he is?"

"We don't think so."

By *we*, Irena assumed he meant those at SI. Which meant Rael had been a topic of discussion, along with the consequences of slaying him.

There was that, at least.

"Perhaps it wouldn't matter to her. Stafford is being groomed by his party, and she's ambitious," Alejandro continued.

Irena frowned. Why not pursue a position of power for herself, then? Women could in this era, and Julia Stafford would have the necessary education and connections.

The crowd cheered again. Rael smiled and nodded.

Perhaps that was why. He had charisma. So many demons did. But still, Irena could not imagine being satisfied by the position her partner attained. What kind of ambition was it to have a powerful husband? It said nothing of Julia Stafford except that she'd married well.

Irena eyed the pearls again. Rael had married well, too. And groomed by his party? Did that mean he would rise higher than congressman? She frowned. Aside from the presidency, what *was* higher than a congressman in America? Irena had no idea.

"How do you know he's being groomed? Do you follow American politics?"

He glanced at her, amusement in his eyes. "You don't?"

Her laugh was lost in the cheering of the crowd. Her question had been as idiotic as his, though for exactly the opposite reasons. Of course Olek followed politics—probably in this country and elsewhere. And of course she didn't.

Rael staggered. Blood spattered over his wife's pearls. She jerked, her smile freezing. Rael fell.

The gunshot cracked over the shocked, silent crowd—the sound delayed by distance, Irena realized. Julia Stafford collapsed, out of Irena's sight. She began to turn, but Olek was at her back. He wrapped his arms around her and waited, waited, his body shielding hers.

Only a second or two. The screams started, the panic. People crouched, covering their heads. Others were running, bumping into one another. No more shots rang out.

"The wife was hit, Olek. Help her."

Alejandro would be safe up there with the demon. Rael couldn't touch him in front of all these people, the cameras.

She felt his nod against her hair. "And you?"

"I'll go hunting. Be safe, Olek."

His heat left her back. He slipped through the panicking crowd, shape-shifting and altering his clothing as he ran.

"Guardian!"

Irena turned. Detective Taylor bore down on her, gun drawn. Though her badge was visible on her trousers' waistband, humans were veering away from her.

Irena pointed. "Your shooter is in that direction. Are you coming with me?"

❧

Alejandro ran up the stairs, flashing his federal badge at the officers who tried to stop him. The scent of blood was sharp here. Demon blood, human blood.

He immediately saw that nothing could be done for Rael's wife. The bullet that passed through the side of the demon's throat had hit hers square on. Beneath the roar of voices and screams, he heard her heartbeat cease.

A woman knelt over Julia Stafford's body, trying to staunch the wound with a folded cloth. Blood covered her hands. Pale hair, Alejandro saw. Her black suit, vest, and starched white shirt were too precise to be anything but a uniform.

Alejandro crouched beside her. "She's gone," he said quietly.

The woman's eyes were flat and gray. "Yes."

Sirens wailed in the distance. Cameramen moved closer to the stage. Detective Preston climbed up the stairs, huffing and flushed. Alejandro glanced back once; Irena and Preston's partner were gone.

Rael rolled over, holding his neck as he crawled toward his wife. He still bled; crimson dripped in a long trail beneath him. "Julia?"

Alejandro didn't suppress his disgust. "You must remain still, congressman."

The demon looked up at him. And quickly—a human couldn't have detected it—used a talon to dig another furrow in his neck.

God damn him. Alejandro *had* to help. The demon's life wasn't in danger, but if his quick healing was discovered, too much could be revealed. Alejandro created a length of cloth, pretended to pull it from inside his jacket, and gave it to the demon.

Rael pressed the cloth against his neck, gathered up his wife, and began to sob.

🔥

Taylor ran flat-out to keep up with the Guardian's trot. What was this one's name? She couldn't remember, only that she carried two wicked huge knives and dressed like a blacksmith stripper with a fur fetish and a deep appreciation for Daniel Day-Lewis's leather stockings in *The Last of the Mohicans*.

Her sprint had just begun to rake at her lungs when the Guardian stopped to study the buildings rising around them. Her head tilted back, the white hood falling away from auburn hair that looked as if she'd hacked at it with a dull ax.

"That building," she said, her voice thick with some eastern European accent. Russian, Czech. Taylor didn't know. "The roof."

Jesus. Taylor turned and eyed the distance back to the courthouse. Six or seven hundred yards. That meant a sniper with a long-range rifle.

"Come with me," the Guardian said. "We will have to do this quickly to avoid being seen."

Do what quickly? Taylor ran after her into a recessed loading ramp at the side of the building. When they were out of easy view of the street, the Guardian stopped and held out her hand.

When Taylor looked at it blankly, the Guardian sighed. "Unless you wish to stay on the ground, I need to hold you against my chest."

Oh. Oh, God. They were going to fly up to the roof. Taylor's stomach dropped to her knees. She could almost see the nail in the coffin that held her career. She was going to have a great time explaining this in her report to Captain Jorgenson. *Yes, sir, after failing to recognize the threat to a demon congressman, I flew up the side of the building.* Yeah. Bye-bye, badge. But what the hell. She moved in closer to the Guardian, and once

Taylor realized they were almost exactly the same height, her debate between facing the woman or turning around became a quick one. She backed up, let the Guardian wrap an arm around her waist.

"The speed will affect you. You might pass out."

Great. "Just get on with it."

Taylor thought the Guardian might have laughed, but in the next second white flashed in her peripheral vision—*holy shit those were wings*—and then her head dragged down to her chest and enormous pressure squeezed her lungs. Bright spots burst behind her eyes, and darker spots swam through her vision. Her stomach ached and roiled.

Oh, God. She was going to puke.

She stumbled, and the Guardian steadied her. Solid concrete lay beneath her feet. Taylor looked up. The Guardian had vanished her wings.

"We're here?" Already? And, what—a second had passed?

"Yes. I smell burnt gunpowder."

Taylor couldn't. She could hear pigeons, the rattle and blow of air ducts—and didn't see anyone. Just the flat, gray expanse of the roof, broken by vents and a stairwell block. From the street, police sirens wailed past the building.

The Guardian took off across the roof. Taylor swore, then went after her toward the south end of the building, where a low wall provided a minimal safety barrier.

A rifle lay in front of it. Semiautomatic, some serious hardware. The scope alone probably cost more than all of Taylor's weapons combined.

"I've got to call this in." Get a forensics team here, call the building management and have security shut the place down. "And for God's sake, don't touch anything," Taylor protested when the Guardian fell to her knees beside the rifle and sniffed. "I . . . you're going to track him?"

"Yes."

Wasn't that handy? "Let's go, then."

She radioed dispatch as she followed the Guardian toward the stairwell block. Jesus, maybe it would be this easy. Only a couple of minutes had passed since the shooting; the guy couldn't have gotten too far.

The Guardian reached for the stairwell door. Oh, shit.

"Wait!" Taylor caught her wrist. "Fingerprints. Maybe." Okay, probably not a chance in hell that the guy had left prints, but they couldn't take even that small risk.

The Guardian looked at the metal fire door as if sizing it up. She turned and gave Taylor the same once-over. "Will you let me take you through?"

"How?"

Her stomach wobbled as the Guardian stepped *through* the door as if the steel were water. The metal warped around her body and solidified again into a flat surface. Taylor's mouth dropped open. The Guardian's forearm poked back through, and her fingers curled in a beckoning gesture. Taylor took her hand, a deep breath, and hurtled through the door. Being sucked through a vat of dark JELL-O might have felt weirder, but not by much.

Taylor half-expected to be in some other realm when she opened her eyes. But on the opposite side of the door, the beige walls of the stairwell were refreshingly normal—and quiet.

The Guardian cocked her head, listening. "I hear no one on the stairs."

"He got off on one of the floors, maybe." Good. They could search the building room by room. "What's your name, anyway?"

"Irena." She skipped down the stairs, stopped to sniff at the door, then skipped down another flight. She paused on the landing. "Here."

Instead of a knob, the door opened with a press-down bar. Taylor drew her weapon and pushed her hip against the end of the bar, sweeping into an empty hall. Tall plants flanked a bank of elevators. The directory at the end of the hall pointed to a suite of law offices on the right, accountants on the left.

"Which way?"

Irena headed straight for the elevators.

"Dammit." The arrows above the elevators were unlit,

and there wasn't a floor indicator to show where the cars had stopped. "You can search the building super-fast?"

"Yes. But if I find him, I cannot detain him."

That's right—a Guardian couldn't prevent someone from exercising free will. That was why she'd asked before flying up here, before pulling Taylor through the door.

"A description and a location would help."

Irena glanced at her, her brow creased. "How will you explain that to your courts?"

"I'll say that I saw and followed him."

"You would lie?"

About this? "Yes."

To Taylor's surprise, Irena seemed pleased by the answer. She nodded. "I will search."

Irena disappeared, and the rush of wind told Taylor that she hadn't simply vanished, but run. She must have taken the stairs—and hadn't even bothered to open the door.

Taylor looked toward the directory again. Someone in the offices might have ridden in the elevator with this guy—

"I picked up his scent again in the underground garage," Irena said beside her, and it took every bit of Taylor's control not to shriek and jump. "But he wasn't there. He must have taken a vehicle."

Her heart still racing, Taylor nodded. "Security cameras might have caught it." Fat chance. The guy moved too smoothly. It screamed of a planned hit; he'd have taken steps to avoid identification. And if it hadn't been a professional, she'd eat her badge.

If Jorgenson didn't shove it down her throat first. Shit. Taylor headed back upstairs to secure the scene. From this point forward, she'd go by the book.

Her phone vibrated at the same time Irena tilted her head. "The police are here," she said.

Taylor nodded and answered her phone with, "We lost the shooter, Joe. Found the site, but he took off."

Her partner bit off a curse, which told Taylor he wasn't alone. In the background, an ambulance siren blared. "Julia Stafford didn't make it. I'm en route to San Francisco General with the congressman and Agent Cordoba of Special Investigations."

The other Guardian. Of course.

"This isn't going to be ours, Andy," Joe added in a low voice.

"I know." The FBI would take this one—or Special Investigations would. SI had been grabbing every case involving demons and vampires for two years, and covering up the supernatural involvement to make it look human. And even if the feds didn't take it, the case wouldn't be Taylor's. Jorgenson wouldn't risk it. She'd been skating too close to the edge.

And doing a damn good job of taking Joe along with her. Jesus, they'd been assigned to *crowd control* . . . and a woman had died on their watch.

Just screwed, all around. But she was going to make damn sure her partner didn't go down with her.

Unfortunately, she didn't know how the hell to do that. With a sick feeling in her gut, she finished up the call and stopped at the top of the stairs. The Guardian pulled her through the roof door again, and she blinked at the bright sun.

Irena glanced at her. She'd probably listened in on the conversation. Only God knew what the Guardian saw in her face— or how much of her emotions she could read.

"What is San Francisco General?"

"A hospital."

Irena frowned. "Do you and your partner know the congressman is a demon?"

Well, if she hadn't known he was a demon, she would now. Not that it mattered; someone was dead, and someone else had to be held accountable for it—demon or not. "Yes. But we still have a job to do. Questions to ask."

"Yes. Of course." Irena's brows drew together, and Taylor had the feeling she'd either said something the Guardian thought was incredibly stupid, or they'd been talking about two different things. God. She could never figure these people out.

"So are you going to take this one?"

Irena looked baffled. "Me?"

"Not *you* you. Special Investigations." Taylor flapped her hands like little wings. "The Guardians."

Her expression changed—into scorn, maybe. Then frustration. She looked out over the roof and said quietly, "I don't know."

CHAPTER 7

Alejandro shed the appearance of a federal agent the moment he entered the Special Investigations warehouse; he couldn't shed the frustration of spending four futile hours at the hospital so easily. He and Detective Preston had learned next to nothing from Rael—and once the FBI had arrived, he'd listened in on a repeat of next-to-nothing.

According to Preston, Taylor and Irena hadn't found much more.

Beside him, Drusilla shifted into her own shape and unclipped her hospital badge from her lab coat. Frustration twisted in her psychic scent, as well, but Alejandro didn't think hers had anything to do with the little information they'd gotten, or even that the safeguards SI had prepared in the event a Guardian or vampire was severely wounded in public had been implemented to cover up a demon's injuries. No, he thought Dru's frustration came from being in a hospital full of people that she simply couldn't help. In that, Dru was much like Irena: Neither woman could tolerate a situation where they couldn't do anything.

Alejandro had to admit he could not tolerate it, either—the difference was, he'd look for another option. In all fairness, Dru's Gift didn't give her one; she couldn't heal natural diseases or human-caused injuries. But Irena was just too damned stubborn to see—let alone consider—alternatives.

He passed through security and into the corridor leading to the central hub, and halted midstride when he heard Irena's shout from the direction of the gymnasium, followed by Castleford's voice giving instructions and calls of encouragement from the novices.

Shaking off his surprise, he continued on to the hub. He hadn't expected Irena to remain in the city after taking her leave of Taylor. And he hadn't expected her to return *here*. But he'd forgotten about the vampire upstairs—she must be waiting for Deacon to awaken; sunset wasn't far off.

Irena's battle cry rang out—a sound that Alejandro had only heard her use during practice. A second later, Pim crashed through the doors and smashed into the opposite wall. The plaster collapsed around her body. The novice's arm twisted at an unnatural angle, the bone piercing the skin below her elbow.

Drusilla gave a gasp of dismay and started forward.

Irena stepped through the doors and crouched in front of the novice. "It was well done until you lost your balance. You shouldn't startle so easily." Her gaze fell from the novice's pinched features to her arm. "If you heal that, we will try again."

Drusilla reached Pim's side. Unlike Michael, Dru couldn't heal from a distance, but as soon as her hand touched the novice's skin, the warm roll of her healing Gift ran over Alejandro's psyche. The novice's flesh mended instantly.

Irena looked up at the healer with a feral smile. Drusilla's jaw set. Neither of them spoke.

In the silence, Hugh came out of the gymnasium. He slipped his hands into his pants pockets and leaned a shoulder against the broken door frame. Two more novices—Becca and Randall—peeked around him.

Irena looked at Pim. "Why did you not heal it before she did?"

"Healing takes concentration. And I couldn't." She swallowed and darted a nervous look at Drusilla.

Afraid, Alejandro thought, that Dru would be disappointed.

"Because it hurt," Irena said flatly.

"Yes."

"*Could* you have healed it?"

"I don't know. Maybe."

Dru stood. "She's studying anatomy now. Practical application will come later."

"Practical application? What is that?" Irena snorted. "She needs practice."

"We don't see so many injuries that she *can* practice, Irena. It's not like practicing with a weapon, when you can just pick up a sword. We have to wait until someone needs us."

"Then we'll practice now." Irena spread her fingers. "Cut off one, Pim. Then heal it."

Gasping, Pim looked up at Dru, who shrugged. A dagger appeared in Irena's grip and she extended the handle toward the novice. Pim took it with shaking fingers.

She stared at Irena's hand, then swallowed. "I can't."

"You just attacked me with your sword in there." Irena jerked her head back toward the gymnasium.

"That was different. I knew I wouldn't hurt you."

"You could have."

"But not on purpose." Pim looked at Irena's fingers again. "Not like this."

Alejandro read the frustration on Irena's face. She didn't understand that. Practice among Guardians hurt. They almost always drew blood, caused injury—and none of it was by accident. To prepare to fight demons, novices *had* to go for blood. They only held back from a death blow.

"And this is how you will become a healer? By watching and never doing?"

"She *is* a healer," Dru said. "It does her credit that she can't cold-bloodedly chop off your fingers."

He didn't think anyone else would've recognized the hurt on Irena's face. Cold-blooded was the very last thing she was. To her, this wasn't about causing pain, but eventually being able to stay alive through it.

He stepped forward, but Irena looked at Pim again and said, "She is right; it does you credit. I would cut my own finger off if your Gift could heal self-inflicted wounds. I would ask Hugh if you could heal what a human does to me. I would ask Dru, but I know she will not."

And Alejandro could not. Did Irena know that, or did she simply not consider asking him?

He started toward them. "Let her heal mine. Irena can cut off my—"

"No, Olek. *Je ne peux pas.*"

She couldn't. Alejandro stopped, holding on tightly to his shock. What could that mean? She'd inflicted damage easily enough during his training, and they had only grown apart— and antagonistic—since then. Good Christ, the one thing that had never occurred to him in four hundred years was that she might not be able to deliberately do him harm—even knowing that he would be quickly healed.

Even knowing that good would come of it.

Hope started in his chest, and he ruthlessly squashed that fragile flicker. He had lived two hundred years with that hope. If he believed Irena could be his future, then he was doomed never to move forward. For a moment, he hated her for giving him even a spark of hope with those words . . . and he hated himself for latching onto it so easily.

Irena didn't look at him, but watched Pim's face. "There aren't enough of us. We are outnumbered by demons, nosferatu, and nephilim. One day, you'll need to heal Drusilla or one of your friends, and you'll need to heal more than their fingers. You *must* practice, and you might as well begin with me, who you care nothing about."

Pim looked at Irena's hands again, her fingers tightening around the dagger handle. After a tense moment, she shook her head. "I can't. Not like this."

Irena sighed. She had lost, Alejandro thought. She would not stop fighting, but in this battle, she had been over-powered.

"I will." Becca stepped forward, then hesitated and looked back at Hugh. "If it's okay."

Castleford nodded, and when she turned her back to him his lips compressed, as if he were trying not to smile.

Becca's nervousness crawled over Alejandro's psyche like fire ants. She knelt, took the dagger, and placed the blade below the first knuckle of Irena's index finger. Slowly, she began to draw the blade back and forth, wincing as the blood welled.

Irena didn't flinch, didn't change expression, but he saw the subtle way her weight rocked back on her heels.

"Becca!" Both Alejandro and Hugh barked her name. Dru said it in her sharp, quiet manner.

"Quickly, Becca," Dru continued. "Do not *saw* your way through. Chop."

Irena's lips parted. The breath she sucked in trembled with her pained laughter. "Thank you."

❧

Irena vanished the blood as the novices returned to the gymnasium. At the end of the hall, Hugh and Alejandro signed to each other—so that the novices would not overhear them, Irena guessed.

She walked with Dru to the hub and did the same.

Pim was ready, Irena signed. Dru had guided the novice through the healing, but Pim hadn't needed guidance—she'd only needed the confidence that Dru's presence had given her. *Yet you could not do what must be done. Is it because you are in love with her, or because she is with you?*

Dru's flush didn't provide an answer. It could have been either—or both. If Dru didn't return Pim's feelings, she still might be sensitive to them. Combined with her natural inclination to heal rather than harm, such feelings would make the healer hesitate to practice with the novice. And if Dru loved Pim . . . it might be impossible to practice in the manner they needed to.

Dru sighed. *Before the Ascension, someone was always injured from practice or during assignments. Always. We didn't have to chop at each other.*

You should speak with Hugh. He'll find a way to help you.

Dru laughed quietly. *He's been trying.*

But Dru was stubborn. Affectionately, Irena tugged at the healer's blond hair, then rose up on her toes to kiss Dru's forehead.

"Your feelings do you credit, too," she said, and laughed aloud at Dru's embarrassment.

Her laughter died when she saw Lilith come through security and into the hall beyond the offices. The other woman looked tired despite her brisk stride and the precise clip of her boots on the tile. As she walked, she pulled at the back of her hair, and the black coil at her nape unwound over her shoulder.

"Alejandro, Dru. We'll debrief in my office." She glanced at Irena. "You were with Taylor."

"Yes."

"Then I imagine her report isn't accurate. If you fill in the details she left out, it'd be helpful."

"I will."

Lilith nodded. "I'll be with you all in a minute."

Irena supposed that was an order to wait for Lilith in her office, but she turned and watched her walk toward the gymnasium, instead. She passed Alejandro, went straight for Hugh.

"You didn't swear. Was that difficult?" Hugh's amused voice traveled down the long hallway.

Irena couldn't see what Lilith signed to him, but Hugh laughed softly, shaking his head. "Do you want me to come in with you?"

"I'll fill you in on everything tonight, and we'll decide how to go from there." Lilith reached him, touched his arm, then his chest. She signed again, and whatever it was had Hugh studying her for a long moment before he pushed her back into the wall. Irena looked away as his mouth took Lilith's.

Alejandro stopped beside her. *They surprise you,* he signed.

"Her," Irena said. "Not him."

"You surprise me, too."

Had he expected her to tell the hellspawn no? She frowned at him. "A woman is dead, Olek."

"Yes," Lilith said. She walked away from Hugh, but held on to his hand until distance forced her to let go. Not looking so tired anymore—and well-kissed. "And we need to know if they shot at her husband because he's a congressman, or because he's a demon."

Alejandro stepped back, allowing Lilith to pass between them. "If they knew he was a demon, they wouldn't have shot him."

"Unless they didn't know a bullet wouldn't hurt him." Lilith pushed open the door to the office she and Hugh shared.

Irena hadn't been in the room before, but it fit the occupants well, a mixture of old and new. Modern computers with blade-thin screens sat on heavy wooden desks. She shouldn't have been surprised that books lined two walls—both Hugh and Lilith were readers. Irena glanced at the other two Guardians. Alejandro always studied, and even now Irena could see the flat outline of a paperback in Dru's lab coat pocket. Three Guardians and one former demon stood in this room, yet Irena was the odd one out.

And feeling out of place—but Caelum was familiar. She moved to the right, toward the wall covered by a painting of the realm. Dru gestured at the two seats in front of the desk, an invitation for either of the elder Guardians to take one. Alejandro shook his head at the same time Irena did, and the healer gingerly sat.

Lilith shut the door. "The FBI officially has the investigation. Bradshaw is the Special Agent in Charge of the San Francisco office; he's good, and he knows what we are—and more importantly, what *Rael* is—but he can't ask his agents to look in certain directions."

"Will you take over the investigation, then?" Irena asked, remembering Taylor's question.

"I'd rather not." Lilith sighed and dropped into her chair. "I got a call from Washington. There is some concern that SI might have been behind the assassination attempt. I told them to fuck themselves, but—" She rubbed her fingers over her brow. "The call was a warning. Even knowing what Rael is, there are senators on the committee and members of the President's Cabinet who want to protect him, and they'll sacrifice SI if necessary."

Irena hadn't known that. Her breath left her in an angry hiss.

Alejandro glanced at her. "There are others in Washington who want him dead."

"Yes, but their reasons aren't political, and it's not just demons they hate. They wouldn't have a problem seeing all of us gone." Lilith's fingers tapped against her desk, then paused. Her gaze moved between Alejandro and Irena. "What the hell were you two doing at the courthouse?"

That she was just now asking told Irena how occupied Lilith had been since the murder.

"Khavi foresaw the shooting," Alejandro said.

Lilith's brows ratcheted high. "And you still couldn't stop it?"

"She didn't tell us who it was. Only that we were to protect a woman."

"That crazy fucking—" Lilith cut herself off. "Unbelievable."

Irena's own anger burned hot at that. Even if the shooter was a human—whose will they couldn't have interfered with—Alejandro and she still could've done something. Alerted the detectives, or created a distraction that would have gotten Julia Stafford off those steps.

"Perhaps Khavi didn't see Julia Stafford. Khavi showed Irena another woman."

"Her name?"

"I don't know. She never identified herself while I could hear her, but she could have been in Rael's employ. Pale blond hair, a dark suit that might have been a uniform—"

"Margaret Wren," Dru said. "I heard her speaking with an agent at the hospital. She provides personal security for the Staffords."

Lilith wrote the name down. "All right. I'll look at her, too." She glanced up at Irena. "And Taylor?"

Irena quickly recounted their steps from the courthouse to the roof, then listened as Alejandro reported how little they'd gotten out of Rael.

At the end of it, Lilith sat back in her chair, tapping her pencil against her lip. "Do you have anything, Dru?"

"No."

"Then I think we're done." Lilith glanced at Alejandro, then back to Irena. "Except you. Can I talk to you for a minute?"

Surprised, Irena searched for a reason to say no. But a woman was dead . . . and she was just curious enough to stay.

❧

His swords were still strapped beneath his jacket when Deacon woke up. His world narrowed to the pain in his back. Jesus Christ. Sword handles couldn't leave a permanent impression beside a vampire's spine, but it freaking felt like they had.

Had Irena just thrown him on this narrow bed and left him? What a pal.

He supposed it could've been worse, though; she could have left him on the floor. Or she could have discovered the real reason he'd contacted her, and killed him in his sleep.

Fuck. He blew out a heavy breath—and slapped at his mouth when something fluttered against his lips.

Paper crinkled. Though the room was dark, he easily made out the block letters.

DO NOT LEAVE THE WAREHOUSE.
I HAVE BLOOD FOR YOU. IRENA.

Guilt slapped him like a bitch. He crumpled the note in his fist and stared up at the ceiling. He couldn't let guilt stop him; he had to get through this. And maybe his deception wouldn't hurt her—just piss her off. Irena was tough. She could take care of herself.

His people couldn't. Hell, *he* couldn't. And they'd all be dead if he didn't follow through on his agreement with Caym.

Just get a little info on a vampire connected to the Guardians. Save his community. Real simple.

Fucking demons.

He sat up. The small room hosted a desk and bureau pushed up against bare walls. Opposite the bed, a door stood ajar;

through it, he could see a sink and the frosted glass front of a shower stall. He'd wash, but it wouldn't matter—his suit smelled like the woman he'd fucked in Rome. Deacon hadn't wanted her, but the bloodlust hadn't given him any choice. And it marked the first time he'd been with a woman he hadn't desired—or at least been friends with. Bloodlust had never been a curse before.

But it was one he'd use to his advantage tonight.

Five minutes later, he finished in the bathroom, donned his wrinkled clothes again, and stepped out into the hall.

The scent of blood struck him at the same time as the hoots of laughter. He looked toward the sound, rubbing his tongue against his fangs to soothe his stirring hunger. The hall opened into a large rec room, with sofas and sitting areas anchored by blue and green rugs, a huge oak entertainment center against one wall, and a game table at the center of it all. Around the table sat two vampires, and three others—Deacon couldn't tell if they were humans or Guardians.

A dark-haired woman reached forward and gave a water bottle a spin. It came to a rest pointing at the female vampire, who grimaced, squeezed her eyes shut, and held out her hand. After a tiny hesitation—filled by the claps and cries of the others that *You can do it!*—the first woman whipped a dagger out of nowhere and sliced through the vampire's fingers. They dropped to the table in a spurt of blood. The others cheered.

Jesus. He'd seen sicker games in his life, but he hadn't expected something like this here. The cheering quieted as he entered the rec room, and everyone looked toward him but the vampire and a different woman, her black hair cut in a sleek bowl.

The second vampire, a tall, wiry male permanently in his mid-twenties, stood and stuck out his hand.

Deacon cast a glance at the stairs, but realized he couldn't avoid this. He took the vampire's hand. "Deacon."

"Good to meet you. I'm Ben, that's Echo." He pointed to the female vampire who'd just had her fingers cut off. "Pim is the one fixing her up. There's Becca—don't worry, she always looks at new people like that—and Randall."

Becca rolled her eyes. "He's not wondering who we are, Ben; he's wondering what the fuck we're doing." She nodded to the female Guardian who was holding a severed forefinger to the stump, her face a picture of concentration. "Pim's practicing her healing Gift. We're growing balls and helping her out."

Pim muffled a laugh. "Literally?"

Becca flipped her the bird. "You wish."

Echo forced a smile through some obvious pain. "Luckily, growing balls isn't an option for us, because they'd probably just want to cut them off."

There was some snickering, but Deacon stared as a warm, uncertain power pushed against his mind, and the vampire's finger reattached to her hand without a single mark to show for it. A healing Gift. Christ. These three kids were novice Guardians, and each one could twist him into a pretzel. But he hadn't known they could heal each other.

He watched for a few minutes longer before excusing himself—before they could ask him to volunteer.

At the bottom of the stairs waited the Guardian he'd met in Rome. Irena's *friend* who had enough names for a freaking prince—Alejandro de Something la Something. A prince who'd barbequed a nosferatu without a change of his expression or an increase in his heartbeat.

Yeah. All of these Guardians could take care of themselves just fine.

Alejandro inclined his head in greeting. So polite. "Irena should be here presently."

"Great." Deacon glanced down another hall and spotted the one man he'd been told to avoid—Hugh Castleford, a human who could detect lies. Which meant Deacon would say whatever it took to get out quickly and to stop Alejandro from trying to delay him. "Is she going to feed me herself?"

"I believe she already answered you."

Yeah, and considering the vibe this Guardian and Irena had been giving off in Rome, Deacon bet Alejandro hadn't liked the question much. "You're right—she prefers them big and blond, doesn't she? And after she rode one of my vampires so hard that Karl was still limping the next day, I'm not about to offer myself up for the same." Deacon paused. "And you know whose name Karl said she was calling at the end?"

Alejandro's eyes narrowed. That *had* gotten to him, hadn't it? The prince's indecipherable face was as sharp as his swords.

Deacon's smile showed his fangs. "It wasn't yours."

Death slipped into the Guardian's dark eyes. Deacon's death, Alejandro's. Jesus, he knew that look. It'd been in the mirror after Caym had beaten the shit out of him, when Deacon would rather have seen everyone dead—including himself— than admit defeat.

But there hadn't been an *everyone*. There'd been vampires with faces and names he'd known and who he'd sworn to protect, so he'd choked down his pride and accepted that he'd lost.

He wondered how many times Alejandro had done the same.

The Guardian stared him down. "I will let Irena know you've gone."

In other words, if Deacon didn't get the fuck out of Alejandro's sight, there'd be one less vampire sucking blood every night. Perfect. Deacon flashed him a grin and headed for the exit.

At the security desk, an old, stiff-upper-lip type in a somber black suit gave Deacon an identification card with a magnetic strip and code that would let him back in to the warehouse. Deacon walked down the empty corridor, feeling the old man staring at him the whole way, thanking God the demon had taught him to strengthen his psychic shields—and that the Guardians were too polite to go looking without permission.

He stepped into the fenced parking lot with only a vague notion of which direction to go: northwest, toward downtown, where the head of San Francisco's vampire community—Colin Ames-Beaumont—kept a nightclub.

"Lost?"

Deacon whipped around, searching for the female who'd spoken. Impenetrable shadows gathered near the warehouse's entrance. The soft psychic touch of a Gift brushed over his mind, and the darkness fell away as if the woman shed a heavy cloak that had muffled both visibility and her heartbeat.

Deacon stared, his bloodlust sharpening. He recognized her—Rosalia—but she didn't appear anything like he'd last seen her. Now she looked like Snow White with her black hair, white skin, and crimson lips full enough to suck on. Snow White, healed and awakened, and wearing a red sweater that clung to every curve. But he was no prince, so he shouldn't even be thinking about all the places on that body he'd like to kiss.

He found his voice. "I'm looking for a meal. You want to volunteer?"

The second the words were out, he called himself an asshole. God knew what the nosferatu had done to her. The last thing she'd want was another bloodsucker at her neck—or to be reminded of it.

"No." Her calm brown eyes searched his, looking deep. But she must not have seen his soul or his secrets, because she didn't kill him. "You led Irena and Alejandro to me. I'm indebted to you. My blades, my protection—you only have to ask, and they are yours if you ever have need of them."

No way in fucking hell was he taking them. "You don't owe me anything. I had no idea you were there."

And he hadn't known there were three nosferatu feeding from her. If he had, he wouldn't have waited so long to contact this agency. Wouldn't have waited while the bastard demon put whatever plan he had into place. And he'd have warned Irena they were walking into a nest.

He thought of Eva and Petra—and their terror when he'd lain on the ground, beaten.

He was so full of shit. He'd have waited, and done exactly as he'd been told. He'd have used Irena, his one contact among the Guardians, and through her, would've found his way into Special Investigations. And now he'd learn who had the keys to the Chaos realm—whether that person was the vampire the demon suspected it was.

These Guardians could take care of themselves.

Rosalia gave him another searching look, and he had the feeling that she was wondering, questioning, *expecting* something—as if she knew him. "If you need a blood-sharer, I imagine you're going to see the community leader."

"Yes. You know him?"

"No, though I have heard of him—the one who walks in sunlight."

His stomach dropped. In sunlight . . . and in Chaos, too? "I thought that was a myth."

"So did I, and all of the vampires I knew." She stopped. The sudden grief on her face would have made angels weep.

Deacon knew he was closer to a devil, and it still tugged at him. She'd lived in Rome. The nephilim had exterminated the vampires there, so any she'd known were dead.

She dredged up a smile. Even forced, the curve of her lips took her from sultry beauty to stunningly gorgeous and almost knocked his legs out from under him. "I have lost too many friends today. But I would like to meet this myth. Shall I take you?"

"You know where the nightclub is?"

"Polidori's, yes. I asked the novices. But I have been waiting."

"For what?"

"I don't know. For you, perhaps. And now I have a reason to go."

She held out her hand. Deacon took it, and she didn't flinch at the touch of his cold skin. She pulled him back toward the warehouse.

"The shadows are deeper here," she said.

He nodded, expecting her to use the darkness to hide the formation of her wings. Her Gift swept over him, instead.

The shadows opened up and swallowed him whole.

❧

Irena waited as Lilith walked around her desk and leaned back against it. Why change position? To emphasize that she wasn't issuing orders from behind the desk? To emphasize that she was taller than Irena? Or for no reason at all?

The difficulty in dealing with someone like Lilith was knowing when she was—or wasn't—manipulating a situation. Lilith's direct gaze gave no clue; unlike most humans, she could lie without giving herself away. And so the only smart response was to assume she was manipulating.

"I'm going to put Alejandro on Rael," she said.

Investigating the demon's role in the shooting? "Do you think Rael was involved?"

Lilith shrugged. "There are factors that lead me to believe either way. His wife was a political asset: She's good money, and a married politician is always more appealing to voters. Killing her has no benefit that I can see. And in the more than two millennia that I've known of Rael, I've never heard of him doing anything—*anything*—against humans. Never tempted, never pushed anyone to murder, never bargained with one to get something. The only thing he needs for a candidacy to sainthood is a different religion than the one he professes to have."

Irena didn't believe it. Rael hadn't become one of Belial's highest-ranked demons by playing a saint.

Of course, Belial claimed he wanted Hell's throne so that he and his demons could return to Grace. Was it possible that a demon practiced what he preached? That he truly believed it? Or was that just another form of manipulation?

She would be stupid not to assume that it was. "And the factors on the other side?"

"He's a demon."

As if to let that sink in, Lilith left her desk, walked to a small cooler installed behind a wall panel. With a bottle of water in hand, she turned back. "The Bureau can't look where we've got to look. That means your friend Alejandro is going to have to get close to Rael. And I need you at his back."

Irena stared at her. Her laugh started and she didn't attempt to stop it. Lilith's brows arched, and she smiled as she sipped from her water.

She swallowed. "You think it's funny?"

"I was imagining Olek's response when you ask him."

Lilith shook her head. "I won't ask. His pride won't allow him to agree."

Yes, Olek's pride was great, indeed. He'd accept another Guardian's—even Irena's—help, but never for the purpose of protecting him.

Irena studied the other woman. She shouldn't be surprised that Lilith saw it, too. When Lilith had been a demon, she'd had to read the character of men in order to break them.

The character of men *and* women.

"This request makes no sense. I am a risk to you and to SI. You know that I don't care if Rael is guilty; given the opportunity, I will kill him."

"A woman is dead, and we need to know if Rael is responsible. We can't do that if you slay him."

Irena sneered. Throwing her own words back at her was obvious manipulation.

But it was also effective. Impotent anger surged through her, and she began to stalk a path from wall to wall. "If we determine that the demon is responsible, I won't hold back my sword."

"We'll see if you do. Perhaps you'll decide not to slay him." Lilith's gaze remained on her; Irena could feel it. "You did not always hate demons so much."

"You are wrong." She had slain her first demon not a week after she'd finished her training in Caelum and returned to Earth. In the centuries since, she'd lost count of the numbers who'd fallen before her blades.

"I saw you in Walachia after Lucifer made his bargain with Vlad—after I pissed Lucifer off, and was punished for it. Yet instead of slaying me, you told Hugh where to find me."

Yes. Almost six hundred years before, Irena had come across Lilith impaled on a giant pole, weakened and helpless; knowing that Hugh—then a Guardian—had formed an attachment to the demon, she had left Lilith's fate in his hands.

Irena stopped pacing. "*That* was a mistake."

"You think so?" Lilith's smile wasn't friendly. "I think, between then and now, you learned what a demon is."

Yes, she had. Not just tempters, not just beings who collected souls to strengthen Lucifer's armies—but beings who reveled in tearing the souls apart. Lilith wasn't much different. Given a chance, she'd dig up everything Irena kept buried.

Irena turned to leave. "I will do as you've asked, hell-spawn."

"Good. We'll meet here tomorrow, seven A.M." Lilith added as she reached the door, "He said there was no one he trusted more at his back."

Irena's hand froze on the knob. "Olek?"

"Yes. You *are* a risk. But sending Alejandro to investigate Rael alone is a bigger one, and SI can't afford to lose him."

Lose him? Ridiculous. Between his Gift and his skill with the sword, Alejandro would survive any fight with a demon.

"He's reckless," Lilith added.

Irena laughed. Lilith saw much, but she was wrong about that. No one was more careful than Olek. He did not make a move without weighing every consequence.

"I will do this, but you are mistaken. We will not lose him."

So she told herself, but as she pulled Lilith's office door closed and saw him standing at the end of the hallway, dread grabbed her by the throat.

Of course it was possible. It was for any of them. An ambush, a misjudgment of speed . . .

A stone turning beneath a foot.

Her breath sharpened. Alejandro squared his stance as she approached him, and her eyes narrowed. Did she look as if she were eager for a fight?

She was. Oh, *how* she was. "You've become a foolish ox."

"Forgive me." He gave a short bow, and paused at the end of it. "You will, of course, tell me why."

Even bowing, he still looked down at her. "You placed yourself behind me at the courthouse. It was an idiot's decision. Don't do it again."

He straightened abruptly, as if she'd struck him. She had. She'd slapped at his pride, his warrior's pride. "You are the stronger of us—"

"Yes," Irena hissed. "I do not need protection from a bullet."

"*The stronger of us,*" Alejandro repeated, circling her with his silent, deadly stride—forcing her to move in a wider circle to prevent him from maneuvering around behind her. "And we did not yet know the scale of the threat. One bullet might have been followed by fifty from an automatic weapon."

Which would cause much more damage, but— "I would recover more quickly than you."

She put her back to the wall and planted her feet. She would not let him push her off balance.

He stopped in front of her. A muscle in his jaw ticked. "Yet you would have to recover. If I place myself behind you and take that injury, you—the stronger of us—can better face a threat if it becomes larger than we anticipate."

"The stronger exist to protect the weaker, you self-important mule."

"Guardians protect weaker vampires and humans, yes." His eyes darkened. Her breath stilled. Powerful emotions made *her* eyes glow; in his, the color deepened. "But in battle, the weaker Guardian must sometimes be used to hold a threat at bay, until the stronger Guardian is positioned where she is most effective."

Damn him. She'd taught him that. But it only applied when the threat was dire. Not when they faced a bullet.

"That battle and that time was not today."

"I determined that it was, Irena, and I will again." He pushed closer, leaning in. "And I vow that I will cover your body with mine whenever I see fit."

The vow echoed in her ears. His smoky scent surrounded her. Her blood heated. No—her blood was already boiling. She'd been so focused on him, but now her focus shifted to the tightness of her skin. The cool, flat press of the wall against her shoulder blades. The molten heat at her core.

Oh, gods, she was wet. He could push at her, slide inside without any resistance. She'd take him all. Make him hers.

"No." He straightened. His eyes shuttered. "I will not fight. I do not like the man I become with you."

The words stabbed her chest. Reflexively, her hands fisted. Irena held them at her sides, struggling against the fury and hurt that urged her to batter them into his face. He stared down at her, and she thought, prayed, that he might take the words back.

Olek shook his head and turned. "Your vampire friend has gone into the city."

He walked away. Irena watched, her heart hammering.

I do not like the man I become with you.

He should have hit her. She'd have known how to respond to that. But this pain, she did not.

CHAPTER 8

The city sparkled below her. Sitting atop a building that rose into the night sky like a flaming spear, Irena looked toward the bay. The dark water was all she recognized from two centuries ago, toward the end of the two hundred years that she'd spent walking this part of the world. She smoothed her hand over her leggings. And she'd made friends during those two hundred years, even as she'd tried to escape the pain that had brought her here.

Between then and now, you learned what a demon is.

Yes. She had.

She'd known from the beginning that there were three types of demons: one who relished pain and suffering and death; one who cared for nothing but his own ambitions; and one who delighted in shredding souls, ruining lives—who reveled in emotional anguish and despair. She'd known that in the same way she knew letters of the alphabet—she was able to name them, to know their sounds, but when they were put together they shifted around so that she had trouble pinning the words down and wrestling out meaning. But with demons, it was simple—it did not matter that there were three types. She killed them all, and it was a job done well. She didn't need to know more than that.

When she'd found Olek on his back, and the demon's blade against his throat, she'd thought it was the first type of demon. She'd guessed wrong. But even if she'd known, she would've still made the bargain to save his life.

Irena closed her eyes, but the image of Olek and that demon was still clear behind them.

He'd been ready. Alejandro with his swords was magnificent to behold. Sleek and deadly. And so when she'd learned that a magistrate near the southern edge of her territory was a demon, she'd taken Olek with her to the demon's residence. When they'd separated to flush out the creature, her worry had been a soft thing. When she'd come up on them in the gardens behind the house, fear had dug into her throat.

She knew what had happened. The soft earth recorded the tracks of their battle; the fight was as clear to her as if she'd witnessed it. Olek had been on the offensive, the demon falling back. Its blood streaked Olek's sword; drops, splatters, and streams ran over the soil.

And in the dirt lay a rock, as big as her fist, freshly overturned. Olek had stumbled—enough to signal the end in most battles between Guardians and demons. But the demon hadn't killed him. He'd cut off Olek's hands as protection against his Gift, then straddled him after shape-shifting into a lush female body. The edge of the demon's blade had been buried in Olek's neck, blood sliding down the sides of his throat—but not so deep that Olek couldn't talk.

So that the demon could hear him beg, she'd thought. Olek wouldn't. He'd die first.

And Irena couldn't allow that.

The demon had been the one to suggest the bargain. And no wonder—Irena would have killed it. The demon had no way out; if it killed Olek, the demon would be dead a second later.

The bargain had been simple: Irena would go into a room with the demon. She wouldn't fight, wouldn't try to kill him, wouldn't use her Gift against him—and at no time would she use more strength than a human. In return, the demon wouldn't kill either of them. And the bargain would be over when he grew bored.

Irena had known what she'd be in for: pain, torture, rape.

Alejandro had realized it, too. In a voice thick with horror, he'd told her, "You cannot do this."

She'd had no choice. She'd ordered him to silence.

And again, he'd defied her. Argued with her. If he'd responded any other way, if he'd accepted her decision, she did not know if she'd have hated him. But he fought. She'd known then that she loved him as she had no other. Lovers had touched her heart before, but Olek had wrapped his hand around it and taken hold.

But if he'd felt the same for Irena, it had been her decision that destroyed those feelings.

He'd pleaded. For her, he'd pleaded. "Please do not do this. If you trade yourself this way, Irena, I will be nothing. Let me die here, still a man. With honor."

She hadn't agreed. His honor would hold as long as he fought. It hadn't been his honor at risk, but his pride.

And so Irena had chosen between his pride and his life.

She'd wanted to cry, to scream. But she'd held on to her calm and ordered the demon to give Olek back his hands, so that they would heal quickly. Her heart had ached. But she'd walked into the room and used her Gift to seal it.

Her body would withstand this bargain. But if Alejandro came in, fought, Irena would fight beside him and break her bargain—and her soul would be lost. So she'd locked the room, and locked her heart and soul away, too.

The first form the demon had taken resembled Michael. No one could copy the Doyen's appearance, but only try to mimic the bronze skin and close-cropped black hair. She'd expected pain, but he'd been gentle. He'd played with her like a lover. He'd licked and kissed, had whispered compliments into her ears. He'd put himself inside her, easing his way with practiced caresses that her body responded to, but that Irena hadn't *felt*. She couldn't physically resist him without losing her soul, and so she went to the same place she had when she'd been violated as a human. She'd sculpted in her mind, practiced with her swords, imagined the smile of Alejandro's eyes. For two days, maybe three, the demon had used her body—but he didn't touch her. And the only pleasure she'd felt was in his frustration that she didn't respond.

Then he'd shape-shifted into Alejandro's form.

It had been her shock and anger that had done it—formed a tiny crack in her defenses. And for an instant, when his lips had touched her neck, she'd wished it was Olek. Had imagined it was him.

And in that instant, she'd lost. She couldn't physically resist him, and so there was only herself to fight as he'd touched her. By the time his mouth had moved between her legs, she'd raged at him to get off her.

She'd battled the first orgasm—and every one after it. Fighting, resisting her reaction, hating that her need for Alejandro had given the demon a tool to use against her.

She hadn't stopped fighting. It was the only thing about those two weeks that didn't shame her.

She hadn't stopped fighting—but she'd felt the urge to give in. To stop resisting and clutch him to her. To move with him and glory in every physical sensation.

Demons had their own specialties. For that one, it had been destroying humans through their own need. He'd done his job well, and she'd learned what a demon was. Their evil was not just that they hated humans, that they loved pain, that they wanted to destroy mankind; their evil was that they led humans to hurt themselves—and to crave the very thing that destroyed them.

Irena still didn't know if she'd have broken, or how long it might have taken. It didn't matter if she could have resisted for centuries—she'd seen the possibility in herself, and that recognition had been more horrifying than anything the demon might have done.

But she hadn't reached that point. Michael had come looking for them. He'd teleported into the room and beheaded the demon while it labored over her rigid form. Without a bargain to hold her, she'd kicked the dead demon off. She'd snarled at

Michael to leave. And when he'd gone, she'd taken out her rage on the demon's body.

She had no memory of tearing it apart. Only of how shocked she'd been when awareness had returned, and she'd seen what she'd done. There were a few pieces of the demon larger than her fist—but not many.

And so she'd learned that about herself, too—that she could completely lose herself to anger.

Devastated, she'd staggered out of the room to find Alejandro attempting to melt his way in through the thick walls. The deep well in the iron had shown how long he'd been trying. His hands had been burned down to stumps.

The pain that had descended on her then crushed her. She'd wanted to kiss his hands, to hold him—but she'd also been burning with a rage and need that wasn't only for him, and she hadn't been able to separate them. And how could she tell him that she'd almost been broken? She could not. Shame had added its weight. She barely remembered cutting off her braids, vanishing the blood-spattered iron, and telling him to burn it all.

Then she'd flown, and hadn't stopped until she'd crossed an ocean, mountains—until a great forest passed beneath her.

She'd landed between the pines and sobbed until she had no more tears. When she was done, she'd begun to walk. She'd traveled between the two continents almost six times in those two hundred years. And when she'd seen that so much of it had become as Europe had been—when the same languages had been spoken—she'd flown back.

The devastating weight had still weighed on her, but not as heavily. And she'd been so careful when she'd seen Olek. She'd spoken to him, not as mentor and novice, but on equal terms and in the language of the city they were in—and in a language that had always forced her to consider her words, to think about their sound and order before they left her mouth.

But despite that care, despite the need, anger, guilt, and shame stood between them like an enormous wall. The blow to his pride had been too great—as had the stain on her soul.

And so the demon had won.

Irena sighed and opened her eyes. Yes, the demon had ruined something good. Something right. That was all demons offered—ruin, pain—no matter the faces they presented. Their kind corrupted everything they touched. Good might come out of an agreement with one—such as saving Alejandro's life— but something else was always destroyed in the process.

She didn't know why Alejandro couldn't see that the alliance with Rael would taint them, and that they should kill the demon before it was too late. Eventually, the demon would exact a price—one that she feared would be too dear to pay.

The whisper of feathers added to the sounds from the city. She glanced left. Michael touched down on the ledge beside her, the wind blowing at his white tunic and loose pants. His black wings folded and disappeared.

She hadn't expected him. "How did you find me?"

"I came to the highest building in the city." He looked over the edge, straight down. She didn't like doing that unless her wings were already formed—she looked, but not down. "Alejandro said you would be here."

Her laugh came out soft and raw. Olek knew her so well. And he still did not guess what she had hidden from him.

Hidden from him—or had she lied to him?

Her fingers clenched. Guilt coated her throat. Guardians often lied, both directly and by omission, and they often hid truth. But would Olek see her omission as a betrayal?

A betrayal of what? What had been left after the demon was done with her?

But was she only splitting hairs to protect herself from more pain if Olek reacted to the truth as she feared he would?

Whatever it was, her omission was not the same as Michael's, who'd still led them, who'd still allowed them to think he'd been a human man before he was a Guardian. Who'd never told them he was the son of a demon.

When she looked at him, she felt a different weight, but one almost as crushing. Michael had trained her himself. For sixteen centuries, she'd looked up to him. She'd admired his quiet and restraint, his ruthless skill. She hadn't always agreed with him, but she'd always valued his opinion and the millennia of experience behind it.

But those sixteen hundred years had been a lie. And in sixteen hundred years, she had learned to deal with physical pain, but she still could not handle emotional pain. She knew that about herself. But it didn't make her any less angry, or see his deception as any less a betrayal.

And the hell of it was, she took comfort from his presence now. Even knowing how he'd lied, she was glad not to be alone on this ledge.

The wind stung at her eyes. "Why come to me?"

"I have just learned about Julia Stafford. And that Lilith has asked you to help Alejandro."

She laughed. How much of a help she'd be remained to be seen. But she could start now. "What can you tell me of Rael?"

Michael lowered to his heels beside her. "He's ambitious. When he lived in Hell, he battled his way up Belial's ranks. He's ruthless. It did not matter if the demons were Belial's or Lucifer's; if they stood in his path, he found a way to destroy them."

"With his sword?"

"Sometimes. Other times he arranged events so that the demons would fall in status, or be killed by another."

Not just a warrior—a cunning schemer. "And since he has left Hell? When was that?"

"Two or three thousand years ago. I don't know the exact date." He smiled slightly. "And since that time, he has lived as a saint. Apparently."

And appearances were almost always deceiving. "Because that is what Lilith knows of him."

"Yes."

"Do you know of anything different?"

"No."

But Rael had been successful in Hell. Why move to Earth and remain here? Why not defend his position Below? Did he have his own reasons—or did he follow Belial's orders? "Why the change? What does he gain?"

"I don't know."

She met his gaze. His eyes were amber—and they appeared so human. "Why haven't you killed him?"

"He concealed himself well. Not just psychically, but physically. He knows human habits. He was not in the public eye until after the Ascension—and after the Ascension, he was not a priority. Those demons who were trying to harm humans were." His gaze didn't waver from hers. "Now, he is useful."

Useful? Irena clenched her jaw and seethed.

"It makes me no more happy than you."

"But less angry."

He smiled. "Perhaps I should be angry, too."

She wanted something from him, but it wasn't anger. She wanted to believe in him again. "Is Rael's change genuine?"

Michael brows rose, as if she'd surprised him with the question—not the question itself, but that *she* had asked it.

He took his time answering. "Demons cannot be judged by their actions, because even those might have a purpose."

Manipulation. As she'd always thought.

But now, it was why she didn't know if she could take Michael's actions—and his history as the Guardians' leader—for what they appeared to be. "You have said your father was a good man. How do you judge that?"

He looked out over the city. "When the rebelling angels were tossed down from Heaven and changed into demons, I don't know if they were given the corruption that is in all of them, or if the corruption had always been there, and the transformation merely stripped the layers that hid it."

"So you don't know if he was truly good," Irena said.

"I don't know if the dragon blood changed him in the same way," he countered. "It allowed him to have children with a human, but like the transformation from angel to demon, it might have been more than a physical change. His treatment of us—Anaria and I—was not what Lucifer had asked of him. I say with certainty that he loved us—and my mother, too." A quick smile curved his lips. "Loved my mother more than us, perhaps. She was . . . a good woman."

He paused. Irena tried to imagine him as a young grigori, growing up among humans, with a human mother and a demon father . . . and could not. "But that didn't last."

"No. As time passed, he became more demonic again, even

though his form returned to its angelic one." He glanced at her. "And, yes, it is true I don't know if the dragon blood changed him for a time, or if it just allowed him to hide what he was—so well that Anaria and I couldn't see it in him—and let him become the father I knew. Perhaps he was not a good man. He was a good father." His mouth twisted in a wry smile. "Once."

"And your sister? The *light* one." She couldn't hold back her sneer. All the grigori were twins. One dark, one light. And Anaria was the one each of the grigori had thought of as the best of them, the most *good*. Yet she was the one who'd studied with Lucifer, who'd created the nephilim, who'd killed humans. "Is she truly good, or just a good sister?"

"Demon blood runs through us, but the human side gives us more choice in the matter than demons. Anaria's choices have not always been what I would have wished." When Irena did not respond, he added, "I have been searching for her."

"What will you do when you find her?"

He didn't answer. Perhaps he couldn't.

"And Khavi?" Irena asked, and lost interest in the past as she felt her anger well up again. "Did she tell you of the woman she foresaw? The one we are supposed to protect?"

"No." His mouth tightened. Michael did not like Khavi's Gift, either. "Who?"

"She did not say. Perhaps it is the Margaret Wren woman—Rael's employee. Perhaps it was Julia Stafford, and we have already failed. I would like to know for certain."

"I will ask her."

They shouldn't have to ask. Not if a woman's life was at stake. "Ask her also if she knew that Julia Stafford would die, and yet did nothing to prevent it."

She was thankful that Michael did not make excuses for Khavi. His face was like stone. "I will." He looked at her, seemed to hesitate, then said, "There are many reasons I did not say who my father was, and one is that Belial is no longer the father I knew. But I have also remained silent because of the question that no Guardian can afford to ask: Is this demon different?"

"Are they?"

He shook his head. "No. Not in any way that matters. But if I am part demon, and I am part human, what does that mean? Is it possible for a demon to be good?" He gave her a wry smile. "Alice told me that was the first question she and Jake asked after Belial told them he was my father. If we ask, if we hesitate—we are lost. Demons cannot be redeemed; any attempt will fail, and endanger the one who tries."

Because then Guardians would have to judge before slaying. And hesitating to find out if a demon deserved to die was far too dangerous.

"Lilith changed," Irena pointed out.

And how she *hated* using Lilith as an example.

Michael must have known. He laughed. "Lilith was never what they are. She began life as a human, and her transformation did not make her heart a demon's. If it had, I'd have slain her long ago."

He stood, and Irena stood with him. Michael had said exactly what she'd needed to hear. Demons could not be redeemed, and Guardians could not hesitate to kill them.

But Michael knew her well. Knew her *so* well. Had he said it for that reason? Was his answer a demon's manipulation, too?

She said baldly, "I do not know if I can trust a word you say." And it hurt.

She thought it might have hurt him, too. After a long silence, he nodded. "One day, perhaps you will again."

She hoped so. Oh, gods, how she hoped so.

❧

Rosalia pulled him into one shadow and out another. Deacon took one step that lasted an endless time and no time at all, and he was on a downtown street. Muffled techno music and the damp, acrid scent of wet pavement and old exhaust filtered through the suffocating darkness.

She let go of his hand. The darkness receded. He could breathe again—not that he needed to, but within the shadows, he'd been certain that inhaling meant sucking in the night.

Rosalia melted out of the darkness after him. "This way, I believe."

She followed the music. Her stride was long, all hips and swivel. His gaze dropped from her ass to her feet. A black skirt swung at her knees. She'd pulled a pair of spiked heels from somewhere. Appropriate for a nightclub, and they did illegal things to her legs—but they weren't much help to a vampire trying to control his bloodlust.

At the street corner, she came to an abrupt halt. A black lace fan appeared in her hand. Steel glinted at the tips of each rib. Reaching for his swords, Deacon caught up with her.

A line of people—humans, all of them—stretched down the sidewalk. A vampire couple skipped the queue and headed directly to Polidori's entrance. The door was unmarked, and guarded by a . . . *Jesus Christ*.

A nosferatu. Ames-Beaumont's bouncer was a nosferatu. Almost seven hulking feet tall, with pale skin, and as bald as a whore's ass.

Rosalia made a small, relieved noise, and her fan vanished.

Deacon took a second, closer look. The bouncer's ears weren't pointed, and his arms weren't as hairless as his head. Not a nosferatu. Just a vampire who superficially resembled one of the cursed creatures—and who guaranteed a jolt of fear at first glance.

Considering what had been feeding on Rosalia for the past year, Deacon guessed she'd gotten a lightning-sized jolt when she'd seen it.

"Clever," Rosalia murmured, her expression on the tail end of alarm and heading into curiosity. "If anyone planned to challenge Ames-Beaumont, that vampire would give them second thoughts before they even made it to the door."

Clever, yeah. But not exactly a welcome sign for newcomers.

"Do you—" He stopped and stared at her. She'd formed fangs. He pushed away the sudden, hot image of her sucking at him. "You aren't going in with me like that."

"The bouncer isn't letting humans in."

"Yeah, but I'm here to get food. You walk in with me like that, and Ames-Beaumont will tell me I've already got a source. So lose the fangs."

Her tongue ran over the points, and her red lips plumped into a pout. Then the fangs were gone, just normal human canines again.

He looked away from her mouth. "If Ames-Beaumont works with SI, then he doesn't have a problem with Guardians." Maybe that was her reason for the vampire disguise; most vampire communities had only recently learned that Guardians existed, and wouldn't know what the hell to think if someone like Rosalia showed up at their door. "So just flash your wings at the bouncer. Or do your shadow thing and sneak in."

She gave him another searching look, then rolled her hips and crossed the street. All right. So flashing her wings in full view of humans wasn't the best idea he'd come up with, but she had her own idea. She stopped in front of the bouncer. He opened his mouth, began saying something about the line— and her eyes flared a warm yellow. The bouncer opened the velvet rope and held it until Deacon went through.

The stairwell had been painted black. They hit the lower level, paid the cover fee, and as soon as they pushed through the swinging doors, got a face full of air-conditioning that kept the place as cool as the night outside. Definitely a vampire's nightclub; anything much warmer, and Deacon would already have been sweating. The club was huge, with an upper level balcony that wrapped around the walls, leaving the ceiling above the dance floor open. They'd gone for an industrial look, with exposed beams and pipes, and thrown in a good dose of English parlor. A crazy mix, but it worked.

Vampires sat at half the tables. Others danced, although that hadn't gotten going hard yet. A few vampires had drinks in front of them, each untouched. No point in buying a drink except for appearances—they couldn't taste anything and couldn't get drunk.

"That will be Ames-Beaumont's table." Rosalia nodded to a large, horseshoe-shaped booth in the back. The seats were empty. "He'd have a view of everything."

"Then let's make sure he sees us."

"I'll find out if anyone knows when he's coming." Rosalia headed for the lightly attended bar.

Deacon approached Ames-Beaumont's booth, and wasn't surprised when he heard the heavy footsteps coming toward him, the gravelly voice that said, "Not that seat, man. You'll find another—" The vampire broke off. "Deacon?"

Well, damn. Deacon's stomach hollowed out, but his grin was genuine. "Darkwolf. You done traveling yet?"

"I'm settled." The big vampire gripped his forearm, then pulled Deacon in to slap his back. "Are you done being an asshole?"

"No."

"Tell me about it then." Darkwolf steered him toward another booth. "I'd give you the best table, but you being who you are, it just wouldn't look—"

"I'm not here to challenge him."

"I fucking hope not." Darkwolf dropped onto dark blue velvet, stretched out his leather-clad legs. More black leather strained across his massive chest. "Because as good as you are, Ames-Beaumont wouldn't even break a sweat taking you down. Taking ten of us down."

Us? Deacon looked at him hard. "Did you try?"

If he did, that meant something was wrong with Ames-Beaumont's leadership. Darkwolf believed in the strongest leading and protecting, but he wouldn't hesitate to fight against a corrupt leader.

"Hell, no." Darkwolf laughed. "I had to convince the fucker to take the spot. I sure as hell didn't want it, not after what went down here."

Drink in hand, Rosalia slid in next to Deacon. "What went down?" she asked.

Darkwolf looked at him.

"Guardian," Deacon said.

His eyes narrowed at her. "I know the Guardians around here. I don't recognize your scent."

Psychic scent, as Guardians didn't have any bodily odor. At least, not that Deacon had ever been able to tell. Irena smelled like smoke and blood, but it was like a perfume covering up the scent of nothing. The only fragrance coming from Rosalia's direction was the peach and alcohol in the fruity drink she was sipping.

She held out her hand. Darkwolf took it, let go. He'd checked the temperature of her skin, Deacon realized. A demon could shape-shift to look like a Guardian, but it couldn't conceal that.

"All right." Darkwolf's gaze moved between them, guessing, measuring, wondering. "Two years ago, or thereabouts, a nest of nosferatu moved into the city, trapped all the elders in here"—he gestured around them—"and burnt it down."

"These nosferatu," Rosalia said. "Are they the ones who made a bargain with Lucifer?"

"Those are the ones. So the Guardians got rid of them."

Deacon knew that. And he also knew that he was supposed to think "got rid of them" meant the Guardians had slain the nosferatu. But that wasn't what had happened. No, somehow the nosferatu had ended up in the Chaos realm, trapped in a hellish dimension with dragons and God knew what other terrors.

No one had access to that realm. Yet the Guardians still managed to trap the nosferatu there.

"How?"

One question. And if he got the answer, got what Caym wanted—Deacon's people would be safe.

Darkwolf's eyes went flat and wary. "I don't know."

He was lying. Deacon's blood pounded. He could drag Darkwolf over the table, beat it out of him. But getting the answer with violence would just draw attention to what he was doing. Would just jeopardize it all.

But if that risk hadn't held him back, he'd have done it. He would have beaten a *friend* to get what he needed. Caym had made him into this.

And he'd get the bastard what he wanted. Then spend the rest of his life seeing the demon dead.

"Then we had problems with a demon trying to take us over, a nosferatu . . ." Darkwolf shrugged. "Ames-Beaumont got rid of them. He and his partner."

And they'd obviously both secured Darkwolf's loyalty. So even a beating wouldn't get it out of the vampire.

Deacon made a show of looking around, taking a few seconds to calm himself. "This is their place, yeah? They don't let humans in?"

Darkwolf's lips quirked. "We do at ten. Someone's got to buy the drinks, keep this place running. But before ten, it's just the community." He glanced at Rosalia. "And guests."

So that any community business Ames-Beaumont needed to handle could be done without humans observing.

"So, you're here to see him?"

Deacon nodded and steeled himself before admitting, "I lost Prague."

He expected Darkwolf's surprise. Not Rosalia's.

She choked on her drink. "How?"

His pride raged inside. Wanted to rage out loud. He went with the cover story, and kept it short. "One of the nosferatu-born moved in, so I moved out."

"And your consorts?"

Were being held hostage by a demon with a plan. "They didn't want to fuck a beaten vampire."

"When did this happen?"

That was still Rosalia, when he'd expected Darkwolf to be asking the questions. Her eyes were wide as she stared at him. His humiliation was hot.

"About three weeks ago."

"That's why you were in Rome?"

"Yeah." That, and because that's where the demon had told him to go. He grabbed her drink, took a gulp. He couldn't taste it, but it was cold, drowning the heat of humiliation.

"Rome?" Darkwolf leaned forward, and as if sensing Deacon's humiliation, changed the subject. A damn good friend. "Now that's some bad shit, man—those nephilim coming in and killing them all."

"Yeah." Deacon laughed without humor. "Bad for most of them. A few deserved it."

"Acciaioli?" Darkwolf grimaced and shook his head. "Now that's the truth."

Rosalia made a small sound. Deacon glanced over. She stared down into her drink with a lost expression in her eyes. Hell, she'd said she'd had friends in Rome. Lorenzo

Acciaioli, the asshole who'd led the community, probably hadn't counted among them, but he and Darkwolf probably shouldn't start running a list of vampires in Rome who'd deserved to die.

He changed the subject again. "So SI brought me in, but I need a blood-sharer."

Darkwolf frowned. "The Guardians didn't hook you up?"

He thought of Irena, her note. "No."

With a nod, Darkwolf stood. "I'll get it rolling. We have a few threesomes where there isn't any commitment. One of them might want a break."

Meaning that the vampires were in a threesome out of necessity, not desire—and trading in two partners for Deacon didn't make any difference.

A second dose of humiliation didn't get any easier to swallow, but he choked it down. "Thanks."

"Any time."

Rosalia's silence continued after Darkwolf left. Deacon tried to think of something worth saying, and couldn't.

Christ, he missed Eva and Petra. Missed their snarky banter, their softness with each other. Friends didn't come any better than those two. Any real desire between them had faded decades ago, but he trusted them at his side, in his bed.

No real desire, and here was Rosalia, who had him wondering about her breasts, her nipples—not just the taste of her blood. Life didn't make any damn sense.

He looked over at her. "So what's your story?"

A strange smile touched her eyes, and told him there would be more to her answer than whatever she said. "I was killed by a vampire while saving my sisters."

Killed saving someone. That was how it always worked with Guardians. "Any vampire I know?"

"Lorenzo Acciaioli."

"No kidding? And you didn't slay him after you returned to Earth?"

Rome's leader had been more than an asshole—he'd been a cruel, vindictive one. As one of the nosferatu-born, Acciaioli hadn't been challenged by other vampires. And demons had left him alone, probably because they recognized evil when they saw it. Acciaioli did their work for them.

"No." She pulled the straw from her glass and downed the rest of her drink. "You have had dealings with him."

That wasn't a question. "Yeah, him and his queer little brother." Now that was a fucked up relationship. Acciaioli had his consorts, but rumor was, his little brother fed from him, too. And no vampire could drink blood without getting hot.

When Rosalia raised her brows, he explained, "About six years ago, we had a dispute over one of his vampires who defected to my community. It wasn't the first one who'd defected, but I guess it was one too many. Acciaioli wanted to kill him for his disloyalty; I disagreed."

And he supposed that the brother was the reason it hadn't come to a challenge, and Deacon getting his ass handed to him. Instead, the brother had sneaked into Deacon's room and kissed him. He could still feel that freak's lips against his own. He'd stopped short of giving Deacon his tongue, but only because Deacon had been pushing at him—the little fucker had been strong, maybe even nosferatu-born, as well—and Acciaioli had come upon them.

Deacon hadn't known if it was out of jealousy, disgust, or embarrassment—whatever the reason, after seeing that kiss, Acciaioli had given up and hightailed it back to Rome.

Deacon shook off the memory. "Is Acciaioli one of the friends you're grieving?"

"I am not sure if it is grief or relief. He was my brother." Her gaze was steady, deep. Stunned, he couldn't look away. "How would you counsel someone in my place?"

He recovered from his shock. "I don't do counseling."

"But as a man of the cloth, you used to."

He stared at her. Eva and Petra knew he'd once worn a navy chaplain's insignia on his collar, but no one else did. And it was a long, long time ago. "How the fuck do you know that?"

"Perhaps it is recognizing like to like. I was not always a Guardian."

Like to like? "Then you were what? A goddamn nun?"

"Yes."

She smiled slightly, as if she hadn't just dropped about three bombshells on him in the past minute. A nun. Holy shit. And that probably meant the *sisters* she'd been saving weren't her blood relatives.

But she'd still been left with one screwed up family. "So you lost two brothers."

Her brow furrowed, then cleared. "No."

What the hell? So the queer little brother—"Oh, fuck."

It'd been Rosalia. Shape-shifted.

The humiliation just kept on coming, didn't it?

Her laugh was quiet, and didn't last. She sighed. "I could not kill Lorenzo, so I managed him." She pushed her empty glass away. "Tried to."

"And that was all you did?" A waste of a Guardian.

Obviously, she thought so, too. "No, of course not." She frowned at him, but before it could settle on her mouth, she stiffened. Her gaze shifted to the club entrance. "Ames-Beaumont is here."

Deacon turned. Just going by his size, Ames-Beaumont wasn't much to speak of. Tall, but not intimidating. Deacon had a few inches on him—and about thirty pounds of muscle. But muscle didn't mean much to a vampire; their strength depended on age and the blood that had transformed them. The vampire's trousers and shirt screamed money and were as neat as a magazine spread. His clothes might have been called prissy in their perfection, but his blond hair obviously hadn't seen a comb in some time.

Deacon's lip curled. He'd bet anything that messy look had been influenced by a recent vampire movie that had been popular with humans, and where the creatures had *sparkled*. Yeah, *prissy* fit just right.

He couldn't deny that Ames-Beaumont was good-looking, though. Pretty as hell. Deacon didn't usually notice that about men, but with a face like Ames-Beaumont's, he couldn't *not* notice.

"The novices said that the effect wears off the longer you look at him. The better you know him."

"What effect?" Deacon couldn't stop staring at the guy, but

that wasn't an effect. It was damn smart, now that the vampire was walking in their direction.

"I don't—" Beneath the table, Rosalia's hand suddenly gripped his, hard. Her fingers rubbed up and down his knuckles like they were a rosary. "Jesus, Mary and Joseph," she whispered.

Maybe the lights shifted just right. Maybe it was just that Ames-Beaumont had come close enough. Deacon didn't know, but one second he was seeing an overly-pretty vampire, and the next he saw beauty so striking, it was a physical blow to his chest. His fingers clamped down on Rosalia's.

Ames-Beaumont stopped at their table. Jesus Christ, Deacon actually wanted to get up and touch the guy. Kiss him. He sat dumb, transfixed by the impossible beauty of that mouth.

Cool gray eyes met his. Then Ames-Beaumont bent his head, and the small female beside him rose to her toes and whispered into his ear. A low, incredibly fast whisper, mostly covered by the music, but Deacon heard his and Rosalia's names—and "Irena."

Jesus, he hadn't even noticed the slim woman until now, but he assumed it was Savitri Murray, Ames-Beaumont's partner. Deacon forced his gaze away from Ames-Beaumont and focused on her. Her black hair was almost as short as her partner's, but tamed into little spikes. Her cinnamon skin would never pale as many vampires' did. Her face was sharp, her chin pointed, and her dark brown eyes were lively. Eva often looked at him with the same combination of mischief and intelligence that this woman had, but where Eva was sturdy and rounded, this woman was delicate.

When Ames-Beaumont straightened, he wore a slight smile. "Deacon, Rosalia. We did not expect the pleasure of your company this evening."

That accent had upper-class and British all over it. He should have guessed. "You are something unexpected, too."

The vampire's grin sent his heart racing. The bloodlust roared to life in his veins. Fucking unbelievable. Another second, and he'd be sporting wood under the table.

"I imagine I am." Ames-Beaumont threaded his fingers

through his partner's and began to draw her away. "Come join us when it pleases you. We will be here most of the night."

Ames-Beaumont turned his back to them. That was some relief.

Rosalia let go of his hand. Her breath was as unsteady as his. "That was kind of him. Giving us time."

"Yeah." Maybe not kind, though. Ames-Beaumont probably just didn't like speaking with awestruck idiots. Deacon dragged his fingers through his hair. "The novices warned you?"

"Yes, but I didn't understand . . . Wow." She shifted a little on the seat.

Oh, Jesus. Was she aroused? *Wet?*

Nothing Ames-Beaumont could have done equaled the need that raced through him then.

"They said it can be worse if he's upset," she added. "Or if his emotions are worked up."

Worse? What did that mean—an instant orgasm? "What kind of worse?"

"Terrifying. Becca said, and I quote, 'One look makes you cream your panties, the other makes you piss in them.' "

Even quoted, some of those words came a little too easily from her tongue. "It's been a while since you've been a nun, hasn't it?"

"A very long time." She lifted her glass, tipped a piece of ice into her mouth, and started chewing. With a deep breath, she glanced over at Ames-Beaumont's table . . . and kept looking.

Getting used to it, Deacon realized, and did the same. Darkwolf joined the couple, sliding into Savitri's side of the bench. She leaned toward Darkwolf as she spoke with him—and Ames-Beaumont stared at her with an enraptured expression that might have been on Deacon's own face a minute before.

"They are both nosferatu-born," Rosalia murmured.

Hearing that Ames-Beaumont was didn't surprise him, but Savitri . . . ? That small, delicate woman was several times stronger than Deacon was?

"You can tell by looking at them?"

"The novices said she was."

He should have hung around the novices a little longer. "How does he do that . . . effect?"

"They don't know, though they each have their theories: a curse, Michael's sword, he's half-Guardian, or half-demon. Whatever it was, he can walk in the sun, only goes into his daysleep once a week, can't see his reflection—"

"*Can't see his reflection?*" Everything else he could buy, but no reflection was ridiculous. Vampires not casting reflections was just an old wives' tale that Deacon proved wrong every time he looked into a mirror. He searched Rosalia's face for a sign that she was joking, and found none. "You're serious."

"Yes." She nodded. "And the novices also said that he is as strong as a Guardian."

Even a nosferatu-born vampire wasn't that powerful. And it meant that Ames-Beaumont would be able to handle himself against a demon.

So he'd pass that info on. Pass it on and hope it was what the demon needed.

Suddenly, he just wanted to get this over with. "Ready?"

In answer, she scooted out. He should have followed her faster. She slid in next to Ames-Beaumont before Deacon got to the seat. He couldn't protect her from the other vampire if she was between them. Couldn't—

Jesus. What was wrong with him? A Guardian didn't need help from a vampire. And he couldn't protect her from Ames-Beaumont, anyway. That much had been made perfectly clear.

At least Ames-Beaumont's effect wasn't so bad now. The kick in the chest had mellowed into a soft compulsion to look, and Deacon's brain was working again.

Rosalia wasn't looking at Ames-Beaumont yet. Her gaze rested on his partner. "So," she said. "You're Hugh's little sister."

Hugh Castleford? The one who could read lies?

It just got better and better, Deacon thought grimly.

"And SI's resident geek," Savitri said brightly, but her face became more serious as she added, "I'll be helping Jake dig through the church's financial records, tracing any money that went into the upkeep. We'll figure out how the nosferatu managed to stay down there so long without anyone raising an alarm. And I'll keep you updated."

Deacon decided he wouldn't tell the demon that. The fucker had better hope he'd covered his ass and hidden the money trail.

Rosalia looked baffled. "But I know who owns the building—it was my brother's. It is not one of the Church's. It was the vampire community's."

Ames-Beaumont's brows rose. "Your brother?"

"Lorenzo Acciaioli," Deacon said.

Ames-Beaumont gave Rosalia a hard look, as if deciding whether she was something repulsive.

"Oh. I— Okay." Savitri floundered, gathered herself, and glanced at Deacon. "And you need a partner?"

Deacon gave a short nod, and Ames-Beaumont frowned.

"The Guardians haven't made arrangements for you?"

Both he and Darkwolf had asked that. What kind of arrangements could the Guardians make? A vampire had one long-term option for feeding, and that was to drink living blood. And Deacon would rather take it from a vampire who went through exactly what he did than as charity from a goddamn novice, or whoever else they could convince to get into his bed and donate their blood.

"No," he said tightly.

Ames-Beaumont and Savitri exchanged a surprised glance. "Okay," she said. "There's one—"

"Oh, good God," Ames-Beaumont interrupted. "The barbarian has made it through the gate." He looked away from the club entrance and met Deacon's gaze. "Are you *certain* the Guardians haven't made arrangements for you? Because I know that look in her eyes: She's hunting, and she's coming for you."

Deacon turned, caught sight of the red hair, the white fur mantle. His stomach dropped to his knees.

Irena.

Fucking perfect.

🌢

Irena loved Polidori's. Loved the vampires that smelled of sex and blood, and the music that beat like a strong heart. She loved

Hugh's adopted sister, who barely knew how to hold a sword—
and who, through sheer determination, had ripped out a demon's
throat less than a week after she'd been transformed. Irena even
liked the vain, affected, irreverent, cursed, and dragon-tainted
vampire Savi planned to marry.

A vampire who also happened to be Lilith's best friend.
Irena didn't hold that against him.

Despite his numerous faults, Colin Ames-Beaumont *could*
hold a sword. Could stand his ground with it, and damage anyone who crossed him. And she had to admire that Caesar himself probably hadn't had Ames-Beaumont's self-confidence . . .
or his ego.

Unlike another vampire she knew. Her gaze settled on Deacon's trapped expression, and she grinned. It widened when he
turned his back to her.

She vanished her mantle as she reached the booth. Though
she recognized the dark vampire on the other side of the table,
she shoved in next to Deacon. He bumped against Rosalia, who
braced herself against the curve of the seat. Irena's apology to
her was answered with a quiet laugh.

Irena half-turned toward Deacon, leaned her elbow on the
table, and propped her jaw in her hand. "You're an idiot. I told
you to wait."

"I chose not to listen."

His pulse throbbed in his neck, his jaw was tense. Not
trapped now, but angry. Maybe insulted.

Good. A man without pride couldn't be insulted. So Deacon
had a bit left.

The lights flickered before she could respond. Irena frowned,
calling in a knife. When she saw Jake had teleported into the
middle of the dance floor, Radha and Mariko at his sides, she
vanished it again.

Ames-Beaumont muttered, "Bloody hell. Shall we just invite all of Caelum?"

"Oh," Rosalia said on a quiet breath. Her eyes shone with
moisture and joy radiated through her psychic scent. "Oh."

Irena got out of the way, but Deacon wasn't quick enough.
Rosalia scooted over him, her ass dragging across his lap. He

tensed. Looked pained and hungry, all at once. His gaze remained on Rosalia as she rushed out to meet her friends.

Interesting. He'd never looked at Eva or Petra like that.

Irena dropped into the seat again. Jake strolled over, toothpick lodged in the corner of his mouth, his hands in his pockets. Savi looked up at him, her brow creased. "Was that you? The lights?"

"Seems so."

"Your second Gift?"

"Yep. Although I hope it turns out to be something a little better than making the power go on and off." He rubbed his hand over his shaved head. "And that I'll be able to control it soon, because computers haven't been so great around me lately. You got my message about the church, and digging around in the financials?"

Savi shook her head. "Apparently, we don't need to."

"Why?"

"It was the community's church. Her brother's, apparently. Lorenzo Acciaioli."

Jake sucked in his breath through his teeth.

Irena frowned. "Did he know she was there?"

"Knowing Acciaioli, there's a damn good chance of that," Deacon said.

"Yes," Ames-Beaumont agreed.

Then he was better off dead. Irena glanced up at Jake again. "Were there any more nosferatu?"

"Nope, and it's just past dawn there now. If there were, none came back to the catacombs. I'm heading back in a second; Alice is there by herself." He looked around, to where the three Guardians were embracing in the center of the dance floor. Tears streaked Rosalia's cheeks, but her smile could have lit the room. "I, uh, guess I'll be back for them later so I don't break up their reunion."

Ames-Beaumont looked to Darkwolf. "A private room, I think."

The vampire left the table. Jake glanced at Irena.

"One hell of a day, huh?"

"Yes." She'd seen worse, but she couldn't argue with his assessment. "Be safe."

Though she felt the thrust of his teleporting Gift, the lights didn't flicker when he disappeared. Then Savi laughed, her gaze on Irena's hair.

She reached up. Static stood each strand on end.

"You need a ground," Savi told her. "Try touching—"

Deacon hissed as Irena brushed her hand against his, and a painful spark arced between them. She yanked her hand back, shook out the sting. That discharge had been a lot stronger than she'd expected.

"I was going to say one of the metal pipes, but that works, too." Savi leaned back into the cradle of Ames-Beaumont's arm. "Deacon tells us he needs a partner."

"And he will get one, eventually." Irena met Deacon's eyes and lowered her voice until the music covered it from anyone not at that table. "But until you find someone suitable, someone you *want*," she stressed, "there are alternatives. I'll give you the first here. The second, I'll explain later . . . because there simply isn't enough for everyone."

She thought she saw understanding in his face. He couldn't know that the alternative was demon blood from a *living* demon. But he'd have realized that if an alternative was available and word of it became public, every vampire unhappy with their blood-sharing partners would want it.

The Guardians' supply was limited. Just one demon, who was bound in a bargain to give them a pint a day. That amount could feed one vampire, maybe two. Not more than that.

He said cautiously, "What is the first?"

She pulled a lead goblet out of her cache, used her Gift to expand the size of the bowl, and looked to Ames-Beaumont. "No humans are here?" She didn't sense any, couldn't smell any—but it was best to check.

"If there were, Hawkins' disappearing act would have set them talking, don't you think?"

Perhaps Jake's teleporting hadn't, but this probably would. She called in a nosferatu's head between her palms. Blood dripped from its severed neck into the goblet. Savi's eyes widened; Ames-Beaumont began laughing.

There were other noises, gasps. Soon, all of the community would know that a Guardian had given Deacon nosferatu blood. That he was unique among them. And when his shock had passed, Deacon would realize that the community knew of it, too.

"Jesus Christ," Deacon said. "You expect me to drink that?"

Despite his words, his gaze was fixed on the blood. The scent was thick, and because it was nosferatu, strong and dark. The other two vampires didn't appear as affected—but then, they'd probably fed from each other already.

Irena squeezed, hoping to get the blood running faster. Some had drained out onto the ossuary floor before she'd vanished the head. That spilled blood was in her cache, too, but mixed with dirt. At least this was clean.

"It's dead blood, so even though it will suppress the blood-lust, it won't feed you for long." Too many days without living blood and vampires became weak and stupid. "But it might make you stronger."

Need flared in Deacon's eyes and was quickly covered. "I've never heard that."

"Neither have I," Ames-Beaumont put in.

"That is because, as far as I know, no vampire has ever drunk a significant amount of blood from a nosferatu. Have you heard of such?"

All of them shook their heads.

"That is why I said *might*." With two fingers, Irena ripped out the nosferatu's tongue, vanished it, and poured more blood from its mouth. Savi half-laughed, half-moaned, and covered her eyes. "But even if it doesn't do anything, drinking this won't hurt you."

"What makes you think *might*?" Deacon asked.

"Jake," Irena said simply. "He has had two transformations, and has become as strong and as fast as a Guardian four times his age. Vampire blood and nosferatu blood are the only bloods that transform. If you, a vampire already, drink vampire blood . . ." She lifted her shoulder. "No difference. But if it is this? Perhaps it will."

Savi peeked through her fingers. After a brief hesitation,

she said, "Colin and I . . . I am not as strong as he is, but I *am* stronger than when I first began drinking his blood. There was a difference. Some of the changes—like the additional strength—have been slow. Other changes were immediate."

Such as both of them being able to see Chaos in a mirror, instead of just the cursed and tainted Ames-Beaumont being able to. Such as having a strong anchor to Chaos—strong enough that no one but Michael could teleport them anywhere without ending up in that realm.

Irena would not have referred even vaguely to how Ames-Beaumont's blood had affected Savi, but she was grateful that Savi had made mention of it. Even if the blood did not strengthen Deacon, it might give the vampire confidence—however false—until he regained his own.

"There, you see? It is not the same, but it is similar."

Deacon nodded at the goblet. "Will that much do it?"

Irena frowned. "I would know that, how? I have just told you it has not been done before. It is enough to transform a human to vampire, but a vampire to . . . *more* vampire?" She shrugged. "But even if it does not have an immediate effect, I have three nosferatu—two raw, one cooked. The blood of all three is yours if you wish to keep trying."

He apparently did. When she slid the goblet toward him, he reached for it.

Savi moved at the same time, lifting her arm to greet someone, her smile a bright, warm curve. "Andy. Sit with us."

Irena glanced up, and didn't conceal her surprise. "Detective Taylor."

Off-duty, obviously. The scent of coffee and stale cigarettes clung to the officer's jeans, her black leather jacket, her hair. If possible, she looked more tired and drawn that she had that morning. Her gaze fell to the nosferatu's head clutched between Irena's hands.

She didn't blink, didn't blanch. After a brief pause, she looked up at Savi again.

"Join us, detective," Ames-Beaumont said, his voice smooth and amused. "And if you'd like to become a vampire—a nosferatu-born one, which I assure you is the very best kind—our winged friend Irena can assist you."

"Thanks, but no." Taylor looked over at Deacon, who was steadily drinking from the goblet, and took a seat next to Savi.

"Are you here officially?" Ames-Beaumont asked.

"Semi-officially."

"Which means not officially at all."

"Colin." Savi nudged him with her elbow. "What's up?"

Taylor's gaze remained on Ames-Beaumont. "I need to know where you were this afternoon."

Because Ames-Beaumont was the one vampire who *could* have been at the courthouse that afternoon. Irena knew it hadn't been Colin—the scent had been human—but the shooter had been *so* obviously human that she hadn't thought to tell Taylor that. She'd never imagined the detective might consider other possibilities.

Intrigued, Irena looked at Taylor more closely. It took guts to come into a vampire's club and ask him to prove he didn't kill a human woman.

"Around noon, I imagine?" Obviously, the vampire knew why Taylor had asked, but Irena couldn't tell if he was insulted or amused. "I was in my daysleep from dawn until just after sunset."

"Can anyone verify that?"

That irritated him. His brows lifted very slightly.

"I was with him," Savi said. "We went to bed together."

"That's not an alibi. You might as well be dead during the day. He isn't."

Ames-Beaumont sighed. "Pray tell me why I would try to kill the congressman?"

"Because he is a demon," Irena said, vanishing the nosferatu head and the smears of blood from her fingers. She glanced up to find them all looking at her. "That is reason enough for *me*."

Taylor smiled, then pinched the bridge of her nose. "Look," she said. "A human died, so Guardians are out as suspects, and so are demons. Daytime means nosferatu and vampires are out.

If the murderer wasn't a human, you're the only one who could have done it."

She'd ruled out a demon killing Julia Stafford, because the nephilim hadn't come to enforce the Rules and slay the demon. Neither had it been a Guardian, because Michael had not asked any of them to Fall or Ascend.

How did Taylor know that much about them?

"No," Ames-Beaumont said. "I am just the only one who wouldn't have been punished already for it."

"Either way." Taylor spread her hands. "The FBI grabbed the investigation, not SI. And the feds won't know to look your way, or any other way. But if it's a human, they'll know how to go after him."

"So asking me will serve what purpose? Easing your mind?"

"I'm just trying to cover the bases that they can't."

Why had Lilith never recruited this one for SI? Irena leaned forward, began to ask—and to tell her that SI *would* be taking over part of the investigation—but Ames-Beaumont apparently decided to relent.

"Sir Pup was guarding our house while Savi and I were in our daysleep. He can verify that I was there."

Oh, he could not be serious. But with one look, Irena realized that he was. Her laughter burst from her in a howl. She fell back, clutching her stomach.

Taylor rubbed her hand over her face. "You want to use Lilith's *dog* for an alibi?"

"He's perfectly capable of answering your questions." Ames-Beaumont glanced at Deacon, whose perplexed expression set Irena off again. "Sir Pup is a hellhound, not a dog."

Deacon's expression didn't clear. "A hellhound?"

"Big," Taylor told him. "With three heads and teeth like this." She held her hands about six inches apart. "Scary as hell."

"And it guards you on the days you sleep?" Deacon's face lost all expression.

"Yes."

Irena sat up, wiped her eyes. "I can verify that Sir Pup wasn't with Lilith today. And also that the shooter smelled human."

Taylor nodded, and exhaled slowly. Exhaustion seemed to settle over her. Savi reached out, touched her arm.

"You okay?"

Taylor's hand folded over the vampire's. They were friends, Irena realized. Whatever had been semi-official about this visit dropped away.

And, she thought, their friendship also explained how Taylor knew so much.

The lights didn't blink when Michael teleported in. Irena usually didn't notice that he *had* teleported until she heard his heartbeat. But this time, she sensed him immediately—and almost suffocated under the weight of his psychic scent.

She usually couldn't even *feel* his psychic scent.

"Yes. I just—" Taylor glanced to the right. "Never mind. Later."

Irena was not sure if Savi had even heard. The vampires moved uncomfortably, though they didn't look as blanketed with the dark weight as she did.

Then it lightened, though his eyes were fully obsidian. To Irena's surprise, he sat next to Taylor. The detective stiffened, but didn't scoot closer to Savi.

His harmonious voice had a deep, hard edge that she rarely heard. "Who are you?"

Without color in his eyes, it was impossible to know where his gaze was focused—but as there was only one person at the table Michael didn't know, Irena said, "Deacon."

"You found Rosalia."

The vampire looked uncomfortable at taking the credit. "Yes."

"Thank you."

Beneath the table, Irena's hands began shaking. Michael had not done anything, but something about him terrified her.

Something the vampires obviously didn't feel the same way.

Michael drew in a breath. The goblet in front of Deacon vanished and reappeared in Michael's grip. "Nosferatu blood."

Deacon glanced at her. "To see if I'll end up stronger."

The Doyen nodded. "You might. And I should not be surprised that it is Irena who has thought of it. She is the one who made the first of you."

"What? The first vampire?" A wave of curiosity washed away Savi's discomfort. "How?"

"It is a tale for a darker night." Irena's gaze held Michael's. "The story does not end well."

Irena, only a century old, had come upon a young woman trying to fight a nosferatu. Though she hadn't killed the creature—Irena had—the woman had fought with honor. So Irena had cut the heart from the nosferatu's body and given it to her.

Irena hadn't known that the woman would heal with each bite, or that when she'd ingested enough, she'd transform. But they'd both been delighted and amazed when she had. Irena had helped the young woman explore her abilities throughout the night . . . but had not anticipated the agony that the sun brought.

She'd died, screaming.

"It did not end well for that one. But many lives have been saved since." Michael looked at her and spoke in the language of the Mongol Horde. Irena had not heard the dialect in centuries—and, very likely, no one else at the table could understand his words. "It was not a failure. You could not know daylight would kill her."

But she should have guessed. She'd known a nosferatu's weakness. Beneath the table, she laced her trembling fingers together. Why had he used a different language—one that only she would know? "Did Khavi tell you who the woman was?"

"Yes." He angled his head slightly, toward the corner of the booth where Taylor and Savi were speaking with each other. "The human beside me."

Irena's heart thumped a painful beat. "What will happen?"

"A vampire. Khavi does not see how or when it comes about. Only that it does."

And that explained why Michael was here. He would not let it happen. Neither would Irena. "Can it be changed?"

She knew he would say yes. Michael believed that free will dictated the future, not prophecy.

"Yes."

Then why was he so upset? Unless . . . "Was there more? Did she tell you more?"

"Yes." The dark psychic weight pushed her down again—despair. Terror. Then it lifted, as if he'd made an effort to conceal it. "But I will not let it come to pass."

CHAPTER 9

Demon, name unknown. Alias, Fabián Palacio.
   Demon, name unknown. Alias, Roberto Verón.
   Affiliation: Belial, suspected. Palacio and Verón have assumed co-leadership of the vampire community in Buenos Aires. I witnessed blood drawn from vampires and collected, similar to the methods outlined by Sammael (Legion Corporation, Seattle). Further observation indicates that the demons are training a select number of vampires.

And the demons could have used tutoring themselves, Alejandro thought, lifting his pen from his report. His desk chair creaked as he leaned back and looked through the open window of his study. Winter birds chirped and fluttered in the garden. Across the bay, the city of Cádiz was nestled like a pearl between the satiny blue water and the clear skies.

Many Guardians returned to Caelum for moments of quiet and to complete the busy work of their assignments. Alejandro preferred the warmth of his house. It wasn't quiet, but it wasn't *silent*, either—whereas Caelum's silence was so enormous that

Alejandro had difficulty focusing on anything else. He'd have found himself thinking of all those Guardians lost during the Ascension, instead of what he should have been contemplating: a demon's incompetence with a sword.

Palacio's and Verón's skills weren't near the level that qualified a Guardian to teach others. Either the demons weren't invested in properly training the vampires, or there were so few skilled warriors among Belial's demons that they made do with what they had.

The second possibility intrigued him—but Alejandro knew the first was far more likely. The demons wanted a supply of vampire blood, and their offer to train the vampires—to prepare them to fight the nephilim—appeared to be a fair trade. The vampires wouldn't know until it was too late that the protection the demons provided was substandard.

And an illusion. A vampire couldn't beat a nephil in hand-to-hand combat. Their only real protection started with a phone call to Special Investigations and the Guardians.

Tomorrow, Alejandro would use the demons' blood to open that line of communication.

He put his pen back to paper to continue the report. One day, he knew, he would succumb to modern computers. But he enjoyed the scratch of the pen's steel nib against the paper, the coppery scent of the ink—and he could write his reports in triplicate at the same speed a computer saved a file to its hard drive. He glanced over at the waist-high stack of newspapers and journals delivered to his home every week. And he had yet to see a computer that had a data connection fast enough to deliver him the same amount of news in the five minutes he would need to read through that stack—and deliver it in as many languages. Yes, he was quite satisfied with ink and paper.

A community gathering is scheduled for tomorrow night.
I will—

Thunder cracked above the house, rattling the windows. Alejandro called in his swords and leapt atop his desk, listening. Not thunder. The skies were cloudless.

A shout shattered the silence. An ear-splitting crash followed. Alejandro raced through his house toward the solarium. The glass roof had collapsed. The scent of blood, burnt flesh, and ozone filled the room. In the corner, Jake bent over a still form.

Irena.

Alejandro pushed in front of Jake. Electrical burns scorched her forearm and hand, shallow slices and deep gashes bloodied her face and side. Her leather apron had protected her stomach and breasts—not so her arms. "Find a healer, Jake. Now."

"No." Irena clenched her teeth as she propped herself on her unburned elbow. "I will heal."

Jake crouched and picked a jagged shard out of her blistered forearm, wincing at its size. "I'm sorry, Irena. So sorry." He glanced over at Alejandro. "We meant to jump in a few hundred yards up in case Emilia was here. I wouldn't just pop in on you again—"

"You can. She no longer lives here." He watched Irena's expression, but it didn't change, and she didn't look up at him. With the edge of her thumbnail, she pried up a spur of glass embedded in her biceps.

Jake nodded. "Okay. Good to know. So we jumped in, but my new Gift just—*Zzzzt!* Got us. Okay, actually, it got *her.*"

Irena vanished the spur, started pulling out another. "You need to learn control, or it will be Alice next."

"Gee, Irena, thanks. I hadn't figured that out yet."

Her head snapped back. Her glare eviscerated the young Guardian.

Apology rushed through Jake's psychic scent. "Sorry. I know." His throat worked. "It's just that the thought of accidentally doing this to her freaks me out."

Irena's mouth softened, and she sighed. Alejandro fought the urge to flay Jake for his thoughtlessness—and ignored the tug of envy in his chest. Irena *never* let go of her anger so easily with him.

"Try this, Jake." A steel pole appeared in Irena's hand. She looked the metal staff up and down, then glanced at Jake. Her Gift pulsed; a foot-long blade formed at each end. "Use it as an electrical ground every time you teleport, so that the spark will go through it instead of us."

Jake took the weapon, his mouth twisting ruefully. "It's not just a spark anymore."

"No." Irena shifted her weight, lines of strain around her mouth. "Go now. Find me at seven tomorrow morning, San Francisco time."

"Find you here?" Jake asked.

"I'll be here but a few minutes. My shields will be down, so you can jump directly to me." She paused. "But before you do, practice with the staff and without it."

Jake nodded and closed his eyes—getting ready to teleport.

"Jake!" Alejandro gestured toward the garden visible through the solarium's remaining windows. "Do it out there."

A blush stained the Guardian's cheeks. "Right."

As soon as Jake jogged outside, Alejandro turned back to Irena. He called in a jar of aloe from his cache.

She began to protest. "I'll heal—"

"Yes, you will. But it hurts more than is necessary now. This will cool the burns."

She smiled faintly. "You know."

"Yes." He knew burns very well.

Jake's Gift pushed against his psychic blocks. From the corner of his eye, Alejandro saw the young Guardian vanish.

Beside him, Irena seemed to collapse on herself. "This first, Olek."

She rolled over onto her stomach, and Alejandro swore. A six-inch glass shard was embedded parallel to her spine. Blood pooled around the edges. The skin surrounding it had already begun to heal. Gently, Alejandro pinched the slippery glass and pulled. The healing skin tore, and fresh blood ran down the small of her back. Irena bit the side of her hand, muffling her cry.

Alejandro clenched his teeth and continued to pull. Finally, the glass slid free of her flesh. He stared down at the bloodied, triangular shard. The point had stabbed as deep as a dagger.

Holy Mother of God. "You should have asked me to remove it while Jake was here. He should have seen the consequences."

"He felt bad enough."

The tears in her eyes put Alejandro in vehement disagreement. But he held his tongue and formed a clean cloth, pressing it over the wound.

She sat up again, bending her arm behind her back. Her fingers slid against his as she took over holding the compress. Though her breath came in shudders, the wry smile she gave him didn't tremble.

"Pain hurts so much more when I'm not fighting."

Yes. The injuries didn't hurt less—but without an opponent to fight, there was only the pain to focus on.

He retrieved the aloe jar and scooped out the gel. God, he needed to touch her. *Again.* He'd touched her more today than in hundreds of years.

Damn his heart, he wasn't satisfied by it.

Gently, he slid the gel over the back of her hand, onto her wrist. Did he imagine that her eyes tracked the movement of his fingers? He scooped out more aloe.

His gaze followed the winding body of her tattoo. "Have you come to fight?"

"No, I—not to fight." She shook her head. "Michael spoke with Khavi. We are to protect Detective Taylor."

Damn. It shouldn't be worse that Taylor was someone he knew and liked—yet it was. "Protect her from what?"

"A vampire." The softness of her response told him how much she feared being unable to stop it. "Khavi told Michael more—his own future, I suspect—but he would not share it."

"But you think it's important?" Important enough to mention.

"He was . . . not himself." Her tattoos seemed to retreat beneath Alejandro's fingers, as if seeking protection. "He watches over Taylor now. I don't know if I should have watched *him.*"

She didn't conceal the tremor in her voice, and Alejandro's chest tightened. He wasn't certain what to think of Michael's parentage, but he was inclined to trust the Doyen. Irena, however—she had known Michael longer. Had been mentored by him. And she'd always plainly worn her admiration, respect, and loyalty toward him.

Discovering that Michael had hidden the truth from them hadn't only angered her. She'd been disillusioned. And after more than sixteen hundred years, she hadn't just lost faith in the Doyen—faith had been torn away from her.

Yes, he could understand why she felt betrayed and wary around Michael. "Yet you didn't watch him. You came here, instead."

Had come here, though she never had before. He wanted to show his home to her, to watch her face as she looked at each room. He would tear it down and start over if he sensed even a hint of displeasure.

Her gaze remained on his hands. "I want you to pull strings."

"Whose?"

"Whoever we need to have Taylor assigned to SI and this investigation into Rael."

Ah. This was Irena's method of preventing conflict—she removed herself from the equation. Amusement eased the tightness that had been squeezing at his chest. "And so you want me to ask Lilith to pull the strings."

"You are more . . . diplomatic than I. And you know SI better—the American police better—and can imagine a way that will work for Taylor, as well. She doesn't know about Khavi's prediction, and even if she did, I doubt she'd accept protection. But if we involve her in the investigation she'll be working near us, and Michael will not be the only one who protects her."

He capped the aloe and used the action to cover his silence. Dear God, how she amazed him. Irena could be so stubborn, so unwilling to see any view but her own narrow and unyielding one. And yet she was also this. Able to see the nuances of a person's soul—to know how someone thought, how they would react. Able to anticipate conflicts, and maneuver around them.

Always as blunt as a sledgehammer, but never as dull. Little wonder that she fascinated him. He would never understand how she could be a hammer and a sword, all at once.

"I will ask Lilith," he agreed.

"Now."

"She is sleeping now."

Did Irena know that when she flashed that grin at him, he would move mountains for her—and enjoy every second of the effort? Suddenly, irritating Lilith had never been so appealing.

"Very well," he said.

She turned. But not to go, he saw. She stepped out of the solarium and onto the patio, looking out over the bay. The puncture in her back had faded to a pink line.

"This house is yours?"

"It belonged to Carlos Marquez . . . a demon that I killed three decades ago."

This time, her grin twisted him up. Though he'd seen no harm in taking the demon's house and assets, he'd thought she would disapprove.

She turned curious eyes on him. "Why do you keep a house?"

"Why do you keep a forge?"

He didn't expect an answer and didn't receive one. Quietly, she studied the city across the bay.

She probably saw it better than he did. Cádiz was a city of columns and arches, walls and gates. Alejandro was drawn by the city's strong Moorish flavor, which had been most familiar to him as a human—but Rome's powerful hand was still visible, and was the foundation on which the rest of the city had been built.

Not unlike him, Alejandro thought. Though she'd been missing from his life for centuries, she'd shaped a significant part of it.

She turned to him. "It is like Caelum, but with color."

And she saw the other half that shaped him—his Guardian life. "Unlike the tundra."

"The tundra is not always white." She smiled slightly. "And it is solitary."

Except for once. Irena accepted visitors to her forge, but none of them stayed as long as Alejandro had.

God. They weren't even fighting, and the ache filled him. He didn't want to feel this. Not this.

The breeze teased her hair, lifting it away from her forehead. "But you are not always alone here. There was . . . Emilia."

"Yes."

She seemed to take a deep breath. He only recognized how false her smile was because he'd never seen her force one before.

"She didn't please you?"

He stiffened. This was what friends did—they spoke of their lovers. He and Irena were not friends. And if this was what friendship meant, he did not want it. "She tired of me."

Irena began to laugh. His jaw locked. Abruptly, her laughter stopped.

"You're serious?"

Off-balance, he stared at her. She'd thought he was joking? He hadn't expected to be flattered by her disbelief that a woman would leave him—not flattered by the one woman he'd failed too badly to have.

Reminded of that truth, Alejandro recovered. "Yes."

"What were her reasons? They could only be stupid."

"I didn't give her the passion she needed." Pleasure, yes. But Emilia was a woman who demanded more.

Now Irena stared at him as if judging whether *he* were joking. "I've never seen you that you did not burn."

For you. He had little left over for the others.

"Another man burned for Emilia. And so she left." Flinging shoes and screaming. Alejandro's calm acceptance had only made her angrier.

"And you didn't fight to keep her?"

"No."

Irena looked away from him. "Then she wasn't foolish to leave you."

If you stop fighting you should feel shame.

The memory set his temper on his tongue. He snapped out his reply. "We had nothing worth fighting for."

"Apparently not."

Pain scored her voice. Pain—and disillusion. Alejandro shook his head, trying to deny it. Had she thought he meant her, and that what they'd had wasn't worth fighting for? And had she thought the same when they'd met again in France?

What in God's name had she expected of him? Because of *his* stupid error, to save *his* life, she'd been raped and tortured by a demon. She hadn't let him die with honor intact—and he hadn't been able to break or melt through the iron walls to save her. Only Michael, who'd appeared at Alejandro's side and taken a single look at him before teleporting into the iron room, had been able to help Irena. Alejandro had accomplished nothing, and so by the time she'd come out of that room with the demon's head in her fist, he'd had nothing left worth offering her.

But he'd tried to reclaim his honor. Had tried to make himself a man of worth, with a life he could take pride in. That couldn't be done by chasing a woman who didn't want to be chased.

And he couldn't have chased Irena, regardless. She wouldn't have allowed it—she'd have stood her ground and fought him, instead. Was he supposed to have battled her? Forced himself on her? Doing so would have erased any shred of pride he'd had left and destroyed any honor he'd reclaimed.

Yet Alejandro knew that, despite their fights, despite her insults, Irena had never thought he lacked honor.

He could not bear that she thought so now. "That was not the same."

"But similar." She edged backward across the patio—watching him as she would an enemy. "So it was practice, yes?"

He couldn't refute it. After Irena, he'd never tried holding on to even one lover. He gave them his house, his bed, his time as duty allowed . . . but little else. And the passionate women he'd gravitated toward always wanted *more*. So, yes—he had perfected letting them leave without a fight.

And Irena . . . she had perfected walking away.

He turned his back to her, so he wouldn't have to watch her leave. He tried to take in the sound of the ocean. Tried to find calm in the soft chirping of the birds and the sighing breeze. But that calm was only on the surface.

His will cracked, and he went after her.

Too late. He searched the skies and didn't see her. He listened, but couldn't hear where she'd gone. With the ache building, he walked slowly back to his study and stared down at his abandoned reports. Ice settled into him. He hadn't felt cold since an executioner's fire had licked at his feet.

He sat at his desk, vanished his reports, and began to plan. If Irena thought he gave up over everything, then he would teach her differently.

He'd take her down slowly. A fall so gentle, it'd be over before she realized it had begun—before she found ground to stand on. She'd see that they'd had much worth fighting for.

But he would not allow her to fight *him*.

CHAPTER 10

Irena hunted. She'd hoped to clear her mind, to think of anything but Olek and their argument in Cádiz. But it had come back to her, over and over, until she'd examined every word, every inflection.

For so long, her emotions toward Olek had been lumped together, like coal tossed into a furnace. They burned and were too bright and hot to look at for long. But now that she could not avoid him, that she saw him more often, she'd begun to pick out pieces of her emotions, examine the sides. She did not always like what she saw—in him, in herself.

Irena hadn't known, until she'd spoken the words, that she had long thought he hadn't fought for her. She'd always been conscious of all the other factors—what Olek thought had happened in that room with the demon, and her own shame. She could not forget those. But the very simple truth was: He'd let her go and it had hurt. And hurt, she'd been angry.

She still was both. How could she *still* be both? Wounds were supposed to heal. This never had. It only festered.

But it didn't fester so badly now. Only a few hours had

passed since she'd realized how much his failure to fight for her had hurt, but in that time, Irena had been forced to make another realization: She had not fought for him, either.

She hadn't felt as if she *could* fight for him; shame had tied her hands and silenced her tongue. When they'd met again and he had not given her a sign that he wanted to continue what they had begun in her forge, she'd been certain too much damage had been done. Now, she had to accept that Olek's pride had bound him as tightly as her shame. He wouldn't have felt that he could fight for her, either.

Yet where did that leave them now? She did not know. Seeing the effect of her shame and his pride in this new light did not make them—or the past—disappear. Though she hurt less now that she understood why he hadn't fought for her, nothing had truly changed. Everything that had prevented them from moving forward still lay between them.

And even if they could move forward, she did not know if Olek wanted to.

These thoughts plagued her throughout the hunt; though she had sought to clear her mind, when she finished she was more uncertain than when she'd begun. Jake found her as she was cleaning the last carcass, then teleported her to three villages that could use the meat before they returned to SI.

Though the air hummed, Irena didn't even feel a spark as Jake teleported her into a conference room.

Jake hefted the double-bladed staff before vanishing it. "That thing works."

Irena shook her head. It hadn't just been the staff. Jake was getting his Gift under control. After he'd left her at Alejandro's, she'd bet that he'd spent every minute practicing.

"I do not know how you separate two Gifts."

"I'm starting to recognize the feel of it. They're different. It's a different push. The second Gift just needs a little more finesse."

She didn't want to be in here while he finessed it. Irena turned toward the door. "Be safe."

"Yeah. Irena, hold on a second." Jake shoved his hands into his pockets. "Becca's worried that you're thinking of slaying

Lilith. I told her you wouldn't, and if you said that to Alejandro then you were probably just trying to piss him off, but it might help if you tell her."

"It will help what?"

"Well, she's feeling like she has to decide between being loyal to a fellow Guardian, or to Lilith and SI."

What a stupid thing to worry about. "What makes *you* think that I will not kill Lilith?"

Jake shrugged. "Because you're hard, but fair. You hate that Lilith is in the position she's in—and I can't really say I blame you for that—but you also know she's done a damn good job. And if you'd planned to kill her, you'd have already done it."

Irena stared at him. Why did it always surprise her that one so young saw so well?

He shuffled his feet. "Unless I'm totally wrong and it wasn't about your thing with Alejandro."

"What thing? We are friends."

"Yeah. Okay."

How easily he gave ground. Irena frowned. "What do you imagine we are?"

"Well, you both have that smoldering thing going on, especially when you use your Gift. I just assume that after you're done fighting, you find a closet and bang each other. So you're whatever that's called—the opposite of fuck buddies, I guess. Fuck fighters? That sounds like a bad rock band. Or porn-star wrestlers. Not that *that's* bad. Maybe fuck enemies. Fuck nemesis . . . es. Nemeses?" He stopped to ponder the word, and glanced at her. His eyes widened. He took a step back. "Yeah, and now I'm going to find Alice before you kill me."

The hairs on Irena's arms rose when he disappeared. In his hurry, he'd forgotten to use his electrical ground. If Alice bore the brunt of that mistake, he would not forget again.

She turned toward the door again, but paused when it opened and Alejandro came into the room. She felt her eyes widen as she took in the black suit and tie he wore—and he'd bared his chin and upper lip.

Her stomach performed a strange, hollow swoop. A shallow cleft divided his chin. She hadn't known the dent was there. Every time he'd stroked his thumb over his goatee, the sensation must not have felt anything like she'd imagined it would.

And her statues of him were all wrong.

She felt unbalanced, unsettled. She knew this must be his law-enforcement appearance, and except for his clothing and his lack of facial hair, he looked the same. He moved the same. And he still only smiled with his eyes.

He smiled now. Irena thought about finding a closet.

"Good morning," he said, and the world shifted beneath her feet again.

He'd spoken in English, with an American accent. She didn't know what that meant. Was it only because of the role they played today? She'd have to remember to watch her words, to smooth away her own accent.

She said carefully, "Good morning."

He smiled again as he approached her. His steps were still quiet. She glanced down and saw that his shoes were like any other man's on top, but the soles were soft and supple.

"Lilith is still negotiating with Captain Jorgenson, Taylor's superior. We will be delayed past seven."

She already missed the music of his native tongue. "What was decided?"

"A multiagency task force. But Taylor is not the police department's first choice, so Lilith is applying pressure." His voice deepened. "You still have the smell of the hunt on you."

"It was a good one," she said, and watched his gaze slide down her form.

He stopped within an arm's length. "You'll need to change."

Yes. Irena closed her eyes and tried to picture the right clothing. Something like Taylor's. But she could not focus on the details of buttons, of seams. She could only think of Olek, there in front of her. He had the scent of the flame upon him. Of smoke and heat.

"Irena." He passed beside her, and laid a booklet on the conference table, open to a flagged page. "If you need a visual."

She joined him at the table and recognized a clothes catalog. "You carry this with you?"

"No. Lilith asked Selah for it." He tugged on the side of her brief shirt, his fingertips skimming her waist. A shiver raced over her skin. "She has only seen you in this and thought you might need the help."

"And she gave it to you to pass on?"

"I believe Lilith wished to make sure Selah was not harmed in the delivery."

Irena laughed, then turned to study the catalog. She visualized trousers, a jacket, a white shirt. She vanished her clothes and replaced them with the newly created ones. Alejandro's shoes served as the model for hers.

His eyes darkened as his gaze lifted from her face to her hair. His brows rose. She knew what he was asking. The style should be smoother—and better suited to the occupation.

She pushed her fingers through the strands until there were no more tangles. That would have to do. Her gaze dared him to argue. He didn't, but he didn't back away, either. "And these are for you."

She took the identification, credit cards, and wallet that appeared in his hand. Her picture had been altered so that she wore the appropriate clothing and hair. Irena's gaze skipped over most of the data, and she didn't try to make sense of it. She searched for her name, instead.

"Irena *Steele*?" They could not be serious.

Humor flashed through Olek's eyes again. "Savi's idea. Your title is *special agent*, but aside from introductions, we will use surnames."

"And what name do you use?"

"Alec Cordoba."

The name fit him, she thought. Not perfectly, but there was some of this agent in him that felt right. She looked down at the identification again. She ran her thumb over the delicate, looping signature, trying to see it as hers. She could not. Her writing was blunt, heavy.

Uncertainty fluttered low in her gut. Investigation wasn't the same as protection, or even a hunt. Hunting required similar stealth and cunning—but there were few rules to heed while hunting, and no need for a delicate touch.

"You won't have the lead in this."

She glanced up. Alejandro must have read either her face or her psychic scent. Reading his in turn was difficult, but a note of apology had filtered through his voice.

Had he thought she'd be disappointed? In almost every battle they'd fought together, she'd taken the lead. But this wasn't her usual battle, and her skills were better suited for backup and support. She saw no shame in taking the rear and keeping a quiet tongue. Her blade was still sharp.

She vanished the wallet. "If you *had* put me in as lead, I would've named you an idiot."

"And I would have lied and said that Lilith made the decision."

His dry response pulled a short laugh from her. His forefinger stroked down the center of his clean-shaven chin in a gesture as sensuous as it was familiar.

"What do you wonder, Olek?"

The wry smile in his eyes told her he had many questions, but he limited himself to one. "The novices heard you were the first to make a vampire. Several have come to me, asking about the story. I had nothing to tell them."

The novices had gone to him? Because she and Alejandro were well known as *friends*. Perhaps they all thought as Jake did.

"She fought a nosferatu and was dying. After I killed it, I gave her the heart," she said. "The next morning the sun rose, and she died."

Olek *did* know her so well that she didn't need to add more. She saw that he understood it all: her admiration for the girl; the frustration of not anticipating her death; the weight of failure.

Perhaps the novices had been right to go to him.

But he still surprised her when he said, "You saw yourself in her?"

"Yes." The girl had reminded Irena of when she'd been a human. And if the girl had died saving another, rather than fighting for her own life, she would have been made a Guardian, too.

"Do you still grieve for her?"

For the girl Irena had admired but hardly knew, or for the opportunity lost in that life? Was there a difference?

"When I think of her." Which was not so often, now that fifteen centuries had passed. Time could not always heal, but it could offer distance. "When I have to speak of her."

"Then I will not make you speak of her, and will answer the novices' questions for you."

That sounded like protection. Irena didn't know how to respond.

And suddenly, she could not. Everything inside her tensed as Alejandro lowered his head, his gaze holding hers. Her heart threatened to hammer through her chest. Slowly, she watched him descend.

His lips brushed hers, featherlight.

And she was unbalanced when he almost immediately lifted his head. Why had he—

It became clear. Her snarl formed on lips he'd barely touched. Was this comfort? He offered her *comfort*?

The first kiss he'd given her—the first kiss he'd taken—and it was nothing more than what she'd bestow on a friend. That was not what she wanted from Olek.

His dark gaze searched her face. She felt the touch of his mind, seeking out her feelings.

Did he want to know? She would show him.

Catching his shoulders, she dragged him down to her lips, and took his mouth as it needed to be taken.

As she needed to take it.

He didn't fight. But he didn't easily give in—not her Olek. No, he issued a challenge the moment he entered her mouth with a silken thrust of his tongue. The moment he tried to take control.

Irena wouldn't let him. Bracing herself on the edge of the table, she wrapped her legs around his hips. She lifted to him and he slid against her, already fiercely aroused, his erection heated steel beneath his trousers. His kiss was wet, hot. She pulled at his hair, wanting more, deeper, now.

He pushed her back flat against the tabletop and followed her down, his weight heavy between her thighs. Her need burst open. She whipped him around, reversing their positions. When he lay back on the table, she lifted her head and froze.

Olek's skin was flushed, his mouth reddened by her kiss. His face was as sharply defined as a newly whetted blade.

She'd done that to him. A multitude of emotions squeezed at her chest, locking away the words she wanted to find. Words that meant something.

His hands closed over her shoulders and hauled her back down.

Yes. His mouth against hers was enough. This was all that needed to be said.

She came all the way up on the table and straddled his hips, her knees spread wide. She licked the shallow dent in his chin. He rocked up against her core. Her inner muscles clenched with need, yearning to be satisfied, to be filled. She was so hungry. She couldn't be hungrier, and yet it became sharper with each taste.

With impatient hands, she ripped his shirt open. A wedge of dark hair shadowed his chest, thinning to a silken line down the center of his stomach. She followed the trail with her fingers. His flesh burned, feverishly hot.

But nothing like the demon's. She'd never touched that one. Her hands had remained fisted. Now, her open palms slid over his skin, claiming every inch.

Mine.

She took his mouth again. Olek's hands slid to her ass, pressed her sex tight against his thick erection, grinding up against her. She panted and moved with him. By the gods, she was so wet, so empty. His mouth burned a path down her throat. She sat up and vanished her jacket, her shirt. His lips closed around her nipple. His mouth was hot. Oh, so hot. He licked, sucked. Her back arched and the ripples started, deep, deep.

She needed him pushing inside her. Needed to have him, to surround him. It would be fast. And hard.

And long, long overdue.

"Now, Olek." Irena vanished her trousers and tore at his. "I need you in me *now.*"

In his body, she felt a hesitation. In his eyes, she saw calculation.

They both lasted only an instant, but she could think over that hesitation in the same amount of time. By the next instant, she understood.

The night before, she'd spoken of her disappointment that he had not fought for her—for any woman. And Olek wanted her. But *this* was not about fighting for her. He hadn't intended that soft kiss to come to this, but just to sweeten her. And during that hesitation, he'd weighed the consequences of going further than he'd anticipated.

Yes, he'd had some subtle plan, because that was Olek. But not because he'd decided to fight for her. This was about his pride. Whether he wanted to prove something to himself or to her, she did not know.

She did not care.

Irena ripped away, leaving him on the table. He came up halfway, onto his elbow, and looked at her between his bent knees. The beauty of him, reddened by her mouth and disheveled by her hands, struck painfully deep. She'd always wanted to see him this way. The urge to return to him battled with the hurt that awaited her if they finished this for his reasons.

Even if his reasons had been lost beneath his own need. His eyes had darkened. They didn't calculate now, but questioned.

Her body was taut, her voice even. "I do not wish to fuck your pride, Olek."

He didn't answer. And that, she thought, was answer enough.

She recreated her clothes. Her fingers shook when she dragged them through her hair.

"Irena—"

Her fury erupted. She struck at his silk-tongued mouth—and controlled herself at the last instant. She drove her fist through the table surface between his legs, instead.

The wood cracked, buckled. The table collapsed, taking Olek and his pride to the floor.

She left them lying there.

❧

Alejandro sat, his head a heavy weight in his hands and anger burning through him—all of it directed at himself.

He was an idiot. And he should have anticipated her reaction when she realized what he was up to. But he hadn't thought she would realize it. Stubborn, blinkered woman—yet she had seen. He'd prepared for the hammer and hadn't expected the sword.

And he hadn't known that soft kiss would spark an uncontrollable blaze. He *should* have known. Passion had never been a problem between them, even if they had only kissed the once.

Twice now. He could still feel her against him. Could still see her face as she'd pulled away.

God, what an unbelievable idiot he was. And if only he could see what to do now.

He couldn't.

The door opened. Lilith stepped into the room with her hellhound at her side, and stopped short. Her lips pursed as she looked at him sitting in the middle of the broken table, his shirt ripped open.

"You trashed my conference room."

Alejandro rubbed his hand over his eyes. "Yes."

Her heels clipped across the floor. She crouched and picked out the catalog from the remnants of the table near his hip. "Was it because of this?"

"No."

"Damn." She stood, the catalog rolled in her hand. "All right. My office, one hour. And, for fuck's sake, with your prick *in* your pants."

He didn't need to look. "It is."

"No." Lilith's smile wasn't kind. "Obviously it's not, because four walls are still standing, and she's not laid out on the floor next to you."

His fingers clenched. And he'd let her go again. He should have gone after her and explained . . . what? That he'd been manipulating her? That his pride had been stung?

Irena already knew.

The door closed quietly behind Lilith. Alejandro rose to his feet, vanishing the table into his cache.

Even if they moved beyond the past, what of the present? Irena could not compromise; he could not draw as severe a line as she did. How to win her, without yielding his honor and everything he believed was right? It was impossible.

But to accept that it was impossible? To give up?

He could not do that again, either.

❧

Earlier that morning, when Jorgenson had called Taylor into his office, she'd thought the tension in that room had been thick. But the captain could have taken lessons from the two Guardians standing on opposite sides of Lilith and Castleford's office. Irena, in particular, had her death glare down to an art.

And Jorgenson had said *her* attitude needed adjusting. She'd have liked to introduce him to Irena.

So, for the first time in two years, she wasn't the one in the room most likely to go flying off the edge, which meant this whole thing had started off much better than Taylor had thought it would.

Lilith's hellhound lay in front of her desk, practically on Taylor's feet. Sir Pup looked normal today—if normal was a Labrador who sported three heads and was the size of a small pony. The huge teeth and steel-spiked fur weren't in evidence, but Taylor wouldn't be making any sudden moves.

Last night, she'd been thinking of questioning Sir Pup as part of an investigation that wasn't hers. Now it was. That was freaking crazy, but she'd take it.

She glanced over at Preston. Her partner's usually droopy face wasn't so droopy right now, and he watched with undisguised interest as Lilith and the other Guardian—Cordoba—ran through a list of assignments that Cordoba had to delegate while he focused on Julia Stafford.

Joe was eating it up. Her partner had loved the idea of SI and the Guardians since he'd heard of them. Maybe he'd have looked to transfer here, if not for her.

If she'd known about this task force, she'd have asked for a place, fought for it. She'd have swallowed her dislike for Lilith and begged her to include them. Hell, she'd have crawled for Joe if that was what it took. He'd been there every time her family had gone to hell, beginning when she was a rookie and her dad had been killed in the line of duty, and again when her brother's life had been shattered. Later, Joe had faced Hell with her, when Lucifer had come after them to get to Lilith's dog. And her partner had remained at her side through every reprimand, supporting her, covering her ass.

And he'd worried all the while. Quite a few of those lines on his face were hers.

But knowing that Lilith had requested them specifically wasn't exactly comforting. Taylor's history with SI's director hadn't been smooth—and the antagonism was mutual. They'd butted heads more than once . . . and every time, Taylor had been the only one to come away with lumps.

Lilith didn't seem interested in butting heads now. She'd probably had her fill all morning. Since *early* morning. Jorgenson had made a point to let Taylor know that he'd been woken up.

She hadn't shown him enough sympathy, Taylor guessed; she'd barely gotten to sleep by then herself.

Guardians operated on no sleep. Which probably explained why one Guardian had so many freaking assignments—the case load she and Joe juggled was a joke in comparison to Cordoba's. Did the list ever end? And was it normal for Lilith to just trot out the entire list in front of everyone?

Even Irena had stopped giving Cordoba the evil eye and was frowning at Lilith.

Lilith didn't look Irena's way. "And the Argentinean situation?"

"Will be contained tonight. There's no need to reassign. I'll handle it."

Lilith gave a satisfied nod, but Joe leaned forward. "How, if you don't mind me asking?"

Cordoba apparently didn't mind. "Two demons have taken over leadership of a vampire community in Buenos Aires. They've scheduled a community gathering tonight. I'll slay them in front of the vampires, so they will know what will happen if they choose to follow demons again."

"They *chose* the demons?"

"They've been promised protection and training. In exchange, the vampires give their blood, because it weakens the nephilim."

Joe frowned. "If they've chosen the demons of their free will, why not let them lie in the bed they've made?"

"Because they don't know what that bed is. I'll tell them."

"And if they do it again?"

"Next time, it will not only be demons that I slay, but the vampires who fought to put them there." Cordoba turned when Irena snorted. "You disagree?"

She spoke slowly—and to Taylor's surprise, without a hint of the accent she'd had the day before. "Not with killing the demons. But slaying the vampires' chosen leaders and offering nothing in return will only breed resentment. And if you kill the strongest vampires, you leave them with no protection at all."

"And so I should wait, and let the vampires find out for themselves what they've invited in?"

Irena's eyes flashed a poisonous green, but her words were still measured. "You have said the Ascension put a knife to our throat. The nephilim have put a knife to the vampires' throats. If we cannot protect them directly, what would you have them do?"

"Do you think this is how I wish it to be?" His eyes darkened. A hint of Spain bled into his voice. "The vampires *must* choose a side. They don't have to actively join the Guardians' fight, but if the demons come to them, they should take up arms . . . or inform us, so that we can. The nosferatu were cursed because they wouldn't choose between Heaven or Lucifer's rebels, and if that is not a lesson of history for the vampires to learn, I do not know what else could be. And Khavi's prophecy—" He paused as Irena snorted again. "That is your response, and yet you are in this room because of Khavi."

"What prophecy?" Joe said.

Lilith spoke to Irena over him. "Our standard procedure is to send a team of vampires to follow up after Alejandro has slain the demons. Then we'll send someone to train them properly— or have a few from their community come here. We won't leave the community to wonder what comes next."

Irena nodded, her gaze still on Cordoba, but no longer glowing with toxic light. "I see."

"What prophecy?" Joe repeated.

Lilith glanced at him, then at her watch. "The prophecy might have bearing on this investigation, so Cordoba can fill you in after you get to Ohio. In about five minutes, Selah will be here to teleport you; a car will be waiting for you there."

Taylor saw Joe was speechless and stepped in. "Are you going to tell us why we're going to Ohio?"

"*You* aren't. Cordoba and Preston are. You and Irena—"

"Steele," Irena said with an unfathomable smile.

"Steele will be talking to Margaret Wren at Rael's house. As for Ohio, they'll be interviewing Mark Brandt, whose daddy wanted to go public about Guardians, demons, and vampires— and/or wipe us off the face of the Earth. And that was *before* he died and a nephil possessed his body. So Brandt might have heard if anyone is following in his daddy's footsteps."

"Brandt?" Taylor frowned, her memory ticking. "Senator Brandt? Died of a heart attack on the steps of the Capitol Building—that was one of the nephilim?"

"No. That was him." With a slight grin, Lilith nodded toward Cordoba. "The nephil had been slain three weeks before, in Seattle."

That was too much. Taylor turned to Cordoba. "You impersonated a *senator*?"

"Yes."

The way Cordoba said it, so calmly and without humor, deflated most of her outrage. However Lilith saw it, the impersonation hadn't been a game to him. And what would the alternative have been? Announcing that they'd slain a demon-possessed senator?

"So, Cordoba is talking to Brandt, checking in with Bradshaw at the FBI, then hitting Rael's office to speak with his staff. Taylor—you have Wren, the follow-up from that, then Rael. Your appointment with him is at his house, at one this afternoon."

She'd be interviewing the demon? Jesus.

Lilith pushed two folders across the desk. "Wren was CIA.

She went into the private sector about three years ago. Most of her records are sealed; Savi will work on cracking them tonight, but see what you can get now."

What could they get that a regular team wouldn't? But Taylor didn't argue. "All right."

"Taylor," Lilith said as she stood. "I've got Guardians who can kick any demon's ass, but who don't have investigative experience. You do, and that's why I've pulled you in. Now, Jorgenson made sure I knew that Preston and you have been playing real-life good cop, bad cop—with a side of *Kolchak: The Night Stalker* thrown in—and that *you* are one step away from playing real-life mall security guard."

Anger shook through her. She opened her mouth. Lilith held up her hand. "Let me finish, detective. I'm telling you that I don't give a fuck about his issues with you or how he thinks you've gone off the deep end; I just want to know if Rael is the reason Julia Stafford is on a slab in the morgue. So get the job done, however it needs to be done. I'll cover your ass if you have to bend any rules."

Taylor hadn't expected that. Not from Lilith. Her throat tightened. "Yes, sir."

"But try not to bend *the* Rules. You know the ones I mean?" At her nod, Lilith said, "And for fuck's sake, if you play good cop, bad cop during Rael's interview, let Irena be the bad one."

§

"What prophecy?"

Preston's tone told Irena that he wouldn't be teleporting anywhere without hearing this first. She liked that he'd gotten his teeth into it and wasn't letting go. And she'd have wagered he wanted to know *now* so that he could judge Taylor's reaction to whatever they learned. They were obviously close, and moved together with the ease of longtime partners. Like Taylor, he was creased and worn. But unlike Taylor, who looked pale and shadowed, Preston just looked comfortably lived in.

She turned to Alejandro. "Do you have the translation?"

Although she'd made Alice read the prophecy to her until she'd memorized each line, Irena didn't carry a copy.

"You do not wish to recite it?" His eyes held amusement.

Somewhere, she thought, after some time in Lilith's office, they'd both lost the burn of anger that had followed them from the conference room. Perhaps it was only knowing that he was as frustrated as she was by how little the Guardians could help the vampire communities targeted by the demons.

Perhaps it was that she wanted to let the anger go.

"It is too stupid to say aloud," she told him.

"At what point do you begin laughing?"

He knew her well. It was not just that the prophecy was stupid; she could barely make it through the recitation. "Caelum's voice."

"Ah." Triumph filled his tone. He produced a single sheet of paper, held it out for Preston. His gaze remained on her. "I last longer than you."

Her eyes narrowed. As Preston took the paper, she said, "You will not provoke me into reciting it. I will not be your amusement."

"Not my amusement. Enjoyment. That is your laughter: the most incredible pleasure."

She drew in a breath, and held it. Everything inside her seemed to be waiting. She would laugh, she thought. Laugh, just from the pleasure his words gave her.

His voice lowered, inaudible to human ears. "And the deepest pain. I do not know why I ask for it."

Her heart jolted and squeezed, as if he'd dropped it to the floor and stepped on it as he strode past her. Heading toward Selah, she realized. Irena hadn't been aware that the other Guardian had teleported into the hallway with them.

Her breath would not steady. Her emotions rebounded between anger and hurt, but her reaction went unnoticed. Preston and Taylor quietly read over the prophecy. Preston's psychic scent churned with confusion; Taylor's mind was shielded, as usual. Making certain her own shields were strong, Irena looked at Alejandro again, found his gaze on her.

When had this happened? The balance they had maintained for so long, the sharp edge they'd walked . . . it had disappeared beneath their feet. She didn't know whether to find it again, or keep stumbling until they fell to one side or the other: everything, or nothing.

Both options gripped her throat with fear. She signed to him. *What is happening between us?*

His hands briefly clenched at his sides. *I don't know.*

"So what does this all mean?"

Preston's voice filtered through the heavy silence that seemed to surround them. Alejandro blinked slowly, like a human waking, and unsure if he was still sleeping. Irony filled his reply. "We don't know."

Selah scoffed before vanishing and reappearing behind Preston. Standing on shoes that were nothing but ribbons and spiked heels that put her at a few inches over his height, she looked over his shoulder. The detective glanced up at her. Then peered up again, as if once hadn't been enough to take in the waves of light blond hair and the perfection of Selah's features, warmed by the smile she gave him. His gaze dropped a little more slowly, and his lips formed a soundless whistle as soon as he was facing away from her.

"We know some of it," she said, reaching around him to run her fingers over the first line. " 'She waits below'—that is Anaria, Michael's sister. And she's not waiting anymore, because the nephilim found her."

And the rest was nonsense, Irena thought. "And you can explain the next part . . . all the way to the 'dragon's blade'?"

She watched Alejandro, and didn't feel the urge to laugh as Taylor quickly read the lines aloud.

" 'The dragon will rise before the lost two. The blood of the dragon will create one door and destroy another. Caelum's voice will sing it closed with ice and fire and blood, and be lost until she claims her new tongue and the dragon's blade.' " She finished and looked to Selah, who shook her head.

"I have no idea," the Guardian admitted. "But the rest we do know. 'The blood that heals will release the dead unto judgment, and the judged unto Heaven.' That's talking about vampire blood, and how it weakens the nephilim—so that the nephilim can be slain, and the soul of the human trapped in the body they've possessed can be freed."

"We *think* that is what it means," Irena said. "We do not know."

"She is such a stickler. You're going to have *such* fun today," Selah said to Taylor, but her smile faded when she glanced down at the paper again. "The last line is self-explanatory."

And upon the destruction of Michael's heart, Belial will ascend to the Morningstar's throne.

Lucifer's throne. And a compelling reason for Belial to arrange his son's death.

"Except that there might be more than one meaning," Alejandro said. "Michael's heart might be just that—his heart—or it might be Anaria."

"Or something we have no idea about," Irena said past a sudden tightness in her throat.

"Yes." His gaze held hers before moving to Preston. "Rael is one of Belial's demons, and so the prophecy—if he believes in it—might be influencing his actions. Khavi also foresaw the shooting and Margaret Wren . . . but it is difficult to know if any of the events are related."

"So if there are connections, we have to dig them up," Preston said.

"Yes." Alejandro looked at Irena. "Before we go, I need to speak with you."

He led her into a small office—not much bigger than a closet. She could not stop her smile as she waited for him to close the door.

"I intended to give this to you earlier," he said, and a small electronic device appeared between his thumb and forefinger. "But we were—"

"Yes," she interrupted. A reminder wasn't necessary. "What is it?"

"A video recorder. You'll need to conceal it during your interview with Rael. A pendant or a bracelet, perhaps. Whatever you can design that will allow us to see and hear him."

Thoughtfully, she studied the camera. Yes, it would be easy to conceal. "How do I record?"

He showed her, then dropped it into her palm. She vanished the recorder and looked up at him. "Is this so that I don't kill him?"

"I'm certain you wouldn't hide it if you did. It is for Castleford, so that he can watch it later and know which of Rael's responses are lies." His smile came into his eyes. "And now you do not protect me from Rael, but Taylor from a vampire."

Irena laughed. She didn't ask how he'd known what Lilith had planned. "I won't have to protect her from many vampires during the day."

"No. But perhaps we will see what puts her in a position to be threatened by one."

"Being friends with Savi isn't enough?" Irena asked, although she knew Ames-Beaumont and Savi would protect Taylor as they would one of their own vampires. "Perhaps Taylor will only be in that position because Khavi told us it was her fate, and everything we do now drives Taylor closer to it."

"That would not be acceptable." Alejandro's face darkened. "A Guardian should not determine a human's path."

His words were evenly spoken, but she felt the force behind them. How had any of his lovers believed he lacked passion? It still astonished her.

"We agree." She raised her hand to his jaw. Her thumb skimmed the cleft in his chin.

He caught her wrist, then pulled her to him and bent his head. "I would give my life to step away from duty with you today. To discover what is happening between us."

She would, too. "But we cannot."

"No." He pressed his lips briefly to hers. He'd barely lifted his head before going back for another—longer, slower. His kiss offered more promise than heat, but the need still smoldered. She was clutching at his shoulders when he pulled away. "Tonight, Irena. At your forge."

"Yes." Her heart pounded. "Be safe, Olek."

She watched him leave, then went to meet Taylor.

CHAPTER II

Taylor remained silent on the ride through the city. The quiet suited Irena well. Traveling by car was new, and the two vises her hands had become were just beginning to relax when she and Taylor neared the orange steel bridge that led north out of the city. Irena reached out with her Gift to taste the metal, and immediately wished she hadn't. She clamped her lips together and resolved not to think about the sheer weight suspended above the water.

The sky was clear and bright. It was a day for flying, not for being trapped inside a car moving across a massive bridge corroding in tiny bits and rivets that she could feel to her bones.

"Are you going to be carsick?"

"No."

Taylor clearly didn't believe her. "I suppose it doesn't matter anyway. You don't eat, so nothing would come up."

Irena didn't tell her that she *had* eaten that morning. The bites she'd taken of the animals' hearts were lodged in her stomach, doing whatever it was her Guardian guts did to food.

"I am not sick."

"Okay." Taylor slanted another glance at her, then poked at something on her door. The window beside Irena slid down.

Irena tilted her face into the wind. After a few minutes, Taylor shivered and the heater blasted.

"Did you read Wren's file?"

"No," Irena said, and opened her eyes as the acceleration changed. They drove uphill now, where mansions clung like fat vultures overlooking the bay.

Taylor reached behind her, brought a folder up front. "Can you take a look?"

Irena opened to a photo of a woman with the sort of pale blond hair that she often saw on children, but rarely on adults. Her gray eyes were flat and piercing, her face composed in the strong, fierce angles of a Nordic ancestry. Irena recognized the warrior in those eyes and that face, but she couldn't see deeper.

Irena found Wren's statistics and converted the numbers. She and Taylor were almost the same height; Wren would tower over them both.

"She is very tall. Should I be taller?"

"Why? You're already like a mob enforcer."

"I'm like a what?"

"A really big guy. One who's always ready to crack heads. It's the way you move—No, that isn't right." Taylor's forehead creased and she gave Irena a once-over. "Scratch that. It's the way people move *around* you. Even the Guardians at SI. They give you room, and watch you out of the corners of their eyes. Like you take up a lot of space."

That amused her. "So should I take up *more* space when we meet Wren?"

"For the intimidation factor?" Taylor considered it, then shook her head. "She'll already be on the defensive. We'll try to appear non-threatening. Demure."

Irena snorted and read on. It took longer than just the look Taylor had probably anticipated, but Irena made her way through the thin file. There wasn't much more than Lilith had told them. Wren had lived in foster care until she'd entered the military, and gone on to the Central Intelligence Agency. Little information existed about her activities there, and no indication about why she'd quit. After leaving the CIA, she'd trained at a butling academy in the Netherlands.

Irena frowned. "What is a butling academy?"

"She's a butler. You know, they open the door, look down their nose. Sounds about right for a family like Julia Stafford's. New money, so they try to put on the class." Taylor pulled a coffee cup from the holder between the seats, sipped, and grimaced. "Jesus. I thought this was bad when it was hot."

"They burnt it," Irena said, and tapped the side of her nose when Taylor looked at her. "What do you know of Julia Stafford's family?"

"Three generations back, they were bootlegging. Then they got into real estate—some of it legit—and Hollywood during the 50s. That's where they got most of their money, but there was some gambling in Vegas during the 60s and 70s, drugs, ties to the mob. Her dad and her uncles are all politicians now, mostly state and city level. But one of them is a governor, and there's a cousin in Congress. They don't have so many ties to gambling—it's all in oil and land. But that taint is still there, so they've got to keep up appearances. She went to a good school, got a law degree, served on charities, boards—but of course, nothing controversial."

Irena nodded. "So Julia Stafford had resources and connections, but Rael can hold her family over her head if he needs to." An advantage for the demon, both ways.

Taylor pushed her cup back into the holder, fumbling until the paper folded and she smashed it in. "I guess. What I see is a demon who fashions himself as the everyman who pulled himself up by his bootstraps, and who got lucky enough to marry the princess who turned some bad history around. Now they've got a butler and a house on the hill. It's all America, baby, and they are proof of the dream. Who wouldn't vote for that?"

Irena thought her answer was too obvious, and so she remained silent.

Taylor took a deep breath. "Sorry, that turned into a rant. I have, to quote Jorgenson, 'anger management issues.'"

Irena shrugged. "So do I."

A smile brightened Taylor's face, and when it faded the detective looked less tired than she had. "But it's not Julia Stafford that gets to me. Or the money. It's that fucking demon."

Irena liked this woman.

"All of you, actually." Taylor met her eyes without apology. "No offense. Not *you*. The idea of you."

A police officer, bothered by the idea of anyone with different rules and who worked outside the law. Yes, Irena understood that. But that wasn't all that bothered Taylor, Irena thought. Through her Gift, she'd sensed the small silver cross that lay hidden beneath Taylor's collar. The detective was likely going through the same struggle that thousands of Guardians had in the years after their transformation, when everything they'd believed as humans didn't seem to fit what they'd learned in Caelum.

Irena had never experienced that particular struggle herself, but she'd been on the listening end of it hundreds of times. "I do not offend so easily," she said.

The detective didn't reply, but went back to her thoughts. A road unwound before them. The bay glittered under the sun, but a fog bank was rolling in from the west.

"What are we looking for with Wren?" Taylor asked abruptly. "The feds have already questioned her."

"We need to find out if she knows what Rael is." If Wren did, then the questions Taylor asked could be different.

Taylor shook her head. "We can't go in, asking if she knows she's working for a demon. Even if we told her she was, even if you flashed your wings, she probably wouldn't believe it. *I* wouldn't."

Humans rarely did anymore. Centuries ago, convincing humans *not* to believe their eyes had been more difficult.

"It is simple, then." Irena tilted her face into the air again. "We will find out if she believes what she sees."

❧

Clumps of shrubbery squatted between needled trees and provided a screen between Rael's house and the street. A black iron gate guarded the drive. A private security guard checked their identification before waving them through. The house exterior had been constructed with peach stone; block columns flanked the entrance and came together in a smooth arch beneath a clay-tiled roof.

The structure had fewer levels than Irena expected, until she realized that the rear of the house sprawled down the side of the hill. It likely had a balcony, she thought—or several. At night, Rael could leave by air without anyone being aware that he'd gone.

Margaret Wren opened the door at Taylor's knock.

Irena was instantly certain that this woman had killed before. But she wasn't convinced that Wren knew about demons; Wren's emotions were still easy to read. After learning about psychic abilities, most humans slowly developed shields; their desire to guard their thoughts became a reality. Chances were, this woman had no idea—

No. Irena forced herself to slow down. She wouldn't decide right away. Quick judgments had no place here. It was possible that Wren knew about Rael, and yet he'd never told her about his psychic abilities—she wouldn't know that she needed shields to conceal her emotions.

As Taylor introduced herself and Irena, those emotions were layered with irritation, anger, and grief. Wren's expression remained flat. Her eyes quickly measured them both, then settled on Irena. Suspicion bloomed through her psychic scent, but she let them into the house.

Bright bouquets in baskets and vases filled the entry with a suffocating array of perfumed foliage. Irena stopped breathing; she wouldn't be talking, anyway. She mulled over Wren's suspicion, instead. Did the woman suspect that Irena wasn't human? Taylor had mentioned Special Investigations—did Wren know who was employed there?

With long strides, Wren led them across a red-tiled floor to a large, open living area. Sofas and chairs the color of sand sat in the middle of the room. Irena walked to the enormous windows looking out over the water, then circled around to the fireplace. On the mantel, more flowers crowded a wedding picture of Rael and his wife. They both looked happy, their faces bright, eyes shining with love.

Taylor offered condolences, which Wren heard without a change of expression. Her eyes did not miss anything. Irena did not move without Wren noting it.

And despite Taylor's prediction, Wren wasn't defensive. She simply stood with her hands clasped behind her back, delivering her answers like she was reading from a report.

"How long have you been working for Representative Stafford, Ms. Wren?"

"Eighteen months."

"How were you made aware of the position?"

"Through the academy where I received my training."

"And your duties are . . . ?"

"I manage the household, including the daytime staff, and provide security."

"What form of security?"

"If someone threatened either of them, I would neutralize the threat."

"Has it ever happened?"

Failure weighted Wren's psychic scent. Her face was unmoved. "They were threatened yesterday. I did not neutralize it."

Taylor considered that. The detective seemed the more impatient of the two women. *She doesn't like going over old ground,* Irena thought. Wren didn't either, but she gave no indication of it.

"You drove them to the protest yesterday. Is that typically part of your duties?"

"Only when Mrs. Stafford accompanies him."

"Do you think he loved her?"

A jolt of surprise went through Wren's psychic scent, but she didn't hesitate to answer. "It is not my place to judge that. I can tell you she was my priority. He made that clear from the first."

"You didn't remain in the car yesterday after delivering them to the courthouse?"

"The crowd was large, and Stafford asked me to join them."

"Did he relay to you any specific concern?"

"Only that the crowd might be unruly, given the controversial nature of the protest."

Controversial? Would that fit in with Rael's politics? She would have to ask Olek.

And, she thought, it was time to find out if Wren knew what Rael was.

Irena waited for Wren to blink. When she opened her eyes, Irena stood at the opposite end of the window.

Though Wren had been still, only her gaze moving, now even that froze. After a long second, she looked at the spot Irena had been standing, then over at Irena again. Doubt and confusion swirled in her psychic scent.

"Where were you standing when the Staffords were shot?"

Wren didn't look away from Irena. "At the south end of the steps, where I had a view of the crowd. When I heard the rifle fire, I went up to attend to Mrs. Stafford and provide cover if it was needed."

As she spoke, the confusion slowly ebbed. In its place was humor. Either Wren was calling herself silly for imagining Irena's impossibly quick movement—or she had realized what Irena was, and thought it funny.

The humor vanished when Taylor asked, "How do you know it was a rifle?"

Wren's gaze snapped back to the detective. Her voice cooled. "Trajectory and damage. For the bullet to hit both the congressman and Mrs. Stafford, the sniper must have been on the roof of one of the buildings six hundred or six-fifty meters north. A bolt-action, probably similar to a FN SPR or an M40. They're the most accurate from that distance."

"Why bolt-action?"

"Because he missed, but didn't fire again. A semiauto allows for marginally faster repeat fire. If he'd had one, he'd have gotten off a second shot before the congressman collapsed."

Taylor pursed her lips. "What exactly did you do for the CIA, Miss Wren?"

"I worked for them."

"As what?"

Wren blinked; Irena moved again. This time, the doubt was

stronger and tinged with worry. A tiny line formed between Wren's pale brows.

"Miss Wren?" Taylor prompted. "You worked for them as what?"

"As . . . an employee."

"Are you avoiding the question because you can, or because your work was classified?"

"You need to ask them, detective."

Taylor nodded. "We will. Do you live here?"

"Yes."

"Does the rest of the staff?"

"No."

"Are they here today?"

"I have given them the day off to grieve."

"But you're not?" When Wren didn't answer, Taylor let it go. "Have the Staffords ever argued in front of you, Miss Wren?"

"No."

Taylor let her doubt show. "You've lived with them for eighteen months, and they've never argued in that time?"

"Not that I have seen or heard, detective."

Taylor paused, looked her up and down. "You're an attractive woman, Miss Wren. Has Stafford ever made advances?"

"No."

"Have you made advances on him?"

"No." Humor shook through Wren's psychic scent.

Taylor couldn't sense it, so Irena asked, "You find that funny?"

Unease immediately replaced Wren's humor, as if she were surprised that her response had been read. "Only because I know myself."

"You prefer women?"

"I prefer nothing at this point in my life."

"That's a preference I should have had at *every* point in my life," Taylor said dryly, drawing a slight smile from Wren. "So you haven't even thought about it?"

"He's my employer, detective."

Annoyance colored Wren's voice—which, Irena thought,

meant that she'd warmed to Taylor. Wren hadn't shown any emotion up to that point.

"And you are loyal to him?"

"I take pride in doing my job well."

Irena narrowed her eyes. Pride wasn't the same as loyalty.

Taylor mulled over Wren's response, before she finally asked, "Have you witnessed unusual behavior?"

Wren's eyebrows lifted. "Such as?"

"Odd waking hours, meetings with shadowy figures."

There was a flash of recognition in Wren—and humor again as she said, "He is a politician, detective."

"Yes, an up-and-coming one. Did he have any affairs?"

"I am not aware of infidelity. On either side."

"Would you cover for him if your job demanded it?"

Speculation tugged at Wren's psyche. She'd realized that they suspected her employer, but again there was no apprehension or smugness. Irena would have expected those emotions if Wren knew of her employer's involvement.

If he was involved, she reminded herself.

"I would cover for many things," Wren admitted. "My contract requires me to maintain my employers' confidence *except* in the event that I witness him breaking the law. I am not in conflict at this time, detective." Wren checked her watch. "And I must leave in five minutes to pick up my employer."

Taylor pulled a card from inside her jacket. "If a conflict ever comes up, I'd appreciate a call."

Irena waited until they were back in the car. "She doesn't know what he is."

"Are you positive?"

Despite Taylor's question, Irena thought the detective had already come to the same conclusion. "It's difficult to be sure. I feel her emotions, but don't know her thoughts."

"And her emotions were . . . ?"

"Each time I moved quickly, there was no comprehension in her. She doubted, and she worried."

"Why would she worry if she didn't have something to hide? Did she recognize you as a Guardian?"

"The worry felt more self-directed. Perhaps she thought she was imagining things, and unable to perform her duty." Wren's dedication to her job had been genuine. Irena frowned. "When you told her that I was with Special Investigations, she was suspicious. I wondered if she knew Guardians worked with SI, but her later response suggests that it was SI itself. Perhaps she was not familiar with the division." Special Investigations had been established after Wren had left the CIA. "Or perhaps she could see that I am not a federal agent."

"No offense—but no one with Wren's history would ever make you for one," Taylor agreed. "So do we tell her the truth about Rael?" When Irena didn't respond, she went on. "Someone like that—someone with the kind of training I suspect she has—if Rael gets his claws in her, traps her in a bargain . . . she could do some damage, all in attempt to save herself."

"Yes. But that will be her choice."

The detective's jaw set in a stubborn line. "She'd make a better choice if she had more information."

Not always. Some humans would take the easiest route, no matter who it hurt; others would do what they felt was right, no matter how it hurt them. Some humans, upon discovering demons, had tried to turn that knowledge to their own advantage. Not everyone hated evil.

And guessing what Wren would do was impossible. "Perhaps we should wait until Savi gives us more information about her."

Taylor pushed her key into the ignition. "It's your call."

"No. It is not. If you choose to tell her, I won't try to stop you."

Taylor's hands clenched. She looked toward the house, and Irena felt the detective's need to head back, to tell Wren everything.

Perhaps because she recognized something of herself in Wren. Perhaps because Wren was in a delicate position. Or perhaps just because Wren was human.

How difficult had it been for Taylor to maintain this secret for two years?

"Telling her now will make her vulnerable," Irena said. "She has no shields. Rael will know she knows. Her ignorance might be her protection."

"Or maybe she'd wish that she'd never found out." Taylor stared at the house with such intensity and warring emotions that Irena wouldn't have been surprised if the detective was making a deal with herself: that if Wren appeared within a certain amount of time, Taylor would get out of the car and tell her everything. "How old are you, Irena?"

Old enough to know that trusting fate rarely worked out for the best. Free will meant little if it wasn't exercised.

"More than sixteen centuries."

The detective made a soft, breathy sound, somewhere between a laugh of disbelief and a gasp of pain. "So you've been at this a while."

"Yes."

Taylor's lips thinned into a pale line. She shook her head, turned the key. And muttered "goddammit" as they pulled away from the house.

❧

The press of people in the elevator of the federal building eased as they moved up. Alejandro kept his back to the corner, and swept the psyche of each passenger: all humans. The stairs would have been preferable to being crowded in this small box, but thirteen flights was a hardship on Preston. The detective had already been teleported twice—once to Ohio, and once back to San Francisco—dizzied and weaving each time.

As they passed the seventh floor, Alejandro's cell phone vibrated in his coat pocket. His lips thinned in irritation. Lilith had never kept tabs on him during an assignment before; he didn't want to set a precedent now.

But Irena was out there, preparing to question Rael. Perhaps she and Taylor had learned something from the Wren woman— although Alejandro suspected that Taylor would have called Preston if that had been the case.

His irritation became surprise, and then a low, heavy thump in his chest when he looked at the display. Not Lilith.

Irena.

He answered quickly. "Cordoba."

There was a pause, filled only with the pounding of his blood in his ears. "Olek. We have finished with Wren. What have you learned from Brandt?"

He closed his eyes, fighting a laugh. Irena spoke in an over-loud voice, and he realized it was possible that she hadn't talked over a phone before. Like every Guardian, she had been issued one, but she might only use hers to receive messages.

And he told himself that he only felt so unbalanced by her call because it had been unexpected. It wasn't the hope that went along with the realization that, no matter how stubborn she was, Irena could change. A phone wasn't a compromise, just an adaptation—yet perhaps she wasn't impossibly set in her ways.

But now was not the time to wonder if she would—if she *could*—adapt to other circumstances. He concentrated on the question. Mark Brandt.

The young man had been just as helpful as when he'd assisted Alejandro during the weeks he'd pretended to be Mark's father. But this time, Brandt did not have any useful information.

"Nothing." Mindful of the others in the elevator car, he said carefully, "And on your end?"

"We do not believe she knew he was—Is anyone there who will overhear me?"

"No."

"Margaret Wren did not know Rael was a demon. Now we wait for his return. Our appointment is in two hours. We are driving now to speak with one of Julia Stafford's friends." He heard Detective Taylor's voice in the background, and Irena repeated, "And then grab lunch."

Alejandro glanced at Preston. He'd forgotten about the necessity of food. "We are proceeding as planned and will meet you afterward."

"Very well. Be safe."

Be safe. It wasn't personal; Irena said it to everyone. Still, his voice lowered as he said, "Be safe," in return.

He'd never been affected by a phone call before. He avoided

Preston's eyes as he pocketed the cell, uncertain he concealed his response.

"No new information," he told Preston, and left the elevator on the thirteenth floor.

Special Agent Bradshaw, whose voice carried a faint memory of the Deep South, met them at the front desk and said they'd arrived in time to sit in on the debriefing with the agents who were leading the investigation. Bradshaw's medium build, short black hair, walnut brown eyes and skin, and unremarkable features shouldn't have made Alejandro immediately wary. Demons chose flashier forms to wear. Yet Alejandro still tensed, uncertain why the agent had tripped his instincts—until the agent moved.

His walk was not flashy either, but like the dark roll of a seal underwater. Though athletic, Bradshaw's form didn't reflect the discipline and training that Alejandro associated with humans who moved with such fluidity.

But there was more to it. A niggling familiarity seemed to tug on the back of his mind. Softly, he reached out with his senses, brushed against Bradshaw's psyche. Human, with light mental shields. Frowning, Alejandro stabbed deeper, piercing Bradshaw's shields.

Human.

At that psychic level, neither a demon nor Guardian could disguise himself. One of the nephilim could. When in human form, the nephilim matched their psychic scent to the scent of the humans they'd possessed.

Alejandro had difficulty believing, however, that if Bradshaw was a nephil he would have been able to fool Michael, Lilith, *and* Castleford.

Bradshaw led them through a maze of cubicles and into a small room occupied by a table topped with pictures, laptops, papers. Four agents—three men, one woman—sat at the table, two on each side. Though Alejandro preferred not to sit when he was anywhere but his own home, he took the chair Bradshaw offered at the end of the table. Preston settled in next to him, and Bradshaw sat at the opposite end.

Bradshaw picked up a pen, and Alejandro's vague feeling of

recognition solidified into a name: *Luther*. Though Alejandro had taught him how to hold a sword rather than a pen, he would have recognized the shape and tension of the Guardian's grip anywhere.

What had Luther's Gift been? Alejandro couldn't recall, but it must have been a psychic mask, or Alejandro would have identified him before now.

As Bradshaw, he must have to live deeply in his role. Luther hadn't been completely inactive, however; Alejandro knew of several kills—demon and nosferatu—that had been attributed to Luther in the past several years. Now, Alejandro would wager that each of those could be traced to investigations that the Bureau had been handling.

Did Lilith know what he was? While the agents suggested different political and fundamentalist groups who might have had reason to kill Congressman Stafford—all of which Alejandro and Preston had already discussed—he sent a text message.

Luther?

A single name that gave nothing away if she didn't know; if she did, Lilith would realize exactly why he was asking.

Her reply came quickly. You don't know that.

Or, Alejandro guessed, he wasn't *supposed* to know. Rael worked in this building; he probably encountered Bradshaw often. If the demon knew the agent in charge of this office was a Guardian, Bradshaw's life would be in danger. With his Gift, he could hide—but if another Guardian knew his identity and gave it away, the psychic mask wouldn't be worth much.

Bradshaw had been with the Bureau more than twenty years, and at the San Francisco office for fourteen. He'd been Lilith's superior before she'd become SI's director; she'd worked beneath him for a decade. Had she known Bradshaw was a Guardian during that time?

He glanced down as another message from Lilith came through.

How did you know?
I looked at him.
You fucking Guardians.

Which told him that she hadn't known until a Guardian had told her. Castleford, most likely, when they'd gotten together two years ago. Alejandro had recognized Luther because he'd known him, but Castleford could determine demon from human from Guardian, just by observing body language.

Before that, probably only Michael had known; anything else would have been too dangerous for Bradshaw—the previous agent in charge had been one of Lucifer's lieutenants. And although Special Investigations performed a similar function to what Bradshaw did here, the Doyen hadn't changed Bradshaw's assignment after SI had been established and Lucifer's lieutenant had been slain.

Because Rael worked only one floor above?

How many know? he asked her.

You. H & M. Hugh and Michael. Keep it that way.

He'd undoubtedly add an *I* to that list, but he needn't tell Lilith that. He put away the phone, drawing a quick, inquiring glance from Preston. Alejandro shook his head.

"No new information," he said softly.

❧

After the debriefing—in which they learned no new helpful information—Alejandro and Preston climbed one flight of stairs, where the congressman's offices took up one corner of the fourteenth floor. A garden of cut flowers overflowed the receptionist's desk and spilled over to the conference table visible through a glass wall. The office had been decorated in blues and creams, the furniture and paintings both understated and expensive. Stafford walked a fine line. Unless he was different from every other demon, he preferred luxury, money, and power. But as a public servant, he couldn't flaunt them without drawing the wrong kind of attention from his political opponents and risking his career.

Did hiding anger the demon? Or was concealing his nature just part of the game?

Though her eyes and nose were red from weeping, the receptionist greeted them with quiet dignity. Lynne Simmons was human—as was the entire staff, Alejandro discovered after a careful sweep of the office. Sounds of grief came from deeper within the office, and a great heaviness had settled over their psyches. Either Julia Stafford had been well liked—or Stafford was, and they grieved in sympathy.

Their sympathy would mean nothing to Rael.

Alejandro suppressed his anger. The demon didn't deserve this. Perhaps Rael had earned it, through careful planning and advancement, by treating his staff well—but he did not deserve to be serving them. This position required putting the interests of his people foremost. Rael would only serve himself. His voting record wouldn't reflect his beliefs, and Alejandro didn't doubt that no matter where Rael lived, the demon would adopt the values of the majority for the sake of political expedience.

Alejandro let Preston take the lead and introduce them. The receptionist's eyes welled up at the mention of Julia Stafford, though her confusion was evident.

"The FBI just left. They interviewed all of us."

"We're just following up, Mrs. Simmons. Did you know Mrs. Stafford well?"

And did she know what Rael was? Alejandro had difficultly imagining that anyone who willingly worked for a demon would grieve as genuinely as she did.

"Yes. No. We weren't friends. But she was friendly." She waved with her tissue. "She always asked how my daughters are doing."

Faint praise, Alejandro thought. As if Mrs. Simmons had to dig for something kind to say about the deceased.

Preston picked out a round mint from the crystal bowl on the receptionist's desk and began untwisting the plastic ends. "How long have you worked for the congressman?"

"Four years now."

"How would you judge the relationship between the congressman and his wife?"

"Oh, very good." With this response, the receptionist seemed to find firmer ground. "I never heard a cross or impatient word from either of them. And Congressman Stafford, he would always make certain he never forgot any date—her birthday, their anniversary. He would often tell me of tickets he'd gotten for a ballet or show that she'd wanted to see, or a trip that he'd planned for them." She paused. "He didn't buy the presents himself, of course. But he always told his personal assistant exactly what to get."

Alejandro nodded. That sounded like a demon. If he was generous, he'd make certain that everyone knew it. "Is his assistant in?"

"Yes. Yes, of course." She glanced at the switchboard, brightly lit. "He's on a call. I'll slip him a note to tell him you're here."

"Thank you." As soon as she stood and was out of hearing range, Alejandro turned to Preston. "I'll return shortly. If I take longer than Mrs. Simmons does, I ask that you make an excuse for me."

"Are you doing anything I should know about?"

"Not if you value the fourth amendment to the Constitution."

"Considering it's a demon, I'll pretend I don't." Preston popped the mint into his mouth. "And if I happen to turn around, I can honestly say I didn't see anything."

He wouldn't have seen it anyway. Less than a second after the detective looked away, Alejandro slipped through Stafford's office doors. He took in the surroundings in an instant: the thick green carpet, the national and state flags against the wall, the leather sofa, the stately mahogany desk in front of the large windows. The desk held a computer monitor. Not a laptop, but Rael might carry one with him.

Alejandro would make do with what he had. Within moments, he'd disassembled the casing of the desktop computer and installed a transmitter. Every file that Rael looked at, every e-mail he sent would be collected and analyzed. The phone line was next. Savi already tracked the calls to and from Rael's cell phone number—although he might have a phone they didn't know about. Alejandro placed the last transmitter beneath the lip of a visitor's chair to pick up any conversations within the room.

Something SI should have done at the beginning, Alejandro thought grimly. Though Rael wasn't foolish enough to communicate with his demons here, he might be arrogant enough to.

Alejandro took a few more moments to search. No loose papers were spread around the room. Color-coded files had been neatly stacked on a low table in front of the sofa. A glance through them revealed pending legislation, drafts of bills. Alejandro was familiar with most of them. He found an additional folder full of correspondence.

He vanished them all into his cache. Copies could be made and the originals returned. If the shooter had been politically motivated, the answer might be in this pending legislation.

At least, that was what Alejandro would claim if he was asked. But another question had begun to form in his mind. A question . . . and a possible solution. One the detective, as far as he was willing to go, might not agree with.

Alejandro looked around the office. He could do this. He could slay Rael. He could take the demon's place.

No, he decided. He *would* do this. Whether the demon was involved with Julia Stafford's murder or not, he hadn't long to live.

Alejandro left the office, determination and dread filling him in equal parts. Irena would applaud his slaying Rael. But taking over the demon's position meant that Alejandro would become everything she hated.

And if he dreaded her reaction, that must mean that his heart had foolishly begun to hope for a future with her.

He was going to let it.

CHAPTER 12

Irena and Taylor had learned nothing from Julia Stafford's friend except that Julia had suspected Rael was cheating on her about two years ago. He'd still been as attentive, her friend had said, but he hadn't shown any interest in bed. But then, the sex got better, and Julia had stopped worrying.

Irena left the woman's house in a dark mood.

Taylor didn't speak until she'd started the car. "You don't eat, so I'm choosing where we're having lunch. And SI is paying."

"I have the credit cards," Irena said. "And I want meat."

"Don't we all?" Taylor glanced at her. "Rael having sex bothers you. Why? He can't do it to her if she doesn't want it."

Irena struggled with her answer. She didn't often pick apart her emotional reactions like she'd been required to today. "It would not be for his pleasure." Demons could physically simulate arousal, but they didn't feel sexual desire. "And not for hers, either—it's only to keep her with him. To secure their marriage."

"And if he's making that effort, it sits on the side of 'he wasn't looking to kill her.'"

"Yes." Irena heard the anger in her own voice. She'd hoped Rael was responsible for Julia's murder, just so that she could slay him—but the guilt *she* felt for hoping that frustrated her. There was no reason for guilt. She had not hoped Julia Stafford dead.

Perhaps the guilt came from not killing Rael before he'd arranged Julia's death—*if* he'd arranged it.

"So you don't have a problem with a demon having sex with a human."

Irena had a problem with demons existing, not just fucking. "I do."

"What about humans and Guardians?" Taylor laughed at Irena's expression. "I'm not coming on to you. Just in general."

"In general, I have no issue with it. I've done so myself."

"Okay, this place looks like it has potential," Taylor said as she pulled into the parking lot of a small restaurant with green and white striped awnings over the windows. "So you like humans?"

"Yes. I am always surprised by what you have accomplished. And what you continue to accomplish," Irena said, then frowned, bothered by her own answer.

If she was always surprised, did that mean her expectations were low? Did she expect so little of humans? She hadn't thought so.

And pulling apart her responses wasn't good for her. She hadn't doubted or questioned herself this much in centuries.

"You see the bad, don't you?" Taylor broke into her thoughts. "Like this job. If they aren't scum, then they're self-centered or just . . . out of control."

"I see the worst of humanity, yes. But I also see the best." And everything in between. Most of it was in between.

"Do you even consider yourself human anymore?"

"No." She met Taylor's surprised glance. "Because I am not. A human's free will is always honored. A Guardian's is not."

"Is that the only distinction you make?"

"Distinctions?" Frustration rattled against her nerves like a knife against her teeth. "What good are distinctions? There is no comparison to be made. No humans train for a century as

Guardians do. No humans live sixteen centuries. Or longer," she added, thinking of Michael. "Are Guardians what humans would be if they had longer lives? Or have we been changed in an even deeper way by the transformation? It is impossible to know. But I do know that I must honor your free will, and I don't have to honor a Guardian's."

"Or a demon's? Doesn't that make you more like them and less like us?"

Irena stared at her.

Taylor sucked in a slow breath between her teeth, as if preparing to run from a predator, but trying not to startle it first. "Forget I said that. Right now, I guess I'm grateful for those Rules."

Irena forced herself to let go of her anger. Evenly, she said, "Do not compare us to them. We *were* human. If we Fall, we become human again. Demons never were, and never will be."

"Fair enough." Taylor nodded. "And when *you* were a human, what were you?"

When they were sitting at a small table by a window, Irena told Taylor about her mother, who'd come from a defeated tribe of people—Irena didn't know who they'd been. Her memories of life before Rome were only brief flickers sparked by the scent of burning peat, or the gentleness in a father's voice, or a dog's sharp bark. Clearer were the years as a slave—and of watching her mother executed after she'd killed the Roman senator who'd raped her daughter.

"Jesus," was Taylor's reply, and then she said nothing for several seconds. "But I guess you don't have to worry about that now."

"Do you think there has never been a rape in Caelum? A murder?" Irena used her fingers to tear a chunk of bread from the coarse brown loaf between them, and dipped it into the small dish of sweetened butter. Taylor had barely eaten from her share. "They are infrequent, yes. But not everyone transformed has been worthy of their wings."

"What do you do when that happens? It's not against the Rules, is it?"

"It is against decency." Some rules shouldn't need to be spoken. "There is a trial. If the Guardian is found guilty, we are not forgiving."

Irena paused, thinking back over several trials she'd witnessed. Michael had never seemed to enjoy administering the sentence—a Fall or an Ascension. Each time, Irena sensed that Michael thought he'd personally failed by transforming the Guardian who'd committed the offense.

But she didn't know if he had a choice when transforming Guardians. If a human sacrificed himself to save another's life or soul, Michael was called to offer that human a place in Caelum. He'd never said whether he could resist that call.

Quietly, she continued, "But of course, what you say is true. I do not have the same worry now." And after her transformation, she'd have given anything to Michael, who'd given her the strength to prevent her body from being taken against her will. Who'd given her the ability to choose who and when. That had been power far greater than her physical strength.

A power that she'd still had with the demon. The demon hadn't left her without a choice; her heart had. Irena couldn't regret it—her body meant less to her than her heart—but she should never have had to decide between them. *That* was indecency.

And *that* was on the demon's head.

His decapitated, charred, and roasted head. Invigorated by the image, Irena cut into her steak.

"So what did you do after your mom died?"

"I endured. I dreamed of killing them all, but when I finally got the opportunity, I escaped Rome, instead. We traveled—" She frowned, trying to remember how long it had taken. "More than two winters. We walked from Rome until we reached the Black Sea—what is now the Ukraine. There, we settled. Or attempted to. I don't know if we remained after the nosferatu attacked us."

"You killed one?"

Irena shook her head. "I died trying, but injured it badly enough that I saved the others. After Michael arrived, he finished what I'd started."

"Yay, Michael," Taylor said, then set her fork down next to her half-finished pasta.

Irena continued eating. Always, with food, she wanted to savor it—and also wanted to devour it as quickly as possible. She kept a steady pace as Taylor called Preston and left a message for him, updating their progress.

"They must still be in with Rael's staff." Taylor put away her phone. "You were pissed in Lilith's office this morning. Why?"

Irena snorted. "Which time?"

"When they were going through Cordoba's assignments. Do you think they've loaded too much on him?"

Irena had to laugh. At Taylor's questioning look, she said, "No. And I wasn't angry; I was envious. I have a territory, I check in on the vampire communities and slay any demons that I come across, but my numbers are nothing like Olek's. Cordoba's."

Taylor's brow creased. "So Lilith was just sticking it to you?"

Irena didn't know if Lilith or Alejandro had thought of going over his assignments in front of her. It was something both would do. And it was both challenge and declaration, though a subtle one: If Irena would be visiting SI more frequently, then they would use her.

"They know I want more to do. But I am stubborn, and Lilith or Ol—Cordoba will give me assignments in another way."

"You don't seem the type to take orders from Lilith."

Her stomach heaved at the thought. "Not orders. Information, which I choose to act upon."

She wouldn't ignore it, just as she wouldn't have ignored Deacon's request even if she hadn't known the vampire.

"You won't work for SI?"

"No." Irena lost her humor. "Not with Rael behind it."

Taylor nodded and her gaze fell to Irena's empty plate. "The sniper rifle was a semiautomatic. No one knows we found the weapon; that info wasn't released. And Wren might have said all that shit just to throw us off—to make it look like she's trying to help us, when really she's just covering her own ass—but there's also another option: The guy only shot once because he didn't miss. Then you've got the *appearance* of an attempted assassination on the congressman, which I bet he can spin to the voters a million ways, but the wife was always the real target. No one looks at Rael because, well, he was shot, too. And even if someone does, no jury is going to buy that he put himself in the line of fire. Not unless everyone finds out he's a demon . . . but if that happens it all goes to hell, doesn't it?"

Irena regarded her quietly. "You would make a fine Guardian."

"Oh, good. Even if we nail him on the evidence at some point, he's not going down for it—but it's all right because I'd look great with wings and leather garter belts and thigh-highs. Lifetime goal, achieved."

Irena continued looking at her, wondering about the vampire Khavi had predicted—and if, instead of wings, fangs would be in Taylor's future. Had Khavi mentioned death? Or had Michael—and Irena—just assumed it?

Not that it mattered. They would change whatever fate it was. No human should be transformed against their will.

The detective sighed. "Shit. No offense."

"I took none."

Taylor checked her watch. "We're due at Rael's place in twenty. How do I go after him?"

A demon who'd lived as a saint? Who had made creating the appearance of a good man the work of a human's lifetime? Irena thought it over as she finished off the bread.

"Do not go after him," she decided. "Question him as if it never occurred to you that he might be behind his wife's assassination."

"Why?"

"There is a demon beneath the man he shows to everyone. One who wants credit for what he did. *If* he did it. And even if he did not, he will at least expect that we suspect him. Or that you do. If *I* do not, he will suspect *us*." Irena stopped, realizing that she was heading into a circle and confusing herself; planning a deception did not fit her well. She barged through on the course she wanted. "But when you do not do the same—act as if you suspect him—his ego and his pride will be damaged. It might lead him to act in a way where he exposes himself."

"Do you think he'd be that careless?"

"No."

Taylor fell into another of her silences as Irena paid for their lunch with one of the credit cards Olek had given her. As they headed back to the car, she felt Taylor's sudden tension.

"Someone's in the back seat of my car."

Irena recognized the dark braids, the stunning face. "It is Khavi."

"Prophecy Girl?"

"Yes."

Taylor didn't hide her irritation. She dropped into the driver's seat and slammed her door. "You've broken into police property. I should haul your ass to the station."

"I broke nothing. I teleported."

"Then teleport out." Taylor backed out of the parking spot. "And fasten your seat belt, or I'll cite you just for the fun of it." She frowned at Irena. "You, too."

Strapped to a seat, facing forward with Khavi behind her? No. Irena continued sitting sideways, watching the grigori. By the time they were driving along the street, Taylor's irritation had turned to anger.

So did Irena's. "What do you want, demon spawn?"

Khavi's gaze remained fixed on the back of the detective's head. "Will you not ask me about Jason? I have seen futures in which you ask."

Taylor's face paled. "Then I'm going to change that."

Khavi's Gift rushed out in a powerful wave. "And so you have. But even if you never ask, the answer is the same: He will never wake up."

Taylor slammed the brakes. Irena flew forward, cracking her head against the window. Through the stars exploding behind her eyes, she saw Taylor whip around, her gun pointed at Khavi's face.

"Get out! Get the fuck out *now*!"

Khavi vanished.

Her eyes wet, Taylor faced forward and holstered her weapon. She spared Irena a glance, then looked again. "Jesus."

Irena wiped at the blood streaming down her forehead. Until

the laceration healed, vanishing the blood from her face and clothes was pointless. "It looks bad. But it is nothing."

The detective's expression hardened. "Screw *nothing*. I listen to you about Wren, about Rael, all your goddamn centuries of experience. Next time, you fucking listen to mine when I tell you to buckle up." She started driving. After a minute, her lips twitched. "Are you okay?"

Irena started to laugh. Yes, she liked some humans very much.

❧

She hated demons. And as Wren showed them into the same room with its sliding glass doors and windows overlooking the bay, where Rael sat on a sofa with his head on his hands, pretending exhaustion and grief, Irena did not attempt to hide her seething hatred.

But whatever it was that Khavi had said to upset Taylor, whoever Jason was to her, the detective had wrapped it up and shielded it. If Taylor felt anything when she looked at Rael, Irena could not sense it.

Irena took her hate, projected it, pushed it—so that even if Taylor slipped, Rael might not notice that beneath Taylor's questions lay suspicion.

She wondered what the detective saw when she looked at the demon. Rael was undoubtedly handsome, but his sculptor had not been sparing in his materials. Everything lay in the open. Irena found nothing interesting in the perfection of his face— nothing that forced the personality behind it to fill in the sharp edges and to work. She saw no mystery, only bland beauty.

But Taylor might see something different. The lack of mystery was a deception worse than any other—it led people to believe they could know him, trust him. And when he looked back at them, he appeared to understand so much about them, about their troubles. He probably did understand, Irena had to admit. His deception was pretending to care.

One low chair faced Rael's sofa and sat with its back to the bay window. After Rael dismissed Wren, Irena called in a sword. She sank into the chair, set the point of the blade between her feet, her elbows on her knees, her hands fisted around the grip.

The rounded pommel was embedded with jewels and glass and a small camera, and the effect was far more decorative than she liked. She'd rather rip him apart with her teeth than use a sword this ugly and unbalanced. Rael wouldn't know that.

She sneered and flashed her Gift, beginning the recording.

Rael frowned up at Taylor, who stood beside Irena's chair. "Are the threats necessary, detective? I will answer your questions."

"Yes, you will," Irena said, forcing his gaze back to her. She bared her teeth. "If you don't, you stinking pig-fucking demon, I will gut you."

Taylor sighed and sat on the arm of Irena's chair. She rubbed at her forehead, pinching the bridge of her nose as if to ward off a headache—or relieve a current one. Irena could not tell if it was genuine or not.

"No, congressman, we do not need threats." She cast Irena a warning glance before looking back at him. "First, let me say that I am sorry for your loss."

"I'm sorry she's dead," Irena cut in, and let Rael feel the brutal honesty of that. "But I'm not sorry for you, because I know you feel nothing but enjoyment at this situation. Because not only did the human who tried to kill you fail in that attempt, a human who meant nothing to you died. One human is damned, another is dead. I am only surprised you are not dancing, demon."

"You know nothing, Guardian. Julia was a good woman and a good wife."

Taylor's hand clenched into a fist against her thigh. She said smoothly, "Forgive my associate, please. She was also at the protest yesterday and was deeply saddened by what happened. So much so that she has not quite recovered."

"Is that how you would put it?" Rael said.

"Yes. She asked to be assigned to help find your wife's murderer—and has agreed to the condition that *she puts aside her Guardian prejudices*."

Taylor finished through clenched teeth, staring Irena down. Irena sneered at the demon again, but fell silent.

"Thank you, detective." He steepled his fingers. "Might we begin?"

"Yes. Thank you," she said, as if he'd done her a favor. "Of course you've realized that we are here because the FBI cannot follow certain lines of inquiry."

"I have realized that, detective."

"Good. That will make this so much easier. We won't spend any time on your political enemies—"

"Political *opponents*, detective," Rael said. His smile invited her to join in. "We are all on the same side, working toward a common goal. We simply have different ideas about how to get there."

"Opponents, then," Taylor said. "The FBI will look there, and at special interest groups. But do you know if any of your opponents are demons who might be interested in seeing you fall—either in the political arena or as one of Belial's favored demons?"

Rael shook his head. "None would dare."

Did that mean none would dare try to harm him, or none would dare to take office? But Taylor moved on before Irena could ask.

She let her frustration burn.

"What of Lucifer's demons? Wouldn't they like to take you down a peg or two, just because you're loyal to their enemy?"

"Of course they would, detective. But at this moment, they are enjoying their brief freedom while the Gates are closed, and pursuing their own interests—not Lucifer's."

"Don't they worry about the prophecy? The one that states the Morningstar will lose his throne to Belial? Doesn't that prophecy make Lucifer's interests their own?"

Rael's expression went blank for an instant, and Irena realized that Taylor had surprised him by even knowing about the prophecy. Had he thought the Guardians would keep it to themselves?

In normal circumstances, Irena supposed that they would.

A hint of condescension came into his voice. "You must understand, detective, that the demons who follow Lucifer do so not because they are loyal to him. They follow him because he has the power to crush them if they don't—and when my liege takes the throne, they will switch their allegiances without hesitation."

Hugh would find no lie in this portion of the recording, Irena thought.

"All right." Taylor nodded. "What about the other part of the prophecy—the nephilim and Anaria?"

"No," Rael said firmly. "The nephilim would not conspire in that way. Neither would Anaria. She wants the throne. That is all she wants; her efforts will be toward that end."

"So she would not bother with you?"

A brief flash of anger crossed his face. Apparently, he didn't like the way Taylor had phrased that. Irena grinned. Perhaps Taylor had not meant her question to dig as it had, but he'd felt it.

"She would not *bother* with anyone who does not support her, or whose goals do not match hers." Rael glanced at Irena. "She doesn't bother with the Guardians, either. Not even Michael."

"That is good for her sake," Irena said. "Because when we find Anaria, I'm going to cut out her heart and eat it."

Crimson rolled across his eyes, as if he had trouble controlling his fury. Irena grinned, snapped her teeth together.

He regained control, looked at her with disdain, and dismissed her.

Taylor stepped in again. "How many people knew that you would be attending the protest?"

"The rally," he said, and smiled. "Protest is too negative a word for what we hope to accomplish, detective. We rally together to fight against a piece of legislation that should never have been passed—only those who oppose us would want to cast a negative light on it."

Slippery bull-fucking demon. Irena clenched her teeth, held her tongue.

"You don't agree, Guardian?" Rael glanced at her, then back at Taylor. "Where do you stand, detective? Don't you think that people should be with the ones they love?"

Irena could not stand it. She hated him. Not just because he was a demon, but because he used such tactics: If Taylor agreed with him, it gave the appearance that she was complicit in more than just this. To disagree would make her appear cold to her fellow humans. To evade the question would make her appear as if she lacked conviction.

"What would you know of love, demon? You know nothing of love. And if you support it, *rally* for it," she sneered, "it is only because you think that it will be your gain."

He did not look at her, and said flatly, "I do know, Guardian. I have loved. I know what it is to love a woman and to want nothing more than to lay the world at her feet."

"Or put a bullet through her throat so that she lays at *your* feet."

"Tell me how I could have shot Julia, Guardian." He cast her a baleful stare. "You were there. Give me a scenario where that could possibly be true. And then give me a reason why I would kill a woman so valuable to me."

"Hold on." Taylor held out her hands, then looked to Irena. "You know you're off track. Sit back. If he'd done this, he'd be nephilim fodder by now."

Irena sat back and seethed.

"So let's get back to the question: Who knew, besides Miss Wren, your wife, and yourself, that you would be at the rally?"

"A better question, detective, would be: Who did *not* know?"

"Fair enough. So if you are mistaken, and a demon did plan to hurt you—politically or otherwise—they'd have had plenty of notice and opportunity to find a hired gun."

Rael shook his head. "I'm sorry, detective, but your logic is flawed: A demon would know I wouldn't die."

"But you might be exposed. They couldn't have known the Guardians would be there to cover for you. Do you know of any demon who would risk exposure—or who has argued for it? Any vampire?"

"I will have to think on that, detective."

Taylor nodded. "What of your wife? Does she have any enemies?"

"She was well-loved, detective."

"Can you think of anyone who would harm her to get to you?"

He frowned. "You don't think she was the target, do you?"

Answer the question. Irena gritted her teeth, fought to stay in her seat and force him to answer. Hugh could not see the truth if Rael returned every question with a question.

"I have to cover my bases, congressman. Many times, that means just throwing something out—even if I can't see a motive behind it. Other times, we don't even have to ask, because the motive is clear, either for or against: For example, you've already stated—and we *know*—how valuable Julia was to you. Not to mention your career. So that takes you out—you obviously didn't hire someone to kill her, risking exposure in the process."

He smiled, shook his head. "No, detective. I didn't."

They would soon see, Irena thought.

§

It was nearing sunset when Taylor pulled the car alongside the sidewalk a block away from the federal building. Irena stepped out, and had a quick stare-down with Preston before he accepted the front seat she offered him. She slid into the back as Alejandro folded himself into the other side. He had to turn toward the center to fit his legs. He stretched his arm along the back of the seat.

His nostrils flared, and she knew that he'd scented her blood. Though he didn't move, his body tightened with suppressed violence.

Unexpected heat sizzled through her. Did she warm from his protective response or that display of readiness? She didn't know, and didn't try to separate the parts of her reaction. All that mattered was that she'd warmed so quickly and fiercely, because of Olek's response and his readiness. Not her anger, not his pride. They would come again, she was certain. But at this moment, anger and pride were not in the car between them.

And she enjoyed the feeling of what was.

Olek made a single sharp gesture. *Rael?*

No. Khavi appeared after our lunch, Irena signed to him. *Taylor did not appreciate the visit.*

Khavi spilled your blood?

Taylor stopped the car very quickly. Reminded, she pulled the restraining belt across her shoulder and clicked it home. *I did not stop until my head met the glass.*

He rubbed his thumb back and forth over his chin, obviously amused. His gaze left hers when Taylor spoke from the front seat.

"So, we head back to SI and report to Lilith?"

"And Castleford, yes," Alejandro said. "When he watches the recording of your interview with Rael, Castleford will know when the demon lied."

Taylor snapped a glance at Irena. "You *recorded* it?"

"Yes."

Her jaw clenched. She faced forward again.

The detective would struggle with that, Irena thought. Taylor would come to terms with it, or not. The Guardians' methods of gathering evidence were different than the methods allowed by human courts. Demons had already been judged and sentenced by those Above. Rael would never stand trial on Earth, he would never be imprisoned—and, if they chose to kill him, Guardians would be the executioners.

Whether humans liked their methods or not.

Alejandro signed, *Bradshaw is a Guardian. His Gift is a psychic mask.*

A Guardian? She'd had no idea. *Who was he in Caelum? Luther.*

She did not recognize the name. *How long has he been with the FBI?*

Since before the Ascension.

And Rael does not know?

No one does but Lilith, Hugh, and Michael. When Bradshaw is not at the office, he does, essentially, what I do.

Irena smiled, pleased. Carrying out a human life on top of a Guardian's would be difficult, but she could see how Bradshaw's position was necessary. She glanced over at Alejandro; he seemed pleased as well, though she could not decide the reason for it. So much of him was still a mystery to her.

Good, she replied, then spoke aloud to include Taylor and

Preston. "Were any demons among Rael's staff? Did any know what he was? His household employees did not."

"Nor did his office staff."

Disappointment wound through her. A demon like Rael would have subordinates; she wanted to know where and who the demons closest to him were.

"What about the staff in D.C.?" Preston said. He'd produced a bag of peanuts from somewhere; the crinkle of plastic and the scent filled the car. "He's got an office there, right?"

"Yes, but I met with each of them as Senator Brandt. They are not demons."

Taylor frowned. "So where are all of his flunkies?"

"We believe they are at Legion," Alejandro said.

Not in government, but in the corporate world. Irena had no real knowledge of either. She turned to look out the window, once again feeling the uncomfortable fit of this role.

"And how short does he keep their leash?" Taylor asked.

"Not tight enough to choke them."

Alejandro's voice was soft—and nearer to her. Irena looked at him, startled as he reached across and pressed at the buttons on her door. Glass lowered. Night air and frigid drizzle washed her face.

But she did not breathe easier. Her eyes locked with Alejandro's, and she watched their color deepen.

That was the only alteration in his expression. His psychic blocks prevented her from sensing anything else of his emotions.

She wanted to tear the blocks away. To see what lay beneath. To strip away everything that hid him from her, to examine him piece by piece, not just the bits he let slip through.

He wasn't looking at her hands, so she couldn't sign to him. But she could not speak to him in French. That language was for watching her words—and those words had helped hold them apart for four hundred years.

"I want to rip you apart," she said beneath her breath in Russian.

There. Something in his expression. Was it hurt or anger? She didn't know. She wanted, needed to know.

In Spanish, he murmured, "I do not look down at you."

I want to destroy you. Yes, she remembered when she'd said that, too. But her words held a different meaning now.

She shook her head. "So that when I put you back together, I will see what you are made of."

And there, in his eyes—another change. It looked like wonder, or hope. He laid his hand on her thigh, his grip bold and possessive. "Do it, then."

He challenged her. Everything within Irena called for her to rise and meet it.

But if she did, a piece would still be missing. Something that she had not given him. Something she was afraid to give him.

She had to tell him the truth about what had happened in that iron-locked room.

Her mouth was dry. She tried to moisten it and felt as if she'd swallowed razors. And she could have answered Taylor's question now: There was little difference between humans and Guardians. As both, she'd felt fear and dread. As both, there'd been pain.

But, before the demon, there had never been this much shame. Not for anything she'd done, or anything done to her.

Pain hadn't stopped her before, though. She couldn't let shame do it now. Not if she wanted to move forward; not if she wanted to move *beyond* an overturned rock and a bargain.

How laughable that, even as old as they were, Irena did not know if either she or Alejandro could do it. He was only human, as well. Would he feel disgust? Pity? Betrayal? His every possible response would add to the hurt. And she wanted to see his emotions, piece by piece—but she only wanted to see his reaction to this after he'd had time to accept it.

Still, she couldn't step away to give them space and time. Four hundred years of separation hadn't made it easier. She had to tell him, face-to-face. And if it hurt *him*, she couldn't run away from that. She'd never been a coward. She wouldn't let the demon make her one.

And she hoped that the presence of Taylor and Preston would force them to be mindful of their responses.

"Have you already backed down?" He still spoke in Spanish,

his voice soft and challenging. "If you have, Irena, I will come after you."

Would he? Fear became ragged claws tearing at the back of her throat, scraping at her eyes. She had not known fear could bring tears. She laughed at herself, hoping to push the fear away, but her laugh came out tattered by it.

Alejandro's hand tightened on her thigh. Abruptly, he let her go.

She caught his wrist. He must have thought his touch had caused this fear. And why wouldn't he? Alejandro could read her face, her laugh, but he didn't know what lay behind them. She'd never told him.

For the first time in her life, she wished that she had pretty words. Some manner of speech that wasn't as blunt as a hammer strike. But she only had what she was.

Though it would be easier to sign than to speak, she did not let go of his wrist. If he signed a reply, she would have to watch his hands. She wanted to see his face.

She spoke quietly in Russian, as he had in Spanish, and her voice was as ragged as her laugh had been. "What the demon did in that room when I made that bargain—it was not what you thought."

His pulse jumped beneath her fingers. He still didn't understand, though. His silence said he waited for her to continue.

The claws in her throat became daggers. "He never intended to use pain. He wanted my body to respond to him." The last part was the worst, but she forced the words out. "And I did."

She braced herself for disgust and pity. She forgot to prepare for relief.

He didn't—or couldn't—contain it, and his relief lifted through his psychic scent, a sweet release.

"He didn't hurt you?" His voice was hoarse. His throat worked, and the rest was a grateful whisper. "*Gracias, Dios mío!*"

He thanked God? Her rage and pain exploded. She swung, backhanded him across the face. His head snapped to the side, struck the opposite window. Glass shattered.

Preston choked. "Jesus Christ! Were we shot?"

No. Irena stared at Alejandro, horrified. She'd hit him. The back of her hand was numb from the force of her blow. Vivid red marked his cheek. His eyes had darkened to black. Blood trickled from the corner of his mouth.

His lips drew back in a terrible smile. "Do that again."

"What the fuck are you two doing?"

Taylor's voice jolted Irena into motion. Her hand came screaming back to life as she reached for the door. She shoved outside and onto the sidewalk.

Sickness roiled in her stomach. She wanted to curl up, wanted to cry, but she walked, seeing nothing but his face. How could she have lost control? She'd known what she could do if she succumbed to her anger, and she'd done it with *Olek*. It didn't matter that a backhanded slap was nothing compared to tearing the demon apart. Both had been done without thought, without any attempt to check her actions.

And once again, she'd left.

She stopped, her breath shuddering. She couldn't walk away from this. Irena turned—and saw Alejandro had kept his promise.

He'd come after her.

❧

Alejandro didn't know what surprised him more: The harsh pleasure he'd felt when she'd hit him, or that a few moments after she'd done it, he realized that she'd lied to him. The demon *had* hurt her. Alejandro hadn't seen the evidence, but he'd scented it. Irena's blood had been spilled in that room.

He wiped at his mouth and tasted his own blood. Mother of God, he didn't know why she'd tried to revise history or why she'd struck him, but he would not stop until he found out.

Rain splashed against his face as he bolted out of the car. Taylor had pulled over on a street not far from SI. Businesses lined the sidewalks, shabbier than their downtown counterparts. Awnings streaked with dirt were leaking. The scents of nail salons and sandwich shops drifted out through the damp. The sidewalks were almost empty. The humans moved quickly through the drizzle, using papers and umbrellas to shield their hair.

Irena passed each storefront without looking left or right. Her head was down, her shoulders hunched.

Her posture ripped at his heart. He was damned if he'd let her get far enough ahead to escape. Not without settling this between them.

God knew if they could.

He glanced back at Taylor and Preston, each standing behind their opened car door. Alejandro held up his hand, silently asking them to wait.

Preston nodded.

Alejandro took off, narrowing Irena's lead to a few meters. She didn't look to see who was running up behind her. Was she that oblivious to his pursuit—and leaving herself open to attack? Anger joined his worry.

In the shadows between two of the storefronts, she stopped. Getting ready to fly?

Not a chance. When she turned, he charged.

She didn't raise a hand to defend herself. Shocked anew that he *wanted* her to strike him, he caught her waist and lifted her. He'd been hard since her hand had connected with his face, and he fought the hot pleasure of holding her against his body, his erection caught between them. This wasn't going to be about sex. His only intention was to question.

When her back hit the side of the building, his intentions went flying. Amazement shot through him. He stared down into her wary eyes, disbelieving the evidence in his hands.

She was so small. Irena weighed no more than a human. In the conference room, had he been too blind with arousal and surprise to notice it? Because until this moment, even knowing, *knowing* that Guardians were no heavier after their transformation, he'd imagined lifting her would be an effort. Irena had always been so solid, so indestructible in his mind, as if he thought she'd been made out of metal—but she was fragile flesh and blood beneath his hands.

Her jaw set, but he didn't just see strength and stubbornness. She expected a blow in return. Dear God. He leaned his forehead against hers, feeling as if he'd lost his footing, trying to regain it.

He never intended to use pain.

Instead, the demon had used Alejandro's face and . . . forced her to enjoy his touch?

Rage mounted in him, as it always did when he thought of the demon with her. But his feelings on *her* behalf were the same. Relief. An emotion that had made her strike out.

Irena's wet palm cupped the side of his neck. She had to feel his pulse racing. Must hear his heart pounding.

He could barely hear the quick beat of hers over it.

"Olek." She pitched her voice low, and he was astonished to realize that she was trying to calm *him*.

He lifted his head to look at her, and struggled to keep his shields strong. Tried to sound less shaken than he was. Despite that effort, he only managed, "You ran."

Her gaze shifted from his eyes to his cheek, though the mark from her hand must have faded. The back of his head felt as if his skull had shattered—but he could ignore the pain. The shock of the slap had affected him more than the blow.

And her stillness, her silence now—was she afraid she'd hit him again?

He didn't care if she did. "Why did you not tell me before?"

She closed her eyes. What was she hiding? What did she fight?

Then he felt it, faint as a whisper behind closed doors: shame in her psychic scent.

"Oh, Jesus." He tried to find words again. "There is no shame in it, Irena. Forced to feel pleasure is no different than being forced to feel pain."

Her eyes flashed open, glowing a brilliant green. "You stupid ox. Do you think I do not know that?"

He felt her anger, rising hot. His footing was gone, but this was familiar.

And that told him something else; she had not hit him out of anger. She'd been angry many, many times. Always, she had controlled it. This was something different.

"You do not hit me now?"

"You thanked your god, you *grateful* pig. Thanked him,

when there was nothing the demon could have done that would have been worse. I'd rather he'd torn my flesh. Would rather have felt pain."

Because it wouldn't have touched her. Because she could guard against it.

Horror shook his veins as he began to realize. He fought to find his footing again. "You did feel pain. Your blood was in that room."

She closed her eyes again, breathing shallowly.

"Irena." He imprisoned her face between his hands. "Tell me, or hit me."

She snarled. "He put his mouth on me. I would not let myself feel pleasure again. I . . . used my dagger on that part of me." Her snarl faded, and she shook against him. "But he only waited until I healed, and bound my hands so that I could not do it again. Then I bit off my tongue so that I could not beg him to fuck me. Over and over, I did that."

Alejandro couldn't speak. Horror, rage, and agony howled within him, but he couldn't speak.

The anger in her voice faded. Only resignation remained. "I could not tell you, Olek. I only do now because something has changed between us. And I could not go forward until it was said."

Go forward . . . without him?

"And so it is done." She turned her face. "Let me go."

His hands tightened. "No."

Her eyes flashed. She pushed at him.

He dragged her higher up the wall and heard her jacket scraping against the bricks. Though he wanted to, he couldn't be gentle. His words had deserted him, yet he had to make clear that he couldn't let her go.

He lowered his head, took her mouth. Her lips were wet and cool. Her breath shuddered, her thighs wrapped his hips, and suddenly he wasn't showing her anything but was rendered helpless to his need. Raw desire rappelled through him, drawing him up hard and tight against her. Her teeth dug into his bottom lip. His groan vibrated deep in his throat.

As if mollified by the sound, Irena softened. She opened

her mouth beneath his. Her hands buried in his hair, pulling him closer.

He barely felt the pain that lanced through him as her fingers found the lump on the back of his head, but she must have realized what she'd touched. She broke the kiss, breathing heavily.

"Let go, Olek."

He never wanted to deny her will. That didn't mean he'd obey. "I will only come after you."

Her eyes flared again. "I won't leave. I will meet you at SI." Her gaze slid to the left. "It is after sunset. We cannot leave Taylor alone."

Damn duty. Damn everything but Irena. But he could not deny her this—and it would give him time to put his thoughts in order, as well.

He stepped back. She touched his cheek, then stroked her fingers down his bare chin. Silently, she turned and walked away.

He watched until she rounded a corner before starting back toward the detectives. Rain soaked the insides of his shoes, squelching with every step. It dripped down the back of his neck. He changed clothes as he passed through the shadows, trading shoes for his comfortable boots. He touched his jaw where Irena had and formed his beard.

The detectives' car was only a block away when a harmonious voice sliced through the air like blades.

"Alejandro Sandoval de Córdoba y Hacén."

He pivoted, seeking Michael. Across the street, the Doyen perched on the roof of a building, his black wings folded against his back. His obsidian eyes seemed to absorb the light. Alejandro had seen them many times, but they'd never appeared to him as empty—as soulless—as they did now.

They had never appeared as the nephilim's eyes did.

"You left her unguarded."

As if the words snaked through Michael's psychic blocks, the air suddenly seethed with the Doyen's anger. Alejandro's stomach lurched. In five centuries, he had seen Michael cold, had seen him ruthless—but never terrifying.

And he'd never felt the raw, unleashed power that Michael

emitted now. Two years ago, he'd felt something similar from Lucifer . . . but this was worse.

Because he thought he'd known Michael. Thought he'd had some idea what the Doyen was capable of.

He remembered Irena's claim that Khavi had told Michael something more than the vision about Taylor. *Yes,* Alejandro thought. Irena must have been right. And whatever Khavi had told him stripped away some of Michael's layers.

He made a short bow, kept his voice low and respectful. "It will not happen again."

"It will not. From this point forward, she is mine after sunset. You may go."

The hairs on the back of his neck prickled. *She is mine?* That was a peculiar way to phrase it. Perhaps there was more to Michael's behavior than just concern for Taylor . . . but Alejandro would not leave her alone with the Doyen like this. Not until Michael's anger had passed.

"I would, Michael," he said, and crossed the distance to the car. "But I dislike the rain, and prefer to ride back to SI."

He got in, unsurprised to find his fingers shaking. Taylor gave a pointed look at the shattered window before pulling away from the curb.

Preston was laughing to himself. "For a minute there, I thought we'd be citing you both for public indecency."

"Cite both your asses for destroying public property," Taylor muttered. "But I'd still have to explain it to Jorgenson."

If Michael's words earlier had opened his blocks, Taylor's seemed to close them. The Doyen's seething anger vanished. No other emotion replaced it.

Alejandro didn't find that reassuring.

CHAPTER 13

Irena felt the tension immediately upon her return to Special Investigations. As she strode into the hub, she heard the conversation from the novices upstairs fade, as if they were listening. A sigh escaped her. She could not walk into a room without everyone around her expecting a fight.

Standing in the center of the hub, Taylor and Preston appeared to be waiting for Alejandro, who was speaking with Selah, making plans to teleport to Buenos Aires later. After he was done here, he still had more to do.

Irena had something she needed to do, too. She jogged upstairs, across the common room, and into the dormitory hallway, noting how the novices avoided her eyes.

Rosalia waited in front of Deacon's room. Her black knee-high boots sported heels that Irena would have twisted her ankle in. A hooded cloak draped her shoulders, creating swirling shadows that now concealed, now revealed the black form-fitting pants and shirt she wore. She'd strapped a crossbow to her back.

Obviously, she spent far too much time among vampires.

"It is good to see you well," Irena said.

"It is good to be well." Rosalia didn't move away from Deacon's door. "He is in the shower. Are you bringing him the nosferatu's blood?"

"Nosferatu and demon."

"If you don't object, I'd like to give the blood to him."

Surprised, Irena regarded her closely. Rosalia's expression, though friendly, had a strange intensity that Irena couldn't read. She remembered Deacon's reaction to the Guardian at the club. Perhaps that interest was reciprocated.

"Why?"

"Because it is good to be well." A small, sad smile tilted her lips. "And I owe him for that."

Irena still didn't see why, but many Guardians had different notions of debts and obligations than she did. She wouldn't prevent Rosalia from repaying hers.

The novices in the common room remained quiet while she passed the blood to Rosalia. Signing, instead of talking aloud. Irena frowned, her irritation with the novices mounting. Why didn't they just say what they thought? Were they truly so uncertain about her intentions? And if they were—why did it make them so hesitant? What *she* did had no bearing on *them*.

She stalked back to the common room, her shields open and projecting the dull edge of her anger. Eyes wide and wary, the novices watched her approach. Becca sat beside Pim, both twisted around so that they could see over the back of the sofa. Randall, Garth, and Nadia stood stiffly beside the game table. Almost half of all the current novices—and Echo, Ben, and Mackenzie were also at the game table, a few vampires, too. Good.

Irena heard Alejandro's light step on the stairs, but didn't glance that way. She stopped in front of Becca, braced her hands on top of the sofa's back, and leaned in.

"I'm heading downstairs to kill Lilith. What are *you* going to do?"

A heartbeat of shocked silence fell over the room. The novices barraged her with objections an instant later, but Irena only paid attention to Becca's.

Her fists curled. Her gaze held Irena's. "I'll stop you."

Irena grinned. "Will you?"

She grabbed the novice's shoulders, hauled her over the sofa. Before novices or vampires could react, Irena had Becca flat on the floor, her knee in the novice's back and her knife against the side of Becca's throat. The novice struggled to get up. Irena held her easily.

She gave a warning glance to the novices surrounding them—each with their weapons drawn, she noted with approval. Behind her, running footsteps suddenly halted, and a shout was muffled as Olek stopped the only one in the room who, given his feelings for Becca, might have posed a danger— to himself, when Irena defended against his attack.

On the floor, Becca tried to pull herself forward. She gasped as Irena pressed her knee down harder. The rug ripped beneath the novice's fingers.

With a soft sound of alarm, Pim stepped forward, lowering her sword. "Irena, *please*."

Irena ignored her. She bent to speak into Becca's ear. "I'm stronger than you. Faster than you. I could tear you apart without lifting a finger, and you do not yet even have your Gift," she said. "Will you still try to come between Lilith and me?"

"Yes." The novice's ragged breaths were almost sobs now.

"Why?" Irena sneered. "Because you are *loyal* to Lilith?"

"Because it's the right thing to do, you crazy cunt bitch!"

Irena flipped her over. She blocked Becca's fist, then captured her wrists. The novice could have hurt Irena with a knee to her back, but Becca must have realized there was nothing left to fight. She stared up at Irena, absolutely still.

"Yes," Irena said. "That is the right answer. Your loyalty should not be to me, to Lilith, to the Guardians. Only to this." She laid her hand over Becca's racing heart. "*Only* this. Do you see?"

Becca nodded, and Irena knew that the novice did see. This one was the youngest here, but she was not stupid. And if the others were not stupid, they would see as well.

Irena hauled the novice to her feet. "Then you will be worthy of your wings."

She began to turn, but Becca's voice stopped her. "And what if I don't know what's right?"

Irena sighed. She hated questions such as these. "Then ask your friends." She gestured to the novices around them. "Surely one of them will say something sensible. Or ask your mentor, or Micha—" She cut herself off. The novice bit her lip. Irena drew a deep breath and finished, "Or Michael."

Humor lit Becca's eyes. "Lilith?"

Irena chuckled, more amused by the novice's daring than the question. "No."

"You?"

Her laughter took off. When she finally wrestled it under control, she wiped her eyes and shook her head. "No."

The novice looked genuinely perplexed. "No? Why not?"

Irena stared at her. The novice had been afraid that she might kill Lilith—and if circumstances had been different, if Lilith had been different, Irena *would* have slain the former demon—and yet she looked to Irena for guidance? "Why would you?"

"You're . . . you."

Irena frowned. That made no sense. But the other novices were nodding, and so obviously the only person it didn't make sense to was Irena.

"Come to me, then," she said. "But know that my answer will always be 'Kill the demon.' Painfully, if possible."

Becca gave a little smile, as if that pleased her. "Okay."

Still frowning, Irena turned away from her toward the stairs. Across the common room, Alejandro stood with his forearm against Mackenzie's throat and his sword angled between the vampire's legs. Mackenzie's rage had not yet cooled.

Alejandro's tone remained calm, but demanded that the vampire listen. "Your desire to protect your woman speaks well of you—but do not forget that she is a Guardian. You must learn to recognize when she needs protection, and when she does not."

From behind her, Becca snapped, "I don't need protection, you stupid jerk."

Irena wasn't sure if *stupid jerk* referred to Alejandro or

Mackenzie, but the vampire must have thought it was him. Chagrin flashed through his psychic scent before he bared his fangs. "Be quiet, my woman."

The novices snickered. Perhaps they'd seen this argument before. Irena left them to it, continuing toward the stairs.

Alejandro released the vampire, adding, "You'll likely find that when she needs it and when she wants it will rarely coincide."

Irena gave him a look as he caught up to her at the head of the stairs. *When she wants it?* she signed.

The corners of his mouth deepened and his cheeks hollowed. His not-quite-a-smile. But his eyes didn't join in; he regarded her curiously. *Do you not know how the younger Guardians see you? Not just the novices, but all of those who are still young.*

She did not think of it much. *I can imagine.*

Then you imagine poorly. He stopped halfway down the stairs, and she turned to face him. *It is almost with the same reverence that they have for Michael.*

Reverence? She snorted. *It is fear, perhaps.*

And respect. He started down again. *They wouldn't have been so conflicted if they cared nothing for your opinion, and only feared you.*

She followed him, unease dancing through her belly. All of her life, she'd urged young Guardians to find a path true to themselves. She'd never thought they might look to hers as a model.

But it had not always been that way, she knew.

"When you were young, Olek," she began in Russian, and continued with her hands when he turned to face her, *you did not regard me with reverence.*

Yes, I did. I'd heard the same stories as every other novice, he replied. *But after I saw you, I only wanted to sheathe myself between your thighs.*

Her breath caught. Never would she forget her own powerful response upon seeing him staring at her across that courtyard. She thought of his promise to meet her at the forge later, and hoped the evening would pass quickly.

The color in his eyes deepened. Yes, he hoped so, too. They reached the bottom of the stairs; the hub was empty.

"Taylor and Preston are in the conference room," he said quietly. "We wait for Lilith and Castleford to join us—and for Michael."

Though hearing him respond to her in his native language felt so perfectly right, Irena couldn't mistake the unsettled note in Olek's voice at his mention of Michael. *What has happened?*

Nothing. He intercepted her frown, and shook his head. *I do not lie. I'll tell you as we wait with Taylor. Hopefully, the Doyen will be himself again when we next see him.*

Oh. Irena understood all too well; he'd met with Michael, and the Doyen's shields hadn't held firm. And she still had no idea what Khavi had told Michael. *Did your hands shake?*

Alejandro gave her a sharp glance, followed by a reluctant nod.

So did mine, she said.

❧

The giant flat-screened TV mounted behind a sliding wall panel in the SI conference room probably cost more than all of the rolling-cart monstrosities *and* half the detectives' computers at Ingleside station, Taylor mused. If Rael had managed to talk Uncle Sam into setting this up for the Guardians, then the SFPD obviously needed a demon sitting in on the city budget meetings.

She glanced over at Joe, who sat in the chair beside hers, eating candy. He jerked his bushy eyebrows at the screen, then tapped his fingers on the table. Unlike the screen, the long, metal folding table was better suited to Ingleside than here, and clearly didn't match the buttery-soft leather seats that cushioned their asses. She shrugged, then held out her hand so that he could pour M&M's into her cupped palm.

Waiting wasn't so bad, Taylor decided, separating out the red candies to eat first. She'd already called her mother, saying she'd be home late. No surprise there. She'd left a message for Savi, telling the vampire that she'd wait at SI so they could begin digging into Wren's history—which actually meant that

Savi would be digging while Taylor watched her perform magic on the computer.

And by the time Lilith and Castleford showed up, she might have figured out why the hell she and Joe were really here.

Her gaze settled on Cordoba, who stood against the far wall. He hadn't taken his eyes off Irena since she'd come into the room. Irena stood against the wall opposite the tall Guardian.

Guardians apparently had a problem with parking their butts in a seat, but no problems talking. Their hands had been flying in that sign language. A bit rude.

But, to be fair, she and Preston hadn't shared their M&M's, either.

She moved on to the orange. One color at a time, one question at a time.

The first big question was Cordoba. Although the Guardian currently looked less like a federal agent and more like a brooding romantic hero with his black breeches and boots—and a heavy twist of a villain thrown in with that devilish little goatee—the man knew his way around an investigation. Unlike Irena, Cordoba hadn't been in the background. And Joe got a little starry-eyed around the Guardians, but he was a cop to his bones. He wouldn't still be looking at Cordoba with any kind of respect if the Guardian had bumbled around.

And though Cordoba had crossed lines, he hadn't bumbled his way over them.

Lilith had lied. SI didn't need them here.

Taylor picked out a yellow M&M's candy, the only one in the bunch. This one, she'd let melt instead of chewing it.

So SI didn't need them, and yet . . . here they were. Lilith had no reason to do her any favors. And Lilith could be a bitch, but Taylor couldn't see how bringing Joe and her in on the investigation was sticking it to them. Lilith wouldn't stick it to Joe, in any case.

Hell, Lilith probably wouldn't stick it to anyone unless there was a point to it. Whatever Lilith was, at least she always had a purpose behind the bitchiness.

And then there'd been that visit from Khavi. Taylor had gotten the impression from Irena that the grigori was just a nut, but that nut had also had a purpose. Khavi had shown up in her car for a reason—and Taylor didn't think it was just to rip her heart out over Jason.

But why would an ancient grigori give a flying flip about her?

Two greens sat in her palm like little eyes. Taylor stared at them, then let them drop to the table. She swiveled her seat around. Irena was back in her leather longstockings and that white fur mantle. Her Guardian outfit. Not playing agent anymore. Good. Taylor wanted the Guardian in front of her, not the pretend cop.

"Irena."

Irena's gaze left Cordoba. Her brows lifted.

"Is it me, or is it Joe?"

She wondered if the Guardian would lie. Wondered if Irena would pretend not to know what she was talking about.

But Irena didn't even hesitate. "You."

Preston turned in his chair, frowning.

"How?" Taylor pressed before he could say anything. "What'd she see?"

"A vampire. That is all we know."

Fear rose hot and bitter in the back of her throat. She tried to swallow it down. "Why didn't you tell me?"

"I thought you would refuse our protection," Irena said. Something flickered in her eyes, and she added, "And we are not used to sharing with humans."

No shit. But she couldn't even spit that out. Trying to absorb the idea that Khavi had seen her death took every brain cell she had.

"Jesus," Joe said, catching up quick. "Can you change it?"

"We will try."

Which was a far cry from *Yes*, Taylor thought. But she remembered Khavi had said she'd altered her future by refusing to ask about Jason. So it *could* be changed.

And maybe Irena was right; Taylor probably would have told them to go screw themselves if they'd mentioned this to her yesterday. But Khavi showing up in her car had changed that, too.

"I'll take protection," she said. Her fingers didn't shake

when she picked up the two green M&M's and tossed them in her mouth. So she was cool. She was okay with this. Everything would be all right. "I have faith in you guys."

And lucky for her, Castleford hadn't shown up yet, because that was a big fucking lie.

♦

The rooms in the Special Investigations warehouse housed only the necessities and were as austere as a monastery's—but where a penitent might use a cold shower, a vampire used hot. Deacon sweated and gritted his teeth against the scalding blast of water.

He still felt unclean to his soul. Sleep hadn't been an escape, but had given him dreams as vivid and as dark as death. Dreams of Petra screaming, of his bones shattering.

Not just dreams. Memories.

Refusing to look in the mirror, he wiped down, then slung the towel around his hips. He anchored it with one hand, slicked the other through his hair.

Ferocious tension gripped him as he emerged from the bathroom. Someone was in his room. The lights were still off, just as he'd left them. Darkness wasn't dark to a vampire—and he couldn't see anyone.

Then she was there, coalescing out of the shadows.

Rosalia.

Instead of releasing his tension, her appearance squeezed it tighter. She was temptation, every sin in a single package. Crimson silk skimmed her curves from her incredible breasts to her knees and didn't look half as smooth as the pale silk of her skin. The straps of her shoes glittered.

Her smile was sweet and open.

Fuck him. She wasn't sin. Any man could sin. They couldn't have something like Rosalia.

He sure as hell couldn't. "What do you want?"

Unperturbed by his rough greeting, she lifted her hand. A black suit jacket appeared, its collar hooked on her index finger. A pair of trousers draped over her opposite arm. "I brought clothes."

Deacon strode to the foot of the bed, where he'd tossed his pants that morning. "I've got clothes."

Her lips pursed, casting her opinion on the wrinkled fabric.

"*Clean* clothes." Her hips on full swing, she joined him beside the bed. "I can take yours, and they'll be pressed and ready for tomorrow. You'll need at least one change while you're here. Unless you expect to go shopping soon?"

Jesus. He'd rather not. And it was hard to argue with her reasoning. "All right."

"Good." His clothes vanished, replaced by the clean suit, a snowy white shirt, and underclothes. Rosalia sat on the bed next to the pile, selected a pair of black socks, and began picking at the tiny string connecting them. "I went back to Rome."

He'd been about to tell her to haul off, but that stopped him. "To the church?"

"Not the church you found me in. But there was a church, and everything and everyone there was as they should be." Her smile faded. "I found no vampires, though."

Had she thought her brother might have survived? He wondered if she'd hoped to find him or if she dreaded it.

"Do you think your brother knew you were down there with the nosferatu?"

A faint, unreadable smile touched her lips. "Oh, yes."

"He made a deal with them?"

She actually laughed. "A nosferatu wouldn't make a deal with a vampire."

No. Nosferatu hated vampires too much—saw them as an abomination. "Then who . . . ?"

"A demon."

His blood chilled. "You think your brother made a deal with a demon—and the demon made another deal with the nosferatu?"

"Yes." She leaned back. Her warm brown eyes seemed to see through him. "Lorenzo should have known better than to get involved with a demon. It never ends well. It especially never ends well for vampires."

He gave her a sharp glance, but couldn't read anything behind her slight smile. "Now there's no Lorenzo, no vampires. I suppose you won't be going back to Rome."

"Oh, I'll return. I still have obligations to fulfill."

Well, he wasn't going to ask what. And he didn't want to be standing around much longer with her leaning back on his bed like that, the hem of her dress riding high on her thighs. He might be bothered by what she'd just told him, but the bloodlust didn't care. As it was, he was thankful he'd come out of the bathroom holding his towel bunched in the front.

"How about you go get started on those obligations?"

"I am." The bed creaked as she sat up. "I have your dinner."

He allowed himself a glance at her neck. He could dream. "I thought Irena had it."

"She did, but she was going into a meeting. I offered to bring it instead." Two tall glasses appeared in her hands. She hefted one, then the other. "Nosferatu or demon?"

The scent hit him. His fangs ached. "Nosferatu."

Her brow creased. "Are you sure? Too many days of this, and your mind won't be sharp."

Yes, but another day or two on living blood would bring him back to normal. "I'll take that chance."

He'd take any chance that the nosferatu blood would make him even stronger than it already had.

"Did it have any effect yesterday?"

He nodded his head, still amazed by it. A smile tugged at his lips. "Yeah. It did."

A hell of an effect. After leaving Polidori's, he'd returned to the warehouse and joined Echo and Ben sparring in the gym. Older than Echo and Ben, he'd already been stronger, but he judged his speed had increased by half.

His smile faded. Then he'd asked them about accessing the Internet. Ben had helped him secure a laptop from the tech room for his personal use—and Deacon had come upstairs, written out everything he'd learned about Ames-Beaumont, and e-mailed it to Caym.

Rosalia leaned toward him, handing over the glass. "Then I guess it must be worth it."

Her forward movement made her breasts sway. Jesus. Deacon turned his back to her and downed the blood in a few long swallows. There was no reason to savor the taste. As incredible as the scent was, the blood had no flavor.

And it didn't matter that drinking soothed both the hunger and the bloodlust. The combination of Rosalia and the scent left him rock hard.

He continued facing the wall. "You've got one second to get out of here, sister, and then I'm dropping the towel."

"That sounds like reason to stay."

What was she, a tease? His brows lowered, but a buzzing from the dresser stopped him from whipping around and seeing if she'd follow through on that.

In two steps, he grabbed up his phone. The text message shoved his arousal into low gear, but left his anger running.

Send everything you know about Irena. Her territory, her haunts.

Fuck that.

Irena's info isn't part of the deal, asshole.

He sent his reply and turned back to Rosalia. Her dark eyes regarded him steadily, her expression serious.

"Problems?"

He remembered her promise to protect him. Though she was a far cry from the weird, playful vampire she'd pretended to be six years ago, there wasn't anything about her that suggested a warrior. Even with her business face on, she just looked sweet, soft, and sexy.

Irena, though . . .

He shook his head. He wasn't going there. Irena and her band of merry Guardians might tear a nosferatu nest apart, and he knew damn well that she could take care of herself—but the moment Caym sensed anyone coming, he'd kill Eva and Petra. Guardians weren't *that* good. They weren't *that* fast. And Deacon wasn't going to take that risk.

"No problem at all," he said. He slicked his hand through

his hair, trying not to feel impotent and naked . . . and failing. "Why the hell are you in here?"

This time her eyes didn't brighten when she smiled. A wealth of vulnerability sat on the rich curve of her lips. Men harder than Deacon would have been softened by it.

"Because I know you," she said quietly.

So, after losing everything, she was looking for someone even remotely familiar to hold onto. Christ. He couldn't be that. No matter how much he wanted to.

His phone buzzed again. Irritated, he snapped it up.

The picture on the screen showed a knife with a demon's taloned fingers wrapped around the handle. Its blade cut into Eva's throat. Her eyes held terror . . . and a stark plea. The message was short.

New deal. You have 10 minutes.

Deacon deleted the message, looked over at Rosalia. "You don't know me. I don't want to know you, and I don't give a shit about what you think you owe me. So get the fuck out of my face."

Her mouth compressed, her eyes glinted, and for an instant he thought he was wrong about soft. Thought he might be wrong about sweet.

Then she smiled. "I won't bother you again."

The oppressive darkness of her Gift shoved against his psychic blocks. The shadows beneath the bed undulated like tentacles, slithering out over the wooden floor. Deacon stumbled back, but they didn't come after him. Thick tendrils wrapped around Rosalia's heels, coiled up her legs, over her chest, thinning and spreading. In less than a second, the shadows engulfed her in a transparent black cocoon.

They sucked her under the bed as if she were no more substantial than fog.

Good Christ. Deacon dropped to the floor, bending his elbows in a push-up, searching for a sign of her. Only shadows lurked beneath the iron bed frame. Only *normal* shadows.

He rocked back heavily onto his heels, feeling as if his chest had been lined with lead. He thought of Eva, the plea in her eyes. The image forced him to move. He strode to his desk and opened his laptop.

Rosalia had been wrong: She would bother him for a long time. But everything else he'd done—everything he was about to do—was going to bother him more.

❧

A man had to know when to protect his woman . . . but that was difficult when Alejandro wanted to strangle Irena himself.

Strangle her, or fuck her boneless. Maybe for two seconds, while he was deep inside her, her skull would soften enough for him to get through to her thick brain.

But he couldn't now. Not with Michael—himself again—standing at the back of the room. Not with the detectives sitting at the table. Not with Lilith perched on the arm of Castleford's chair, her hand stroking the back of the hellhound lying beside them.

But, good Christ, Irena deserved at least a good shaking. She'd *taunted* Rael. She hadn't put the camera in a bracelet or a pendant, but a sword. And even with the camera facing the demon, Alejandro knew that she'd regarded Rael with a disdainful sneer.

"Julia was a good woman and a good wife."

"Truth," Castleford said quietly.

"He *believes* that is true," Lilith corrected. "She might not have been."

Castleford smiled. "That is true, too."

Alejandro focused on Lilith, trying to read her. He knew Lilith had put Irena on this investigation to watch his back—and then Taylor's, after hearing about Khavi's prediction. Was she regretting that as she watched this recording? For Christ's sake, she thought *him* reckless?

He couldn't tell what Lilith thought now, but Irena was pleased with herself. She watched the video with a sharp smile, her eyes glittering.

Waiting for a lie.

Her voice on the recording caught his attention again.

"Because when we find Anaria, I'm going to cut out her heart and eat it."

Kill Michael's sister.

The tension in the room suddenly thickened. Alejandro rose up on the balls of his feet, ready to put himself between Irena and Michael. His gaze swept to the back of the room.

The tension became a hot lead weight. Michael was frowning at Irena, his brows heavy over his eyes. Not obsidian anymore, but amber, almost human.

Alejandro looked over at Irena.

She steadily held Michael's gaze. Alejandro couldn't see any tension or fear in her. It was only in the rest of them.

Dear God, was she foolish in this, too? While they'd been waiting for Castleford and Lilith to arrive, Alejandro had told her about his encounter with Michael and the Doyen's strange behavior. Irena had seemed to take his concern seriously then. Did she have no sense of self-preservation now?

"Why does that anger him?" Michael asked.

Lilith paused the video. "That's what I want to know."

Know what? Alejandro frowned, wondering what he'd missed. Realization swept over him.

He'd been so focused on Irena and Michael, he hadn't questioned the demon's response. But Rael *should* be trying to kill Anaria, too.

"I didn't think to ask," Irena admitted. "I was too pleased that I'd angered him."

She didn't look amused now, Alejandro saw.

Taylor sighed. "I could've asked, if I'd known. Why isn't it supposed to anger him?"

"Rael is Belial's lieutenant," Michael told her. His frown was thoughtful, Alejandro realized. Not upset. "Rael and all of Belial's demons at Legion have been allying themselves with vampires, because Khavi's prophecy says that vampire blood will destroy the nephilim and will be followed by Belial's rise to the throne in Hell."

"Okay, we got that earlier when we read the prophecy," Taylor said, flicking a glance at Alejandro. "But Anaria?"

"Considering Michael's relationship with Anaria, Rael

might not have known what the Guardians intended to do when we found her," Alejandro said. When he saw that both Taylor and Preston still looked confused, he added, "Anaria is Michael's sister."

Taylor's mouth fell open, and she glanced from Irena to Michael. "Oh. Boy."

Michael smiled faintly.

"And so when Irena said she'd kill Anaria, we expected a different response from Rael," Alejandro said.

"Anaria's death should please him." Michael's gaze remained on Taylor. "She is the nephilim's mother—they are loyal to her. She has to die before Belial can ascend to the throne; it doesn't matter who slays her."

Taylor seemed unnerved by Michael's flat acceptance of his sister's eventual death. "Do you believe that prophecy?"

Michael didn't change, but the sudden psychic heaviness in the room reminded Alejandro of the terror he'd felt earlier. He saw Irena's fists close. Sir Pup's heads lifted. The hellhound's eyes glowed red; his hackles rose. Lilith placed her hand on his back, murmuring to the hellhound in the demon tongue.

"I believe we need to change it," Michael said quietly. His gaze on Taylor was fiercely protective—or threatening. It was difficult to determine. "But not for Anaria's sake."

Taylor swallowed. "Okay. That's just super."

Silence fell, uncomfortable, as charged as static.

"All right," Lilith said, restarting the video. "We'll follow up on this, but unless it relates to Julia Stafford's murder, it's not a priority."

Alejandro met Irena's gaze across the room. She was not listening, he could see, but thinking . . . and unhappy with her thoughts.

What is it? he signed.

Her jaw tightened. *Rael deserves my hatred, but I am stupid to let it blind me.* She sneered and added before he could respond, *Do not say I should not hate demons so much.*

I would not say that.

He wouldn't have. He'd done the same here in this room: let himself be distracted by concerns outside of the investigation.

Her eyes narrowed at him, as if that had just occurred to her, too. *You have also been blinded. Because of my quarrel with Michael—and his recent behavior?*

Aware that the Doyen could see their conversation, he said, *Yes.*

You stupid ox.

Her smile softened the words, and he thought of pushing her up against the wall, down to the floor, into the office next door. He thought of a promise he'd made four hundred years ago and not kept.

Next time, it will not be my hands, but my mouth.

Castleford sat forward. "Replay that."

Alejandro caught himself, forcing his attention back to the screen. One smile from Irena, and he'd *still* been distracted. He couldn't have said what had caught Castleford's interest.

"I know what it is to love a woman and to want nothing more than to lay the world at her feet."

Castleford shook his head in disbelief. "That is truth."

"He loved his wife?" Taylor looked shocked. Alejandro thought her expression spoke for all of them.

"No. Two years ago, Lilith asked him if he loved her. He said yes then, and it was a lie." Castleford asked Lilith to play it again. When it ended, he said, "I don't think he's speaking of his wife."

Taylor and Irena exchanged glances. Taylor said, "Her friend told us that, two years ago, Julia suspected he was having an affair. Then their sex life got better. Could there have been someone else then?"

"Me," Lilith said, and Castleford pinched the bridge of his nose, obviously holding in laughter. "I threatened Rael. I knew he probably didn't screw his wife often—and guessed he was a lousy lay when he did. So I told him I'd use Sir Pup's venom to paralyze him, stick Hugh on top, and take pictures. If he was cold in bed, his wife would probably believe them. So would the *Enquirer.*"

Irena's laugh was low and appreciative. The sound set off the detectives—Preston snorted and Taylor's lips pressed together.

Alejandro fought not to be distracted again. "But your threat gives him a motive, does it not? Without Julia Stafford, you have no hold over him—and cannot threaten his political career."

Lilith considered that, then shrugged. "He might be all right at a local level, but nationally, photos of him having sex with a man could damage his political career whether he was married or a widower. And it's been two years."

"Demons have long memories. He may be speaking of someone dead," Michael said.

"Or not," Irena countered, frowning. "Everyone avoids mentioning this in front of me, as if I will tear Caelum apart if I'm reminded—but Belial's demons *did* try to obtain Anaria for themselves."

Yes, one of Belial's demons had traded a Guardian's life for Anaria while she'd still been locked in her underwater prison. The nephilim had reached her first, however.

Although the Guardians didn't know who had authorized the negotiation, Alejandro assumed that Rael had approved the trade before the demon had brought it to the Guardians for their consideration. The gathering in Caelum, during which the bargain had been discussed, had drawn lines between the Guardians. Irena had wanted to kill Anaria—and had been vocal in her opinion of the grigori, saying that the demons' spawn could be trusted no more than the demons could be.

After the gathering, Guardians—particularly those who worked at SI—had tread lightly on the topic when Irena was in the room. Alejandro thought that a few Guardians expected her to lead a revolt against Michael.

They didn't know her well. The revelation about Michael's parentage had hurt her, deeply. But Irena wouldn't slay Michael for the offense of being born to a demon—and she wouldn't think highly of anyone who waited for *her* to move, if *they* believed Michael should die.

"Why did they want Anaria?" Though Preston's psychic scent burned with curiosity and mild frustration, he didn't ask why they feared Irena might tear Caelum apart.

A diplomatic man, Alejandro thought.

"She studied with Lucifer and created the nephilim," Michael said. "She has extensive knowledge of the symbols and their magic. And so Belial's demons believe she can tell them how to have children, as well."

Taylor held up her hands and looked at Irena. "Okay, wait. So you're saying: Rael falls for some lucky girl . . . and then kills his wife to get her out of the way. And he gets pissed when Irena says she'll kill Anaria, because Anaria might show him how to have little demon babies with the lucky girl. Is that what I'm hearing?"

"I've only said that Belial's demons wanted Anaria alive, despite the prophecy." Irena's eyes glowed with amusement. "I am trying to consider details. You are the one who put them together."

"So I did." Taylor dragged her hands through her tangled red hair. She turned and studied the frozen image on the screen, as if trying to see past the human face Rael wore. "And I can't buy it. I mean, where is this woman?"

"It's a stretch," Lilith agreed. "Pure speculation."

"Yes." Michael nodded at the screen. "We'll pursue the question of the woman later. For now, let's go on."

Alejandro watched the remaining questions, his body tensing through each one. On the recording, Taylor danced closer to the one they wanted to hear, and he couldn't shake the sudden, heavy feeling of impending disaster.

"You obviously didn't hire someone to kill her, risking exposure in the process."

"No, detective. I didn't."

"Lie," Castleford said.

A breathless silence hovered over the room. Alejandro absorbed it, his stomach twisting.

With a feral smile, Irena pushed away from the wall. "That is it, then."

She strode to the door. Alejandro recognized her gliding, effortless step. Irena was on the hunt. She meant to slay Rael now.

Lilith shot to her feet. "Irena—"

"Lilith," Michael said sharply. "No."

Alejandro didn't wait to hear what either had to say. He caught up to Irena as she left the room.

"You have come to talk me out of it." Her accusation echoed in the narrow hall. "Don't try. He killed a human."

"I don't want to stop you."

She cast him a hard glance. "You lie."

"I won't stop you. But I ask that you wait."

Her mouth twisted in a sneer. Her pace increased, and she formed her wings.

His patience snapped. He caught her wrist, twisted, and slammed her face-first into the wall. He shoved his body against her, her wings tight against his chest.

He snarled into her ear, *"Wait."*

Between them, Irena's fingers clamped around his wrist, mirroring his hold on hers. Aside from that small movement, she stood still, her cheek flat against the wall. Her eyes shone bright green.

She could kill him without turning around, he knew. She could break him a thousand ways. But she didn't move.

"You deliberately push me," he realized. "Why?"

"Because you can take it," she snapped. Before he could feel the pleasure of that compliment, her lashes swept down, hiding the glow of her eyes. "And I wanted to see what you will fight for."

His hand tightened on her wrist. "I do *not* fight for Rael." His voice and his fingers bit into her, but he couldn't make himself ease back. This was her opinion of him? "A woman is still dead, Irena. Rael pulled the strings but he didn't pull the trigger, and if you slay him now, we may never know who did."

Her vicious smile appeared again. "I'll make him tell."

"And if he does not? Then her killer is never punished."

"Our purpose isn't to police humans, or to help humans punish each other."

"Not our purpose. But when demons have destroyed human lives, helping to pick them back up should be our *duty*."

She didn't respond, and he prayed she was taking his argument in and giving it due consideration.

In a softer tone, he continued, "That is not the only reason I ask you to wait. Rael must be slain . . . but SI must keep *Thomas Stafford* alive. I need time to prepare for that, Irena. It has to be done carefully."

Her brow creased as she puzzled through his words. He felt the moment she understood. Visceral rejection ripped through her psychic scent. She tore her wrist from his grip.

Alejandro stepped back. He had his reasons solidly outlined, but he couldn't voice them past the tightness in his throat. God, how he'd hoped she would accept his decision. She'd been pleased to hear about Bradshaw's role at the FBI. But she obviously didn't feel the same about his intention to replace Rael.

She turned, pressing her back to the wall. Her wings created a soft frame of feathers around her rigid form. Her eyes glittered.

"That deception will be no different to the people you would serve than Rael's deception is now, Olek."

He saw that it was different. But he knew that every argument he made, Irena would call splitting hairs.

"So be it," he said. "It must be done."

Anger stabbed through her psychic scent. She closed her eyes, averted her face.

He waited, feeling as if his heart was clenched in her fist. It squeezed tighter when she pushed away from the wall. Without looking at him, she strode down the hall toward the exit.

"Irena—"

"I'll wait, Olek. Go do what you must."

Her agreement didn't ease the ache in his chest. He watched until she turned the corner, then listened until he could no longer hear her quiet footsteps.

He drew a deep breath, then returned to the conference room. Michael nodded once, indicating that he'd heard Alejandro's plan to take Rael's position—and was giving his approval.

The Doyen must have already signed the exchange to Lilith and Hugh. Alejandro couldn't read Castleford's face; Lilith regarded him with a bemused expression.

"We should have done this two years ago," she said.

It was too much. He had Michael's approval and Lilith's, when he could not have Irena's. He could not remain here without breaking.

"If we are finished, I have duties to attend to in Argentina."

Duties that required Alejandro's swords to draw blood. He had never looked forward to it more.

"We are." Lilith glanced at Taylor. "Except you. You're staying until Savi comes?"

Taylor nodded. "We'll let you and Cordoba know if we find anything on Margaret Wren."

At the moment, Alejandro didn't care if Wren had enslaved Rael with a bargain and had arranged Julia Stafford's murder herself.

He bowed stiffly and left.

CHAPTER 14

Taylor didn't smoke often—just often enough that a collection of ash had gathered in the one of the empty flowerpots that lined the small balcony of the second-level apartment she and her mother shared. And just often enough that she knew how slowly to open the sliding door so that it wouldn't squeal and wake up her mother—who'd come out, see her lighting up, and give her a look. The daughter of a nurse should know better. *Did* know better. But sometimes didn't care.

She drank a lot more often.

Tonight, she did both.

She didn't have a view, except for her mom's flowerpots—mostly empty for the winter—and the contemporary stylings of a brick wall about three feet from the rail. She glanced down, into the tiny space between houses. Though gates blocked each end of the gap, a vampire could sneak through there, and easily leap up. No vampire was there now. Just garbage cans, a red plastic wagon tipped on its side, and what looked like a beheaded Cabbage Patch Doll.

Fun. The kid living in the house next door was probably

someone she'd meet again, in about twenty years. Then again, maybe not. Sometimes they started out bad, and ended up okay.

She took a sip of her red wine—a glass a day kept vampires and heart disease away, so tonight she was having four. She looked up at the dark sky. Just clouds, and a few wires. She didn't see a Guardian. Somewhere out there, a novice was probably practicing his stalking skills.

Unless they weren't. Maybe they were like the tree in the forest. If she didn't see them, were they there? If they were, she didn't need to raise her voice.

Quietly, she said, "If you're here, you might as well come have a drink with me."

She waited. No wings in the sky. No one hopping over the gates in a single bound. Figured. She turned to stab out her cigarette. She hadn't really expected—

Oh, shit. A large hand came out, covered her wine before she sloshed the contents all over his white linen tunic.

She really should have stopped at just one glass. She blinked up at Michael.

She hadn't expected anyone—but she really hadn't expected *him.* Not the Doyen. And he was the last one she'd have wanted here. Irena might give off mob enforcer vibes, but Michael was the one who scared the crap out of her. Part of it was that he seemed to try to appear nonthreatening, like some kind of guru, but underneath that tunic were ropes of muscle and the chest of a gladiator. Did he think he could *hide* that? And his bare feet— they were fine, as feet went—but the point was, he obviously didn't have to go all out with the steel-toed boots or even the soft leather stockings that Irena wore. His bare feet screamed: *I could rip apart a demon and I'm not even wearing shoes.*

God knew what he could do to humans. And he definitely wasn't one. All the right parts were in all the right places, but he was built like he was solid stone. And he was perfect. Not beautiful in the way Savi's partner was, but more like someone had taken Taylor's idea of masculine perfection and put it in an untouchable, unfeeling form. Like a cosmic joke—except that she wasn't important enough to bother playing it on.

He released her wine. She couldn't decide whether to stop now or just throw it all back in one gulp. It wasn't as if the damage hadn't already been done.

Enough damage that she told him so. "I've had a little too much to drink."

"Is that why you offered to share it?"

His voice made her shiver. Or it was just the cold. "Yes. I sure as hell wouldn't have asked you here sober."

"I know."

Of course he did. He could probably see right into her head. She forced her head back into work. "Savi got the information on Wren—some of it. Butlers make a hell of a salary, apparently. And Wren is making transfers. Big ones." She took another sip. What the hell. "But the CIA stuff? It's not on any computer. There's a list of records, but not the records themselves."

Michael nodded. "I will get them."

"Do I want to know how?"

"No." He studied her wine, her cigarette, as if looking for the reason behind them. And he nailed it in one. "Khavi visited you."

"That she did." With a big smile, she pushed her cigarette out, gestured for him to follow her inside the apartment.

She liked it, mostly. Clean, well-built, nothing fancy. She couldn't imagine what he thought. She'd seen the paintings of Caelum, including his temple—a huge, Parthenon-like structure of shining marble. A whole freaking temple to himself, with columns and statues, and room enough to fit ten of her apartments inside. Maybe twenty.

Welcome to my digs, Doyen. Behold the luxury that can be had on a cop's salary, a widow's pension, and a brother's medical bills.

She didn't have to open Jason's bedroom door—it was never closed. The night-light gleamed off the rails of the hospital bed, the equipment beneath, his eyes. They were open; she hated it when they were open. When they were closed, she could still pretend that when they opened, he'd wake up.

She felt Michael in the doorway beside her. "Can you heal him?"

"No."

Her chest seemed to fold in on itself. She hadn't even admitted to herself how much she'd hoped his answer would be different.

"Would you if you could?"

"Yes."

She turned, walked back out to the balcony. She could do tears. Tears were quiet. But if she got louder, she didn't want her mom to hear, and wake up, and have that burden, too.

Michael said nothing. He stood quietly beside her, his arms folded over his chest.

After a few minutes, she wiped her cheeks. "After Savi was transformed last year, I tried to get rid of her. Stopped talking to her, e-mailing her. But she was such a stubborn little . . ." Taylor shook her head. "She shows up at the station. Somehow, she'd found out about Jason, and she tried to heal him with her blood—a transfusion." She swallowed hard. "My mom doesn't know."

Taylor wouldn't give her hope, just to take it away. They'd gone through that too many times already. A small change in his status. A noise that would sound like a word.

And always, it ended up as nothing.

"Transformation would not work, either. There is too much damage."

"We figured that, and didn't try." She stared at the brick wall. "It was just a stupid, stupid accident. He was on his bike. Hit a pothole. His helmet didn't do what it was supposed to do."

"I'm sorry."

She thought he might mean it. But she didn't want to look at his face and see stone. "Thank you." A deep breath seemed to clean her out. "I've accepted it, mostly. It's been eight years."

"Khavi did not help."

That was the understatement of the year. She lifted her glass to him, finished it off, and said, "So, that's the painful story of my brother. I hear you've got one about your sister. Anaria. What kind of name is that?"

"It is demon, for *sun.* There isn't one in Hell."

"Where does the light come from, then?"

"Pain."

Jesus. That sounded like a joke, except she thought he wasn't kidding. Was he?

Michael sighed.

Michael. "Your name isn't demon."

"No. I was named after a friend of my father's."

She stared at him. "An angel?"

"Archangel. And one of the seraphim. Before the Second Battle, and while I was a boy, they were frequent visitors at my father and mother's table."

When his father had been something other than a demon. Something more, or something less? "What were they like?"

"Beautiful. Kind. I loved them." He smiled slightly. "And I was terrified by them."

Her mouth dropped open. She didn't know which shocked her more—that Michael could *admit* to being terrified, or that something could terrify him.

But she believed him. Aside from that smile, which wasn't exactly full of joy and amusement, his face didn't give much away—yet his eyes had become obsidian.

"Why terror?"

"They make you want to serve them. They cannot help it, and they do not intend their effect—yet it is there. And it is why humans thought they were gods. With angels, the line between free will and compulsion is blurred."

And that alone had frightened him? "Were they very powerful?"

"They could level mountains. They *could* heal your brother."

The emphasis in his voice made her guess, "But they wouldn't?"

"No. Because everything that is not done of free will, is *His* will. And so they would feel sympathy, offer comfort, but they would not change it." He paused. "We would."

The Guardians? "But you can't."

"No," he said. "We can't."

"Why would you change it? Don't you think it is His will— or, or . . . fate?"

"No. It is only chance. If fate determined anything, I would

have no reason to be a Guardian. Nothing we did would matter.
Free will wouldn't matter so much—the Rules wouldn't hinge
on it—if everything is left to chance."

"Even though the *angels* believe it's His will—?"

"Lucifer was an angel once. He made a mistake. They might
have, too."

She had to laugh. "That's one view of the Guardians that I
haven't heard before. Not better than angels—just a little more
willing to admit their mistakes."

"Yes." He smiled again, and the intensity of his look deepened. "Would you become one of us?"

Would she? "Yes. But probably not for the right reasons,"
she admitted. "I'm too much of a coward to die."

His obsidian eyes seemed to absorb the light. "So am I."

Even with the door standing open to the frigid tundra, the forge
was too hot. Irena had fed the furnaces too much before she'd
left, and returned to stifling air that wrapped her in a suffocating cocoon. Each crackle from the hearth fire exploded in her
ears. She couldn't push the heat out.

But she could shut her eyes against the firelight. A tall iron
block stood before her, and she ran her hands down the smooth
sides. She made her mind as shapeless, emptying it of images
and concentrating only on her emotions.

She focused. Her Gift gathered her emotions and shoved
them into the iron, sculpting the metal without her direction.

Irena stepped back and looked. This one was uglier than
usual, pitted and misshapen. Spikes grew out of irregular
lumps, as if a warty boar had belched cactus spines. Twisting
iron ropes with razor edges surrounded dark hollows. She circled around to the back, found a semi-transparent tendril curling over a spike. She flicked her fingernail against it, listened
to the clear chime.

Smiling, she continued her circle. She never knew what to
expect, or what to make of these sculptures. She'd discovered
her Gift this way, in an outpouring of strong emotion. Practice
had lent her control, until she could form an eyelash from steel.

Within three hundred years of her transformation, she'd been able to manipulate metal into lifelike movement, a skill she'd taken great pleasure in.

Yet these mindless sculptures pleased her almost as much. Seeing them always lightened her mood. She'd long thought that her method of creating them was not much different than drifting. Guardians didn't sleep, and most cleared their minds of emotional and psychic buildup by meditating; Irena cleared hers in one push of her Gift.

Despite the similarity of method, however, the sculptures unsettled most other Guardians. Several times, she'd put a selection in the courtyard near her quarters in Caelum so that she could see them as she came and went, and she couldn't help but notice the unease with which Guardians—young and old—had skirted around them. She'd heard their theories about her emotions and state of mind—almost all which had pushed her into laughter. The sculptures she made in her best moods were just as ugly as when she was angry.

Alejandro was one of the few who knew that. It had only been a week before their encounter with the demon, she remembered. They'd spent hours arguing over an essay about nature and beauty that he'd found in Caelum's library and read aloud to her here. Olek had been in agreement with the author; Irena had not. It was that simple, but afterward, Olek had stalked from one end of the forge to the other, reading the essay again—probably looking for a point he could use to sway her. Irena had not minded; the sight of Olek, stalking and determined, had been worth watching.

Until she'd realized that the hungers she'd buried were being uncovered with his every step. Then she'd formed her iron block, blanked her mind, and shoved her emotions into it.

She'd felt Olek's astonishment when he'd turned to see what she'd created. He'd examined it from every angle, then looked at her.

With a hint of laughter around his eyes, he'd said, "This is not anger."

No. Her Gift stripped her emotional shields, and he'd felt

everything she'd put into the block of iron: her contentment, her desire, the deep pleasure of being here with him.

Of course, he'd thought she'd been making an argument of her own.

"I see your point," he'd said. "When there is no will to shape an object, then the only meaning it has is what the person seeing the sculpture gives to it."

She'd been about to remark that his conclusions also said more about him than about her sculpture, but then he'd added, "And when your will shapes the metal, the result is nothing but what you intend it to be. All of those statues of me—they are just that: me. No one could mistake them for anything else, or read any more meaning into them."

She could not answer then—she had been laughing too hard. If anyone with eyes looked at the statues she'd made of him, they would know instantly how beautiful she'd thought him. How every plane and angle of his body had become a new landscape to explore beneath her hands. How she had fought to understand why the tightening of his fingers had so many meanings, in what combination his brows and eyes and lips would tell her what he thought. It was all there, in each sculpture she'd made.

Olek hadn't seen it, but he'd never seen himself as she did. She'd laughed as he declared that she'd misunderstood his arguments. And he'd finally tossed away the essay, and invited her to spar with him, instead.

That had been a memorable day—one of many memorable days with him, in a life that had grown very long and the years indistinguishable.

Irena sighed and returned to the front of her latest sculpture, running her fingers over one of the ridged bumps. She missed those days almost as much as she treasured them.

And it had been so long since they had fought so well together. She wanted to recapture it . . . but once again, she had no idea how to move forward. If he would take a demon's role, she didn't see how it could be done.

Icy air touched the back of her neck. The forge had finally cooled. She walked to the open door and stopped, shielding her eyes and looking out over the windswept snow.

In the brilliant midday sun, the plain shimmered a blinding white. Half a kilometer distant, three figures trudged through the snow toward her forge. Two men, one woman—each dressed in a bright, bulky coat, synthetic pants, and heavy boots that told her they'd come from a city.

A psychic probe confirmed they were human. Irena searched the horizon behind them, but didn't see any vehicles. They'd been traveling for a while, then.

One of the men lifted his arm. Irena waved, then headed back inside.

Unease prickled at the back of her neck. She paused, glanced over her shoulder. Another psychic probe confirmed the first: They were human.

It wasn't the first time travelers had stopped here, whether lost or simply heading through. Reindeer farmers moved their herds across these plains during the summer, sometimes camping within a stone's throw of her forge. There had been tourists, surveyors. She'd never turned anyone back.

She would, however, be careful.

With a mental pull, she called in her pantry from her cache. The fifty-year-old bread would still be fresh, and there were enough canned goods to feed the three humans for a week, if necessary. She set the rustic table near the central hearth, called in an aluminum hip bath and a stuffed tick mattress piled high with furs.

When she was done, her forge looked like the home of an eccentric sculptor who lived very simply. She'd learned years ago that calling herself an artist provided unspoken answers to many questions about her lifestyle.

She returned to the door and looked out. They were making good time. Her unease began to crawl down her spine.

Inhospitable or not, she didn't want these people in her home.

Without giving herself a chance to reconsider, Irena formed her rabbit-fur mantle over her shoulders, and walked out to meet them. If she had to, she would carry them back to civilization.

An icy crust lay over the snow. Her feet broke through with every step, sinking two or three inches to the compact snow beneath. Now and then, she sank farther—up to her knee, or thigh.

They were doing the same, she saw. Stupid of them, and a sign of their inexperience in this terrain. If they'd walked in single file, the one in the lead could break the trail, and the others could follow in his steps. They'd be exhausted by the time they reached her. As far as they'd come, they probably already were exhausted.

But they should have been breathing harder than they were.

Irena watched their mouths, the frozen puffs of air. Each was as even as hers. Impossible.

Dread dragged over her skin like icy fingernails. Her psychic probe *had* encountered an unshielded human mind. A demon couldn't mask that. Which meant they had to be nephilim.

Three nephilim.

Terror bulged in her chest, rose thick and acrid in her throat. She swallowed it down. She strengthened her psychic shields, refusing to let her fear leak through. The nephilim hadn't tried to reach out to her mind yet—doing so would reveal the demon inside theirs. So they were hiding. Probably waiting until she came closer.

In their human forms, nephilim were weaker than vampires—but they could shape-shift almost instantly.

Fifty meters separated them now.

Her heart pounded. Irena hoped they couldn't hear it yet. She pinned on a smile and prayed they'd be fooled by the welcome. Prayed they'd let her come closer. Prayed she'd have time to slay just one before they shifted to their demonic forms.

According to Drifter—one of two Guardians who'd fought the nephilim—in their demonic form they were many times stronger and faster than he was, a century-old Guardian. Irena was much faster than Drifter, too. But was she fast enough to survive against three nephilim?

Despair cried out beneath the fear. She silenced it and forced herself to think. Tried to grab onto something amidst the slippery slope of hopelessness.

Olek.

Olek had once slain a nephil by using explosives. Irena didn't have any. But she had her Gift. She knew how to fight on this snow-packed plain. In her cache, she carried the vampire blood that weakened and slowed them.

Hot determination suddenly burned away every other emotion.

Ten meters. The male in the center had pretty blue eyes and thick brown eyelashes. His frosted breath covered his upper lip. He smiled and called out a greeting in Russian.

They *all* smiled, the boar-fucking bastards.

Irena grinned back at them. *Look well, hellspawn. I might die, but these teeth will be in your throat.*

The male on the left took a step and broke through the ice-crusted snow to his hip. It was an advantage Irena hadn't expected. She didn't waste it.

Irena leapt, shooting toward him with her knees close to her chest, making herself as small a target as possible. Before she'd covered half the distance, he shape-shifted. His clothes vanished. His frame lengthened, muscles bulging beneath pale skin that deepened to crimson as it stretched. The whites of his eyes hardened to obsidian stones. Huge black feathered wings whipped open, flinging snow. A sword glinted in his right hand, and he swung the blade into the path of Irena's leap.

She called in an iron block, let it fall heavily in front of her and followed it down. Snow crunched. She flattened herself against the side, using the block as a shield. The nephil's sword struck a ringing blow on the opposite side.

He hadn't expected the block. She pictured him on the other side, his arm extended, his sword shivering from the impact.

She shoved her Gift through the iron. She didn't have to see the deadly blades that razored out from the block and sliced toward his neck and chest. She heard the rending of his flesh, felt the resistance of bone.

To her right, the female shrieked with rage. She plowed toward Irena with terrifying speed, a stone battle-ax over her head.

Irena couldn't outrace her. She'd barely have time to start running before the female was on her. Heart in her throat, Irena formed handholds in the block and flung herself up and outward. The female veered in the same direction, throwing her ax.

The ax struck Irena midair, a glancing blow to her arm. It knocked her aside, forced her to spin, but she managed to create a smooth disk beneath her as she hit the snow. The aluminum disk raced over the icy crust, carrying her away from the female, who'd set her feet in anticipation of Irena's landing.

Part of Irena's arm lay on the snow next to her. A trail of blood followed the path of Irena's sled.

With a burst of laughter, Irena looked down at the stump below her elbow. Not a glancing blow. And a good thing she'd prepared for this. Her lips drew back from her teeth, and she leapt off the disk. The female was almost on her again, ax in hand.

Focusing her Gift, Irena shaped a new forearm and hand of steel and clamped it around the stump. She called in her shield over it, just in time to block the nephil's ax.

The blow staggered her. The impact tore through her body. Feeling as if she'd been ripped apart, Irena dug her feet into the snow, and barely recovered in time to intercept the next swing.

The nephil was fast. Too fast for Irena to mark the male nephil's position. She needed every instant to track the female's movements, to defend against the stone weapon. Looking away for a moment meant death.

Not looking away to find him meant the same.

She couldn't hear his steps or wings over the crash of the ax and shield. He wasn't in her field of vision. Behind her, then. And so this would be the end.

Despair screamed a dire warning beneath her racing heartbeat. Irena barely avoided a pummeling blow that would have shattered her head, and searched desperately for an opening for her blade. She pulsed her Gift constantly, forcing the heavy steel arm into natural motion, waiting for the strike of a sword against her neck from behind.

She felt an electric charge sizzle through the air, instead. A familiar Gift hummed against her psyche.

Jake. Oh, sweet Jake. She had never loved the young Guardian more.

The nephil felt the psychic hum. As she brought down the ax, her eyes darted to the side, as if to check *her* back.

Irena lunged. She vanished her shield and caught the edge of the stone ax in her steel palm. Pain shot through her shoulder, bearing the force of the blow. She clenched her teeth and swiftly unraveled her metal forearm. Within the space of a blink, thin steel wires spun out, wrapped around the ax handle, and pierced the nephil's wrist. Irena forced the wires into the nephil's arm like hungry worms. They coiled around bone, stabbed through the muscles in her shoulder to her neck.

The female's eyes widened with shock and terror. The veins in her throat bulged and exploded through her crimson skin with gouts of blood.

Irena yanked her arm back. The wires ripped free in a scarlet spray. With her right hand, she followed through with her blade, slashing through the shredded flesh and spine that remained.

Spinning around, she remade her forearm and prepared for another attack. The nephil wasn't behind her. Alice raced toward her instead, her black skirt flapping like crow's wings. Fifty meters beyond Alice, beside the iron block, Alejandro battled the last nephil. Their swords rang in a flashing frenzy of steel, Alejandro falling back before the nephil's speed.

Irena's heart climbed into her throat. She'd barely taken a step toward them when Alice's shout reached her.

"Get down!"

Irena automatically looked up at the sky, searching for a winged threat. Nothing. She started for Alejandro again.

Jake teleported in behind the nephil. Irena had an instant to realize that the young Guardian was slinging a belt of plastique and wires around the nephil's waist before Jake teleported and reappeared behind Alejandro. They both vanished—and reappeared beside Alice.

Irena met Alejandro's eyes. He dived, catching her legs, and tumbling her into the snow. His body shielded hers, his hands covered her ears.

The explosion rocked him against her. Pressure swelled in her head. Hot air whipped past them. Irena's exposed skin tightened, felt like it would split. Alejandro swore and his Gift sucked in the heat like a sharp inhalation. The air cooled.

After a long second, pieces of charred flesh rained down in heavy splatters.

Irena lay stunned. *She was alive.* Alive, with snow melting against her back, Alejandro's taut body pressing down on hers, his ragged breath in her hair. He murmured her name.

Then his mouth found hers and invaded in fierce possession. Irena welcomed it. He tasted of fire and blood, and she drew him deeper, chasing away the dread and despair that had threatened to devour her whole.

The moment was too brief. The shattering pain of battle engulfed her body. Taken by surprise, Irena made a sound deep in her throat. She turned her head and clamped her lips to prevent it from escaping as a whimper.

Alejandro's mouth touched her jaw, and then he was standing, holding his hand out for hers.

Jake's voice rumbled distantly through the ringing in her ears. "See? Just friends. That was *exactly* what friends do."

Irena sent him a killing look as Alejandro pulled her up by her real hand. Beside Jake, Alice's prim expression lost its fight against a smile.

"Then you and I must be quite good friends," Alice told him. Her brown hair had come loose of its braid. She held Irena's bloodied forearm at her side, caught in the shifting folds of her skirt. Her pale gaze met Irena's across the snow, and she lifted the severed arm. "How ridiculous you are!" she called out. "If you had wanted practice, you know there is a queue of former students waiting to chop off a piece of you. You did not have to call on the nephilim."

Irena couldn't manage a smile—couldn't even manage a breath. She could, however, use her Gift to lift her steel middle finger in a gesture that expressed her feelings perfectly. Despite the amused *tsk*ing sound Alice made, concern filled her psychic scent.

Jake frowned. He called in his electrical ground and vanished.

When Alice reached them, Alejandro took the arm. He turned to Irena. "Are you ready?"

Irena nodded. She closed her eyes and vanished the steel arm. Agony shrieked up from the stump and through her shoulder.

They worked quickly. Within seconds, Alice had wrapped her arm in black silk bandages, and created a sling to support its dead weight. Irena opened her eyes as Alice knotted the straps of the sling together.

"It is crude," Alice said as she vanished the blood from her hands. "But it will hold your arm together until Jake returns with Drusilla."

Irena's nod set off a series of stabbing pains through her chest and stomach. Warm liquid heaved into her mouth, and she spat blood. Slowly, she sank to her knees. She just had to remain still. Very, very still.

Alejandro crouched beside her. He reached for her, but stopped himself, clenching his hands into fists by his thighs. They remained that way, silent, until Jake's Gift crackled through the air.

A second later, Dru dropped to her knees in front of her. Her blue eyes widened as they ran over Irena's face. "Oh, Lord, you're a mess." She reached for Irena's hand. Her healing Gift probed gently, testing the injuries. Dru sucked in a breath. "Jesus. Did they pulverize you?"

"They didn't have to." The bitter cold froze Olek's words into thin icy clouds. "She blocked the nephil's ax. Even Irena can't absorb those blows without damage."

Dru nodded. Her Gift slid deeper, and warmth spread through Irena's muscles. Sensation returned to her arm, first as a tingle over her skin; then feeling returned in a sweet rush. Her shoulder slid painlessly back into place.

The constriction around her lungs eased, and Irena breathed out a thank-you.

Dru smiled tightly. She eased back on the heels of her red tennis shoes. She turned her head, as if taking in the churned, bloodied snow, the shallow crater, the overturned iron block.

She looked back at Irena. "It was close?"

The constriction was suddenly there again, around Irena's throat, squeezing her heart. She clenched her teeth and nodded, then dropped her chin against her chest.

Dru turned to Alejandro. "I can leave her with you?"

"Yes." He bit out the word, as if he couldn't believe she'd had to ask.

"Good." Unfazed by his anger, Dru rose to her feet. "Jake, Alice—we're out of here. Now."

She used the tone that only a fool would argue with. Neither Jake nor Alice protested, and a moment later, they vanished.

Alejandro only had to touch her. His fingers brushed her cheek, and the raw despair Irena had fought to keep in check welled up.

Curling forward, she buried her face against his chest, holding in a scream of desolation. Death had been *so* close. If Jake had been a second later. If the nephil hadn't looked to the side. She'd felt death at her back before, but never, *never* had it been so pointless and empty. Never had she stood to lose so much for nothing.

Alejandro's arms tightened around her. Her fingers bunched in his shirt.

She had almost lost so much.

Alejandro lifted her up against his chest. His wings formed. Silently, he turned toward the forge, and carried her into the air.

CHAPTER 15

The moment Alejandro stepped over the threshold, he felt every second of the four hundred years he'd been gone.

Everything was the same. The furnaces along the back wall. The central hearth that Irena kept lighted for no reason that he'd ever seen. The pantry and table that she'd used for guests, the hip bath. Centuries of footsteps had trampled the earthen floor into a surface as hard as stone.

Everything was the same but them. The two Guardians who had left here together four hundred years ago were not the Guardians who returned.

And when they left again, he vowed that something would be changed between them. They would not leave with everything unsettled.

He paused a few steps inside. He turned away from the bed, though part of him wanted to settle that first—but not while she still shuddered with fear and relief. He moved toward the bath just as Irena lifted her head.

"I need to wash," she said.

He nodded and set her down. Dru had vanished the blood.

Irena probably didn't know how she'd looked before that. Her face had been as crimson as the demon's, painted with their blood and hers.

But Irena wasn't washing for that reason, he thought, pushing the tub closer to the wall and turning on the taps. A system of pipes ran from the cistern outside—one pipe heated by the furnaces so that hot water filled the tub. Four hundred years ago, he'd thought her bath was the most amazing luxury. They'd both used it often.

Now, she climbed into the tub fully clothed and submerged herself completely. Taking solitude, Alejandro realized. Walking away and hiding her vulnerability, but this time without leaving.

The quiet of the forge was only disturbed by the crackling of the fires, the steam in the pipes, the drip from the taps. He heard the indistinct beat of her heart, muffled by the water.

He was glad of the moment to himself.

As soon as Alejandro sank onto the sofa, shaking overtook him. A delayed reaction, he knew. He'd felt it before. When his youngest son had been eight, the boy had darted into the path of a galloping horse. Alejandro had seen him knocked beneath the pounding hooves. But when he'd pulled Eduardo from the ground, the boy hadn't suffered more than muddied knees and a skinned elbow.

It had been one of the few times in his life that Alejandro had raised his voice. He was not a man of violence, although he would use violence when duty demanded it. But that day, without demand or prompt, Alejandro had shaken and shouted at the boy until Eduardo had been in tears and trembling.

Only afterward, when he'd been alone, had he fallen to his knees and thanked God.

The sheer force of his will had prevented him from doing the same to Irena today. After the explosion, after he'd kissed her—it had taken all of his strength not to shake her. And as they'd waited for Dru to arrive, it'd taken all of his strength not to hold her to him and weep his thanks to God.

He knew that modern science had given names to it. Adrenaline. Endorphins. Those chemicals might work the same in

Guardians as in humans, when struck with the sheer terror of realizing how close his world had come to shattering.

Irena, he thought, had realized it, too. She knew how close it had been.

When his shakes eased, he rose to his feet to study the sculpture she'd left near the center of the forge. He'd wager that she'd made it after she'd left him at SI. He wished it gave him some insight into what her feelings had been. Had she begun to accept his decision? Or was her rejection still as strong?

He fed the hearth fire, burning low in the shallow iron bowl set within a waist-high ring of stones, then wandered the room and examined the few changes she'd made. On a shelf sat a plastic winged monkey that was a recent gift from Drifter's partner Charlie—Alejandro had heard about the gift, even if he hadn't seen it before.

From beside the monkey, he lifted a framed icon and quietly regarded the Virgin's mournful eyes and adoring face. Irena had never owned—or sculpted—many religious objects. The small icon might have been a gift from one of the villagers Irena helped support during the long winter months, as was the rag doll propped on the shelf. He remembered her receiving another doll four centuries earlier. Perhaps it had rotted by now— or at some point, she had offered it to a different girl.

He replaced the icon and continued on. New weapons topped the discard pile next to the wall. Though she always said she'd find another use for the metal, she never had. At the bottom of the pile were rusted swords almost a thousand years old. Alejandro knew some of his would be in there.

He'd lied to himself. All these years, he had lied to himself. Two hundred years ago, when she'd returned from her self-imposed exile, he'd told himself that he'd accepted they wouldn't be together. That there was no future. But until Alejandro walked back into the forge, he'd been lost.

And all this time, he'd been waiting to come home.

His chest aching, he returned to the sofa where he'd spent so many hours studying—and reading aloud to her once he'd realized that she had difficulty ordering the letters. She hadn't stubbornly remained illiterate, as he'd initially thought; she could read *because* she was stubborn and had forced herself past the difficulty. She simply took no pleasure in it. But she enjoyed listening, and so he'd often read to her.

She probably would not enjoy listening to the files he had pulled from Rael's office, so he read through them while he waited for her to emerge.

Almost an hour later, the ripple of water brought him out of an education reform bill choked with useless additions and meaningless language. Irena was sitting up, the water lapping at her bare shoulders. A small frown creased her brow.

"Why am I not dead? I killed the first nephil, but I could barely hold my ground against the female. Why did the second male not come up behind me?"

Had she been ruminating over the battle all this time? Or was that simply what had pulled her up?

"The first wasn't dead yet," Alejandro told her. "The other male was holding him when we teleported in."

Her eyebrows shot up in surprise. "Comforting him?"

"Yes."

"No demon would do that for another."

"They are not the same as demons. They are siblings." When she remained quiet, he frowned. "I hope you are not doubting yourself—"

"No." She stood and water cascaded into the bath. "They were here to kill me. They massacred communities of vampires. I do not doubt that I should have struck first." She cast him a wry glance. "But I *can* wish that they did not care for each other."

Yes, it was the same difficulty with their mother. Anaria's intentions were good, but if her plans meant that she would prevent humans from acting freely, the Guardians couldn't allow her to carry them out. It wasn't just a difference of opinion and method; agreeing to disagree didn't work when one of the parties insisted on imposing its will over the other.

Irena shook her head vigorously, flinging water in a wild spray. She stepped out of the tub and vanished the rest of the moisture from her clothes.

She walked to the hearth, bending close to the fire and pushing her fingers through her hair, letting the heat dry it. Her mind was still on the battle. "Why did you not have Jake use his blade when he teleported behind the nephil?"

"He likes explosives," Alejandro said.

She glanced at him sharply. Her mouth curved. "And you, too?"

He enjoyed knowing that the nephil hadn't just been killed, but obliterated. "I understand the appeal." When she laughed, he continued, "How did they find you?"

She gave him a look that told him he'd either said something obvious, or something she'd have no way of knowing—but either way, he was an idiot.

A moment later, he realized she was right. "Your Gift," he said. A nephil might have been miles away and still have felt it. "You will want to check on the vampire communities in your territory."

He knew she did regularly, but if the nephilim were in the area, it was best to check as soon as possible.

"Yes. I will visit them each when night falls." Her gaze landed on the files stacked by his thigh. "What have you been reading?"

He felt his chest tighten again. He couldn't avoid this. "The files from Rael's office. Legislation, correspondence. For the investigation, and so that I will have the information I need after I take his position." When she didn't respond, but stood pulling her fingers through her hair, he began roughly, "Irena—"

"No." She straightened and flipped her hair back. "No fighting now. I have had enough for today."

Alejandro battled his frustration, then nodded. "Was it a good fight?"

She took her time answering, poking at the fire and staring into the flames. Finally, she said, "Yes. Yes, it was, though it almost ended badly. It would have, if you hadn't come with Jake and Alice." She looked to him. "What brought you here?"

He would have come anyway, to try to convince her that taking Rael's place would be *right*. But they were trying not to fight. "Jake wanted to compare the spikes that he found on Zakril's skeleton to the spike that had pinned Rosalia."

Irena frowned, but didn't comment on the thousands of years separating the two incidents. Demons often had an individual method of operation—and pounding iron spikes through Guardians and into stone wasn't common. Zakril and Rosalia were the only two Alejandro knew of who'd been pinned that way.

"We will have to compare them tomorrow," she said. Her gaze studied his face. "But that is not why *you* came."

He searched for a reason that had nothing to do with Rael. He stood, calling in one of the swords she had given him in the church. The blade had snapped in half. "I have two swords left," he said. "I need more."

A fierce light came in her eyes. She took the sword from him, examining it. "When did this happen?"

"Tonight."

"In Argentina?"

"Yes. It was a fine sword," he said—unnecessarily, by the chiding look in her eyes. Yes, she knew the quality of her work. "But the demon traded his sword for two maces when I did not expect it."

A risk for the demon, changing weapons midair—but one that had paid off. Irena's gaze ran quickly over him, as if looking for any sign that he'd been injured. She turned toward the furnaces, tossing the sword away. It clanked against the other discarded weapons.

"You are lucky Jake was with you, then."

Alejandro followed her to the worktable. "He was not."

"Who was your backup?" She formed her apron and arranged her tools on the bench. "Have you begun specialization with a novice?"

"I went alone."

Her fingers froze above a hammer. "Alone against two demons?"

"I'd already assessed their skill. They weren't a threat."

"Except for when your sword breaks." She turned on him. "Of all the stupid, reckless—"

"We are not fighting tonight," he reminded her, barely holding on to his own temper. Did she think him an untrained fool?

Her jaw clamped so hard, Alejandro was surprised her teeth did not shatter. She turned her back to him, laid a billet of steel on the anvil, and began to hammer.

The pounding, painful ring stabbed at his ears. Each blow had to be hurting her ears, hurting her arm.

"No matter how hard you wish, that will not be my head."

She glanced over her shoulder. He saw her lips twitch. Her Gift pulsed, and the steel on the anvil became a miniature sculpture of him.

She tapped her hammer against the head. "I will pound sense into you, until you admit it was reckless. It is one thing if you come across two demons and must fight them. But to go into a fight against two? You cannot guard against a broken sword."

He did not point out that his sword had broken, and yet he had still won. He did not point out that a sword could break no matter how many demons surrounded him. She was trying not to fight. So would he.

He held his tongue and let it go. This would not be settled tonight.

She turned back to her anvil and vanished the steel figurine. She laid the hammer on the bench. Her hands clenched on the edge of her worktable, the smooth muscles in her arms hardening. The serpents danced in the firelight, vibrant with life.

When her forearm had been severed, the tattoos decorating the unattached limb had barely resembled snakes. Those crude blue lines had been shaped by an unskilled hand, but *these* were Irena's. Her body shifted to create the designs that moved over her skin. He wondered if she knew that they changed. Wondered if there was anything conscious in the way they seemed to coil, waiting.

Waiting to see if he would fight?

So be it. If only one thing was settled today, it would be that he would not give her up.

He did not try for silence as he approached her still form. Her fingers squeezed tighter on the table with his every step. She didn't look around when he stopped behind her.

The tension inside him drew taut. Four hundred years had passed and so much had gone wrong between them. Now, it had to be right—and he remembered one time when everything between them had been fiercely right.

With a silent prayer on his lips, he lowered his mouth to the side of her neck, and pressed a soft kiss beneath her ear.

Irena's breath slipped out as a sigh. She tilted her head, lengthening the bare line of her throat. Damp auburn strands clung to her nape in spikes. He brushed them aside and trailed his mouth lower, opening his lips to the flavor of her skin. Her pulse beat frantically beneath his tongue.

"Olek." Her whisper was as thick as the blood pounding in his veins. "Do not begin this if you cannot finish."

If he could not take her to completion? Satisfy her? He accepted that challenge. But he would never be *finished*.

In answer, he flattened his hands to her sides and slipped them beneath her apron, the heavy leather dragging against his knuckles. She wore nothing beneath. The swell of her breasts filled his palms. He found her nipples, stiff with need, and gently pinched the rigid peaks. Irena arched into his hands, a rough sound of pleasure in her throat. Her desire spilled through her psychic scent, pouring over his mind and body like heated oil.

Holy God. Need speared through his shaft, bringing him to instant, aching hardness. He fought for control. Fought the urge to lift her onto the table and plow deep.

He couldn't control the heat flaring across his skin.

Irena's psychic shields were open. Her felt her hunger—and in quick succession, her rejection, her shame, her anger—before she closed to him. Alejandro froze.

The demon's skin would have been hot, too. No other man's would have been. No vampire, no Guardian. Only Alejandro's would remind her of the demon in this way.

His heart tightened painfully. He couldn't do this to her.

He began to draw away. Irena clapped her hands over his, holding his palms to her chest. Though her apron separated their fingers, he felt the trembling in hers.

"Can you not finish, after all?"

Alejandro closed his eyes. And so this was why she'd made the challenge earlier. She'd known she might react this way to his touch. She'd known what his response to *her* reaction would be.

"Irena—"

"It is *here*, Olek. In me, though I hate it. Though I've fought it. Though I *know* it is not him. That it is not you. It is not—no." Her voice cracked, then hardened with brittle determination. "This is not what I mean to say."

His throat a burning knot, he waited, calling himself a fool. He'd thought to turn back the clock four hundred years, but that was impossible. He could not ignore those centuries.

They'd been four hundred years in which she'd fought what the demon had done to her. In which she had feared not being able to separate the demon from Alejandro. In which she'd thought that his guilt upon causing her any kind of pain would be greater than his need to stay, that he would have left her alone because his bludgeoned honor demanded he atone for his failure.

He wanted to shake her. Wanted to shout that he wouldn't have given up if she'd given *him* one damn sign that she'd needed him with her. Always, she'd faulted him for the size of his pride.

Irena's pride could fill oceans.

But he could not go back and prove himself. He could only stand with her now.

"What do you mean to say?"

Her deep breath lifted her breasts against his hands. "I hunger for you. The rest is"—she flicked her fingers toward the pile of discarded swords—"damaged. But I will make another, and I will make it better."

Ah, Irena. Her memories of the demon could not be discarded so easily—and neither could his reluctance to remind her of them. And unlike the swords, they could not replace flawed steel with new materials; they could only reshape what they had with the strength of their will.

And heat.

Alejandro bent his head to her nape. He could reshape this, too. Rather than trying to recapture the past, he would use it to give her security. She could prepare herself for his next touch. He'd only follow the path he—and the statue she'd made of him—had taken before. A kiss down her back. Then his fingers in her slick, silken heat. And he would not rush, he promised himself.

No matter how difficult she made it for him to keep that promise.

Beneath his hands, Irena responded like a flame, tiny flickering movements fed by a sweep of his thumbs, the touch of his breath. A flame, but she was still controlled, contained. He needed her burning higher.

He lowered to his knee, kissing his way down her spine. Her skin shivered under his tongue. His fingers found the apron's ties.

In his mind, he had done this a thousand times. Bared her. Watched her head fall back, with the firelight warming her throat. It had never been with this enormous pressure in his chest. Or the frustration of being unable to see her face and read her emotions.

These small flickers of movement, the tiny sounds of her response, were not enough.

Patience, he reminded himself.

But patience was slipping away.

"You hold yourself back, Olek."

The accusation in her voice was a sharp prod. His hands on her hips, he surged to his feet and spun Irena to face him. He lifted her onto the table, bringing her almost level to his height, and pushed between her leather-clad legs.

Her gaze targeted his mouth. Her eyes glittered.

He tangled his fingers into her hair. Brought his lips a razor's width from hers. "You hold yourself back, too."

"I wait to see what you will do."

What *he* would do? As if he would do nothing.

His blood pounded and urged him on, but it was with slow deliberation that he claimed her mouth. Slow . . . slow. He savored the taste of her, teased her lips open. Then Irena's fingernails dug into his back and he thrust against the rough heat of her tongue, need riding over him.

With effort, he slowed again. Irena growled in her throat. He tore his mouth from hers, spoke harshly against her jaw.

"I will *not* take you in a frenzy. I have waited too long." He ground his erection against her sex. She lifted to him with a husky moan that almost pushed him over the edge. "And if I come inside you now, I will *come inside you now.*"

"I have waited, too. So I will take it."

His eyes closed. "Perhaps you will. My pride will not."

She laughed, and he pulled back to see her face. His heart kicked, hard. By all that was holy, she was stunning. Strong. And he had to see more of her.

"You want to know what I will do?" He hooked his fingers in the neckline of her apron. "I will remove this."

"That is all?"

His gaze fell to the vee of her thighs. His stomach clenched with need. "No. I also have a promise to keep."

She hesitated. Her lashes dropped, hiding her eyes.

No. Brash, earthy Irena wouldn't look away when a man spoke of taking her with his mouth. But she would if she felt vulnerable or afraid.

He jerked his hand back. Her gaze snapped to his. He sensed her sudden anger, and his temper rose to meet it.

"I *will* finish this, Irena." But not in anger. And not with Irena battling herself every step of the way.

Curse that bastard demon. Irena ripping the creature apart hadn't been enough. Alejandro would've given anything to put the demon back together just to rip him apart again.

Feeling his control slip, he turned abruptly away from her to stalk across the forge. The light from the hearth fire stung at his eyes. How had this happened? He could never have imagined these hesitations when they finally came together, these false starts. One touch had always been enough for need to take over. Christ, they hadn't even had to touch. All it took was a look. Need had never been a problem. The problem had been preventing himself from going to her, stripping her naked, and staking his claim in the most basic, barbaric way a man could.

Yet now he had to force himself to push forward. Force himself to kiss her, and try, for God's sake, to forget that she had to *give herself permission* to enjoy it. The very thought revolted him; he could only imagine how fiercely Irena hated it.

But he also couldn't stomach the thought of avoiding her again.

The path they were on now was right. They had kept from each other for too long. But, by God, he simply could not find his footing.

He stalked past the bed lying next to the wall. He wanted to burn it. Wanted to slash the furs to pieces. He could go back to her now with this frustration pounding at him, this hurt, and they would fuck on her worktable or the floor and he would lose himself in her. He knew it. Passion rode that edge with them, and never allowed for hesitation.

But why was it so damned impossible to make love to her without anger between them?

He stopped at the hearth and slipped his hand into the shallow bowl of fire. Pain licked at his fingers before he drew on his Gift and pulled the heat from his skin. With a soft nudge of power, the dying flames roared upward.

This, he could control.

But where was Irena's fire? She responded to him, yes. But she had always burned hot on her own. Where was that now?

Without warning, she grabbed his arm from behind and wrenched it back, out of the flames.

"You stupid ox," Irena hissed. "If you must burn yourself . . . to . . ."

Her voice faltered as he spread his fingers. She stared at the unmarked skin. He watched her fists clench, and the hard fury come into her eyes.

"You didn't tell me you can do that," she said with a carefully neutral tone that might have terrified a novice.

She wanted to hit him, Alejandro realized, and suddenly he felt like laughing. "In four centuries, there is much I haven't told you," he pointed out. In a single movement, he caught her waist and swung her up onto the stone ringing the hearth. Before she could flinch away from the flames, his Gift surrounded her. "Such as discovering that I only burn when I must create my own heat."

Her brow creased. "You aren't hurt by any other fire?"

"No. And this close, I can also protect you."

Her gaze held his. Deliberately, she leaned back, suspending herself over the dancing orange and yellow tongues. Only his hands at her hips prevented her from toppling over into the bed of coals.

He didn't need to ask if she trusted him. Earlier, she had given him control—even though that wasn't her nature, any more than it was his nature to control her.

Perhaps that was where they had stumbled.

He pushed aside a charred piece of wood, sending up a shower of sparks. When there was an even bed of embers with no sharp edges, he lowered her into the hearth. She lay before him like a pagan sacrifice, her upper body surrounded by fire. The air shimmered around her; her eyes glowed as fiercely as the coals.

"Tell me, Irena." He slid his fingers beneath her loosened apron. "Tell me to keep my promise . . . and to keep you safe."

Irena vanished the apron. Her nipples were the delicate pink of an oyster's shell, brushed with coral by the orange light of the fire. It took everything in him not to bend his head and suck at her wildly.

A smile curved her mouth. "Keep your promise, Olek."

She didn't say the rest, he knew, because she thought it was both obvious and stupid. *Of course* he would keep her safe.

Still, he didn't move. "Tell me how."

Her eyes narrowed. "Put your mouth on me before I kill you."

Better, but not enough. "If you kill me, you will burn."

With a snarl of frustration, Irena reared up and grabbed his hair. She dragged him down into the flames with her, shoved his lips to her breast.

At the first lick, her snarl softened into a moan. Pleasure skimmed over her psychic scent, then plunged as he drew her deep into his mouth, circling his tongue around her hardened nipple.

She pulled at his hair. "More."

Both the demand and gentle pain rippled through him, sweet and hot. Yes. This was what he'd needed, too. For Irena to make demands, so that he could fulfill them. He licked and teased his way across her chest. He rocked against her, his heated shaft grinding against her core. Sparks shot into the air around them.

"More," she said, and this time the word was both a demand and a plea.

His fingers tore at the laces of her leggings before he remembered. He stopped.

"Tell me, Irena."

She looked at him down the length of her body, past her heaving breasts, the tips reddened from the heat of his mouth. "Keep your promise."

He tugged a lace free. "How?"

"Push my legs apart and taste me." Her hands fisted around burning charcoal. "And do not stop, even if I scream."

He wouldn't. She'd scream his name, hers, and every one of her gods before he finished. But that was not what his promise had been.

"Even if you *beg*," he corrected.

Her laugh dared him to try. "We will see who begs."

His fingertips met, as if the lace had been plucked from between them. Alejandro looked down and struggled not to forget his promise, not to ram inside her heated depths and pound against her. Her leather stockings and leggings had vanished. He wouldn't have to push her legs apart. She'd already spread them to make room for his hips, and braced her heels on the edge of the stone ring. At the juncture of her sleekly muscled thighs, a small triangle of auburn curls guarded her glistening pink cleft.

He'd have begged. Oh, yes, he'd have begged. And then worshipped. Her beauty destroyed him.

He stepped back so that he could bend and press his lips to her bare hip. "I make a new vow, Irena."

"First fulfill this one—*if* you can from that position. My hip is too far north."

A soft laugh escaped him. Gliding his mouth over her flat stomach to her navel, he flicked his tongue into the indentation.

"I vow that your ankles will soon be on my shoulders," he said.

Her hands tightened in the coals. Pale gray ash dusted her fingers. "That is . . . a good vow."

With the barest pressure, he stroked his fingertips up the inside of her thigh. "I vow that I will soon sheathe myself in you, inch by inch, until I can push no deeper."

Her eyes closed and her hips rolled, as if she imagined taking him inside her. An ember popped, sending a glowing chip to land on her stomach. Alejandro brushed it away. His tongue traced the crease of her torso and thigh.

"*Lower*, Olek." She unfurled her fist, scattering crushed charcoal and ash. Her fingers threaded into his hair, directing him to her center.

She stopped, holding him there. He looked up and met her eyes. She had hesitated, but it didn't have the flavor of anger or shame.

"I haven't allowed this. Not since—" She moistened her lips. "It is too . . . open."

Alejandro nodded his understanding. Fucking didn't require intimacy. It didn't make her vulnerable. The same couldn't be said when tongue and teeth were against the softest, most unprotected part of her.

She released his hair and let her hand fall back into the fire. "It is easy to open myself to you, Olek. But know that I expect the same in return."

She already had it. With his Gift protecting her from the fire, she felt his every emotion. His awe, his overwhelming need. She might have even felt his vulnerability, that she held his heart in her hand.

He swallowed past the tightness in his throat and dipped his head lower. He spoke to prepare her; anticipation made his voice rough.

"My mouth will be hot."

A sound like a purr vibrated from her chest. "I know."

Not just his mouth. He parted her soft cleft with a lick and the clenching need tore through him, stiffening everything but his lips, his tongue. One lick, and he was on the burning edge of release. One lick, and Irena became still, so still—but the serpents on her arms writhed in a primal dance. She felt as he did, then. She would contain this, or shatter.

He drew his tongue through her center before circling her clitoris, sucking lightly. Irena's body shook. His hands clamped on her hips and he increased the suction. Irena broke into motion, her upper body twisting violently. She cried out. Alejandro held her, stunned by the frantic throb of her flesh beneath his tongue.

That quickly? He glanced up. Irena lay still again, her heart racing. Flames heightened the flush on her cheeks; heated air currents moved gently through her hair.

She looked down at his expression and laughed. "It has been a very long wait, Olek. And then I looked at you. Your lips were . . ." Her body made a single, rolling undulation. "I could not hold after that."

"You should close your eyes." Amused, Alejandro slipped his fingers down, sliding them through her silken wetness. "For although you are already spent, I am not near to finished."

"I am not spent." Her eyes glittered with challenge. She didn't close them.

He would wear her out, then. So be it. Alejandro lowered his mouth and began to play. *Slow,* she told him, and so he moved faster, until she gasped and tried to break away. He slowed, and she moaned for him to quicken his tongue. He eased his fingers between her slick folds, and had to withdraw his mouth and tease until the need to taste her again overwhelmed the desire to work his shaft into the tight heat his fingers invaded. She snarled in frustration and he devoured her. She shook and he didn't stop when she closed her eyes, when she twisted and screamed his name. Then she lay still for a brief second and laughed again.

It *had* been a long wait. And he still wasn't finished.

He drove her hard, his mouth and fingers ruthless. Had it been any other woman he would have stopped, would have tired of it, would have been ready to seek his own pleasure. But he'd never found as much pleasure as this, watching Irena try to hold back, watching her give in. Listening to her breathless laugh each time.

He felt a gradual change in her response, a softening beneath his mouth and hands. She *had* opened to him, yet the tension within her hadn't only been erotic. And she'd reveled in her arousal, but now, she luxuriated in it, like steel that had heated to melting. Still hot, but no longer trying to hold a shape.

He eased up, each lick a long slow taste, sliding his hands up her sides. Irena arched, her head tilting back.

"You lied, Olek." Her breath was ragged. "I am burning."

But not from the fire. His Gift still kept her safe. She came, not with a violent twist, but on an endless cresting wave that lifted her against him, her fingers clutching his hair—not in demand, but as an anchor.

He lifted her out of the hearth and found his legs would not stand. With Irena's thighs circling his waist, he sank to his knees. Her lips found his in a slow melting kiss.

He settled her over his erection, felt the heat of her sex through his trousers. That would be all for now. And it would be enough. For although the need in his body still raged, hers was satiated. She would welcome him in, meet his every thrust, and find another release with that liquid ease. But her anticipation, her urgency would not match his, and he needed her wound as tightly as he was more than he needed to bury himself inside her.

She must have noted the change in his touch. Her lips left his, and she leaned back to study his face.

"You do not fulfill your second vow?"

To his relief, Alejandro couldn't sense any disappointment in her, only curiosity. "Not this night."

Her mouth curved. "You have finished me well. It would be difficult to follow that."

For an instant, his pride demanded that he prove her wrong. Then he admitted, "Yes."

She laughed and wrapped her arms around his shoulders, rocking forward against his shaft. He tensed; she stopped.

When she looked at him again, her eyes flashed with green fire. "You *did* come. I felt you."

"Yes." Only a man of iron could have tasted her, could have watched and sensed her pleasure for that long and not found his release. But his erection hadn't softened. For a Guardian, the spirit only needed to be willing, and the flesh was capable. "I am finished, Irena."

"But not satisfied." She pushed her hand between his legs, pressing her palm to his heated shaft. "And *not* finished."

"I do not need—"

Irena threw herself at his chest. Unbalanced, he fell over, his back smashing into the hard earthen floor. Irena rode over with him, straddling his stomach. Her mouth fastened to his.

This time, it was no slow, melting kiss. She licked past his lips to duel with his tongue. Alejandro's body ratcheted tight, as if she'd already wrapped her mouth around his shaft and drew on him. Her hand stroked beneath his trousers. Almost deranged by pleasure of it, he fought for sanity.

"Irena—" He could barely speak. He would explode at any moment. "I don't need repayment," he forced out.

Her hand froze. Her gaze clashed with his. Heat filled it, followed by determination—but no anger. Softly, she said, "You stupid *man*."

He couldn't remember her using *man* as an insult before. Briefly, he wondered if he should pride himself in being the first who drove her to it, and tried to appear as if he had a modicum of sense left. "You will enlighten me, I hope."

"You think women do not take pleasure in it. *Repayment*." She repeated the word like a curse.

He struggled against his pride. "Many do not." And sensing emotions was not always an advantage in bed. "Not for themselves."

And he could not enjoy the act if his partner didn't.

"Because they could not own you. Because you did not open to them." Her fingers unfastened two of the buttons on his shirt before ripping away the rest. "I would not bother to suck you, either, if you gave me nothing in return."

Just as she'd said they'd been right to leave. She watched him with a steady gaze and he fought not to throw his psychic shields up.

Her hands moved to his trouser fastening. "And so you give pleasure with your mouth, and you take your own when you fuck. But that is not how it will be with me. You will be taken, Olek. And I will enjoy it all."

Taken. A part of him rebelled, though he realized this was what she had demanded from the beginning.

He hissed in a breath as her fingers circled his erection, aroused to the point of pain. She raised his straining length toward her mouth. His anticipation was a physical ache in his shaft, through every muscle in his body. Her tongue wet her bottom lip. His hands fisted.

She met his gaze and opened her shields.

Her desire jolted through him like an electric shock, more powerful than any physical sensation. She hungered to please him, to taste him—hungered for *him,* as fiercely as he had for her.

She lowered her head, and wet heat engulfed him in a steady, deep slide. Alejandro clenched his teeth, trying to hold onto sanity, onto control. *God!* Is this what she had felt? This ecstasy as he'd taken her with his mouth and his Gift open? He'd never experienced anything like it. He hadn't prepared for it.

And she had softened beneath his lips, but he became harder, steel forged by the heat of her mouth, shaped by the strike of her tongue. Folded and worked until he thought he might fracture beneath the pressure.

She made him. She could destroy him. And if she ever tossed him aside, he would be nothing.

Panic threatened, and he fought not to push her away. His fingers dug into the floor. His body shook, and he stared up at the wooden beams supporting the forge's metal roof.

He looked down when he felt a light touch against his hip. Irena's fingertips traced his skin. As if she was forming a statue, her Gift pulsed, and her emotions washed over him, more than need and desire. Reverence. Admiration. Joy. Her fingers moved higher, and his body shaped the trail her fingers took.

Alejandro unclenched his hands, sought hers. At his hip, her fingers threaded through his and tightened. Her mouth took him deep, and she drew so hard he dizzily thought that she would also take his heart, his soul.

So be it.

The orgasm lunged through him with teeth and claws, ripping away his breath, throwing his head back. Irena growled her satisfaction deep in her throat and drank him down. When he could breathe, when he could think, he saw that she watched him. With a few leisurely licks, she finished, and crawled up his body until she lay on his chest. Her fingers stroked his hair. He closed his eyes, certain he'd never felt this lassitude, this contentment in his life.

He was stretched out naked on a dirt floor. He'd never been happier.

"I should have come back before this, Irena." No—he should have made the forge his home while she'd been gone those two centuries, and been here to welcome her when she returned. "I have missed you."

"I have missed you," she said, her cheek against his shoulder. "And I should have dragged you back."

He smiled and passed his hand over her hair. They had not settled many of the problems between them.

But they had settled the most important one.

Deacon left the warehouse, hit the sidewalk, and started going, headed for nowhere—and wishing that he could still get drunk. A nice, falling down stupor.

Unfortunately, nothing could make a vampire less than clearheaded but drinking live blood—and he couldn't stomach the thought of it now. Couldn't stomach his own company, but he was stuck with himself.

Three nephilim. And Irena.

It didn't take a fucking genius to figure out that the message he'd sent had pushed them straight to her. She'd survived, but according to the description Dru had given the novices, it had been close. Closer than Deacon had ever gotten at the hands of the demon.

Maybe Guardians couldn't take care of themselves against this.

So he'd go back. He'd tell them everything. And he'd probably die.

He started back, anyway.

About four blocks from the warehouse, a black car with dark-tinted windows rolled up beside him, kept pace. He could sense a human in the front, but that wasn't what was behind the rear window. It slid down, revealing a blond male with a little too much polish to be hanging around an area like this—at this time of the night. He smiled at him.

"Mr. Deacon."

Deacon kept walking. He'd seen the news, heard the buzz around the warehouse. Demon, with a murdered wife.

Irena had been involved in that investigation, too.

"Mr. Deacon, please get in. You are done here. I am taking you home."

"I've got friends who can fly." Not many would be left. But it was much better than what a demon might offer him.

"And *I* am an associate of Mr. Caym's. I only have to make one phone call to him, Mr. Deacon, and tell him that I am displeased—and you will have a few less friends."

God *damn* them. Deacon stopped.

"Get in."

He got in.

A dark partition divided the front and back seats. He couldn't see the driver, only an outline.

"That's Maggie," the demon said. "She can't hear us back here, and she won't help you. She's very loyal. And she has a contract."

Maggie, whoever she was, might be loyal—but she was clearly broadcasting worry, and a distinct sense of uncertainty. But maybe the demon liked that, too. Maybe, he'd get her to a point where she wasn't sure what was going on, but she felt scared and trapped—then he'd offer her an out.

And she wouldn't know until too late that the out he offered was worse that being in.

He eyed the glass. Was she watching them? Could she see anything other than shadows?

When the demon smiled at him, Deacon grinned back, showing every inch of his fangs. Surprise and doubt dropped into the mix of Loyal Maggie's swirling emotions. Doubt, then rejection.

The demon laughed. "No humans believe what they see anymore, Mr. Deacon."

"Fuck you."

"That is what you have left?" The demon smiled at him again, but Deacon sensed a little disappointment. Or maybe he was *supposed* to sense disappointment, and react to it. He remained silent.

"All right, Mr. Deacon. I understand—you must be at the end of your rope. Perhaps you've just discovered how some of the information you've given us has been used." He sighed. "It's so difficult to lose a friend."

A friend . . . *Irena*? The demon thought Irena was dead?

She should be. It'd been close. She'd gotten lucky.

But Deacon wasn't going tell this demon differently.

"Fuck off," he said.

And he realized the demon was right—that pretty much *was* all he had left.

The demon sighed again. "You are almost done, Mr. Deacon. You have just one more task. You'll spend the day in my home, and we'll fly to Prague tonight. And you *will* be on your best behavior around my employee, Mr. Deacon, or I will make that call. Just do as you're told, and everything will end well."

Deacon closed his eyes. What had Rosalia said? "It never ends well."

It especially never ends well for vampires.

"Mr. Deacon, that *is* disappointing," the demon said. "You should have a little more faith."

CHAPTER 16

Irena had known weeks and months—even years—when she'd done little but wander her territory, searching for demons and nosferatu. And then came days like this, when she wondered how she would complete everything she needed to—particularly when her duties sat on opposite sides of the world, and the window of time to meet with vampires lasted from sundown to sunrise. When the day began in San Francisco, night would not fall for three more hours in her territory.

Thanks to Selah, she could start at SI and not lose too many hours flying to and from the Gates.

Before she and Alejandro left the forge, she quickly made him four swords with her Gift. She would craft others later, better suited to his growth in speed and strength these past four centuries.

Every moment in the forge with him had been perfect—almost unreal, as if in a dream. She did not mind. Irena hadn't slept in sixteen centuries, had not dreamt. It was time for one: a waking dream.

And she was trying to remind herself of that when she stood

in the conference room with Taylor, Preston, and Lilith, looking down at the files Michael had brought regarding Margaret Wren. Irena barely listened as Michael told them he'd teleported into a secured CIA facility to obtain them; she only felt the conflict in Taylor's psychic scent. Irena wasn't sure if the conflict stemmed from Michael's method of retrieving the files, or the information within.

Irena looked up at Olek, who'd read through the reports within a few seconds. "What are we looking at?"

"An assassin."

What did that matter? "She wasn't the shooter."

"No." He flipped through another folder. "But she was issued and used the rifle. Going by the serial number, it's the same weapon. She'd listed it as destroyed during one of her assignments."

Assignments she no longer had. "Why did she resign?"

"She only stated 'personal reasons,'" Alejandro said. "But for her last assignment, she was ordered to assassinate a fellow operative. An operative that she knew well: She'd trained with him, completed assignments with him. He saved her life twice."

So they'd pushed her too far, Irena realized. Perhaps they'd thought her loyalty to the job would override any other consideration.

"Did she carry out the order?"

"Yes."

Irena frowned.

"There's more," Taylor said. "Savi dug into her financials. Wren's been funneling cash into a few bogus businesses and charities, which then head to a numbered account."

Irena had no idea what that meant. "What does that say?"

"That she contacted someone she knew, and paid them to shoot Julia Stafford for her," Preston said.

"Do we believe that?"

"Good question." Lilith tapped her fingers against the table. "Let's bring her in to ask her—but not here. Bradshaw can handle it, and hit her with the gun and the money."

"Why?" Irena frowned at her. "Is it not obvious she's being set up?"

Lilith indicated the files with a sweep of her hand. "We shouldn't have these. Through regular channels, we'd have had to fight harder for them than this. That's not easy or obvious; a month from now, a frustrated investigator is supposed to finally get this info and say, 'Aha!'" Lilith shook her head. "But Rael doesn't know that *we* already know he hired someone."

Taylor pursed her lips. "Hired them through Wren?"

"That is the question. But since Rael doesn't know we know that step, let's keep it that way. We'll use Bradshaw."

Taylor nodded, and Irena realized that was the end of the meeting when Alejandro cleared the files from the table. She fought her discomfort and frustration; she wasn't useful here. Unless they needed her to kill a demon or protect someone, she had no reason to accompany them to this interview with Wren. Alejandro could cover Taylor. Hugh could read the truth in Wren's responses. And Irena could catch up on what they learned later.

She stopped Lilith in the hall. "You don't need me here."

Lilith's brows arched. She glanced over her shoulder, where Olek had halted to watch them. *Perhaps not. But, considering that five hours ago you were almost killed by three nephilim, I'm not sure if one of my agents will be on his game if you're not in his sight.*

Irena laughed. Olek might worry, but he'd never be stupid. "Don't be an idiot."

"I won't; I leave that to Michael." Lilith's expression became speculative. "After you've checked on your vampires, I have a few files you might find interesting."

"I might find them interesting if they do not come from an agency supported by a human-murdering demon."

"But that will change soon, won't it?" Lilith said, and turned to follow the others down the hall.

Alejandro's face darkened. His gaze held Irena's, and she shook her head. Not now. She did not want to discuss it now.

Lilith turned, walked backward for a few steps. "Deacon didn't come back to the warehouse this morning, but his things are still here. Colin hasn't heard from him."

Irena frowned. Vampires didn't like to bed down in unsecured locations. "I will ask Rosalia."

"Do that."

Irena looked to Olek again, watched him approach while the sound of Lilith's heels faded.

"Where shall I find you later?"

After speaking with the vampires in her territory, she had to find Jake and compare the iron spikes. "Caelum," she decided.

He pushed his hand into her hair. His lips captured hers for a long second. When he lifted his head, his smile shone from his eyes. "I believe we have just stunned everyone in the warehouse."

From the direction of the gymnasium, Drifter called, "I reckon we're just astounded neither one of you is bleeding."

"Or killing another conference table," Becca yelled after him.

"Or breaking through a closet wall," Michael said in his harmonious voice, and shocked into silence anyone who had considered adding their own. The warehouse became deathly quiet.

"He's been talking to Jake," Irena said.

Alejandro closed his eyes, shook his head.

She grinned and touched his chin. "Be safe."

§

Taylor supposed that she couldn't complain about the Guardians' secret sign language anymore. She knew a word now: *truth*.

Chances were, Rael had positioned himself within the federal building so that he'd be able to hear Bradshaw's questions for Wren. This wasn't about Wren at all, Taylor had realized— but leading Rael to think the investigation was headed in the direction he wanted them to go.

And the Guardians didn't intend to let the demon know that Castleford watched the interview from the back of the darkened observation room, reading the truth and lies in Wren's answers.

He stood to the left of her, with Cordoba on the other side of him. In between them and the one-way mirror, two FBI agents watched Bradshaw thank Wren for coming in for a follow-up. Michael stood on her right. The Doyen had shape-shifted into a sixty-year-old black man—an identity he'd apparently used before, because he had a Special Investigations badge to go along with his appearance, and the agents had greeted him by name. A different name. Until Cordoba had whispered his real identity to her, Taylor hadn't known who'd been standing so uncomfortably close.

When she'd woken up that morning, Michael had been standing at the foot of her bed, arms crossed over his wide chest. The arch of his black wings had almost brushed the ceiling. Even in the predawn darkness, she'd seen that his eyes were fully obsidian, and she hadn't known if he'd been watching the door, the window, or her.

And she wasn't sure if the tremor that had raced down her spine meant that she'd been freaked out or a little thrilled.

It hadn't mattered. Either reaction was a reason to grab her weapon from her nightstand and order him the hell out of her room.

She had; he'd gone.

Bradshaw settled into his chair. Joe sat at the end of the small table, looking over at Wren with his careworn, I'm-your-favorite-uncle face on, which had guilted more than one person sitting across from him to break down and confess their sins.

Margaret Wren didn't. She sat rigid in her chair, speaking only when spoken to.

Bradshaw laid a picture of the rifle on the table. "Do you recognize this weapon, Miss Wren?"

Her gaze flicked down and back up. "Yes. It's a Heckler & Koch PSG1 semiautomatic rifle."

"A sniper rifle."

"Yes."

"According to CIA records, you were the last person to have this particular rifle in your possession."

Wren's face didn't betray any emotion. "I could not say whether I was."

Truth, Castleford signed.

"You won't tell us where you last had the weapon?"

"That, too. But I also do not memorize serial numbers."

"Perhaps you'll be more familiar with other numbers, Miss Wren."

Bradshaw read off two bank account numbers, then a list of transactions. At the one-way, the agents frowned and shifted their weight. Taylor had difficulty holding back her own protest, reminding herself that Bradshaw wasn't trying to go hard on Wren. He was just laying out what he had for Rael to hear.

Cordoba and Michael exchanged a glance and rapid-fire sign language.

Taylor frowned at them. Michael bent low and murmured into her ear so quietly she had to strain to hear—and then forced herself not to shiver as his breath warmed her skin.

"Her heart races. She's frightened and angry."

Surprised, she shot a glance through the window. Wren appeared ice cool.

Bradshaw finished his recitation and leaned back. "These are your accounts."

"Yes."

"Have you allowed anyone else access to them, Miss Wren?"

"No."

Truth.

"Do you know who might have obtained access?"

"No."

Truth.

"Did you make these transfers?"

"No. I wouldn't be that stupid."

Even before Castleford signed *Truth,* Taylor knew that it would be. Wren wasn't that stupid. And Taylor would bet that if Wren had been behind Julia Stafford's murder, she wouldn't have left a trace of it.

Wren glanced at the one-way mirror, then at Bradshaw. "I won't take any more questions without my lawyer present," she said flatly.

"Very well. Thank you for your help so far, Miss Wren."

Michael bent toward her again. "Her anger is cold now. Her fear is gone."

Taylor gave a nod of satisfaction. Wren had figured out she was being set up. She might open her mouth a little more once she realized her employer was behind it.

The agents grumbled; Taylor tuned them out. Michael and Castleford left quickly—they would teleport back to SI before Rael realized they'd been here.

Fifteen minutes later, she stepped out of the building with Joe and Cordoba, and pulled her coat tight around her. She almost wished she'd teleported with Michael; the wind was cold enough to make her forehead ache.

And what fun—the demon was making his way across the plaza toward them.

Joe harrumphed, as if she hadn't noticed. Cordoba watched Rael's smiling approach without expression. The Guardian didn't talk much. Not unless he had to—or unless Irena was in the room with him. Other than that, he seemed the quiet, deadly type.

Not the demon. He effused warmth, and instead of dark and brooding, he was handsome in a clean, rugged kind of way—tanned but not *too* tanned, with a few wrinkles next to his eyes for character, and sprinkles of gray through his sandy hair. In Hollywood, he'd be the kind of actor who only got hotter as he aged, the kind who looked at home in a suit and private jet or on horseback trekking through the mountains.

He stopped. The wind whipped at his dark wool trench and his red scarf. "Detective Taylor, Detective Preston. It's nice to see you again."

Taylor frowned. "Considering your recent loss, Representative Stafford, I'm sure that can't be true."

His sad smile managed to show off his perfect white teeth. "I always try to find the good in every situation, detective."

Taylor actually felt chastised, like she shouldn't be a surly bitch. Her badge entitled her to that, at least. So did the fucking wind.

"I didn't expect you to be done with Maggie so quickly," he added. "I was just taking a walk to clear my head when she called me. It's easier to think without the distractions in the office."

So he'd been walking and not listening? Right. "I bet," Taylor said.

He smiled again. "And I like to see our new building from all angles." His face tilted up, and he stepped back as if inviting them all to turn and look at the federal building. "She's quite a feat, isn't she? An amazing architectural accomplishment. Beauty and efficiency, in one package."

"It's great," Taylor said and glanced at Cordoba. His face was still unreadable—and the demon hadn't addressed him or acknowledged his presence. Was Rael trying to piss him off?

Joe didn't look back at the irregular building. "I dunno about *great*. It looks like a parking structure after a quake to me. And every time I walk out, I get this feeling someone's going to follow me home and yell at me for living in my little place made of wood that probably came out of some slashed-and-burned forest."

The demon smiled. "Our responsibility for our future should not mean we have to denigrate the past. We couldn't have built what we have now without taking those early steps—even steps that we later discovered were destructive."

Joe shrugged. "I don't care about that. I just want to put some butter on my potatoes without clutching at my chest."

"Ah, yes." The demon laughed quietly, as if he thought Joe had been joking, and looked to Taylor. "You must be pleased to be working with your partner again. I suppose yesterday's team up with Irena did not work out."

It'd worked out fine, but why tell the demon that? "Not really."

His expression became a picture of sympathy. "It's a pity she didn't make it today."

What did that mean? Was he trying to wheedle out her take on the interview with Wren? As if she'd give him anything.

"Yeah, it sucks to be her," Taylor said.

"Yes. Good day, detectives."

As soon as the demon's back was turned, Joe gave her a *What the hell?* look. Taylor shrugged and shook her head. But

Cordoba, she noted, was staring after Rael with eyes that had darkened to black.

He waited until Rael had disappeared into the building. "Please excuse me while I make a call."

Quiet, and so polite. She gestured toward the plaza. "Knock yourself out." They'd just hang around and freeze.

He strode away. She watched him lift the phone to his ear, then squeeze his eyes closed and tighten his mouth in the universal sign that he'd been dropped into a voice mail instead of reaching the person he'd wanted.

Free will or not, sometimes Guardians seemed very human.

She thought of Michael, and waking up to him at the end of her bed. *And sometimes . . . not.*

She glanced at Joe and asked before she could stop herself, "Would you become one of them—one of the Guardians?"

"In a heartbeat." Joe studied her face. "Are you worried about this prophecy thing?"

"No." She shoved her hands into the pockets of her jacket. "Let's go see if we can find some coffee from a field that's been proudly slashed and burned."

❧

No one knew where Rosalia was, or how to reach her. But since Irena was back in her territory and had to visit Prague's new community leader anyway, she would drop in on Eva and Petra first. She knew Deacon cared for them; he might have kept in touch.

If nothing else, she'd find out why they hadn't stood by him.

She arrived in Prague a few minutes after sunset, and flew directly to Deacon's place on the north side of the city. She landed behind the tall stone building as the sun's orange glow faded from the sky. Thirty years ago, Deacon had converted the second floor of a textile factory into a living area for him and his partners. Through the square, barred windows on the ground floor, she saw the two antique automobiles Deacon had been restoring—both sat abandoned, tools still laid out on a cloth spread over the hood of the vehicle in the first bay.

Irena frowned and vanished her wings, feeling the first stir-rings of unease. Those cars were Deacon's; they didn't belong to the community, and his personal property wouldn't be trans-ferred to the new community leader after he'd been defeated. Why hadn't he at least made arrangements to have them stored until he could come back for them?

Khavi appeared beside Irena as she was walking up the steps to the apartment. The small woman was almost swimming in a bright yellow slicker and boots. Rain from wherever she'd teleported still streaked the plastic.

Irena paused to let the demon spawn go ahead of her. "Why are you here?"

"Because I finally have enough boats in my cache."

Boats? Irena eyed the back of Khavi's braided hair. Two thousand years in Hell *had* driven the grigori insane.

Irena knocked, then used her Gift to unbolt the locks when the vampires didn't answer. The scent of stale air and old blood filled her lungs. Destruction met her eyes.

The living room and a portion of the library had been torn apart. Beside an overturned sofa, a body-sized, irregular patch of dried blood discolored a cream rug. Deacon's blood, Irena realized. She'd assumed he'd been challenged at one of the community's gathering places, but Deacon had been beaten here in his home. Perhaps that explained why Eva and Petra weren't at the apartment—and hadn't been for some time. They might have felt too vulnerable to stay.

An hour later, she'd crossed the city four times, and had to face the terrible truth: It wasn't just Eva and Petra; *all* of the community was gone. She hadn't detected a single psychic whiff, let alone a living vampire.

She left the final, empty gathering spot, her hands in fists, ready to fight—but no one was here. Khavi tromped along next to her, ridiculous in her yellow slicker. Irena could not even sneer at the grigori; at that moment, her dislike of the demon spawn wasn't half as sharp as the hate she directed at herself.

She should have come earlier. She should have come back when Deacon said he'd been beaten by a nosferatu-born vam-pire. She'd wondered then if it had been a demon masquerading as a vampire; she shouldn't have assumed that Deacon's impressions had been right. Maybe a demon could temporarily fake cold hands; maybe, in the midst of being pulverized by a demon's fists, a vampire could mistake their temperature. Maybe it had been one of the nephilim.

But she couldn't linger here and try to flush out the demon. She had other communities to visit and to warn.

Then she had to find Deacon and tell him what she feared.

She turned, looked out over the city, felt the cold bite of the night wind against her cheeks. Maybe, after the change in leadership, the community had just moved to another location. Maybe one of the other communities would have heard.

She could not even convince herself of it.

With a heavy heart, she glanced at Khavi. Teleporting to the other communities would be faster.

"You will ask," Khavi said and held out her hand. "I will say yes."

❧

Rael waited before coming to SI, but no longer than Alejandro had anticipated. Just enough time had passed—the time it might take for a close-mouthed butler to give in and tell her employer why Bradshaw had asked her to come in for an additional interview. Of course Wren hadn't, but Rael claimed she did. And in Rael's place, Alejandro would have done the same thing.

Knowing that didn't bother him; thinking like the demon would be an asset later. He escorted Rael into the conference room where Preston and Taylor waited and took the opportunity to study the demon's walk, the way he nodded as he greeted the detectives. Alejandro knew Rael called his receptionist by her first name and his personal assistant by his surname. Later, he'd watch recordings from the floor of the Senate, interviews, and campaign speeches.

But the congressman wouldn't be the same. He'd sell his house and take a modest apartment in the city. He wouldn't be as outgoing, he wouldn't smile much, and he wouldn't attend as many functions. He'd be passionate about his work, focused—

if somewhat solitary. The changes would be blamed on his recent personal loss. Grief would do that to a man.

Not a demon. Rael sat at the conference table with barely contained energy, like a child waiting for a gift.

He spread his hands as he addressed the detectives sitting at the end of the table. "I'll get right to it. You are looking at my personal head of staff, Maggie Wren. You're looking in the wrong direction."

Alejandro rested his back against the wall directly across from the demon. "That is not what the evidence suggests," he said.

Rael's frown managed to be both earnest and irritated. "Then you aren't looking hard enough, Guardian. I don't expect *you* to take my word for this—but she's a good woman."

"She was an assassin. She made her living by murdering humans," he said, laying it on thick.

Alejandro saw a distinct difference between government assassins and murderers, but he preferred Rael to think of him as a narrow-minded, sanctimonious Guardian. The demon would be less likely to expect what came later.

"You don't believe a human deserves a second chance? That's all I've wanted, to offer her—" He broke off. In a human, Alejandro might have believed the suppressed display of emotion. "You must see that this is the work of a demon—one of Lucifer's followers—who is looking to hurt me, and to discredit me and mine. And the FBI are following the clues they've laid like dogs. You need to dig deeper—"

Khavi appeared at the end of the room, with Irena beside her, blinking through her disorientation. Rael's shock hit Alejandro's psychic shields.

"Khavi!" The demon's greeting was surprised and welcoming.

And Alejandro believed *that* display of emotion. A leaden weight formed in his gut. "You know each other?"

Preston sat forward, as if uncertain whether he should be standing—either because the women had appeared or to get out of the way. Irena began to walk along the table on Rael's side, toward the detectives.

"Yes," Khavi said, making no effort to approach the demon.

"He was a friend to Zakril, Anaria, Aaron, and me in the centuries after Michael ordered Anaria's execution. We hid from the Doyen together, fought together." Her smile was sharp. "It is lovely to see that he is a friend to the Guardians again."

As if uneasy, Rael looked away from Khavi. He glanced to his side, as if just noticing Irena walking past him. For an instant, he seemed surprised again. He quickly recovered, flashed his smile at her, and turned away from her to look at Khavi again.

Idiot, Alejandro thought.

Irena smashed the demon's face into the table. The impact cracked as loud as a gunshot. Taylor jumped up, her hand flying to her weapon. Preston rocked back in his chair, his face slack with surprise.

Her muscles visibly straining, Irena held the demon down, her fingers clamped over the back of his head. "I am not your friend. And when the time comes, I *will* kill you."

Rael forced his head up. Blood dripped from his nose, his mouth. His teeth clenched, he gripped her arm, and tossed her over the table. Apparently finished, Irena went without resistance. She landed on her feet beside Alejandro.

Rael laughed as he stood, holding a white handkerchief over his nose. He glanced at Khavi. "You will tell her, I hope, that she has not a chance of defeating me."

"Oh, you are safe from her. She does not slay you." Khavi's eyes softened. "Anaria will."

Rael's smile faltered. Khavi vanished.

Alejandro thought Rael appeared almost lost for moment. Then the demon recovered, and looked across the table.

"Please remember what I said about Maggie. You're looking in the wrong place."

He left. Alejandro followed him to the door, and watched until the demon reached the hub and turned for the exit. He looked over at Irena.

You don't have your cell phone? he signed.

It's in my cache.

Where the device was absolutely useless. But he let it go. Trouble darkened her eyes—he didn't think Rael had been the cause. The demon had only been the recipient of her frustration.

What has happened?

The Prague community is gone.

Christ. *The nephilim?*

No. They have always left bodies, and I couldn't find any sign of the vampires—dead or alive.

And Deacon is missing as well?

No one in the nearby communities has heard from him.

Do you have any thoughts on what has happened to them?

No.

Guilt weighed heavily in her psychic scent. Alejandro signed, *Ames-Beaumont and Savitri are scheduled to be here after sunset. We'll use their contacts. Perhaps they will uncover something.*

At the table, Preston cleared his throat. They both glanced his way.

"So . . . is anyone else sitting here wondering if maybe we are looking in the wrong direction?"

Irena frowned. Alejandro quickly summarized Rael's visit.

"Oh." Irena turned back to the detectives and sighed. "He is very good at what he does."

"Maybe. So he sets Wren up in the most obvious way, then comes to argue against it. Why?"

"Because playing with us gives him pleasure," Alejandro said.

Taylor's gaze was steady. "There's no doubt in your mind? Castleford couldn't have misread the video or Wren?"

"No," he and Irena said together. She continued, "Demons were made to create doubt. That is what they do. And so Rael has."

Taylor and Preston exchanged a glance. Alejandro couldn't read that look, but they seemed to settle something between them when Taylor shrugged.

Irena must have thought so, too. She turned back to him. "Rael was surprised to see Khavi. Did he not know she was alive?"

Alejandro didn't think Rael had known. But he was more

interested in the demon's reaction to Irena's appearance. "He was surprised to see Khavi *and* you."

He watched her take that in. Alejandro had wondered that morning, during Rael's conversation with Taylor, if the demon had known of the nephilim's attack on Irena. He hadn't been sure then, but seeing Rael's surprise here had erased his uncertainty.

Irena's brow creased as she asked the same question that plagued him. "How did he know?"

Taylor stood. "I don't know what you guys are talking about, and we're going to leave you to figure it out. We've got some things back at the station to take care of."

Sundown was in less than an hour. Taylor wouldn't be leaving here without protection.

Alejandro met Irena's eyes. She raised her brows, silently asking if he had other obligations. He shook his head. "Have you had an opportunity to speak with Jake?"

"Not yet."

"Then I will accompany her," Alejandro said.

Taylor sighed.

Irena laughed and started for the door. Her fingers trailed a warm path over his hand as she passed him. "You'll meet me in Caelum afterward?"

"Yes."

Until then, he'd work through the gnawing suspicion that Rael had been behind the nephilim's attack on Irena, and decide whether the suspicion had teeth or if it was a distraction to be ignored.

That morning in the federal building plaza, the idea had bit and he'd dismissed it as impossible. Because the prophecy said Belial would only rise to the throne after the nephilim were destroyed, Belial's demons—and therefore Rael, Belial's lieutenant—were enemies of the nephilim. But after witnessing Rael's reaction to Khavi and learning they'd once been friendly, his suspicion had taken hold again. Rael's pleasure upon seeing Khavi was genuine.

It made Alejandro wonder if the demon's best memories were several thousand years old.

Taylor and Preston spoke little as he rode with them across the city. With new eyes, he reexamined pieces that shouldn't have fit, turned each one, and watched them fall into place.

Rael had loved a woman. Alejandro briefly considered Khavi, but Rael's response to her had been wrong. Even a demon, seeing the woman he'd loved for the first time in more than two millennia, would have wanted to go to her. He'd want to touch her, to confirm she truly stood there. And even a demon's pleasure would be tinged with pain when he held himself back.

Anaria, however . . . Anaria fit.

Anaria was Belial's daughter. Even if fatherly love hadn't been a reason to protect her after Michael ordered Anaria's execution, her knowledge of the symbols and magic were. Anaria had power, and she wanted to challenge Lucifer for his throne. Even if she didn't succeed, surely her attempt would weaken Lucifer, giving Belial an opportunity to take the throne for himself. *Yes*, Alejandro thought. He could easily see how Belial's lieutenant had become an ally to Anaria and her husband, Zakril, while they'd hidden from Michael—and Khavi hadn't yet given Belial the prophecy, on which his need to destroy the nephilim was based.

Zakril had been murdered before Khavi delivered the prophecy, too. Murdered, and his body left with a message for the nephilim, telling them where to find their mother. A demon couldn't open Anaria's prison—only the grigori, Lucifer, or the nephilim could.

But Khavi had been trapped Below, and Aaron, her husband, had been slain by Belial; they couldn't have freed her. Michael and Lucifer would have killed Anaria if they'd been the ones to find her, and the nephilim hadn't been released from Hell until two years ago, when the Gates to Hell closed.

Rael had waited more than two thousand years—and lived as a saint during that time. Trying to make himself worthy of Anaria when she returned? Or just giving the appearance of it—to a demon, they were the same.

Now, the husband Anaria had loved was long dead—and within months of her return, Rael rid himself of his wife, too.

Cold certainty settled over him, but Alejandro turned each piece over again. They settled in the same way. Parts were missing, but the shape was clear.

Rael had killed Zakril. He'd waited for Anaria. And when she appeared, he'd killed Julia Stafford. The demon had removed every obstacle he saw standing between them.

Every obstacle except the Guardians.

Had Rael already been in contact with Anaria? Had he approached her as a friend, offering his support and fealty?

Alejandro sighed, knowing that if Irena had been with him, she'd have given him a look. Obviously, Rael had—and he also had the ear of Anaria or the nephilim. They'd shown up at Irena's forge within hours of her telling Rael that she'd slay Anaria.

That hadn't been coincidence. That had been Rael.

And suddenly, slaying the demon and taking his position had become far more complicated than it had once been—and more imperative.

CHAPTER 17

Caelum's silence wrapped around Irena the moment she stepped through the Gate. Earth could be quiet, but even on the tundra, background noises filtered through: the whisper of air currents across grasses or snow, the crack of ice and the drip of water, the settling of the soil as it warmed and cooled. Caelum's silence wasn't a deep quiet, but an absence of sound—and of life. It pressed on Irena's chest until she pushed it back. Until she heard her heartbeat, her breath, her steps.

Caelum stood empty—but never abandoned.

And it was not completely empty, either. Somewhere in Caelum's eastern quadrant, Khavi's hellhound puppy roamed. Lyta hadn't yet been on Earth; the puppy had only recently left Hell, where Khavi had been her only companion, and they were uncertain how Lyta would react to humans . . . and to Sir Pup. Like Sir Pup, Lyta was abnormally friendly for a hellhound, but that only meant they didn't rip apart and eat every living thing they encountered.

Irena did not mind the hellhounds. She found their unwavering loyalty to their chosen companions admirable—even if their companions were Lilith and Khavi.

She formed her wings and took to the air. Her feathers ruffled, and each beat of her wings ended with a satisfying snap. Here was wind, and sound, though of her own creation. She flew toward the edge of the northern quadrant. The never-moving sun shone overhead; below her, the city rested in an endless, waveless sea, an enormous white disc on a smooth bed of brilliant blue.

The buildings surrounding Odin's Courtyard were stockier, less graceful than the temples and spires in the rest of Caelum. Alice's quarters only consisted of a single building, but every Guardian considered Odin's Courtyard hers. Irena landed at the edge of the courtyard. She coughed loudly before vanishing her wings and walking toward the giant marble elm tree that sheltered the square.

She was thankful she'd given Alice the warning when the Guardian emerged from her building, her skin flushed and her hair unbound. Alice's giant tarantula ran out after her, claws clicking on the white stone tiles.

At the sight of the spider, Irena wanted to climb into the tree—but she wasn't certain if Nefertari couldn't jump that high.

Alice had told her that bigger spiders crawled in Hell, creatures many times larger than the Coliseum in Rome. Irena had lived more than sixteen centuries without stepping foot in Hell, and was glad of it. The demons didn't frighten her; she'd have liked to kill legions of them. But she feared she might run away screaming if she spotted a monstrous spider.

She held her ground as Nefertari skittered toward the tree, and hid her relief when, with a soft word and a touch of her Gift, Alice commanded the spider to remain at her knee.

A second later, Jake appeared beside her—just as flushed, and wearing a broad grin. He seemed to be waiting for her to say something.

Irena eyed him, then realized what was missing: the staff that served as his electrical ground. She hadn't felt the now-familiar sizzle of his second Gift, either—only a faint push of his teleportation Gift.

She nodded. "Well done."

"Hah! Wait until you see this." Jake held his index fingers an inch apart. His electric Gift hummed, and a white current arced between his fingers. "I'm a Taser."

"I now see what had you so excited when you came to get me." Alice's mouth quirked, and she began braiding her hair. "I wonder if this is what Khavi meant when she said you would be known as 'the Weapon' among the demons. How utterly terrified all of Hell will be when you whip out your Taser."

He grinned at her. "Just wait until I figure out other applications."

Alice pressed her lips together, flags of color on her cheeks. Nefertari purred and rubbed her hairy body against Alice's skirts.

Jake turned back to Irena, who was fighting a shudder and the urge to swat at her own leg.

"So does that rock or does that flippin' rock?"

"We *are* susceptible to shock," she agreed. But what he'd just shown her seemed worthless. An injury from that tiny electrical arc would be an irritation at worst. Unless . . . She stepped forward, took Jake's hands, and put one on each side of her head. "Now, try—"

Her vision burst into a white hot flash. Then there was nothing.

❧

Irena opened her eyes to Alejandro's worried gaze. She felt the marble tiles beneath her back. Alice's lap cushioned her head. She prayed her feet weren't within biting distance of the tarantula.

The worry faded from Alejandro's eyes, replaced by amusement. "Jake fetched me."

"Not a healer?"

"I believe he was more concerned about what you would do to him when you awoke."

She looked past him. Jake stood with his hands linked behind his head, his face pale. Not with fear, she saw, but guilt.

Sitting up only made her head swim a little. Whatever his Gift had done to her, it hadn't hurt—or she'd healed while she'd been unconscious. She had to moisten her lips before she spoke. "I am impressed, Jake. But I will be more so when you can create that arc between two swords."

Relief lightened his psychic scent. Speculation lit his eyes. "That would do some damage."

"And might melt the metal, so do not use the swords I made when you practice." All of her dizziness gone, she rose to her feet. "We'll experiment with different conductors and weapons."

"Not today," Alejandro said.

She looked to him. Anticipation rose within her, sudden and hot. "Taylor?"

"Michael replaced me at sunset."

She must have been unconscious for at least twenty or thirty minutes, then—and she still had not completed the task she'd come here to do.

To Jake, she said, "Do you have the spikes?"

When he called them in from his cache, she immediately saw that the two spikes Jake and Alice had found pinning the wings of Zakril's skeleton matched the one she'd pulled from Rosalia's forehead.

She called in that spike. A touch of her Gift to each one confirmed her suspicion. "They are the same."

Alice frowned, looking at the spike in Irena's hand. "Are you certain? They do not look at all alike."

"I changed this one when I freed Rosalia." With a pass of her Gift, Irena reshaped it. "But I am not certain because of the appearance—the composition of the iron feels identical. That only happens when iron is smelted from the same ore. They were probably molded at the same time, as well."

Jake shook his head in disbelief. "So some demon has been carrying a stash of these in his hammerspace for two thousand years plus?"

"They could have been distributed to more than one demon," Irena said, though she doubted it.

She sensed that Alejandro also doubted . . . and that he wasn't surprised that the spikes were from the same source. "Find Khavi," he said to Jake. "Ask her if she knew any demon who made or used weapons like these."

Jake nodded. "Zakril was her brother, so I'm guessing she'd like to know that whoever spiked him might still be running around."

"I wonder if she would," Alejandro said quietly. "But we will ask her, regardless."

"All right." Jake held out his hand for Alice's. "Let's get going."

As soon as they disappeared, Irena formed her wings and said, "And we should ask the demon who was a friend at the time."

Alejandro looked at her, his expression unreadable. What went on behind his dark eyes? She did not know, *still*. But she could imagine. No one had suggested that Rael was responsible for Zakril's murder, and yet she'd immediately put it out there based on a flimsy connection to Khavi.

"I am ready to blame him for anything," she admitted.

"Perhaps. But that isn't reason *not* to look at him." He took a step, and his wings arched out behind him.

She waited on the ground as he launched himself into the sky. Watching him was sheer pleasure. She loved the way he flew, his body as straight as an arrow, each powerful flap of his wings. Smiling, she lifted into the air and joined him. The wind caressed her feathers with silken warmth, teasing the tips. He'd headed southeast—not toward his quarters, but hers.

Mine. He was. But this time, she would hold on to him.

He glanced over as she caught up with him. "Consider this scenario: The woman that Rael loved is Anaria."

Irena fought her immediate response—that a demon couldn't love. But they did, in their own twisted way. "Zakril had helped imprison her. So Rael murders Zakril to help Anaria . . . or to get her husband out of his way?" Whatever the reason, Rael would be helping himself.

"And then kills his own wife after Anaria returns to get *her* out of the way."

"Julia Stafford wasn't spiked through the head."

"No. But we found Rosalia just before his wife was murdered. And that murder has been a distraction enough that we haven't looked hard in Rome's direction. Deacon was the one who led us to Rome; now Deacon's community is gone."

Something in her stomach twisted. Caelum passed below in a blur of white and cream. "Do you think Deacon is involved?"

He shook his head. "That is not what I suggest. Only that a demon like Rael would be able to broker a deal with Acciaioli and the nosferatu in Rome—and if Rael was angry with Deacon for interfering, he might have punished him for it. I am also suggesting that if Rael was once a friend to Anaria—perhaps still is—he might also be a friend to the nephilim, who massacred the vampires in Rome before touching any other city."

Friends with Anaria? "And so he was angry when I said I would kill her."

"And the nephilim arrived at your forge not long after."

The magnitude of what Alejandro suggested finally hit her. Rael positioned himself as loyal to both Anaria and to Belial. Would not Belial's other demons turn on him? Or had he convinced them that he was manipulating Anaria with the appearance of friendship? Did they know he played both sides?

She could not imagine the balance necessary to walk such a dangerous line. "Do you believe he could do all of that?"

"He did not become Belial's lieutenant by thinking on a small scale. It's impossible to say how many roles he plays, and how many plots he manages. But he didn't attain his position by juggling only one or two."

"And how many will you take on?" She immediately regretted the question. It would lead to a fight, and she'd stir from this waking dream. But her anger was swelling from deep within, and she couldn't stop it. "How many, Olek?"

His jaw tightened. "As many as I must."

"Will you lead Belial's demons? Will you marry a human to forward your political career?"

"You goad me."

She did. Dropping her left wing, she slipped past a needle-thin spire stabbing high into the air above Caelum. She'd once known a Guardian who'd impaled himself on it.

"You take everything on yourself, Olek. A rock turns, and your honor is destroyed for four hundred years. You plan to deceive thousands of humans by continuing a demon's deception, and your honor is not touched."

"Millions of humans," he corrected softly. Too softly. His anger had risen as hot as hers. "And it was not the rock. It was you, offering yourself in trade for my life. And yesterday, I discover that what he did was *worse* than either of us thought it would be."

"That trade was never about you. I had to do it no matter the feelings between us—and I would have done the same for anyone with a knife at their throat." Her breath hitched painfully in her chest. "And you would have made exactly the same choice if I had been in your position, even if I begged you not to do it."

His eyes darkened. Alejandro must see that she spoke the truth. And she knew that if their positions had been reversed, he would never have thought she was dishonored. And she . . . would have hated herself for falling, for placing him in a position where that terrible decision had to be made.

"And my decision is not about you, Irena. Rael must die, but we must be able to keep the resources we have through SI. And so I will take his place, despite the feelings between us." Though his voice was even, his tone stung like the lash of a whip. "But *do not* tell me that what you felt had no influence. You would have held out against the demon if you had not wanted me."

Irena snapped upright, hovering. Her throat burned, tight with tears and shame. "*You tell me.* Tell me that you wish I didn't want you. That you wish I hadn't loved you."

His face whitened. He stared at her, motionless but for the quiet beat of his wings that held him aloft.

"Tell me, Olek, that you would trade all of my shame and take back your honor in exchange for my heart."

"I cannot," he admitted hoarsely. "I would wish both of us through Hell first."

So would she. Her laugh was short and bitter. "If you step into a demon's role, you will take us there."

This time, fury paled his skin. He turned away from her, and silently dove toward her courtyard. Irena followed him, vanished her wings, and dropped the last few feet, landing in a crouch.

He glanced back at her as she pushed her Gift into steel, forming his new swords. She tossed the weapons to him. "They are yours."

Alejandro hefted their weight, his displeasure obvious. "Why the alterations?"

"You have used the same swords for four hundred years. They no longer suit you."

"Perhaps not. But I'm accustomed to them."

She sneered and called in her knives. "Can you not use other weapons?"

"I can. But there is no reason."

"There *is*. Your old swords do not fit, and I will not make any more for you. So you had best learn these."

His jaw clenched. Then he lifted his left sword, sweeping his right behind him. "Then we begin."

Fighting did not release her anger. Seconds stretched into minutes, and it only grew harder, shining brilliantly, like the sharp edge of a diamond. She blocked his every strike with her knife. He feinted low. She whipped around, plowed her elbow into his stomach. When he bent over, she smashed the back of her head to his face.

She didn't get a chance to follow through. His blade slipped in from the side and pressed against her throat. She froze, and he laughed softly into her ear. She scented the blood on his breath.

"These *are* good swords, Irena."

He pushed against her. His erection prodded against her back.

She almost stumbled. What was this? A moment ago, he hadn't been aroused. There had only been anger between them, and the fight. Until she'd hit him.

His thigh pushed between hers. His lips skimmed the side of

her neck, unexpected heat that plunged straight through to her core. Her knees weakened.

She reached back, yanked his hair. Alejandro instantly reacted. He vanished his swords and his hand dove down, cupping her sex. He lifted her up to grind between her legs from behind. A cry wrenched from her, shocked and desperate for more.

"Again," Alejandro commanded.

She tore out of his grip, faced him. "What is this?"

With the edge of his thumb, he wiped blood from his bottom lip. "I do not yet know. But there is apparently nothing you can do to me that will not make me want you. You could cut my chest open and I would beg you for more."

She shook her head. "I don't want that."

"And I don't need pain to want you. God knows, I want you without it." His mouth twisted. "But don't tell me you never want to hurt me. When you do—and you *will*, Irena—know that no harm is done. It is only foreplay."

She didn't want that kind of freedom, that much power over him. Did she? Excitement crackled along beside her anger, her astonishment.

His laugh was harsh. "You balk? Last night, you sucked my soul into your keeping. Do you not take this part of me, too?"

He dared bring last night up now? Rage shook her. She made herself remain still. "I do not want to fight."

"About this? About Rael? What else about me will you not take?"

Not take? Her throat tightened. "Olek—"

"No!" He started toward her, then stopped. His hand slashed through the air in a gesture that felt too close to finality. "I have accepted all of you. You cannot do the same."

How could he believe that? "I do."

"No. You cannot make a good weapon of faulty steel." His voice roughened, and she did not know if it was in anger or pain. "And you cannot imagine that I would see the same faults you do, but transform them into something good. That I can take a demon's deception and create something honorable. Or that I could step into a corrupted role and use it in the right way."

She stared at him, his accusation echoing between her ears. While she tried to take it in, he shook his head and walked away. Her heart leapt in fear. She stalked after him.

"Face me, Olek!" *Let me fight for you.*

Panic surged through her when he didn't stop. She didn't give him warning. In a burst of speed, she launched herself onto his back, rammed her knee into his spine and pulled at his hair.

He turned on her like a predator unleashed. His fingers digging into her arms, he hauled her over his shoulder and slammed her back to the ground. He came down over her. Fury stretched his body as tight as a steel wire. She stared up at him, tried to catch her breath to speak. His thighs pushed between hers, spreading them wide.

His lips drew back from clenched teeth. "I have taken you! Your anger and your stubborn head and all of you." He reached between them, ripping her leggings. "One way or another, you will take me!"

Surprise held her motionless before need swept it away. *Yes.* She'd take him just like this, wanted him just like this. Irena vanished her leggings and his fingers scraped her bare skin. Her blood racing, she felt his clothes disappear, and the heat of his flesh against hers.

Bracing his hands beside her shoulders, Alejandro loomed over her. The blunt tip of his shaft parted her wet folds. Shaking with anticipation, she lifted to him.

He shoved inside, huge and thick, and her body screamed with the pleasure of it. Oh, gods. Fierce joy pierced the heart of her. She'd measured his length, but hadn't known what it was to be taken by Olek, finally. She arched, trying to force him deeper, and cried out when she did.

He froze at the sound, awareness sweeping through his psychic scent like an icy wind. Irena hauled his mouth down to hers. No stopping. No thinking. She bit his lip and tasted blood.

With a feral growl, Olek kissed her back, hot and wet. His hips swung, hammering deep with every stroke. *Yes.* By the gods, yes. Finally, taken. Finally taking. Each heavy thrust sent her heartbeat racing faster, wound the ecstasy tighter. Her nails raked his back, digging furrows in his skin. He groaned and licked deeper into her mouth. Her frantic breaths filled their kiss. He pinned her hips and twisted his and she slammed into orgasm, slick muscles clamping around his thick shaft.

When she fell out of its grip, Olek lifted his head. Remorse darkened his eyes. "Again," he demanded hoarsely. "Forgive me. Again."

She breathed his name and his mouth reclaimed hers. No fury heated this kiss. Only need. Only the feel of him against her, inside her. And although the anger between them was spent, his skin was still fire. His lips burned.

Without breaking their kiss, he lifted her ankle to his shoulder. He worked into her in a relentless rhythm—in and in, slow inch by inch, he kept his vow and repeated it. Pleasure became the sweetest pain, sizzling across her nerves. Every endless thrust, every kiss stoked it higher, brighter, until her senses immolated in white-hot flares.

She'd barely come back to herself when he said, "Again, Irena."

She'd melted, and he wasn't done. Half-panting, half-laughing, Irena pushed him over onto his back. "Stupid, prideful man."

"Not pride." His voice was low, his heartbeat as rapid as hers. "I cannot believe I'm here with you like this. And I don't want it to end."

Her heart clenched. For a moment, she took in the sheer beauty of him before lowering her head.

She kissed him slowly as she rode him. His hands held her hips. He rocked up to meet her, faster and faster. Between kisses, between licks to his throat and his jaw, Irena whispered to him, urged him on. Her voice, the slide of their bodies, the pounding of their hearts filled the silence of the courtyard. His smoky scent filled her lungs, her mind, and she buried her face in his neck, drawing it in deeper. *Olek.* No, she didn't want this to end, either—she wanted to devour him all, to take all there was to take. To glory in the tight stretch of her body around his, the taste of him on her lips, his ragged breaths in her ears.

But although she wished it, they couldn't stay here forever, and there would always be *again*. Her fingers slipped between them and circled his length, following the slick rise of her sex. He groaned and it was a harsh, tortured sound. When he began to shake, she pulsed her Gift. He came silently, his teeth gritted and his body arching into a taut bow, lifting her with him.

Irena clung to his shoulders, barely able to form a thought except that they were both well finished.

Olek must have agreed. His mouth found hers and he did not stop kissing her until his flesh softened, until she smiled against his lips and raised her head.

He sighed. "I did not intend—"

"Do not regret this," she warned.

"I do not. But I didn't want anger between us."

She ran her finger down the soft point of his goatee. His lips were still reddened. Hers must have been, too. "Idiot. With us, anger is clumped with the rest—not always at the forefront, but always there. And if our anger ends like this, it is not so bad, yes?"

He kissed her in response.

When he lowered his head again, she held it cradled in her hands, his hair thick against her palms and Caelum's marble hard beneath. She searched for the right words to say—and realized he'd said them many times.

"Forgive me, Olek."

His brows drew together, but he didn't speak. He waited for her to explain.

"I have lost faith in many things of late. And I have lumped them all together." Stupidly, blindly. She swallowed and pushed on. "I should have separated you out of them. I should have trusted that you would do right. And I will try to see your taking Rael's position as you do."

He closed his eyes. She thought he might have breathed a prayer as he raised his mouth to hers and kissed her. Kissed her as if he'd never stop, kissed her as she'd always thought a man might kiss when he loved a woman and she had just given him the world.

He shivered beneath her; his body tightened.

No. Alejandro hadn't shivered. *Caelum* had. And Alejandro had stiffened in reaction.

Irena sat up. "What was that?"

Shaking his head, Alejandro rolled over onto his knees, forming his clothes. Irena did the same, and reached out with her senses. No one. But something felt different in the back of her mind. Something had changed . . . something new. Something with the same resonance in her psyche as a Gate.

By the gods. *A Gate*.

Her stomach dropped, and then she was on her feet, sprinting toward central Caelum. In the middle of the city, near Michael's temple, lay a huge courtyard that no one but the teleporting Guardians could enter. Gates surrounded it, made of marble arches; between them, buildings and temples created walls.

Those walls had shifted, their shape had changed. Irena raced around them until she found the new archway.

A *new* Gate. Somewhere on Earth, a Guardian had sacrificed herself to save another. At that spot, a new portal had formed, linked to this Gate in Caelum.

And whoever had killed a Guardian was on the other side. Irena called in her knives.

Steel glinted in Alejandro's hands. "I am at your back," he said.

CHAPTER 18

The coppery scent of vampire blood struck Irena the moment she rushed through the Gate into an enormous room. A *familiar* room—the gymnasium at Special Investigations.

Echo and Ben lay in the center, chests split open, eyes wide with surprise in death. Their weapons lay beside them, un-bloodied. Whoever had done this hadn't given the vampires a chance to defend themselves.

And she would not give *them* time.

Her gaze darted around the room—empty—and she turned as Alejandro came through the Gate. She saw his shock as he recognized the gymnasium, then his cold fury when he spotted Echo and Ben. She looked past him through the open double doors, where the Gate had formed. Her blood ran cold.

A single red shoe lay in the hallway.

No. By the gods, *no*. Not Dru.

Alejandro caught her as she stumbled forward. "The Gate, Irena. You can't go through the door."

She'd end up back in Caelum. Her voice trembled. "Make one."

He nodded, and passed in front of her. She tried to prepare herself, stepped forward until she stood only a small distance from the Gate.

Grief hit her, almost doubled her over. Pim sat in the hallway, cradling Dru's body against her chest. Though her arm was limp, Dru still gripped her sword. Blood soaked her white lab coat and pooled on the floor beneath them. Pim held Dru's blond head against the body's neck, and the frantic thrust of the novice's healing Gift carried her terror, her grief, her denial.

Swallowing hard against her own, Irena whispered, "Pim."

The novice looked up, her eyes glassed over and cheeks wet. Her voice was high and thin. "I can't fix her. I can't fix her."

No. Dru couldn't be healed. Her vision blurred, and Irena wiped at her eyes. *Not now. Not yet.* A loud shredding sound ripped through the room, and she glanced over at Alejandro. He'd lifted his swords over his head, speared his blades through the wall, and was dragging them down to the floor. Within seconds, they'd be out of the gymnasium.

"Who did this, Pim? What are we facing?" When the novice didn't answer, Irena sharpened her voice. "Pim!"

"The nephilim." Her healing Gift shook against Irena's psyche again. "She pushed me behind her. I can't fix her."

A shout came from farther within the warehouse, followed by a desperate scream. Irena's gut tightened. That had been Savi.

"Hurry, Olek."

In answer, he slammed his foot into the wall, sending the piece he'd cut out crashing into the hallway.

She followed him through.

They didn't have to go far. Beyond the end of the hall, at least four nephilim stood in the hub. They'd shifted to their demon forms. Their black wings blocked her view of the opposite hallway, which led to the warehouse entrance, but she could hear several racing heartbeats, someone choking on their breath, a soft keening. Panic and pain raged through psychic scents, all too chaotic to separate.

She drew abreast of Olek at the end of the hall. He took the right side, she the left.

No nephilim were guarding the mouth of the corridor. Across the hub and to her left, five stood in a large semicircle that cordoned off a quarter of the room. Each nephil faced outward—protecting someone behind them. Through the gaps between their wings, Irena saw a woman holding Colin Ames-Beaumont against the wall.

Anaria.

Though she'd been called the light twin, Anaria had the same coloring as Michael. Bronze skin, waist-length black hair. Beneath a simple linen sheath cinched with a narrow leather belt, her form appeared small and delicate. Her legs looked no more substantial than a yearling doe's.

Irena couldn't doubt her strength, however. The grigori had lifted Ames-Beaumont aloft with one hand around his neck. The vampire was as strong as a novice, but though he pulled at her wrist—was probably trying to crush it—Anaria did not appear to feel his efforts.

Blood slicked the front of the vampire's black shirt. A leather-wrapped hilt protruded from his chest. Anaria had impaled a sword through his ribs, pinning him to the wall.

But not through the heart, Irena saw with relief. Not yet.

Farther left of the nephilim, near the head of the corridor leading to Lilith's office, Sir Pup stood in his demon form—taller than Alejandro, his eyes glowing crimson. But the hellhound wasn't threatening the nephilim; instead, he restrained a struggling figure beneath his forepaws, the jaws of his middle head gently gripping the back of her neck. Savi.

Irena stepped out of the corridor.

The nephil closest to her spoke. "No Guardians will die if you do not fight us. We have no quarrel with you."

Were they cow-fucking idiots? When they'd killed Dru, Echo, and Ben, they'd established a monster of a quarrel with the Guardians. She glanced at Alejandro. He'd stolen farther into open space on the right side of the hub and crouched, attempting to look past the nephilim and the hellhound, into the left corridor.

Her heart careening against her ribs, Irena glanced back at the stairs. Three novices—Randall, Becca, and Nadia—had gathered at the top, their swords ready. Though their faces were pale with fear, they looked to her for a signal to attack.

Irena shook her head. *Stay there,* she signed.

Three novices, a hellhound, Alejandro, and her—against five nephilim and Anaria. It would not be a fight. It would be a slaughter.

The choking she'd heard earlier repeated, a tortured gurgling breath.

"Lilith," Alejandro said softly, and glanced up at Irena.

She walked toward the center of the hub, almost within a sword's length of a nephil, and took a single glance into the corridor. Hugh held Lilith tightly to his chest, agony carving deep lines beside his mouth. Blood slid from between Lilith's lips. Her body convulsed, but like Dru, she still gripped her sword. Had she tried to protect Ames-Beaumont from Anaria? The grigori would have stopped her with barely a flick of her hand.

And to a human, even a human as strong as Lilith, a flick of Anaria's hand was a crushing blow.

Irena turned and sprinted back down the gymnasium hall, where Pim sat rocking Dru's body.

"Pim, you are needed."

"I can't fix her. I can't—"

No time for this. Irena ripped Dru's head out of the novice's hands. Pim's shriek became a scream as Irena grabbed a fistful of her black hair and ran, dragging the novice down the hall. She raced into the hub, skirting the nephilim, past the hellhound.

Hugh glanced up. The desolation in his eyes became a fragile hope.

Irena shoved the novice down next to Lilith. "Heal her."

Doubt seized Pim's features. "I—"

"Now!"

The novice scrambled to her knees. Her Gift reached out, searching for Lilith's injuries.

Irena turned, stalked back into the hub. Savi struggled beneath Sir Pup's giant bulk. Irena's stomach performed an uneasy dive. Savi's eyes glowed as red as the hellhound's. Her bare feet had stretched and lengthened. Her desperate cries had become growls and whimpers.

The hellhound watched her approach with his left head, his razor-sharp teeth bared. He'd obviously been ordered to protect Savi, but Irena didn't know whether Sir Pup could hold the young vampire if she shifted.

Irena sank to her heels. She didn't need to get low to speak to Savi, but it offered her a better view through the nephilim's wings.

And she could see Olek now—and he, her. He held his cell phone. She briefly met his eyes. He shook his head.

Anaria must have put a shielding spell up around the warehouse, he signed.

Which meant that they couldn't call out for help—and no one could come in, either through the warehouse entrance or by teleporting. Only through the Gate—and unless Michael happened to go to Caelum, he wouldn't know the new portal was there.

But he wouldn't teleport to Caelum. Michael was only a few miles—a few *seconds*—away, watching over Taylor.

Feeling as if her stomach were lined with lead, she studied Anaria. From this angle, the grigori stood in profile to her. Her black hair was pulled back in a tail at her nape, revealing the graceful line of her neck. Like Khavi, Anaria possessed startling beauty—but she had none of Khavi's fierceness. Her composed features suggested a deep and reassuring calm.

The serenity of her expression didn't alter as she slipped a dagger from the belt at her waist and slashed Ames-Beaumont's wrist. His blood ran. A bowl replaced Anaria's dagger, and she held it beneath the crimson stream.

Bracing herself, Irena glanced at Ames-Beaumont.

Terror ripped through her. Her muscles trembled with the need to turn and run. Her heart galloped, her blood racing into her head in a dizzying rush. Clenching her teeth, she fought the psychic effect, strengthening her mental blocks. She kept looking.

Ames-Beaumont's face was turned in her direction, his

beauty a physical pain, a burning behind her eyes. His tortured gaze had fixed on Savi. His lips moved silently.

Beside Irena, Savi whimpered and begged the hellhound to let her up. The nephilim in front of them edged closer together, preparing to catch the vampire if she burst free.

Quietly, Irena said, "They'll kill you, Savi."

Heedless, the vampire struggled to pull herself forward. "Please." Savi's voice had become an almost unrecognizable growl. "*Please*, Sir Pup!"

"Do not let her move, pup." Ames-Beaumont's plea was hardly more than a whisper squeezed past Anaria's choking grip and the sword through his ribs. "Do not fight him, sweet. I can bear this pain. I cannot bear you hurt."

Savi went still, her growls dissolving into anguished sobs.

Anaria slashed his wrist open again. Irena's fingers clenched at her thighs. She glanced over at Olek, knew he saw her helpless rage.

He smoothly stood, and she could only see his tall boots, his black trousers. She didn't know how he managed to keep his voice even, concealing his anger and revealing only his strength when he spoke.

"You've murdered one of us, Anaria."

The grigori turned slightly, looking first to Olek, then over at Irena. Her amber eyes were friendly. Her harmonious voice pulled at Irena, drew her in like a warm embrace. "We told the young one not to fight. My children defended themselves."

For an instant, Anaria's explanation made perfect sense. Irena almost found herself nodding before the words penetrated.

By the gods, what kind of power was that? Terrified, seething, Irena rocked back on her heels, mentally putting distance between herself and Anaria.

She saw Alejandro brace his feet slightly farther apart. He'd felt that, too. This time, his voice held the barbed silk of aristocratic disdain.

"And the vampires? Your children needed to defend themselves against young vampires, as well?"

"No." Anaria vanished the bowl of blood. "Vampires are abominations. Bloodlust is a curse never meant for mankind."

"But you obviously need *that* vampire," Alejandro said.

Anaria tilted her head as she looked up at Ames-Beaumont. With a soft smile, she stroked her fingers down his face. Weakly, he tried to jerk away from her touch, his fangs bared.

"This one cannot hide what he carries within him. My Zakril was the same; he could not hide his light." A deep sorrow filled her expression, made Irena want to weep. "But although this vampire has the look of an angel, it is not light that lives inside him. It is only Chaos."

Abruptly, her hand fell to the handle of the sword sticking out from his chest.

Irena called in her knives. "Anaria!"

Anaria paused, glanced at her. Across the room, a pyramid of bricks appeared in front of Alejandro. He kneeled beside them.

Irena swallowed hard. Not bricks. Plastique. Enough to destroy the warehouse, possibly more. The explosion would kill everyone inside, but the sacrifice was well worth it.

Irena could not prevent Dru's death, or Ben and Echo's. But if one more died here, then the nephilim and Anaria would, too.

She projected the full force of her anger and hate. "If any more are harmed, demon spawn, we will not have mercy on you."

"I do not wish to harm you. I would persuade all of you to join us."

Irena turned, began to slowly circle around the nephilim toward Olek. She needed to touch him again first. "Join you for what?"

"We will take the throne Below, and slay the demons. We will free the humans in the Pit from their torture."

Oh, how Irena wanted to. She forced her gaze away from Anaria. On the stairs, the novices stared at the grigori, their faces yearning, frightened. Irena vanished one of her knives.

If she kills Ames-Beaumont, Alejandro and I will fight. You will run. Find Michael. He is with Taylor.

Becca frowned. *But—*

You. Will. Run. Each word was a hard, sharp gesture.

Becca shrank back. Each of the novices nodded, agreeing to flee.

Her heart aching, Irena wanted to order Alejandro to do the same. She knew he wouldn't.

"And the humans here on Earth?" Alejandro asked.

"No more will be destined for the pain of Hell. My children will ensure there is no sin."

She spoke with such conviction, Irena almost believed her. But the uncertain push of Pim's healing Gift reminded her of the truth behind Anaria's words.

The nephilim hadn't done that to Lilith. Only Anaria, who didn't have to follow the Rules, could have injured a human without consequence. And once she took over Hell's throne, her children would have the same freedom.

"Say what you mean, demon spawn. You and your children would prevent all sin by crushing human free will."

Anaria turned to look at her, a sad smile curving her lips. Ames-Beaumont's hands wrapped around the handle of the sword through his chest. She stopped him from pulling it out with a single finger against the pommel.

"You sound like my brother," Anaria said, her gaze following Irena. "The angels exercised free will, rebelled, and became demons. Humans make demons of themselves, and they, too, suffer Hell. But we will show them the way. They will have free will, and they will be free to choose only kindness. Only love."

Was she insane? "As if humans are children."

Anaria nodded. "And I will be the mother who guides them."

Cold horror crawled up the back of Irena's neck. Anaria wasn't insane, she realized. Just utterly certain that she was right.

That was far more frightening. Irena reached Olek's side. She touched his hand. His fingers squeezed hers before letting go. Irena called in her knife again. Alejandro held a sword in his right hand—and what she thought was a detonator appeared in his left.

"So will you join us?" Anaria's question included them both.

Irena shook her head. "No."

The grigori sighed and turned back to Ames-Beaumont. "If you have any regrets, vampire, perhaps you will think on them now."

A terrible keening filled the room. Savi struggled beneath the hellhound, scratching wildly at the floor. No, that young vampire would not stop fighting.

Neither would Irena. She adjusted her grip on her knives.

"I have no regrets," Ames-Beaumont said hoarsely, his gaze on Savi. "I loved you well, my sweet Savitri. Even in death, I will love you."

The warmth projecting from his psychic scent echoed his words. Irena's heart constricted into a tight knot.

Anaria hesitated. She stared up at the vampire's painfully beautiful face, then looked over at Savi. "Perhaps we will not be too hasty," she said softly. "I may have need of your blood again."

She yanked her sword from his chest, and he crumpled to the floor. Without another glance at any of them, Anaria strode to the corridor leading to the warehouse entrance.

The nephilim filed after her like ducklings.

Sir Pup let Savi go. She scrambled forward, gathering Ames-Beaumont into her arms. The hellhound turned toward Lilith.

Irena entered the corridor after the nephilim, Olek at her side. The last nephil did not even turn to watch his back.

The sliding door at the security station had been ripped away. Inside the station, a novice lay bleeding and unconscious, but still alive. Irena didn't stop.

The four-inch thick steel door leading outside hadn't been smashed in, as Irena had expected. Anaria had a keycard. She slid it through the lock and stepped outside. The nephilim followed her, one by one.

Beside the door, Alejandro wiped away the blood from the carved symbols that had created the shielding spell around the warehouse. Noise from outside the building rushed in.

Irena stood in the entrance, her palm flat against the steel door, watching the nephilim disappear into the night sky.

"Do we go after them?" Alejandro asked quietly.

And be killed? She shook her head. "We can't."

She walked back into the warehouse, but had to stop a few feet inside. She couldn't breathe. The corridor shrank around her.

Alejandro touched her back. There. Always there.

And, by the gods, she was a Guardian. She didn't *need* to breathe. She whipped around, punched her fist through the wall.

Again, and again—until the walls stopped closing in on her.

❧

Taylor worked to clear everything off her desk that might give Jorgenson a reason to chew her ass out once she got back to regular duty. Almost an hour after she was ready to go home, and forty-five minutes after Joe took off and she had nothing but his empty chair to look at, Michael—in his SI agent form—appeared beside her. Or maybe he hadn't just appeared. Maybe he'd walked into the bullpen and she hadn't noticed. God knew, he'd sneaked up on her before.

"About time." She grabbed her jacket, knowing she sounded irritated and ungrateful—but, goddammit, she *was* irritated, and not feeling so grateful. She'd been on edge since sunset. She'd thought Khavi's prediction would feel less real as time passed; instead, it weighed a little heavier with each tick of the clock. "This isn't going to work if I'm stuck waiting for you to show up before I can go anywhere. Isn't the idea that you stay where I am, making sure I'm not vamp bait?"

He could have at least looked apologetic. He only said, "I was here."

Great. Nice to know *now*.

Like everyone else in the bullpen, the desk sergeant had a phone growing out of his ear. She tapped her fingers across his desk as she passed. He waved her on without looking up.

No surprise. Even when they weren't busy, no one in the bullpen looked her in the eyes much anymore.

She kept silent until they hit the stairs at the rear of the station, leading down to the parking lot. "You were really here?"

"Yes."

"*Where?*"

"The roof." The glance he gave her might have been wry. She couldn't tell. The face he wore looked softer than his own, but the same man still lived behind it. "Waiting for you to leave."

Was he serious? She stopped, shaking her head. "Hold on. This supposedly worries you guys so much that the Doyen himself takes time out to sit on the roof of my station—yet you expected me to walk outside at night when I don't know you're there?"

Michael frowned and shifted back to his Doyen-sized body, and she suddenly realized how *big* he was. Even without his wings, even in his loose pants and tunic that couldn't have been less threatening, he seemed to fill the narrow stairwell. She suppressed the urge to take a step back, to give herself more space.

"I assumed you knew that I would be nearby, even if you cannot see me."

Unbelievable. "I don't work that way. There are two people in my life I trust enough to assume they'll be there. One is probably about ten minutes from his recliner, a beer, and a basketball game on the tube. The other's waiting for me, cooking and reading a cozy mystery—because it's *cozy*, and the detectives always make it back home." She turned her back to him and continued down the stairs. "I don't know you well enough to trust you like that."

"When you do, you still will not."

Taylor was trying to figure out that softly-spoken statement when he appeared at the bottom of the stairs ahead of her. He must intend to go through the door first. She didn't plan to argue.

When he looked back at her, the cast of his face resembled carved granite. "Margaret Wren awaits you outside."

"What?" Rael's butler, here? Taylor was glad he'd told her now; she could hide her surprise later. "How is she feeling?"

"Determined. Uncertain."

Which could be anything. Wren could be here to confess or

to shoot up the station. "She hasn't been turned into a vampire, has she?"

He smiled slightly. "No."

"Then let's go."

He didn't change back to his agent persona, although his clothes altered and became a suit. She eyed his size. He didn't have *mob enforcer* written all over him, but he definitely had the intimidation factor.

Because he couldn't protect her from Wren, she realized. If he interfered with a human's free will, even the Doyen would have to Fall. The thought made her vaguely sick.

"Don't do anything stupid," she said as she followed him through the door.

She thought he might have sighed. "You must stop talking to Lilith."

Taylor smiled, her gaze sweeping the lot. Wren wasn't attempting to hide. Her uniform starched and pressed, her hair almost white beneath the lot's security lights, she waited beside Taylor's personal vehicle. How she'd known which was hers, Taylor wasn't going to ask.

Not right now.

Her phone vibrated in her pocket as she walked across the lot. She ignored it.

Wren's hands were out in the open. A good sign. Her flat gray eyes skipped to Michael before meeting Taylor's. "Detective."

"Miss Wren. Just out for a walk?"

"No. May I speak with you in private? I am conflicted."

Conflicted—had Wren witnessed Rael do something illegal? Taylor barely stopped herself from doing a fist pump. She glanced at Michael. He nodded once and moved a few parking spots down. He could still hear everything, but Wren didn't need to know that.

"I am not going to reach for it, detective—but I have my employer's driver's license inside my jacket pocket."

Taylor frowned. "I don't—"

"He is currently operating a motor vehicle without a license in his immediate possession, which I believe is unlawful," Wren continued in a flat tone, but put a little more emphasis behind the rest, "and may endanger the party he has with him."

Taylor got it. She didn't understand the code this woman lived by, but she understood that Wren was doing her damnedest to deliver a message in a way that didn't break that code.

"Where are they headed? Perhaps we can inform this other party that he's riding with someone who shouldn't be operating a vehicle."

"The airport. My employer told me that Mr. Deacon has almost completed a job for him. They are returning to Prague, where it will be finished."

A *job*? Oh, Jesus.

And why did *Deacon* sound familiar? Had she run across it in one of the files?

Wren went absolutely still, her gaze fixed over Taylor's shoulder. Taylor glanced around. Michael stood just behind and to the left of her. His eyes weren't black, but they might as well have been. The intensity of his amber gaze burned.

"Describe Deacon, please."

Wren's gaze darted to where Michael had been standing a few seconds ago. "How—"

"Describe him."

Without moving, Wren seemed to draw herself up straight. "Six-three, two-ten—all muscle. Brown hair, shoulder-length. Green eyes. Scars here"—she drew her forefinger in a line across the knuckles of her left hand— "and in a crescent below his jaw." She hesitated before adding, "Theatrically altered teeth."

The vampire from Savi's club. Oh, shit. Taylor was almost afraid to look at Michael now. She did. He appeared calm.

She wondered what was going on below that.

But the important thing here was that Rael had brought a vampire close to Wren. If the demon wasn't trying to hide Deacon, what else would he be revealing to her? And what kind of bargain would he use to keep her quiet . . . *if* he didn't have her killed, too?

Michael must have been thinking something similar. He gestured to the car. "Will you please come with us, Miss Wren?"

Wren didn't move. "Where, and why?"

"Special Investigations," Taylor said. Her phone vibrated again—just once. A text. "For your protection, and to explain a few things about bargains—and why you won't want to make any in the near future."

Wren only hesitated for a second before nodding. "I'll come with you."

"Good. Take the passenger side." She preferred to have Michael at her back; she thought Michael preferred that, too.

As Wren rounded the hood, Michael said softly, "She's not concerned for her safety. She's curious."

Taylor would have been freaked out, but it took all kinds. She got in, checked her message as she waited for Michael to slide into the back.

She frowned and turned to look at Michael. "It's Cordoba. He says, 'Michael is needed at SI.' And that's all."

But it was apparently enough. Michael's eyes flashed obsidian. Her breath caught. Suddenly, the man wasn't someone she wanted anywhere behind her, but something dangerous, frightening.

"SI," she dimly heard Wren repeat. "That is where we are going?"

"Yes," Michael said in the deep, harmonious voice she hadn't heard him use around other humans. In the confines of her car, it sounded utterly *in*human. "We are going now."

Taylor braced herself, realizing what was coming, but she didn't see him reach out. His hand touched her shoulder and the world dove into a flat spin.

God. Even before she opened her eyes, she smelled the blood. Michael held her against him, his arm like a rock across her stomach. Metal flashed in front of her eyes; he had a sword in his opposite hand.

Wren weaved dizzily on her knees next to them. She'd gone for the gun in her shoulder holster, but hadn't pulled it out yet. Her eyes were wide, her face white.

"I can stand," Taylor forced out.

Michael let her go. She stumbled a few steps, but thank God, remained upright. Their surroundings came into focus: the hub at the Special Investigations warehouse. A novice sat on the stairs, sobbing. Standing at the head of a hallway, Cordoba turned their way, lowering his phone. He started toward them, his hands flying in the Guardians' sign language.

Taylor's quick scan screeched to a halt. To her right, Savi sat with her back against a wall, Colin in her arms, her hands clamped tightly together over his chest. Blood covered them both.

"Oh, Jesus." Taylor rushed forward. "My God, Savi—what happened?"

"She got in." A bubble of hysterical laughter burst from the vampire. "Anaria was in our base, killing our dudes."

Colin made a soothing sound, though his eyes were closed and he was in some obvious pain. Savi gathered him somehow closer, burying her face in his hair. Tears slid over her cheeks.

"Where is he injured?"

Taylor glanced to the side. Wren knelt beside them, stripping out of her jacket. She folded it, obviously planning to make a compress, and Taylor thought now was probably not the time to tell her that, if Colin wasn't already dead, he'd be fine within an hour or two. Less, once Michael got his ass over here.

She looked at Savi. "This is Wren. Let her help you, okay? Whatever she does might make it easier for him."

Not really, but it gave them all something to do.

The vampire pulled in a sobbing breath, nodded. She unclamped her hands, and Taylor had a second to see the deep gash in his chest before Wren covered the wound with the jacket.

"Just hold that tight," the butler said, her lips thinned into a pale line. She touched his arm, apparently searching for the source of the blood there.

"It looks worse than it is," Taylor told her before rising to her feet. At the end of the gymnasium hallway, she saw Michael crouching beside a still form.

Her stomach rolled over. Oh, damn. She knew that one. Dru.

The body vanished. Michael stood again as Irena came out of the gymnasium doors, her hands fisted. The tattoos on her arms seemed to constrict, like rattlesnakes coiling before they struck. They stared at each other for a long second, until Irena's breath hissed through her clenched teeth.

"We could do *nothing*."

Her accusation didn't appear to touch him. He said simply, "You kept the others alive."

Irena turned her face away. Her chest rose as she took a deep breath. "It is not enough."

"No. It never is." He sounded as if the weight of the world pushed out his reply. "But it is what you have."

Irena nodded. She touched his arm as she passed him, continuing down the hall. Michael looked after her. Taylor thought the expression on his face might have been surprise, but it shuttered when he met her gaze. He strode into the gym.

When he emerged a second later, his face had set like stone. "Any others?"

"No." Though Cordoba spoke to the Doyen, he watched Irena, who was walking toward him. "We'd sent the team out to Buenos Aires. No other vampires were here."

Michael disappeared. She heard his voice a second later—behind her.

A young woman, her black hair in a bowl cut framing her tear-streaked face, kneeled beside Lilith. SI's director sat holding Castleford's hand. The hellhound lay on his belly next to her, licking blood from her cheek.

Michael touched the young Guardian's shoulder. "Well done."

He left the corridor, stopped next to Colin and Savi. Taylor felt *something*, like a compression of air through her chest. His healing Gift, apparently. Colin's grimace of pain vanished on a sigh. With a murmured thank-you, he pushed away the compress Wren held against his wound.

Wren stared at the now-healed skin showing through the tear in his shirt. The poor woman. Taylor wouldn't have blamed her for running out of here, screaming mad. Maybe Wren had been planning to before she glanced up at Colin. She reached forward, caught herself, and sat completely still. Her gaze didn't move from his face.

Taylor had felt like that the first couple of times she'd seen him up close, too.

"Did she take your blood?" Michael asked.

Colin nodded. "Two or three pints."

Michael glanced at Wren, then over to where Irena stood beside Cordoba. "Deacon is with Rael. The vampire completed a job for him."

Irena's face whitened. The serpents on her arms seemed to shrivel, drawing out into long, fragile lines. Cordoba closed his eyes, as if struck by a sudden, deep pain.

"That is all we know," Michael continued. He looked to Taylor. "You will stay here."

She didn't consider arguing. "Maybe Savi can—"

"Dig up Deacon?" The vampire's normally friendly smile was cold and sharp. "His computer is upstairs. We have his cell number. He's mine."

"No. He's mine." Irena pushed forward. Her knives appeared in her grip. Obviously, she meant *right now*. "Michael, can you teleport to him?"

"No. He is shielded."

Wren shook herself and glanced away from Colin. "They should be at the airport."

Irena frowned. "Why would Rael need an airport? He can fly."

The butler seemed to take that information in stride. "Then they are flying to Prague. That's where Deacon will finish the job."

Irena turned to Michael. "You will take us to Prague."

"Deacon would not be there yet, Irena," Cordoba said. "Whether by airplane or if Rael carries him, it will be several hours."

"Wait," Michael agreed. "We will see what Savitri can find." He glanced down at Colin—who, Taylor thought, seemed perfectly content to continue sitting on the floor with Savi's arms around him. "If Anaria took your blood, she is looking for access to Chaos. You will need to monitor the realm."

Colin clenched his jaw, but nodded. He stroked his hand over Savi's arm. "Go with Taylor, sweet. I'll watch the mirrors in the chamber upstairs."

"But—" Savi stopped herself. She sighed. "Okay. I'll be up soon to help you. Take this first."

A glass appeared in her hand. She gave it to Colin, held her arm above the rim, and sliced her wrist open with a dagger.

Taylor looked over at Wren, whose expressionless features still managed to convey horror and shock—and the curiosity Michael had mentioned earlier. Taylor realized that she was likely going to be the one stuck with the explanations.

She hoped Wren was ready for them.

Dawn had just begun to lighten the eastern sky when Olek found her standing on the building's edge. She heard him land behind her. When he slipped his arms around her waist, she leaned back against him, grateful that he could be a quiet man, and that he could leave her to her thoughts without leaving her alone.

Savi had been brilliant. Within an hour, the vampire had found within Deacon's computer an e-mail about Ames-Beaumont's oddities, and another describing the location of Irena's forge. She'd recovered his phone records, too—including a text that had requested Irena's info, Deacon's terse reply, and a photograph of Eva.

By then, discovering that Anaria had used Deacon's keycard to enter the warehouse hadn't mattered. She could have broken in, anyway.

Irena hadn't let herself think after Savi had laid out everything she'd found. The pain had been too sharp; she'd been too angry. She'd walked up to the second floor of the warehouse, and watched from a darkened observation room as Ames-Beaumont fought his terror in a chamber of mirrors.

The images of Chaos he'd projected still festered behind her eyes. Rivers of molten rock twisted across a bleak landscape of black stone. Wyrmwolves raced in packs, tearing pieces from one another as they ran, and swarming like a plague of rats when carrion fell from above.

Ames-Beaumont hadn't looked up often. When he had, he'd flinched as if the enormous dragons darting through the air passed within feet of him. He'd projected iridescent scales, gaping jaws with shreds of putrid flesh caught between serrated teeth, but couldn't project the scent that made him gag and retch. And although she couldn't hear the screams of the damned, she saw them clearly—their bodies dangling from a frozen ceiling, as if Chaos was a cavern beneath the bowels of Hell.

But Chaos wasn't *beneath* Hell. The ceiling formed a barrier between the two realms, but not a physical one. Within Hell lay a territory of ice and silence, and frozen within the ground were the faces of the damned—demons and humans who'd failed to fulfill their bargains. After death, their faces were eternally frozen in Hell, but their bodies rotted in Chaos. And like vultures picking over a battlefield, the dragons devoured the bodies—which regenerated, eventually to be eaten again. In Hell, the tortured souls remained aware of every second of it; there was no relief for them.

Irena didn't know if Deacon had been forced into a bargain with the demon. Perhaps the demon hadn't needed one—the lives of Deacon's lovers and his community were probably worth more to him than his soul.

But it was his life that Irena had to consider now. She and Alejandro would be heading to Prague soon.

She smoothed her hand over his forearm, signaling that she was ready to talk—if he was. Behind her, he shifted his weight, and a light tension seeped through his body.

"Have you decided what you will do?"

Straight to the point, her Olek. Irena thought of Eva's picture, her face a mask of fear. And she saw Dru's red shoe. "I will slay him."

He didn't reply, but she felt his response in the hardening of his psychic scent.

"You don't agree?"

"I cannot see that any of his decisions were made of his free will. Instead, I see a man who was broken and used by at least two demons."

Yes. They'd discovered that, as well. The origin and time of the messages hadn't matched Rael's movements. Another demon—probably one of Rael's subordinates—had been pulling Deacon's strings.

But Deacon could have cut those strings. "He made a decision when he contacted SI. He made one with every message he sent—"

"And attempted, in one, to refuse their orders. He did not stop fighting."

"But he gave in. He decided to do as they asked. He could have decided to come to me." Her throat was tightening. Her insides felt as if they'd been flayed. "He could have told us. We'd never have refused to help him. He *knew* I would fight for him, yet he decided against it, every time."

"Perhaps he did not believe that we could."

Her heart twisted. "That is our purpose. He knows that's what Guardians are for."

"But we don't always win. He would know that, too."

He sighed when she didn't respond. She didn't know how to tell him that she remained silent *not* because her answer was obvious, but because she had no answers.

"I do believe punishment is appropriate, Irena. But I do not think that death is."

What sort of punishment could possibly be appropriate—what was even an option? "Shall we beat him again? Shall we lock him away with only pig blood? Guardians have never been jailers."

"Perhaps we should start." He paused. "Are you slaying Deacon to punish him, or to punish yourself for bringing him to SI?"

She couldn't answer that, either. "You see too many sides, Olek."

"That doesn't sound like the insult is used to be."

"Because it is not."

He pulled her closer. She turned, wrapped her arms around him, pressing her cheek against his heart. His wings folded forward, the white feathers coming around her in a warm, weightless embrace. How had she ever thought she didn't want comfort from him? This was comfort, and more. And she'd had no idea how much she'd needed it. Especially now.

Her voice was thick, the words a physical ache. "When will the gathering for Dru be?"

"Selah and Jake are sending word to the others. It will be in two or three days."

Her eyes burned, and she pressed her face harder into his chest, as if the pressure could hold back the tears. "She fought me. Every step of the way, she fought me."

Olek held her, his hands running up and down her back. Irena gulped in air. The pain threatened to rip her apart. And she felt it. By the gods, how she felt it. She turned again. His wings parted. Cool air swept her face.

"You can never prepare for this," she whispered, and her chest would not stop shuddering. "The hand, the leg. You can be ready when you lose them. Not this."

"As it should be," he said softly.

Her breath hitched. And when Olek said, "I am at your back," she let go and screamed. She doubled over and he held her as she screamed and screamed. Her grief echoed through the city's metal canyons, sent startled birds winging into the heavens.

But it could never be loud enough.

CHAPTER 19

When Deacon awoke in his own bed, he knew he was dead.

A demon wouldn't care about his comfort—and if everything had gone right, Eva and Petra would be here with him. But, no. This wasn't Heaven or Hell or a dream, but a demon's way of twisting the blade in his gut before chopping off his head. Of making him hope before ripping hope away.

But it didn't matter. He didn't need hope. He just needed to follow this through, so that tomorrow, Eva and Petra *would* be waking up in this bed.

Even if he wasn't here with them.

He could hear Stafford and Caym talking in the living room or the library—he didn't recognize the language they used. Someone else was out there with them, but not saying much. A human. His psychic shields were soft; Deacon slid inside them easily. He sensed anticipation and fear, and a coldness similar to what he'd felt from the congressman's butler—but with a fragile edge, like ice that had been chipped into thin slivers.

Probably not someone who was here to help him.

Deacon sat up. Whoever had tucked him in had also stripped

him down to his trousers, but they hadn't taken his weapons. His swords and the gun that prince Alejandro had given him lay atop his bureau, clearly stating just how much an armed vampire concerned the demons: not at all. Just another little twist of that blade, he thought.

They could twist it all they wanted. He was ready to finish this.

Resolute, he dressed and strapped on the weapons. The demons didn't know that he'd been drinking nosferatu blood. He couldn't equal their speed, but he might take one by surprise. Once his community was safe, he had nothing to lose by trying.

His resolve almost failed at the bedroom door. A shudder ripped through him. He stopped, panic and dread tearing through his blood. *Nothing to lose.* Jesus Christ. Just his life. And he was scared shitless.

Silently, he pressed his shaking fist to his forehead, got the fear under control. He walked out of the bedroom like he'd been stone-cold from the moment he'd woken up. They might take everything from him, including his life—but he wouldn't give them the pleasure of knowing how much he wanted to keep it. How much he wanted to wake up with his friends tomorrow.

He passed the library. To enter the living room, he had to step around an upended chair—*still* there from when Caym had beaten him down. No one had been here to right it. He'd known the demon had taken Eva and Petra to another location, but seeing his empty apartment hammered home how much power the demon had over him. Not that he'd needed the reminder.

To his right, Caym stood in his demon form, his skin crimson, his leathery wings folded. Obsidian horns curled back from his forehead. The demon rhythmically flipped a dagger in his hand, catching it by the blade in his taloned fingers. When those hands had been pulverizing him, they'd looked human; Deacon wasn't certain whether this display was for the man who'd taken up the chair in the corner of the room or him.

Cadaverously thin and strung tight as a wire, the man watched Deacon with a cold, flat stare that didn't quite hide the hunger behind it. He was bald as a nosferatu, and around his eyes, his swarthy skin appeared delicate, irritated. Deacon couldn't smell the sickness that was killing the man, or the chemicals that had been treating it, but his desperation stank with the eye-watering punch of undiluted bleach.

Deacon might have felt pity if he hadn't had the sinking realization of what "final task" Stafford required of him.

Unlike Caym, the congressman hadn't shape-shifted. In a black suit and red tie, he took up the corner of Petra's dainty, powder blue sofa, his legs crossed at the knees and his arm resting along the curved back. The demon regarded him in the same way Irena sometimes examined a sword, the same way Eva looked at a painting, and Deacon was suddenly certain he hadn't fooled Stafford for one second. He'd bet the demon knew every thought that had passed through his mind since he'd woken up—not by looking into his head, but just by reading his face . . . or maybe just anticipating his every reaction, from strapping on his weapons, to his determination not to show them a hint of fear. Deacon thought he'd fooled Caym, though. And although Stafford had introduced himself only as Caym's associate, he realized the demon with the power here wasn't the one who'd beaten him. Caym was just the thug who got his hands bloody.

He remained facing Stafford. "Where are my partners? I've done what you asked."

"Yes, you have." Stafford gave a pleased smile. "The nephilim visited Special Investigations today, using your identification to get in. They'll collect Ames-Beaumont's blood, the others will try to stop them . . ." He waved his hand as if to say, *And you can imagine the rest.*

Deacon could, all too well. His stomach threatened to heave. "Eva and Petra. Now."

"I need one more thing from you first, Mr. Deacon."

"Fuck you. I've finished my part of the deal."

"But I have not." Stafford's pleasant smile disappeared, replaced by a reptilian stare. "I have made a bargain with Mr. Lukacs—he takes a life, I help him gain immortality. He has completed his part. I do *not* like having my part unfulfilled."

Deacon glanced at the man. Lukacs's hands shook against

his bony knees. It didn't take a giant leap to guess that a few days ago, those hands had been steady enough to hold a rifle. If Lukacs became a vampire, they'd be steady again—but he'd never look any healthier. "You don't need me to turn him. Any vampire could do it."

"True. But if you insist on honesty, I can tell you that I haven't needed you for any of this, Mr. Deacon. I never thought you and the Guardian that SI sent to Rome would survive the catacombs, and that the Guardians' search for the nosferatu would provide a distraction while Mr. Lukacs carried out his task."

The demon might as well have slid a knife between his ribs. Stafford hadn't thought he'd get out of the catacombs? That meant the demon had never intended to let Eva and Petra go, or to let his community live. The pain of that failure almost brought him to his knees.

Don't show it. Maybe the demon could read him, but Deacon would be damned if he'd give the fucker one visible sign of his misery. "What a shame, then, that Irena killed your nosferatu."

"A shame?" Stafford leaned forward, and every word was a twist of the knife. "Dead nosferatu or dead Guardian—both outcomes are equally enjoyable. As was the entertaining diversion you provided holding up your side of your agreement with Caym. But no, Mr. Deacon—I did not need you even then. You told us nothing that I didn't already know about Ames-Beaumont, and the one piece of information I didn't have—where to find Irena—resulted in failure. The only thing that you have ever been useful for is transforming Mr. Lukacs."

And *then* Deacon was dead. Yet Eva had been alive only a day ago, when he'd received her picture. Somewhere, she and Petra waited for him.

But even if he discovered where "somewhere" was, he couldn't let the demons leave here alive—Deacon would never win in a race against them. Once Stafford and Caym were dead, Deacon would have time to search for the women.

He needed to buy some time *here* first, however, so that he could figure out how to do the impossible.

"All right. I'll do it." He nodded toward Lukacs. "But you've got to bleed out first. I'm not drinking from you."

"My cancer won't—"

"No shit. But I don't want to fuck you. So open your vein, and when you're down to nothing, I'll give you mine."

Lukacs nodded, his face tense. Caym passed him a dagger, and the human sliced it over his wrist.

Deacon stopped breathing so that he wouldn't inhale the rich fragrance. The bloodlust didn't differentiate between the blood of a murderer and the blood of a newborn baby; it all smelled good to a vampire.

Lukacs had cut deep, was bleeding fast, but a human body carried a lot of blood. Deacon had a few minutes now.

As if bored, he leaned his shoulder against the wall and scanned the apartment, searching for inspiration. He couldn't make a stand out here. This room was too open; Stafford and Caym could come at him from too many directions. The front door offered escape, but it wouldn't lead to Eva and Petra. Deacon glanced toward the southeast corner of the apartment, where Eva had set up her studio. The screened partitions she'd used to divide the area from the living room offered no protection, but the exterior walls were stone; he could get his back against one and still have room to move, to fight.

More room than he remembered. His eyes narrowed. The shadows seemed deeper behind the screens, as if the studio extended farther back than the building's walls did. And even to his vision, the shadows looked *dark*, almost like . . .

Oh, Jesus. His heart pumped faster. He fought a sick sense of unreality. Was Rosalia here? Or was it just wishful thinking? He hadn't felt her Gift—but then, he hadn't felt it outside the SI warehouse the first time, either. Not until she'd come out of the shadows.

But if she was here, he didn't want to alert the demons to her presence. He forced his gaze to move on.

Stafford rose from the sofa. Deacon tried not to tense as the demon walked over to him. He failed.

The demon managed to give a good impression of sympathy. "I understand what you're feeling, Mr. Deacon. Truly, I do."

"Fuck off."

Stafford breathed a disappointed sigh. He turned and pressed his back against the wall in front of Deacon, and slipped his hands into his pockets.

"I *do* know," the demon insisted on continuing, so Deacon prepared himself for that blade to screw deep. "I know what it is to do anything for the one you love. You betray your friends and your brethren. Your liege. All so that you can lift her to the throne where she belongs and stand beside her. And I know what it is to pray that she thinks well of you."

Wherever Stafford had been trying to stick that knife, he'd missed. Deacon didn't feel anything but sick that this demon thought they were similar in any way.

"You don't know shit." And if Stafford could read him, the demon would know he meant that.

Deacon left him standing there, and crossed the room. Lukacs lay half-dead on the floor in a pool of his own blood. Deacon considered leaving him to die. The world would be all the better minus one murdering asshole. Someone like that became a vampire, someone like Deacon would inevitably have to put him down.

But the same reason he'd had for everything else pushed him forward. He used Caym's dagger, still lying on Lukacs's lap, and slashed the blade over his own wrist.

The wound wouldn't stay open long. He sealed his arm to Lukacs's mouth. Quickly enough, the man began drinking. Lukacs wasn't a vampire yet, so it didn't feel good—didn't feel bad, either, except for the self-disgust that clung like a slug's slime trail at the back of Deacon's tongue.

When the man had taken enough, Deacon pushed him away. Lying on his back, Lukacs breathed slowly, his eyes wide with wonder. His teeth had already lengthened.

Deacon turned to Stafford. "Eva. Petra. Now." He bared his fangs. "Or is this when you kill me?"

Stafford laughed, shaking his head. "Oh, Mr. Deacon. We aren't going to kill you. The Guardians are—and it'll probably be your *friend* Irena. After all, she's the one you hurt the most. And although she might hate what she has to do . . . she'll do it anyway."

The slime seemed to fill up Deacon's lungs, his stomach. Irena had warned him about demons like Stafford—the kind that loved to tear people apart without ever touching their flesh. Told him they were the worst ones. Yet here he was, sick because he'd run headlong into everything she'd told him to avoid.

But Caym was the kind that got off on the physical pain. So what had been in this for him? Standing just a few feet to Deacon's left now, the crimson demon wore a smile that exposed his fangs. He looked a little too pleased for a demon who'd only gotten one beating in.

Another must be in Deacon's near future. Not killing him, but not letting him go without a scratch, either.

Deacon braced himself, nodded at Caym. "And him?"

"He had his fun, too."

A clay urn appeared in the demon's hand, its rounded bottom nestled in his palm. A small knob centered on the lid. Caym opened the lid with a flourish, and with his gaze on Deacon's face, tipped the urn to the side. Gray sand poured onto the floor.

Deacon's stomach lurched. Not sand. *Ash.*

"Eva, I believe," Stafford said.

The agony of grief staggered him. He stumbled to his knees beside the remains, knowing his pain howled from his chest, uncaring if the demon heard.

Another urn appeared in Caym's palm. Stafford added, "And there's Petra. Returned to you, as promised. I'm afraid Caym wasn't so good to package up the rest of your community the same way. They are in his cache if you want them."

Deacon looked up at the demon pouring his life onto the floor. His grief ripped away, left only rage and revenge. Nothing else remained of him.

"I want them." But he'd take his people back by cutting them out of the demon himself. He'd take them back, or he'd join them in death.

Deacon reached for his swords and sprang, surprising the demon, buying an extra moment of time. With the nosferatu blood, a moment was all Deacon needed. He stabbed his right sword upward beneath the demon's ribs. Flesh split, and he dug into the heart. Caym fell back, gaping soundlessly. Deacon pushed forward. Hot blood spurted over his hand. With the heart destroyed, the demon was dead, but Deacon wasn't done. He whipped his left blade up, sliced open a smile beneath the demon's chin.

He swung around. Stafford was already on him, sword in hand. The demon struck fast, disarming Deacon with two flicks of his wrist, blows that felt like they'd shattered the bones in his forearms. Stafford vanished his sword, wrapped his fingers around Deacon's throat.

Deacon kicked at the demon's knee. Stafford didn't react. He slammed Deacon against the stone wall. His eyes glowed crimson.

Stafford's lips peeled back from his teeth. An iron spike appeared in his left hand. "Now *that* was a shame, Mr. Deacon."

The demon stabbed the spike toward his forehead.

Rosalia didn't save him.

Thank God.

❧

The scent of blood—human, demon, and vampire—assaulted Alejandro the moment they teleported into Deacon's apartment.

Jake sucked in a breath. "Jesus flippin' Christ."

Stepping around the young Guardian made Alejandro aware of a fine grit beneath his boots. He didn't glance down to see what it was. He stared at Deacon, pinned to a stone block wall in the same manner Rosalia had been. Blood—still wet—covered his face, but didn't obscure the relief and gratitude in his expression. His short swords had been stabbed through his palms, holding them outspread, as if in welcome.

Alejandro looked over at Jake. Horror filled his eyes, and beyond him, Irena's face was stricken.

Quietly, Alejandro said, "Leave us, Jake."

Jake glanced at Irena, nodded, and disappeared.

Irena's throat worked. "Rael knew I would come to kill Deacon."

"Yes." If Rael hadn't been counting on that, no doubt the

vampire would be dead instead of pinned—waiting for Irena to finish it.

Her eyes closed. He could feel the debate raging within her. The decision to slay Deacon had been hard enough; now she fought her instinctive need to act opposite of what a demon wanted from her.

Alejandro knelt, ran his fingers through the gray powder. Only a small amount dusted the wooden flooring here, but piles of it were heaped near the wall, more had been trampled and saturated with blood. Two urns lay broken and tipped on their sides. He rubbed the powder between his fingers.

"Irena." When she opened her eyes, he said, "It is vampire ash."

She blinked slowly. Her gaze sharpened, and when she looked around the room again, he knew she was reading the story of the blood splatters, the footprints in the ash. She crouched next to the pool of human blood, and slid her knife through it. The blood had already thickened.

"This was first," she murmured. "But there was no violence. The human lay quietly here while he bled, and later walked away." Frowning, she reached for a dagger half-hidden beneath the edge of the sofa. She brought the blade to her nose, sniffed. "Human, vampire."

"Transformation," Alejandro realized.

"Yes. The ash was spilled after the human's blood. And the demon's blood after that." A bitter frown bent her mouth. "I think Deacon did what they asked, and they gave him back his partners."

Mother of God. He looked up at the vampire again. "Tell me, Irena, which punishment is worse: killing him now, or forcing him to live?"

Her eyes narrowed and flared a poisonous green. Then she scanned the room again, her gaze softening and deepening as she looked. The grief and sadness in her psychic scent pulled him to her. "Living," she said. "Killing him now would be mercy. A part of me wants to do it for that reason alone."

"And the rest of you?"

She stood and strode toward Deacon. Some of her earlier

anger returned, hardening her voice. "Is going to make him live with it. Let us get him down."

Irena had changed her mind. Alejandro tugged Deacon's swords from the vampire's hands, feeling as if a sledgehammer had pounded into his chest. Dear God, how he loved her. Not because she'd agreed with him, but because she'd done exactly as she'd promised in Caelum: tried to look from different angles.

He hadn't known if it'd been something she vowed only in the aftermath of their lovemaking. And he hadn't been certain she *could* do it, if he would always be the one to compromise, just to stay with her. He would have, endlessly, if giving in had been the only way to fight for her—though it would eventually leave him with little pride, and leave her with a companion not worth having.

But Irena was fighting for them, too. And perhaps they would never agree again, but her effort alone told him how much he was worth to her.

Irena reached for the spike. Her Gift pulsed.

Another Gift echoed it, like a dark, thick slide beneath his skin. He looked over his shoulder.

Rosalia stepped out of the shadows behind a screened corner, her cloak swirling around her. She lifted her crossbow to her shoulder when she saw them. "You are not slaying him."

"No," Irena said calmly. "We are not."

She yanked out the spike. Alejandro caught the vampire, dragged him over to a blue sofa.

Rosalia lowered her weapon. "Caym is dead."

"You killed a demon?" Alejandro asked. Rael's accomplice, most likely.

"No. Deacon did."

"You watched," Irena said flatly.

"Rael didn't intend to kill Deacon—and I had not yet decided if I would." Her brown eyes, usually warm, were tortured as she looked to Alejandro. "Is it true that the nephilim invaded the warehouse? Or did Rael lie?"

"It's true." Irena knelt, vanished all of the vampire ash, leaving the human and demon blood behind. "We will have a gathering for Dru within a day or two. Perhaps Ben and Echo, if they wished to have their remains rest in Caelum. And now, these vampires."

Rosalia closed her eyes, nodded. "I will not be there. But I will pay my respects."

Guilt colored Rosalia's psychic scent. Alejandro frowned as suspicion bit at him. "Did you know Deacon would betray us?"

She crossed her arms beneath her breasts, as if hugging herself. "No. But I knew that something was not right with him. I'd hoped . . . I'd hoped he might reveal what troubled him. He did not." She swallowed and looked down at the vampire. "I intend to take him."

"Take him?" Alejandro looked around at Irena, saw similar surprise on her face. "Why?"

"I haven't decided." A faint smile curved her lips. She flicked the hood of her cloak up over her hair, hiding her features in shadow. "Either I will chain him to my bed, or give him a five-minute head start before hunting him down with my crossbow."

Irena came to stand beside Alejandro. "He's completely broken. He will not be good for fucking or hunting. He wanted to die, and so he might not even run."

"Then I will let him go kill himself. I will not be stuck for another two centuries, caring for someone who cannot care in return." Rosalia's Gift pushed out, carrying a hollow yearning, as if she'd made a wish she already knew wouldn't be fulfilled. Shadows crept from beneath the sofa and wrapped around Deacon's still form. "I have not been in Caelum for years, and so perhaps my voice and opinion do not matter. But I cannot understand how Rael was given enough room to maneuver as he has. His bargain with my brother, what he has done to Deacon, his association with the nephilim—all could have been prevented if we had slain him instead of allying ourselves with him."

"Yes," Alejandro admitted.

SI had never trusted Rael, so they'd thought that if the demon turned on them, they'd be prepared to counter him. And so their decision to align themselves with him, born of desperation—

or arrogance—had led them down a grievous path. Alejandro couldn't deny that, or the knowledge that his decision to replace Rael and sever SI's ties to the demon had come too late.

Irena, of course, did not respond. And she could have easily indulged in an *I told you so*, yet he knew she never would. She'd rather have been wrong; being proved right had cost far too much.

"Good. And when you find Rael, perhaps save a little piece for me." Rosalia paused, then added, "After Rael and the human—vampire—left, I followed, but did not find an opportunity to slay them. Rael called him Lukacs, and I am almost certain he killed Rael's wife in exchange for immortality." She projected an image of an emaciated man, his eyes dark and hungry. "If that is not his true name, perhaps he will have a medical record. He'd been through chemotherapy."

If Lukacs was a vampire, his true name would not matter much now. He would never face a human court. "We'll find them both," Alejandro said.

By the movement of her hood, Rosalia nodded. "I trust that you will. Be well."

"Be safe," Irena said.

As soon as Rosalia and Deacon disappeared, pulled into the shadows beneath the sofa, Irena turned to Alejandro with a frown. "Why did I do that?"

"Let her take him?"

"Yes."

She would probably not admit, even to herself, that she still hoped for the best for Deacon; her pain and anger were too sharp. But Alejandro could turn her away from them for a moment.

"Because you regret never doing the same to me." When her frown deepened with confusion, he said, "Hunting me down and fucking me."

A laugh as loud as Irena's should not be able to lift quietly through him, gently lightening his own spirits, yet it did. But they were not in a location where laughter could last. When she sobered, her soft steps took her through the apartment. She paused now and then, as if remembering a time when life had filled each room.

Finally, she returned to the living area. "I liked these women," she said. "And I will not be able to hold my blades back much longer."

She did now only for him. But even if Alejandro had not been ready to take the demon's place, the attack at the warehouse had changed everything. Perhaps Rael thought the Guardians' reliance on his support in Washington would save him. The demon couldn't have been more mistaken.

"When you next see Rael," Alejandro told her. "You do not have to hold back at all."

CHAPTER 20

Irena didn't see Rael.

She didn't see Alejandro, either, except for in passing. For two days, she and Jake followed the sun's path around the world, visiting the heads of vampire communities—she'd lost count of how many. Some, she only had to give contact information, and remind them about the dangers the nephilim posed; others, the reminders and warnings had bordered on threats.

She'd slain four demons posing as vampires. It would have been five, if Jake had not used his teleporting advantage to race ahead. As soon as he could better control his electrical Gift, she thought he would not even have to teleport to slay a demon ahead of her—but she had only let him practice that Gift on her twice. They had too much to do; she could not lay unconscious for hours at a time. And after Cambodia, where she'd seen him throw off a lightning bolt that had struck a limb from a tree and left the vampires too frightened to do more than nod at them, she realized that *unconscious* might have traded up to *dead*.

Jake had talked constantly. Some of it, she knew, was his natural inclination. Grief drove the rest, and after Cambodia, nervous energy and dread, so Irena hadn't put a stop to his chatter. Every region they visited, he'd told her about the military history or described in detail archeological ruins particular to the area, and she'd learned more about forty-year-old rock music than she'd ever cared to know. By the time they'd finished, and returned to the SI warehouse for the final time, her need for quiet was a physical ache.

So was her need to see Olek.

Irena knew what he'd been doing, even if she had rarely seen him. She and Jake had frequently jumped back to SI to check in. There, depending upon the hour, Lilith, Hugh, or Michael updated them on Alejandro, Preston, and Taylor's search for Laszlo Lukacs—who, it had not taken Savi much time to discover, had been a sharpshooter for the Hungarian police. It had taken less time for Lilith to construct evidence that implicated Lukacs in Julia Stafford's murder. Once they found the vampire, a money trail and physical evidence would surface, wrapping Lukacs up neatly. The vampire himself would be slain.

And as soon as Rael surfaced, his blood would run, too. But Congressman Stafford's hands would stay clean.

She could accept that, Irena decided as she climbed the stairs to the second floor. And she had to admit a sense of satisfaction, knowing that a Guardian would take over—and make good—a role a demon had created for his own ends.

She still didn't know exactly how Olek planned to do it, but she *did* believe that he could.

When she reached the second level, quiet hung over the common room like a pale shroud, but it was not the kind of quiet she sought. The novices whispered in careful tones; their laughter only sounded in quick and uneasy bursts. The pall of grief dampened their psychic scents. The fragile tension would have to break soon—but Irena would not be the one to smash through it. She only spoke with them briefly before heading into the corridor that led to the soundproofed, mirrored room.

She opened the door and paused. Michael stood in the center of the observation area, facing the mirrored chamber, his hands clasped behind his back. His thinking pose.

"Stay," he said when she began to back out. "I will not speak much."

No. Like Olek, he rarely did. She closed the door, muffling the noise from outside. From the beige sofa at the side of the room, she would be able to see his profile. She seated herself in the corner, drew her legs up. Neither of them breathed. She heard her heartbeat, his, and little else.

And for the first time in months, she did not feel angry in his presence. The pain of his betrayal didn't spear through her chest, forcing her rage up to her tongue. She didn't ask why. She accepted the difference, and closed her eyes.

Perhaps a half an hour passed before Michael said, "Khavi has foreseen a dragon, come to Earth."

The hairs on the back of her neck prickled, and a shiver worked down her spine. She looked up at him. "The dragon from the prophecy? The one who will rise?"

"I do not know if it is the same." He stared into the mirrored chamber with obsidian eyes. "This one, she has seen escape Chaos through a portal that Anaria creates. I have no words to describe the devastation it can—" His jaw clenched. He faced her. "Everything that can burn, does. Cities, villages. Forests and the plains. People. So *many* people."

He projected images that made her throat close, pushed her stomach up against her heart. Humans—children. No one had escaped it. The world burned, and demons rode the dragon's back.

"This was the Second Battle?" When Michael and the other grigori had fought with the angels to stop the dragon and Lucifer.

He nodded. "We chased the dragon across half the world before we stopped it."

Before Michael had cut through its heart with his sword— but not without a price. Irena had only recently learned that, too.

"You died."

"Yes. I would again, to prevent another from coming here."

Irena's blood chilled. She remembered his dread, his fear. "Does Khavi foresee this dragon killing you?"

"No." He looked away from her, toward the mirrored chamber again. "But it is why, if Colin or Savitri sees that Anaria has made her way into Chaos, we will have to lead the others in after her."

By the gods, Irena hoped that would not happen. But if it did, she would do what needed to be done. "What would she want there?"

"If her goal is the same—Lucifer's throne—she will want both a dragon, for its power, and access to Hell. She will try to break through the frozen barrier, and mount her attack on Lucifer."

"With only her nephilim?"

"There is no *only* about the nephilim, except on Earth. In Hell, they are not bound to the physical forms they've had to inhabit here." He glanced at her, and she read his worry in the line that formed between his brows. "I do not know how strong they will be in Chaos."

"Khavi can't see that?"

"Khavi cannot see what she doesn't know."

"What does that mean?"

"No one but Khavi knows. And I am not always certain that *she* does."

The exasperation in his reply sparked her laugh. He laughed quietly in return, and that was how Olek found them a moment later, followed by Detective Taylor.

Irena's heart tripped against her ribs. She remained seated, but her gaze feasted on him, the graceful swordsman's stride that brought him a quarter of the way into the room, the lean strength of his hands as he reported to Michael in the space of two steps—and with his report finished, the darkness of his eyes as they fastened on her, the shallow dent in his chin that she wanted to slide her thumb across, to kiss before searching his lips.

I have not seen you enough, he signed. *Now I cannot look away.*

He never had. *You have always watched me.*

It has never been enough. But it was what I had.

They had more now. Her thighs tightened as she recalled the

surge of his body into hers. And a slow melting warmth stole through her when she remembered the strength of his arms around her as she'd grieved. She'd never needed anyone to do that for her before—or perhaps she'd never allowed herself to admit that she wanted it. But want or need, Olek was an answer to both. A lover, a friend—she didn't think the two had ever combined so well. And still there was more.

She held back her reply as Taylor hesitated beside Olek, then came to sit at the other end of Irena's sofa. Michael had fallen silent when they'd come into the room; now his eyes—amber again—tracked the detective's every move.

"It is sunset?" Irena asked. She did not know what time it was here—or even what day.

"Almost," Taylor said, looking up at Michael. "Which means that I'm all yours."

And she didn't need Olek to protect her now. *Do you have another assignment?* Irena asked him.

Not immediately.

The color of his eyes deepened. Irena squeezed her legs together. Anticipation curled low, a smoking flame.

"You have the scent of Rael's house upon you, detective," Michael said abruptly.

Taylor's eyes widened. "What does that mean? What the hell does his house smell like?" She lifted the lapel of her jacket to her nose and sniffed.

Irena was not certain whether to take pity on Taylor or Michael. She chose Taylor. "He is joking. Alejandro has already told him that you visited Wren."

"Jok—" Her mouth fell open in disbelief as she stared up at the Doyen. "That's your idea of a joke? You're, what, a billion years old? Aren't you supposed to have razor-sharp wit by now?"

"If anything, detective, time dulls the wit," Alejandro told her. "As evidenced by the eldest two here. Now, you will see that Irena's only response is—"

She threw a dagger at his head. Without a change of expression, he sidestepped and plucked the blade out of the air.

She would have missed anyway; she was laughing too hard for accuracy.

"—to kill something," he continued without a pause. "Michael's is to sigh."

Michael sighed, then frowned.

"But also, detective," Alejandro said, "the type of humor you expect depends upon slippery words and double meanings. That is the language demons use. So Irena is blunt, and Michael does not speak much at all."

Understanding dawned on Taylor's face. Understanding, and a sharp recognition. "So you are hiding something?" she asked Michael.

"Many things." He smiled, obviously intending to soften truth with another joke, but it failed again.

Uneasy, the detective glanced away from him.

Michael sighed and looked to Alejandro. "Why does Wren not leave Rael's home?"

Taylor answered him. "She feels obligated to fulfill her contract with Julia Stafford, if not the congressman. She's staying until the funeral on Friday—which she's been making arrangements for, in Rael's absence."

Taylor's tone had taken on a slight defensive edge. Not against Michael, Irena realized, but on behalf of Wren. After Anaria's attack on the warehouse, Taylor had spent almost the entire night with the woman, explaining the Rules. Apparently, Taylor's already sympathetic stance toward Wren had begun to deepen into friendship—or just a bond between two women who had recently been thrust into a new world. She'd formed a similar attachment to Savi, Irena remembered.

"Will she let us know if he returns?"

"Yes," Taylor said, and her lips twisted in wry acknowledgment. "Although I suspect that part of the reason she's staying on is so she can put a bullet in his head if he shows up."

Irena frowned. "It wouldn't hurt him."

"No, but it would feel good, wouldn't it?" Taylor said and reminded Irena why she liked the detective so much. "Regardless, she'll leave after the funeral."

Irena glanced at Alejandro. "Do you think Rael would miss his wife's funeral?"

"No. His grief could excuse his absence, just as it has these past two days—but the publicity would be too politically valuable."

"So I kill him at the funeral."

Alejandro just looked at her.

Taylor stuck her fingers into her ears. "I'm not hearing this."

Irena grinned and said, "I will do it quickly. He will not expect it in public. I vanish the body, you step in. And if Wren is arranging the funeral, she will know where the cameras and security are, so that we can avoid them."

"It is still a risk," Alejandro said slowly. As he considered it, his thumb followed the carved line of his jaw, his forefinger swept down his chin. "But a bigger risk would be losing him again."

"I agree," Michael said. "And will help you slay him."

"La la la," Taylor sang. She pulled her fingers out. "I'll ask Wren for the security details."

Michael frowned. "Are you certain you want to involve—"

"Oh, come on." Taylor gave him a hard look. "You know I'm on my way out of there anyway."

His face became stone. "Khavi's prediction will not come to pass."

"Not that. Jesus." Taylor rubbed her face, as if trying to scrub away the reminder. "I'm talking about being one step away from having my badge stripped or burning out. Either way, I'm just fucked all the way to—" She stopped, pinned Michael with a stare. "You'll give Joe a place here at SI, right?"

"You will have one, too."

"Yeah. Thanks, but no thanks. I'll do better without all this." She let out a long breath, as if she'd just let go of a huge weight. "So, I'll ask Wren. I'll help you kill a demon. And be done."

Taylor was mistaken if she thought that would be the end of it for them. Not with Khavi's prediction still hanging over her head. Irena glanced up at Michael. His eyes were obsidian again. Yes. Taylor might not know it, but leaving them behind did not mean she would not have protection.

But the detective must have realized it, too. "What's the save-me-from-the-vampire plan while you guys are having your gathering in Caelum?"

"I've scheduled it to coincide with dawn here, tomorrow," Michael told her. "I realize you will not agree to be locked away in Caelum—"

"You got that right."

"—so I will accompany you to your station and return before sundown. The warehouse will be closed; Lilith, Hugh, and Sir Pup will be guarding Savi while she sleeps. Colin will be with us—he is the only vampire who could possibly harm you during that time."

The detective shook her head. "Colin wouldn't—"

"Not voluntarily," Michael agreed. "But if a demon threatened Savi, then I believe he would destroy half the world."

"And then we'd have to kill him," Irena said.

Alejandro's gaze lit with his laughter. "Or give him to Rosalia."

For hunting and fucking? Irena narrowed her eyes at him and rose from the sofa. "Michael, have you anything else for us?"

"No."

Good. She passed Alejandro. He turned and followed her. When he closed the door behind them, she spun him into the corridor wall. He lifted her. Her legs circled his waist. His mouth found hers, hot. She opened her lips, took him deep. Not enough. She kissed his chin, his cheek, his neck. She needed to touch him everywhere.

"I have missed you," she breathed between kisses.

"Irena." His fingers clenched on her thighs. "Irena."

As if that was all he could say, he took her mouth again. She'd thought kissing him would be a release, but now she wanted more. Here, if she had to, Olek hard inside her, until she came and came.

Footsteps filtered through the haze of need, followed by

Ames-Beaumont's bored voice. "It is just like the tube in London, sweet. Barbarians copulate in dark corners."

The cursed dragon-fucking bloodsucker. Without breaking their kiss, Irena slid her hand from Olek's hair and extended her middle finger.

His fangs gleaming sharp in his grin, Ames-Beaumont passed them, his features ridiculously beautiful even half-glimpsed in profile. Then Savi went by, holding her hand like a blinder beside her eyes and shaking with laughter.

Olek, the stupid ox, had begun laughing, too. When the door to the observation room opened and closed, she leaned back against the wall.

"I hate this place. There is no privacy." They could easily find privacy in Caelum, but unless she had no other choice, Irena was not yet ready to use Dru's Gate. "We will find a roof outside," she decided.

He shook his head. "It is raining."

She laughed and pulled him down for another long taste. When she heard the observation room door open, and Michael's sigh, she took Olek's hand. She didn't look back at the Doyen, but walked quickly down the corridor toward the common room.

Her steps faltered when the psychic pall settled over her. Irena stopped, blocked their grief and sent out a sharp stab of anger. The novices looked over at her. Pim and Becca weren't among them, she saw.

"Perhaps none of you is old enough to know what a gathering is," she told them. "But you will not bring *this* to Caelum. Grief, yes, for she is missed. But you all sit as if *you* are dead, and the gathering is about her life, not death. If you cannot shed this, stay here." She opened her shields, so that they would know she meant every word. "Because if you bring this death there, I will hunt you down and skin you all."

She felt their resentment, their anger. Good. Better than the dull nothing. Still holding Olek's hand, she crossed the room.

He slowed on the stairs, and she glanced back at him. His eyes were alight.

She frowned. "You laugh? I am serious."

"I know. I laugh *because* you are serious. There is so much of you that amazes me."

"I do not understand that." But her heart did a little jump anyway. "Anyone my age ought to be as skilled as I am."

"Yes. But apparently you have not noticed, Irena—no one is your age. And I do not speak of your skills. You would amaze me if the only weapon you possessed was the blunt edge of your tongue."

He stopped in the hub, looked in each direction. With a firm step, he started toward the hall leading to the conference room.

"Do you know, Olek, that it is not just demons who use slippery words? Roman senators—politicians—did as well."

"I do know." He swung open the conference room door. "This must be difficult for you."

She shook her head as she stepped inside. "No. It is you, and so it is easy."

He closed the door, pushed her back against it. His palm ironed up her spine, burned up her nape, until his fingers buried in her hair. He braced his left hand on the door above her shoulder. He didn't kiss her, but watched her with steadily darkening eyes.

Anticipation prickled her skin. Her nipples tightened. She tried to rise up, to bring her mouth to his, but his hand fisted in her hair. Her muscles tensed. Need unfolded through her as she imagined him holding her still, working into her with slow, measured strokes.

"Do you need oil, Irena?" His murmur swept over her ears in a velvety caress, and she became intensely aware of the liquid heat at her core.

"No, Olek." She let her gaze challenge him. "I could take you in now."

She felt him stiffen. He wanted to. But he apparently had something else in mind. His fingers still clenched in her hair, he slid his left hand down her naked back. "I will judge for myself."

She would not argue. But— "Kiss me first."

"I'll kiss you when you're ready."

She snarled. Expectation silenced her when his hand pushed down the front of her leggings. His fingers teased the curls just above her clitoris. She lifted onto her toes. He delved deeper. And stopped.

She snarled again. "Do you want me to hurt you?"

He gave her a look that was both amused and speculative. "No. But I would not mind."

Her laugh became a breathless gasp when his fingers sank into her, the heel of his palm pressing against her clitoris. He made rough circles with his hand.

Ecstasy spiraled outward. Irena's knees weakened and she clung to his upper arms, her nails digging into tightly sculpted muscle. He pumped his fingers and her hips rocked, pushing against him, pulling him in. She tried to look down, to see. She only saw his face, carved into austere lines by his own need.

She could hardly gather the breath to say, "Don't deny yourself, Olek."

"I do not." He glanced down. The heat of his skin against her, inside her, flared hotter. "Learning you pleases me."

He'd already learned well. Though he'd left everything untouched but her sex, the tips of her breasts ached. Her skin stretched over passion-seared nerves, her clothes a constriction that bound and teased. Warmed by her body, the wooden door pressed into her shoulder blades. Beneath her hands, his biceps flexed with each thrust of his fingers, each clench of his fist tilting her head back farther.

But if he was determined to learn her, then she would help him. Back arched by the pressure of his hand in her hair, she vanished her shirt. Though she couldn't see, she knew her nipples were tight beads. "I want your mouth on me."

"*I* want my mouth on you."

Then why did he not put his mouth on her? She shrieked in frustration. In response, he cupped her sex, lifted her. Her feet left the floor. His fingers drove deeper. She held on, shaking, working her hips into his hand, release just out of reach but flying nearer, nearer.

He buried his face in her throat. "You burn so hot."

"You don't?" Her voice was thin, trembling as she poised on the edge.

"I do. Too hot." He moved his hand, his thumb strumming over the slick bundle of nerves. Her inner muscles clamped around his fingers, and the silken warmth of his voice roughened into a groan. "I'm almost insane with it. I will take you here, Irena, and here." His fingers slipped from her center, teased farther back. "No part of you will I leave untouched."

By the gods, she wanted that. She strained toward him. He plunged his fingers deep inside her again. His mouth covered hers, taking her cry as she writhed into orgasm. She dragged it out long, riding his hand.

Her breath raced against his lips when she was done. Releasing her hair, withdrawing his fingers, he carried her to the table. With a laugh, Irena saw that they'd replaced the temporary one with another of solid oak.

"I should have hit you," she said when he seated her on the edge. "I feel like I might." No, that was a lie. But she might yank on his hair.

"So I'll lose my head?"

"Yes." And take her over and over again.

"I will. But I had to make certain you were satisfied first. Because I cannot keep my head if I am kissing you"—he lowered his head to hers, plundered her mouth in a long, hungry kiss— "or tasting you. And I am hardly finished."

He caught the tips of her heaving breasts with his teeth, his fingers. Anchoring herself with her hands flat on the table, she arched and lost herself in the rapture of his touch, his heated tongue. Had he truly thought he might not satisfy her? He only had to look at her, and she ignited.

"You are mad, Olek."

"So I have told you." He brought his face to hers. She read the tortured need in his eyes, but more lurked there, a ravenous predator waiting in the darkness. "And when I do this, Irena, I have no hope left of sanity."

She looked down as the broad head of his shaft parted her cleft. They both groaned as she took him in, but she was the one to whimper when he drew back again. She glanced up. Olek's teeth were clenched, his body trembling with effort, his gaze locked on her face. He stroked forward again.

And she saw. Yes, Olek had been burning. *Too hot.* But he hadn't wanted to repeat Caelum; he hadn't wanted to take her in a frenzy. And now he tormented them both by containing that heat. Slowly, he pushed deeper. Pleasure rippled outward from her core, tiny waves that tightened nerves, muscles, and skin in their wake, but she held herself still, held his gaze as her slick inner walls gave way to his invasion.

When he'd breached her to the hilt, she whispered, "You are mine."

Fierce possession exploded through his psychic scent. He pulled at her legs, hooking her knees over his hips, forcing his cock deeper. Pleasure stabbed through her, a sweet blade. Irena's elbows gave out and she fell back, flat against the table. Olek leaned in, braced his hands beside her shoulders. His gaze skimmed down her length, lingering on her arms, her breasts, and finally, where they were joined. She could tell that everything he saw pleased him.

When he looked back at her, the challenge in his eyes was unmistakable. "We will see who belongs to whom."

She grinned up at him and tensed, ready to hold out against a hard fucking, but he came into her again in a liquid surge, a fluid roll of his hips. Her throat captured her surprised cry. He rocked into her again. Her hands scraped at the table, then clamped on his arms when his next surge pushed her along the smooth surface. He dragged her back to the edge, back over his cock, and the slippery heat of her arousal made each stroke a luscious glide, the wetness heightening the overwhelming sensation of every thick inch stretching and pushing within.

Deliberately, she tightened her inner muscles around his shaft, and gasped as that intimate clench set off tiny spasms through her core. Olek's eyes half-closed before he locked his gaze with hers again.

Every stroke of his cock pushed her closer. Her hold slipped, and she clawed for orgasm, desperate to fling herself over, but it was all heat and wet without rough edges to give her purchase. One hard, sharp thrust and she would—

Olek gave it to her. She screamed and arched, her spine a rigid bow. Convulsions ripped through her. His face taut with need, Alejandro reared back and clamped his hands beneath her ass and lifted her to slam deep. Finally letting go, he fucked her with heavy strokes that had her tightening again, flying over. He stiffened, his hips jerked. His release pulsed hot inside her—but he was silent.

He fell forward, bracing his hands again. His chest heaved.

"I screamed," she said breathlessly. Her legs were still around him; she couldn't bring herself to let him go. "So I think I have won."

His shoulders shook with quiet laughter. "If you have won, it is only because you can still think."

Not very well. Remnants of their passion still sparked in her veins. Emotion filled her chest, her throat. She turned her cheek against the tabletop. Only a few days ago, she had been in a rage here. Only a few days ago, she'd refused to fuck his pride. Had he brought her here to make reparations for that? Did he know he didn't have to? They had both made mistakes, but they did not have to pay for them forever.

"Why this room?"

His hand swept down her arm, his thumb tracing a winding pattern over her skin. "It is soundproofed, holds the sturdiest table, and the door is reinforced."

So pragmatic, her Olek. "The others expect us to tear down the warehouse. You will disappoint them."

"So be it." His eyes smiled as he lowered his head, and he said against her lips, "You are mine, Irena."

That they belonged to each other was far too obvious. And so her only response was to open her mouth for his kiss.

❦

Three hours later and four thousand miles south, Irena sat beside Alejandro at another table, trying to remember that strangling a man was not the rational way to win an argument. Sensible, perhaps, but she didn't think she could declare a real victory.

She'd accompanied him on his assignment to determine whether a drug lord who had rapidly been gaining power in Colombia was a demon—and if so, to slay him. On the flight from a Gate outside Caracas, she'd told Alejandro about her conversation with Michael, and Khavi's predication that a dragon would escape Chaos. She'd watched his expression tighten when she showed him the images Michael had projected into her mind, of the demons riding the dragon as it torched the Earth.

After that, she'd been looking forward to killing a demon—more than she usually did. But the drug lord and everyone else at his jungle compound had been human. Upon seeing her disappointment, Alejandro hadn't hidden his amusement, and asked whether she'd have killed the man if he'd been a vampire.

She'd answered with an unequivocal yes. Alejandro disagreed, stating that his decision to slay even a vampire drug lord would depend upon the circumstances, and the consequences of power changing hands in the region. She'd given him a look. He'd laughed and winged his way toward electric lights that clustered at the edge of the jungle. The village seemed half-tourist destination and half-trading post, with Mission-style hotels, thrown-together shops, and a marketplace set up with stalls that had only begun to close for the night.

At the north end of the village, an open restaurant had drawn her in with the music of a steel drum and a guitar, and the rich scent of grilling meat.

The kitchen was housed in a long shack that consisted of a stove, a worktable, and a bar, surrounded by three reed-thin walls supporting a tin roof, with a circle cut out for the stovepipe. The open-fronted kitchen overlooked a patio that was nothing more than a cleared rectangle of swept dirt, its dimensions marked off by discarded tires. A string of flickering electric lights connected the broad-leafed trees that, during the day, would provide shade for the patrons. Most of the tables were filled—primarily by the hotel clients, Irena guessed by their new clothes, pale and sunburned skin, and the variety of languages they spoke. Her longstockings and brief shirt had raised a few brows among both tourists and locals, but they were quickly forgotten when Alejandro chose a table in the corner farthest from the kitchen to continue their argument.

With a surface made of rough-hewn planks cobbled together to form a circle and held up by toothpick-narrow legs, the small table didn't seem sturdy enough to rest her elbows on, let alone the platter heaped with chorizo and fried steak, rice soaked in coconut milk, sweet corn bread, avocado and fried bananas—flanked by two bottles of tequila—but Irena did her best to lighten its burden. Over the next hour, she fed herself and Alejandro, offering him bites from her fingers, and while his mouth was occupied, used the opportunity to tell him all the ways he was wrong.

And while she steadily sipped her way through the tequila, relishing the fiery slide from her tongue to her stomach, Alejandro held her hand, kissed her fingertips, her wrist, trying to weaken her by adding seduction to his arguments.

She appreciated his technique very much. So much that she decided not to strangle him.

The night wore on. Her senses were intoxicated—by the burn of peppers and alcohol, the quiet heat of their argument, the lazy strum of the guitar, the lush fragrance of the jungle. By Olek, the darkness of his eyes and the music of his voice. By his liquid grace that made him appear at once completely relaxed and yet poised to strike, though seated in a spindly chair with uneven legs and a rigid back. She wanted to crawl into his lap, tell him to run his lips beneath her jaw, to feel the soft brush of his goatee over her skin.

The argument waned, and they both let it. Claiming that Irena's earlier mention of Khavi's Gift reminded him of an essay he'd read during the two centuries she'd been gone, Alejandro produced a pamphlet from his cache. A red ribbon marked the page he wanted; he'd written her name in the margin. He read to her in Arabic drawn long by his accent, and she sat listening with her heart full to the point of pain.

Four hundred years.

She could not be sorry for all of it. She'd needed time after the demon had almost shredded her into nothing. Olek had needed time to regain his pride. But a single vow, a word to each other would have brought them back together long before this. A single vow, and she'd have known he'd fight for her; he'd have known she'd intended to return to him.

Olek stopped midsentence, looking at her over the top of the page.

His face had softened and blurred, and she spoke through the ache in her throat. "We are both fools, Olek."

He reached for her hands, pulled her to him. "I will not argue that."

CHAPTER 21

The novices all wore red tennis shoes.

Irena smiled as she watched them swoop gently to the ground, their wings spread wide to slow their descent, their landing almost soundless. For the past fifteen minutes, Guardians had begun gathering on the eastern shore of Caelum, where the city's marble edge seamlessly met the smooth blue plane of the waveless and silent sea. Overhead, the cerulean vault of the sky stretched cloudlessly to an infinite horizon.

Irena stood where she had a view of the Guardians coming in by air and on foot. Laid out before her, flat marble pavers extended to the curving edge of the city and created a long, crescent-shaped terrace, a hundred feet deep at the center. Behind her, its walls forming the crescent's interior arc, a round tower jutted into the sky, crenellated at its crown like the battlement of a castle. Dru's quarters comprised the upper levels of the tower, a location she'd chosen because her rooms overlooked the sea, and so Irena felt no surprise that the healer had requested her body be laid to rest beneath the waters. Some Guardians chose Caelum; others, Earth. Irena had no preference for hers, but she knew the ceremony would be important for anyone she left behind. She'd chosen the tundra, and a pyre. A *big* pyre. Alejandro had probably chosen a ceme—

Her heart gave a painful jump. She couldn't finish the thought. She glanced over at him, standing quietly beside her wearing his customary black. She looked away again, quickly, and for a moment the small crowd of Guardians swam in front of her vision.

No. She could not even contemplate it.

She shifted closer to him, until she felt the heat of his hand against hers. Glancing up again, she saw the query in his dark gaze.

She might as well set it in stone now. "I will go first."

He looked out over the sea, his jaw white. "No."

"Do not argue."

"Do not pretend you can determine which of us will—" He shook his head, sharply. "No. I will be first."

"I will drag you down from the laps of the angels Above and kill you for leaving."

"You threaten me?" He narrowed his eyes, and humor came into their depths. "We will never agree on this, Irena. Admit defeat."

She sneered. "I will eat spiders in Hell first."

"Then you might as well surrender now. Even a woman of your deep hungers could not chew beyond the second leg."

She looked away before her laughter burst out. Two dozen Guardians quickly glanced in other directions. Most were smiling—or trying to suppress one. Good. Much better than quietly running as far out of the line of her and Alejandro's fire as possible. And now they would all know why he stood at her side instead of watching her from a distance, as he had at every other gathering.

Wearing a gauzy dress the same color as the sea, Selah teleported in to the center of the terrace, bringing Drifter with her. The tall Guardian looked around, spotted Irena and Alejandro. He touched Selah's arm, and they teleported again, reappearing next to Irena.

Irena's stomach rolled into a hard stone. Selah's greeting was as sunny as usual and Drifter offered a smile, but his demeanor struck her as *too* casual. And although his posture was long and easy, she read his tension in the barely-perceptible twitch of muscle at the side of his neck.

"What is it?"

He blinked, as if it'd taken him by surprise, then glanced out over the terrace. He shook his head, and turned his back to the terrace so that his body blocked the movement of his hands. *It can wait. Selah and I decided not to cast a shadow over—*

I'll be wondering now, anyway, Irena interrupted.

"As will I," Alejandro said.

Drifter sighed. He exchanged a look with Selah, who nodded.

All right, he signed. *About twenty minutes ago, Jake came to get Charlie, and take her to where Castleford and Lilith are looking over Savi for the day.*

Irena frowned. Drifter's vampire partner and Jake had developed a relationship that reminded Irena of siblings, and he was almost as protective of her as Drifter was. But Charlie lived in Seattle—and because she didn't have the same taint in her blood as Ames-Beaumont and Savi, wasn't a target in the same way that they were. And Drifter often left her alone in her daysleep, with just a protection spell around her room. Why had Jake thought that wouldn't be sufficient today?

I did the same for Lucas, Selah said. *Which might be an overreaction, I know, and maybe I'll have him back in Ashland before the sun goes down—but I want to make certain that he knows what has happened as soon as he wakes up. Not worrying, and waiting for a call.*

Irena closed her eyes. She didn't need to see what they'd sign next. She knew. Anaria had made her portal to Chaos, and the Guardians would be going in to stop her.

They might not all return.

Alejandro's palm flattened against her lower back, warm and supportive. She opened her eyes.

Drifter was signing, *Ames-Beaumont is still in the mirrored room, giving Michael an account of what Anaria and her nephilim are doing. They'll be here shortly. I figure once the gath-*

*ering is over, Ames-Beaumont will be opening his portal, and
we'll be heading through.*

Irena nodded. Fear coated the back of her throat, but she
would do what had to be done.

Alice and Jake arrived by air rather than teleporting. Irena
guessed that Jake must have retrieved Alice from the Archives
or her quarters, and told her about Anaria on their way here.
Alice's narrow face seemed pinched, but she made a visible
effort to clear her expression as they landed. They looked at
each other for a moment, then parted. Jake walked to where the
novices waited; Alice searched out Irena, and moved toward
her with an inhumanly graceful stride instead of her disjointed
one.

Irena almost laughed. Like Drifter, Alice must have decided
to wait until after the gathering to speak about Anaria—and in
the meantime, she made an effort not to creep everyone out. Alice probably did not care that the unexpectedness of her gliding
step drew almost as many looks as her spidery movements did.

She slipped between Drifter and Irena, and linked her bony
elbow with Irena's. Her long skirt brushed Irena's leggings.

"You have heard?" Alice murmured.

Irena nodded.

Alice's pale blue gaze remained on Jake, who'd reached the
novices—and who, until only a few months ago, had been one
of them. After the Ascension, Pim and Jake's friendship had
formed the heart of that close-knit group. The dynamics had
changed since Jake had been promoted, but Irena saw their
friendship had not. Pim looked up at him. The brave face she'd
been wearing suddenly collapsed. Jake hugged her to him, and
the young healer sobbed against his chest. Becca wrapped her
arms around them both.

Irena swallowed hard. "You have been a fool now and then,
Alice. But you chose well with that one."

"Yes."

"I reckon the kid's the one who got lucky," Drifter said.

Irena gave him a look that put color into his cheeks. Selah
laughed and bumped him with her hip.

"How obvious you are, Ethan," Alice teased him. Her gaze

rested on Irena's face for a second, before moving beyond her to Alejandro. When she looked ahead again, a slight smile curved her mouth.

Irena smiled, too, and looked out over the terrace, to the horizon. In all her years, she'd had many friends, but she'd never had this before. Olek, silent and strong on her left, his hand a comforting pressure on her back. Her closest friend stood on her right, and next to her, two Guardians that she'd been proud to train and to serve with, and whose opinions she valued as much as Olek's, as Michael's. They gathered with her, and she'd never before felt how much she had. And what was missing.

Her gaze fell to the novice's red shoes. "Dru had a reason for wearing those shoes."

As if the name were magic, the conversations around the terrace quieted. Beside her, Alice drew up a little straighter, her lips trembling before they firmed.

"Tell us," Alejandro said.

It was a signal to start. Michael wasn't yet here, but many things, Irena had learned, began in their own time. As difficult as it was to say each word, she also could not hold them back.

"I'd never trained a novice slower than Dru," Irena said. "Nothing I said made her move faster. She couldn't land a punch or a kick. I would chop off pieces of her, and instead of moving out of the way, she would just pick them back up and put them back on. She'd tell me she hated rushing around for no reason."

Michael arrived, teleporting into the north end of the terrace. Ames-Beaumont was with him, his eyes haunted, his beautiful face tired. The vampire paused, as if uncertain where he should stand. Selah beckoned to him.

Khavi teleported in behind Michael, wearing a simple white shift. The Doyen met Irena's gaze, and nodded for her to continue.

Irena wiped at her eyes. "I told her not to be stupid, of course, because if she was slow she'd just end up dead. At our next practice, she arrived with those red tennis shoes on. And she told me—" She began shaking with laughter, and for a second couldn't speak. "She told me that not only would they make her faster, but *so* fast that the only way her opponent would see her coming was by looking for the streak of bright red. And I was laughing so hard . . . I didn't see her coming. With one kick, she crushed four of my ribs and my right arm, then followed through with a roundhouse that broke my cheekbone, my jaw, knocked out half my teeth and popped my right eye out of its socket."

Stunned silence fell, which made Alejandro's soft laughter seem loud. Shaking his head, Michael broke into a grin. A muffled snicker came from somewhere to her left. Within seconds, it was difficult to separate those who laughed from those who wept.

"In sixteen hundred years, no novice has *ever* gotten the drop on me like that. But Dru wasn't done." She choked on another laugh, wiped her eyes again, drew a breath. "She put her foot on the back of my neck, and held me down while she healed each bone and each tooth, one by one. She took about a half an hour; my eye had almost healed on its own by then. And she told me she was just teaching me the difference between slow when it mattered, and when it didn't. Then she said that when someone needed her to save them, she'd be fast enough." Irena looked over at Pim, who watched her with wet cheeks and shining eyes. "And she was."

At some gatherings, a heavy quiet stretched between the memories. Not this one. Drifter immediately stepped forward to fill it. Irena leaned back into Alejandro, and listened to Drifter's long, lazy tale from a century before that ended with Dru swearing off men and kicking him out of her bedroom, where he'd landed, "right about thereabouts." He'd pointed to where the novices stood, which seemed to signal to Becca that it was her turn.

Not everyone shared their stories; Irena shared several. Michael did, Alice, even Ames-Beaumont. Each one gave her more of Dru, and reminded her of how much she liked the Guardians here, whether from their memories or their reactions to the stories they heard. And when Alejandro offered his, she not only had more of Dru, but something of Olek from the years they'd kept apart.

No gathering would be worthy of Dru, or capture what she'd been to any of them; but by the end, Irena thought it had spoken well of them, too. Perhaps that was why Michael had begun the tradition.

She looked across the terrace at him as Guardians slowly began to leave. He met her eyes, then made his way across the terrace toward their small group. Khavi walked beside him, frowning. She said something to him in the demon language; Irena couldn't understand it, but Alice stiffened.

Michael stopped. His eyes shifted to obsidian. His black wings formed. They opened, the feathers appearing to absorb the light from Caelum's sun. Sweeping down, his enormous wings launched him straight into the air.

Irena watched him rise and fly beyond sight past the wall of the tower. "What did she say, Alice?"

"She said, 'Will you not sing? Much time will pass before she hears your voice again.'"

She? Irena feared Khavi hadn't meant Dru.

Alejandro pulled in a sharp breath. Her heart a tight knot, she turned to look at him, saw the same dread. "Caelum's voice," he murmured.

By the gods—the prophecy. What had it said? *The dragon will rise before the lost two. The blood of the dragon will create one door and destroy another. Caelum's voice will sing it closed with ice and fire and blood, and be lost until she claims her new tongue and the dragon's blade.*

Khavi had predicted that a dragon was coming. And Caelum's voice would be lost.

Irena shook her head. Each lungful of air she drew felt like wind sawing through a dried clump of grass. "We will not let it—"

A vibration ran up her legs as if the ground beneath her feet shivered. But this wasn't the brief tremor of a new Gate—the sensation amplified until the marble around them began to hum. A song rose from beneath, from above, swooping and rising through words she didn't know.

Michael. Irena felt for Alejandro's hand, her eyes filling, though she thought she couldn't possibly have more tears. She looked up—she couldn't see him, but she searched the skies, backing away from the tower with Alejandro. The others moved with her, faces tilted up, slowly circling.

His voice swelled, harmonious, almost bringing Irena to her knees. Always, Michael's voice had been several voices in one but now more were held within it. She heard the mournful howl of a wolf and the rush of cold wind over her face. The roaring heat of a fire, the soothing murmur of a lover, the trembling heartbeat of fear, a sweet longing—sound that became sensation, emotion that became song, and Caelum responded to its touch.

Marble ivy appeared at the base of Dru's tower, climbed as if seeking the sun. In the distance, a thin spire flattened and stretched, forming a bold dome against the cerulean sky.

A new building knifed upward, as smooth and narrow as a blade, rising high above the others. Fierce recognition tore through Irena. She had never seen any structure of its type, but everything within her leaped forward at the sight of that building, claimed: *mine.*

The song faded. Irena strained to listen, trying to hold onto the music of it as long as she could. Already grieving its loss.

But it faded, and silence filled Caelum again—except for the heartbeats and breath of those around her. Those Irena trusted and loved; those who, like her, were rigid with astonishment and awe; those who were just as terrified for Michael as she was.

"Khavi may have predicted it," she said, and clenched her fists. "But we will *not* let it come to pass."

❧

From inside a hollow iron structure as big as the Special Investigations gymnasium, Alejandro watched Ames-Beaumont kiss his partner a final time. His face taut and pale, the vampire strode to Michael, who waited nearby. They vanished.

Somewhere in Chaos, Ames-Beaumont would begin writing the symbols that would allow them to create a portal. Until then, novices, Guardians, and a few vampires waited in the cold empty room, and the only relief from the sight of the iron walls was the mirrored chamber that had been reassembled in the far corner.

Standing next to Mariko and Radha, Luther caught Alejandro's eye. Larger, darker in his Guardian form, he gave a wry nod before returning his attention to the women. With a Gift that allowed her to manipulate glass in a manner similar to Irena's Gift with metal, Mariko was small and quick, and light armor guarded her forearms, chest, and thighs. Radha wore little more than two strips of red silk and her long black hair; she'd painted her body blue. Her Gift allowed her to pierce the strongest psychic shields—painfully—and disorient her target with illusions.

With luck, her Gift would affect dragons, as well.

Beside him, Irena sighed. Alejandro studied her face, memorizing every feature . . . again. He couldn't see her fear any more, just as he no longer felt his. It had settled into determination—and in Chaos, they would both wield their determination like another sword.

And he could not see the reason for her sigh. His breath froze to a vapor in the frigid air. "What is it?"

She glanced up at him, and smiled faintly. "I had the thought that if Ames-Beaumont hadn't had any friends, we would not be here."

Alejandro could imagine many meanings behind her statement, but he knew she only meant one: that if Ames-Beaumont had not made a blood-brother pact with his childhood friend when he'd been human, his blood could never have been tainted by Michael's sword.

The weapon that Michael had used to pierce the dragon's heart during the Second Battle still carried the beast's power within it. The blade cut through stone like water and could blaze with magical flames. And it could leave within a small human boy an anchor to the Chaos realm—and when that boy was transformed into a vampire and cursed, offer him a glimpse into that realm through any mirror.

But Alejandro thought it was not just one human boy and his friend—there had been others that led them here. If Ames-Beaumont had not been friends with Lilith, he'd never have been accidentally teleported to the Chaos realm with Selah. If Ames-Beaumont had never cared for his friends, he'd never have allowed his blood to be used to send a horde of nosferatu into the Chaos realm. If Ames-Beaumont had never been friends with Castleford, the vampire would never have met Savi—and while trying to save her, discovered the combination of symbols that were tied to his blood and made a portal between Earth and Chaos.

And without friends, the secret of Ames-Beaumont's blood would never have leaked out. Rael and Anaria would never have known to come for him.

Where that had led them, however, Alejandro saw only what Irena did: here.

Here was atop an Arctic ice sheet, hundreds of miles from anything human. But its isolation wasn't the primary reason they'd chosen this spot; the unending winter night was.

Once he returned here, Ames-Beaumont couldn't open the portal without a psychic connection to his partner, Savitri; Savitri couldn't help him unless she was awake and holding her psychic shields open. This far north, where the sun wouldn't rise for another week, Savitri could remain awake until the Guardians' mission was completed.

Once, Michael could have used his sword as an anchor to the realm and teleported the Guardians to Chaos without Ames-Beaumont's and Savitri's assistance, but the powerful weapon now rested in Belial's hands.

Unfortunately. If Michael could have taken the weapon with him into Chaos, the sword's value would have been immeasurable—as enormous as the value of the lives it would probably save.

And if Irena could, she'd have probably made a thousand of them.

He looked at her. Had she ever tried to replicate it? They had once seen a sword almost identical to it—Zakril's sword. But that one hadn't had any of the other weapon's power. "What was the difference in Michael's sword?"

Irena hesitated, as if uncertain. Could she not describe it, or had she never felt it?

"Did you never try to sense the bronze with your Gift?"

"I did." She touched her forehead. "I woke up with blood coming from my nose and ears. I did not try again."

"That's what happens to me." Drifter came up beside them, towering over Irena. "My apologies for listening in—couldn't help it. But that blood . . . that's what happens when I use my Gift to bust through the lock on the shielding spell. Except it'll burst all the vessels in my eyes, too."

Irena smiled. "Perhaps it did mine, but I could not see it."

Drifter nodded. Faint worry lined his eyes. "It's a shame we can't make another like it. It'd be right handy."

Alejandro tensed for the barest moment when Jake suddenly appeared in front of them. Christ. The young Guardian would end up with a sword through his heart if he made a habit of that.

Or a knife. Irena vanished the weapon in her hand, shaking her head.

Jake only looked a little chagrined. "Okay, so we don't have Michael's sword. What about anvils? Big ones. We can just drop 'em right on their heads, knock 'em out of the sky."

Irena gave Jake a look. To amuse her, Alejandro said, "The dragons, the nephilim, or the nosferatu?"

Her mouth dropped open in disbelief, and she stared up at him. Her eyes narrowed when she realized he was joking. Her gaze promised retribution.

With a grin, Jake said, "Any of them."

"I dropped a truck on a nephil once," Drifter said. "It mostly just shrugged it off."

Irena glanced up at him, frowning, then settled on Jake. Alejandro knew she debated between demonstration and telling—which was rarely as effective. But if a demonstration went badly this close to a fight, the shields and determination they'd all built out of fear might weaken.

She settled for forcing Jake to figure it out himself. "Why didn't I drop iron blocks on the nephilim at my forge?"

Alejandro watched the young Guardian's expression sharpen and the humor turn to speculation. Jake had a fine brain behind that mouth—he just had to use it.

"Because if they managed to catch the block, they'd whip it back at you—or use it for a shield," Jake said.

"Yes. Never *give* your enemy something that they can use as a weapon against you." She looked at Drifter. "Unless you are absolutely desperate."

"I was pretty damn desperate. I reckon we might be again." His brown hair spiked up when he dragged his hand through it. "How do you figure we kill these things? Nephilim, nosferatu—we know it's the head or the heart. But the dragons? What do we do—just throw anything at them?"

Alejandro had wondered the same. From the images Ames-Beaumont had projected, he could clearly picture the creatures' heavy frames, their bodies similar to a rodent's in shape, with powerful haunches and slightly weaker front limbs that ended in sharp talons. They were enormous, some appearing a hundred feet in length, and as they flew, their bodies possessed a serpentine grace. Fast and sleek, the dragons could dart as quickly as a hummingbird, and dive like a hawk. The iridescent scales that covered their hides were most likely armor, and they belched fire from a maw big enough to swallow five Guardians at once.

"It is best not to leave it to guesswork," he said. "We know from Michael that the dragons can be slain with a sword through their hearts. So I suggest two strategies: either strike for the heart or run as quickly as you can."

Irena nodded her agreement. The speculative look in Jake's eyes deepened. He quietly teleported away. Alejandro glanced around the room, didn't see where he'd gone.

"He probably figures he doesn't have enough explosives," Drifter said.

§

Irena didn't know if explosives would help them.

Michael and Ames-Beaumont returned, reeking of rot and sulphur. Ames-Beaumont painted two symbols on the wall in his blood, which immediately froze to the iron. When the vampire and Savi lowered their psychic shields, wyrmwolves in Chaos would swarm to the symbols he'd written in that realm, and begin ripping at each other. With enough wyrmwolf blood, the portal would open, creating a bridge from Chaos to the symbols here.

They might only have to wait minutes after the two vampires opened their shields; they might wait hours. They readied for it now.

Michael projected a picture of where the portal would open—a sheltered, rocky crag at the base of a black mountain. He called in a large table and spread a sheet of paper over the surface. They gathered round.

In black ink, he drew a circle in the center. "This is the mountain. On this side is our portal"—he drew a black X on one edge of the circle, then another on its opposite edge— "and here, halfway up the mountainside, is the mouth of a cave system. Several nephilim have been guarding the entrance against wyrmwolves, and more nephilim have been moving in and out of these caves in teams of ten."

Even without the image Michael provided, it was easy to picture the nephilim like bees at the entrance of a hive. Irena frowned. "Is their portal inside—and their queen?"

"I am not certain about the portal," Michael said, "but it is a strong possibility. Anaria has been outside the caves, however. She's been focused on the barrier and on the dragons."

The ceiling between Hell and Chaos. According to the diagram, the mountain sat near the edge of the enormous, circular span of dangling bodies. "Is she hunting a dragon?"

Michael nodded. "Once she has its blood, if she casts a spell to open the barrier between the realms, the magic of the symbols will be that much more powerful."

The blood of the dragon will create one door and destroy another.

Irena pushed it away, refusing to glance at Khavi standing next to Michael. Their life would not be determined by prophecy.

"What is our primary objective?" Alejandro asked.

"To close the portal is the most important task. We cannot allow a dragon into Earth. Alejandro, Irena, and Alice will search the caves. Khavi and I will clear the entrance for you first, then Khavi will prevent any nephilim from coming in behind you."

A cave that might be full of nephilim. Irena swallowed the hot lump of terror, of denial. She *would* allow Khavi at her back—and Alice, with her razored spiderwebs and quick blade, was the perfect choice to accompany them inside.

Jake's mouth tightened. He shifted on his feet, his gaze repeatedly scanning the small diagram Michael had drawn, but he remained silent.

"The symbols Anaria will have used to make the portal won't be in Chaos; you'll have to destroy the portal from this side on Earth."

Alejandro exchanged a glance with Irena. "How will you know if we've been successful?"

"I will know," Khavi said. "Roads that have been open will close. Certain possibilities will cease to exist."

Possibilities, such as a dragon passing through a portal? Why did Khavi never speak clearly?

Irena clenched her teeth and held in her response.

Drifter asked, "And the rest of us?"

"Anaria has focused her nephilim at the ceiling. They have almost killed all of the nosferatu—and we will not make an effort to stop them."

He paused. Irena said, "You will not find an argument here."

Michael smiled briefly, before continuing, "Our second task is simply to stop the nephilim from completing *their* task at the barrier. They are writing symbols between the bodies. We have to interrupt that."

"How?" Jake asked.

"Whatever manner that you can, according to your Gifts and your strengths. We are also a distraction until Irena's team closes the portal, but none of you will take unnecessary risks or make sacrifices," Michael said. "You will be in teams of three—each team will have one teleporter. Drifter, Mariko— you are with Selah. Radha and Luther, with Jake. If the nephilim converge on your teams, or you find yourselves losing ground, run. The nephilim have a task, and they will go back to it rather than give chase. If choices must be made, you *must* choose to leave Chaos, taking your team with you. I will have no argument in that."

No one offered one—yet. Irena eyed Jake, waiting.

"Do not approach Anaria; I will take her. Avoid the dragons. I cannot heal a dragon's bite, but I will watch for any other wounds, and heal them as quickly as I can." Michael glanced at Jake. "You are the Weapon, so you will be in the lead. Try to kill all of them—dragons, nosferatu, nephilim—before we fly in and engage."

"I thought I'd have a little more time to practice with it."

"You don't."

"Right, then." Jake nodded, once. A long metal tube appeared in his hands, carrying the scent of gunpowder and oil. He hoisted it over his shoulder. "You mind if I use a couple of these first?"

Khavi frowned. "What is it?"

"Rocket launcher," Jake said, never taking his eyes from Michael. "And I've got a few other ideas, too."

Michael gestured at the table, inviting Jake to lay them out.

Jake vanished the missile launcher, called in a pen. "All right. So we've essentially got a whole mess swarming around beneath those bodies. The dragons, because that's where they're feeding, and the nephilim writing their symbols. And we're looking to scatter the nephilim, confuse them, just keep them from doing what they're doing. So we should be doing that over here." He made an *X* beyond the edge of the dangling bodies, a small distance from the mountain's cave entrance. "If we come out our portal, circle around behind the mountain and use it for cover as long as we can, then set up shop here, we can start blowing shit up from a distance, aiming right into those bodies—and we can keep an eye on that cave entrance, so that Khavi can be freer to move around like Michael, keeping Anaria and the dragons off our ass."

Crossing his arms over his chest, Michael studied the lines Jake had drawn. "Go on."

"Irena, Alejandro, and Alice are still our best bet in the caves—they're our strongest on the ground and in tight quarters, and Irena's and Alejandro's Gifts play both offense and defense. But the rest of us, we need to form a line here." He tapped his finger on the *X*. "Luther, Drifter, Selah—their Gifts don't have long-range capabilities, so I say we stick them with these missiles and let them go to town. I'll try to get my light-ning working, but if I can't, I'll pull out my own. So we'll be the offense. Mariko and Radha, they've got good short-range de-fensive Gifts that can weaken the nephilim before going hand-to-hand. A nephil or two breaks off, comes after us, Radha and Mariko intercept it as a team, try to take it out."

Mariko nodded. "We can do that."

"Right on. Now, if the nephil gets closer than that, or if there's more than one or two, we've got these." Jake replaced his pen with an automatic rifle, and tilted the gun as if he were displaying a trophy. "These AK-47s will fire six hundred rounds per minute. We aren't going to get minutes, and shooting their bodies isn't going to hurt them enough—so we'll aim for the wings. We're all stuck flying—unless we want to go swim-ming in lava—but so far, I've only seen the nephilim carrying swords. So until they're right up on us, we'll just rip the hell out of their feathers. Maybe their eyes, if you can get an angle on them. After that, I've got tranquilizer darts filled with vampire blood. We'll send them crying back to Mama."

Irena snorted. Jake grinned, vanished his gun, and shoved his hands into his pockets.

Michael's expression didn't change. "You have ten minutes to train them."

"Hot damn." Jake seemed to bounce a little, like an ener-getic puppy.

"But the stipulations I made before still hold: no sacrifices. If the nephilim come at you en masse, and your weapons can-not hold them back, teleport out of the realm. Alive, we can re-group and return. Dead, we cannot." Michael waited for Selah's and Jake's nods. "As soon as we have gone into Chaos through the portal, the novices here will erase the symbols, and kill any wyrmwolves who make it through before the bridge closes."

At the end of the table, Becca gave a thumbs-up. Pim nodded.

"Khavi and I will bring Irena's team out if they can't find Anaria's portal. If anyone is left behind, return to our portal site—or run. Ames-Beaumont and Savitri will find you through the mirrors, and we'll return for you." He swept his amber gaze over each of them, his face hard. "We will not fail."

"No," Khavi said softly, and when her Gift dragged across Irena's psyche, it revealed a heavy sorrow behind Khavi's quiet expression. "We won't."

CHAPTER 22

Flying into Chaos, Irena hit a solid wall of screams. She thought she'd prepared for them, but they ripped at her ears, her heart. Tortured, terrified, pleading—the noise filled her, combined with the hot fetid air, squeezed into her lungs as if trying to force her own scream.

She slowed, waiting for the others. Michael and Khavi had already gone through; now they flew with incredible speed around the mountainside, where they would clear a path to the caves. Below, wyrmwolves writhed and squirmed. The stench of their blood and exposed flesh rose on heated currents. To her left, the bleak landscape stretched, ribboned by the rivers of molten rock. Far above, she saw the whip of a tail and a flash of scales against the frozen black ceiling. Her heart clamored, the racing of her pulse in her ears adding to the crushing weight of sound.

Not just her heart. The others' raced, too, as they gathered beside her. She glanced back as, finally, Alejandro came through, bringing up the rear. She met his eyes, and the pressure of the noise receded. As soon as he was in position, she led them forward.

As they rounded the side of the mountain, Jake's group broke off, angling upward. Irena skimmed close to the rocks, aware of the bright target her white wings made against the dark granite. They came in above the cave—Michael and Khavi had already completed their task. Three nephilim lay dead beside the entrance, their black feathers the same color as the rock beneath them.

Irena landed and vanished her wings. Michael stood, bloodied sword in hand, looking out over the swarm of nephilim and dragons. A flash of white briefly lighted his face. Lightning forked across the sky. A nephil fell; a dragon dived after it.

Michael glanced at Alice. "You will tell him it was well done."

"*You* will," Alice countered. Her face pale, she swiftly unwound steel-strong spider silk from a coil the size of Irena's fist. The strands were gossamer thin and difficult to see unless Irena looked for them. "I will tie one end near the mouth of the cave. If you come for us, this will lead you to our location—but mind your step. I intend to set traps, should any nephilim try to follow us inside. I will mark them with a drop of blood."

The first explosion tore through the bodies. A dragon shrieked, drawing up as a ball of fire roared toward it. With a flick of its wings, the dragon rolled into a sinuous back somersault, changing direction. A second, then a third explosion came quickly after.

A smile touched Michael's hard mouth, and he lifted into the air. "Be safe."

Irena turned as Alejandro slipped into the cave, his blades gleaming in the dark. She followed.

The mouth of the cave narrowed into a single tunnel that sloped sharply down into the mountain. Ames-Beaumont and Selah had hidden in these caves before, and had given them a description as far as they could recall: After five hundred yards, this tunnel opened up into a large chamber, which split into three directions. The tunnel on the right, they'd warned, was eventually a dead end, but with enough chambers to hide the nephilim. They'd taken the left tunnel, which in turn broke off into other directions, tiny crawlspaces, abrupt chasms.

Beside her, Alejandro inhaled, and looked to her with a question in his eyes. "Human?"

His nose was better than hers. Irena could barely detect the scent of human blood and bodies beneath the reek of rot and the wyrmwolves' stale musk. But it wouldn't be human—it was the nephilim. The scent would give them a clearer trail to follow. Irena motioned for Alejandro to take the lead.

The noise from outside slowly faded, the screams, thunder, and explosions faint in the background. The corridor narrowed until Alejandro was forced to walk at an angle to make his shoulders fit.

Remembering Khavi's prediction, Irena frowned. "How would a dragon fit through this space and find the portal?"

"Perhaps there is another entrance," Alejandro said. "Or a very small dragon."

Alice sighed. "Never would I have imagined myself saying this, but I miss the friendship you shared, when you only spoke to each other in French. How absurd I feel, following a conversation in which one half is Russian and the other Spanish."

Alejandro spared a brief glance back. "And now more than half. You choose Russian?"

"I feel absurd, not foolish. I know better than to poke a bear with a fox's blade."

Irena grinned. The tunnel widened, and she felt Alejandro's relief as he once again had more room to maneuver. Ahead, the first chamber arched overhead like a cathedral, and stood empty. The scent led them to the far tunnel.

Of course, it had to be the one tunnel they knew nothing about, Irena thought.

With his swords, Alejandro gestured to the right and left. "Shall we close them?"

Yes. Even if any nephilim hid in chambers or chasms, Irena could seal off the mouths of the corridors and prevent the nephilim from coming around behind them. She called in several tons of steel from her cache and set it at the entrance of the right tunnel. When she pushed her Gift through it, the steel flowed upward, outward, radiating into a thick door. She slammed the edges into the stone, setting the door into place. She repeated it at the left tunnel while Alice set an elaborate trap with her webs at the end of the corridor that had brought them to the chamber.

They made enough noise, Irena thought, to bring an army of nephilim down on them . . . but none came to investigate the sounds or the use of her Gift. Dense stone *could* muffle psychic senses—but if the nephilim hadn't heard her ramming steel into stone, they'd have to be much deeper into the mountain.

Or in human form.

When the nephilim used their demon forms, their psychic scent didn't match the humans'—and the body rejected their presence, as it might fight off a sickness. The longer the sickness, the longer the nephilim needed to heal once they reverted to human form.

Perhaps the nephilim had not been in and out of these caves using the portal. It might simply be the safest location to recuperate.

Alejandro must have been thinking the same. "I had expected them to seek us out."

Irena nodded. "They had guards at the mouth of the cave; I cannot imagine they would not have more inside, particularly if their brethren are vulnerable." It was what Irena would do, if she had to watch over weakened or injured comrades. "If they are in an easily defensible position, they'll wait for us to come to them rather than leave their brethren alone."

And unable to hide their approach, she, Olek, and Alice would walk into an ambush. Alejandro stared down the darkened corridor, his thumbs rubbing against his sword handles. It was, Irena knew, a gesture that meant the same as a stroke of his finger down his beard: He considered alternatives. He weighed priorities.

Irena slipped into the corridor, listened. Nothing. The darkness deepened at the end of the tunnel; soon, the dark would be absolute, and they'd have to use a light source to see—making them a brighter target than their movements would.

She already felt completely blind. The narrowness of the first tunnel had convinced her that the portal could not be this way—no dragon could squeeze through. Yet her certainty came from Khavi foreseeing the dragon passing through the portal; a future which, itself, was uncertain.

It was an endless knot that she couldn't untangle. But she did not know if it was time to draw her sword and cut through it.

Her eyes searched the darkness. Fear gripped her throat in its ragged claws. As frightened as she was of the nephilim waiting, the consequences of taking the wrong path terrified her far more.

Khavi cannot see what she does not know.

Maybe Khavi didn't know that the tunnel was tighter than a dragon's ass.

Irena turned to Alejandro. "We must decide—"

"We go back," he said.

"Back," Alice agreed.

Irena laughed, nodding. "Yes. But let us do what we can here first." She glanced at Alice. "Did Jake give to you any of those missile launchers?"

Alice's relieved expression flattened into a disbelieving look. "That question is just slightly more stupid than asking if he gave me only *one*." Smiling, she joined Irena at the mouth of the tunnel. "Do you want to collapse it?"

"Or worse. I do not know how long a door would hold against them if there are many."

"I have worse," Alice said. "Namely, a tactical nuclear device."

Irena stared at her.

The Guardian shrugged her thin shoulders. "Jake considered using it out there, but he didn't know if exploding one against the ceiling would weaken the barrier."

Irena wasn't certain if shock or amusement had prevented Alejandro from replying. But now he recovered, and said, "What is the yield?"

"It is small—only ten tons. About two city blocks."

"On a timer?"

"Yes."

Irena found her voice. "And so this is your plan—we set it and run? But what if they take hold of it first and toss it back at us?"

"We carry it farther down this tunnel," Alejandro said, gesturing toward the darkness beyond Irena. "We can see that it narrows. When it widens again, you create a steel box for it, wide enough that they can't move the container beyond the narrow gap, and with the metal embedded into the stone so they cannot vanish the box into their cache without first hacking it free. *Then* we set it and run."

Alice nodded her agreement. "If we take it to that depth, we'll also be safer once we are outside."

How could this sound reasonable? Either it *was* reasonable or they were desperate. Perhaps it was both.

"Get it ready, then." Irena crouched in the mouth of the tunnel and looked into the shadows. "And I will watch your back."

She glanced around once; Alice worked quickly over a device she'd taken out of a green barrel. They decided upon a five-second timer, with Alice in the lead to guide them around her traps as they ran outside. Alejandro only agreed to let Irena bring up the rear after she pointed out that, if something kept them in the tunnel longer than five seconds, she could create a thick steel shield to protect them.

She did not know if it would—she knew nothing of nuclear devices. She only knew that if they ran late, she would take the brunt of the explosion.

Alice finished, drew a deep breath, and vanished the device into her cache. "We are ready."

The shadows in the corridor deepened. Irena couldn't remember when she had last seen such darkness. She listened for heartbeats, heard only theirs. The human scent grew stronger. The tunnel narrowed. Her heart thumped when she heard a scrape behind her. Only Alice's boot, and yet knowing didn't ease her fear.

The tunnel wall angled wider. Alejandro watched the almost-complete darkness as Irena quickly formed the box. Alice called in her device, slipped it inside. They looked at each other. Alice reached forward, turned a key, touched a button, Irena sealed the box—and they ran.

The chamber passed in a blur. Alice raced ahead, springing

traps with her blade, darting around others. Five seconds was an eternity. The screams from outside became louder and louder. White light flashed down the tunnel. Thunder crashed as Alice breached the entrance. Alejandro turned, grabbed Irena's hand, leapt for Alice. They smashed to the ground.

Irena formed a thick, domed shield, surrounding them in six inches of steel. They waited. One second, two, three—

The steel shuddered beneath them, as if the mountain had been rocked by a small earthquake. A tiny tremor followed. Then all was still.

Irena lifted her head. Her fingers shook. She untangled Alice's skirts from her legs. "I expected worse."

"As did I." Alejandro rose onto his knees, ducking his head beneath the low dome.

"We shall shower Jake with our disappointment." Alice took a deep breath. "We're blind."

Yes. Irena called in her knives, crouching. Alejandro brought in the heavy swords she'd made him. She waited for Alice's long-bladed naginata to appear in the Guardian's hands before she said, "On three, I'll unfold the dome, and give us a wall. The mountain should be at our backs. As soon as we are on our feet, I'll vanish the steel. On three."

She counted, then rolled her Gift through the metal. The dome opened like an oyster shell, flattening and rising to form a wide shield in front of them.

Something hit the other side. Before Irena could react, the wall slammed into her. She smashed into granite. Bones snapped— not hers. Beside her, Alice's eyes were closed, her body limp. Pinned by the steel wall facing Alice, Irena couldn't see Olek. She tried to push forward. Her feet slipped. On blood?

She struck with her Gift. Steel spikes stabbed outward; Irena heard a feminine gasp of pain. The pressure of the wall eased. Irena folded the thick steel sheet, snapping it closed like an Iron Maiden. She missed.

Alice crumpled to the ground. Black dust and smoke filled the air around them, above them, obscuring the frozen ceiling. Only flashes of lightning and the never-ending screams penetrated the dense cloud. Irena vanished the steel wall.

Black dust streaking her beautiful face like tears, a sword in her hand, Anaria lunged out of the darkness toward Irena.

Olek got there first. The blade meant for Irena's heart stabbed through his stomach.

Irena caught the tip as it pierced his back. Her Gift raged through the sword, peeling thin wires from the blade. They climbed Anaria's sword arm. Irena wound them tight, biting into skin and muscle.

Anaria froze.

Her chest heaving, Irena slipped her right arm around Olek's waist. She couldn't see Anaria's face. She couldn't release the sword. "Let him go."

A sob caught in Anaria's voice. "You killed my children."

I would kill them all. Irena didn't dare say it. Not when Anaria still held the sword. Not when her strength could tear dull steel up through Olek's heart, not when Anaria's speed far exceeded Irena's. Even if she softened the steel, the grigori could punch through Olek's heart.

She did not know how to respond, what would get them out of this.

Olek did. And despite the sword through his gut, when he spoke his words were the smoothest silk. "You will not kill her, Anaria."

"No?" The reply devolved into a laugh, high and pained.

"No. And if you vow you will not, I will tell you the name of the demon who murdered Zakril."

The laugh stopped. The sword quivered against Irena's bloodied hand. "Who?"

Olek waited.

"If you speak true, I will not kill her," Anaria promised.

Irena's body trembled. Olek bargained with Anaria as he would with a demon. "Him," she said. "You won't kill *him*."

"Her," Olek said firmly, and before Irena could reply— "Rael murdered your husband. Rael stabbed a sword through Zakril's chest, pinning him to a stone wall. He pounded iron spikes through Zakril's wings, and used his desecrated body to leave a message for your children, so they would know where to find you."

"No." The sword jerked. Olek tensed, but didn't make a

sound; Irena clenched her teeth against the terrified scream rising in her throat. "I can see lies, and Rael has never lied to me. He has said he is a friend to me."

"If you also see the truth, you know that *I* do not lie."

Anaria's breath shuddered once, twice. Her reply held less conviction, yet more determination—as if she were trying to convince herself. "He has *never* lied to me."

"Then perhaps you have never asked him the right questions." Olek's voice hardened. "Starting, perhaps, with his definition of friendship."

Movement flashed at the corner of her eye. A winged shadow passed through the dark cloud. Irena couldn't determine size or shape.

Olek must have seen it, too. His heart beat faster. His weight shifted, almost imperceptibly—preparing to move.

When she spoke, Anaria's harmonious voice had lost all emotion. "Do you have any regrets, Guardian?"

Irena stiffened, prepared to liquefy the sword. She searched her cache. An anvil. A rock. It did not matter—*this could not happen.*

"Just one," Olek said. "And enjoying every moment of what Michael does to you now isn't it."

A dark form streaked out of the cloud, slammed into Anaria's side. Her sword ripped from Olek's stomach.

Michael. He flew headlong into the mountainside, smashing Anaria face-first into the granite. His face rigid with fury, he wrapped his arm around her neck from behind, caught her in an unbreakable hold.

Irena didn't understand a word Michael shouted at his sister, but his rage needed no translation. Anaria kicked at the granite; the ground beneath Irena's feet shivered.

She turned back to Olek and formed her wings. "If they begin to fight, we don't want to be caught in the path of it."

"Yes."

With swords in his hands, he stood over her as she bent to Alice. She lifted the Guardian against her chest. Alice's skirts and side were slick, wet. Irena's heart clenched as she searched for the source of the blood. Her hand came away clean.

Not blood. Not blood. *Water.*

She sniffed her hand and looked up at Olek. "There's water. Sea water."

"From where?"

Irena stood with Alice in her arms, her gaze scanning the ground. Drops over there, splattered as if from high above, traveling away from the cave entrance. Farther away, another drop, and another. But here, beneath Alice, there hadn't just been drops but a puddle. As if someone flying had spilled the water, and—still wet—had left more drops in his wake.

She glanced up into the sky just as Michael shouted her name. A huge shadow arrowed toward them from high above, taking shape at terrifying speed. A shimmering blue-green dragon, its black wings tucked, its talons outstretched, like a hawk preparing to snatch a rabbit from a field.

Fear speared through her, hot and thick. She reached for Olek, pulled in steel for a shield—

The dragon vanished.

Irena blinked.

"The portal," Olek murmured. "Holy Mother of God."

Michael flung Anaria away, ran toward them.

Give me Alice. I will inform the others, and we will be right behind you, he signed, even as he roared a single word that drowned out the screams.

"GO!"

♪

Alejandro dove through the portal into cold water. The still-healing gash in his stomach burned. He tasted salt, and vanished his wings when the weight dragged at his speed. Stone ruins lay half-submerged in the sand around him. Somewhere among the ruins, Anaria must have written the symbols to open the portal. He would not stop to find them now.

Above, he spotted the dragon, swimming with the undulating grace of a serpent toward the moonlight piercing the surface of the water.

Fewer people would be on the sea, but the ruins suggest they probably weren't far from land. He glanced over at Irena.

Though she'd come through the portal after Alejandro, her powerful arm strokes had already caught her up to him. He couldn't see her feet through the churning of the water she kicked.

Her knife was clamped in her teeth. Her eyes glowed a brilliant green.

A hunt, like they'd never had before—one they could not lose.

The dragon skimmed along the surface of the sea before lifting into the air. Distance blurred its shape into a dark smear.

Irena's scream of rage boiled from between her teeth.

Michael appeared in front of them. He reached for Irena's hand, grabbed Alejandro's. They teleported out of the water into the sky.

Alejandro fought the disorientation, formed his wings again. The dragon flew below.

Irena dropped without wings. Michael circled around beneath the creature as Irena landed on its massive back. Calling in her saber, she lifted the weapon high and drove the blade straight down into the dragon's shoulder.

The steel snapped against the scales. The dragon twisted its body, rolling in the air. The pale green scales of its belly and chest were exposed for a brief second. Alejandro dove. The dragon changed direction mid-twist and he rocketed past it. From beneath the dragon, he saw Irena lose her seat, scramble for a grip on its glossy blue hide, and slip. The dragon backflipped and snapped enormous teeth at her as she fell.

The dragon missed. Alejandro's wings beat several times before his heart did again.

Michael teleported beneath the dragon. His sword stabbed deep, but must have missed the heart; roaring, the dragon raked his hind claw at the Doyen, catching Michael's leg, sending him spinning toward the water. Before the dragon could dive for the falling Guardian, an iron block dropped on its head. The dragon shook it off.

Hovering, Irena shouted, "*Here,* you sheep-fucking snake!"

The dragon circled around toward her, seemed to gather itself. Alejandro streaked between them, began pulling his Gift before the dragon opened its mouth. Fire belched forth.

The flames billowed toward Alejandro on a wave of heat, licked at his skin, ruffled his feathers. It surrounded him, a bright orange, dancing light. His power slid through the fire, grabbed hold, but it slipped through the fingers of his Gift; he could not control it. The best he could do was turn the flames back toward the dragon.

The creature shrieked and drew up, flashing its pale underbelly. Rolling to its side to avoid the flames, the dragon snapped its wings, whipped its tail. It darted west, far faster than either Irena or Alejandro could fly.

They needed Michael—or any other teleporter.

"Olek!"

Irena reached him. Her eyes were frantic, her hands moving over his body as if searching for burns. Her expression froze, and she brushed her thumb over his lip. Crimson streaked her skin.

"Don't do that again," she whispered.

He wiped the blood from his nose and ears. "Only if you do not taunt it again." He still wanted to shake her for that.

To his surprise, she nodded before glancing around them. "Where is Michael?"

Alejandro didn't see the Doyen, either. But though they could not catch up, neither could they wait. They started out after the dragon. They flew at Alejandro's fastest speed, and for the first time, he had a moment to look for something that might reveal their location. Water stretched north and south, but to the east and west the faint lines of low-lying land masses darkened the horizon.

"We are between Sardinia and Italy!" Irena shouted to him over the rush of the wind. "And—"

She broke off, a look of horror coming over her face. He only saw her mouth move. *By the gods.*

The dragon surged upward. Alejandro's gaze searched higher, and his stomach rolled into a ball of ice. Moonlight reflected off the silver sides of a west-bound commuter jet slicing through the night sky, leaving a vapor trail like blood welling behind a blade. The dragon chased after it, closing in fast.

He and Irena were both flying faster than the jet, but they could not make up the time the dragon had. They could only watch. The dragon dipped into the vapor trail, darted closer—from nose to tail, its body was longer than the jet's, its wingspan double the length.

"We will try to catch them!" he shouted to Irena.

Perhaps her Gift could hold the fuselage together, even if the dragon ripped the aircraft apart. How many humans could he carry at once? Ten, perhaps, if they clung to him. If the jet was full, it likely carried forty or fifty. Perhaps they could stretch a metal sheet between them like a lifeboat . . . and leave themselves and the humans defenseless against the dragon's attack.

He prayed.

Michael appeared between them, Khavi and Alice ahead of them. Jake and Selah dropped into formation behind, flanked by Drifter and Luther, Mariko and Radha. Michael took a single glance, and gave the signal to teleport again.

Too late. They appeared beside the dragon as it snatched at the jet like pulling a fish from the water. Metal shrieked as claws scored the aluminum fuselage. The jet seemed to bump across the air.

Hysterical screams sounded from inside.

Alejandro searched for Jake, saw the young Guardian had already teleported beneath the jet and flattened his palms to the metal skin. His electric Gift sizzled across Alejandro's mind, filled the air with static. Through the small oval windows, Alejandro saw the lights inside the cabin flicker and burst in showers of sparks. The dragon jolted and screamed, releasing the fuselage and diving toward the sea.

The engines sputtered and died. With sickening inevitability, the nose sloped downward. Michael teleported, braced his hands behind the hatch for the forward landing gear. His black wings quadrupled in size, their span as wide as the jet's.

Michael shouted, "Khavi, Mariko, Radha, Alice—with me!" He looked to Irena. *"You must stop it."*

Her face pale, she nodded. Irena flew over the fuselage,

dragged her hand over its surface, sealing the claw marks with her Gift.

She glanced at Alejandro, and they dove after the dragon.

§

Either strike for the heart, or run as quickly as you can.

Running was no longer an option—and Irena found that getting to its underbelly proved almost impossible, even for the teleporters. The dragon seemed to sense Jake and Selah coming, and raked with its hind claws before they could do enough damage with their blades. Bullets bounced off the scales. It moved too quickly to target with a missile or explosive. They'd been able to do little more than fly alongside it, teleporting when the dragon flew ahead, trying to herd it north without success.

The west bank of Italy approached with terrifying speed. The images Michael had once projected flashed through her mind. People would burn if they didn't stop the dragon. Until they stopped it, *everything* would burn.

Both armed with machine guns, Jake teleported with Drifter in above the dragon's head, aiming for the eyes. The dragon snapped its jaws back, almost quicker than Irena could track, and caught Drifter by the left leg.

The Guardian set his jaw, shoved the muzzle of the rifle between the dragon's teeth alongside his thigh. The burst of gunfire down the dragon's throat didn't slow it. Jake teleported behind Drifter, disappeared with the big man, and teleported in beside Selah. Drifter's leg had been severed mid-thigh.

His face white, Jake disappeared with Drifter again, and came back without him. Lightning snaked out. The dragon screamed and twisted around, but didn't slow.

Lightning and fire—the only two things that frightened it. Twice, she'd seen dragons, when faced with fire, pull upright. Twice, they'd left their bellies exposed for a brief second.

Maybe they burned, too.

Irena called in a steel spear. With her Gift, she textured the smooth shaft so that, if bloodied, it would not slip in her hands.

Forcing away the memory of blood on his lips, leaking from his ears, she signaled to Alejandro, flying alongside her.

I am not going to taunt the dragon—yet I need you to break your vow, and use its fire against it again.

He waited.

As soon as you draw its fire, Selah and Jake will teleport in above to distract it, while I come in below.

If you are in the path of the fire, you will burn. I cannot control its flames.

I might burn. But I will not die.

His lips thinned as if he prepared to argue, but he nodded. She signaled to Jake, to Selah.

Jake took her arm, Selah took Alejandro's. They teleported west, and flew back to meet the dragon head-on—the two tele-porters and Alejandro flying slightly ahead and above Irena. They drew closer. Its blue scales gleaming in the moonlight, the dragon roared as if recognizing the challenge.

Alejandro snapped upright, hovering. He spread his arms. A spiraling inferno roared between them, and he threw it toward the dragon, a funnel of flames that lit the dark sky.

His own fire. Horror lurched through her stomach. Irena only had an instant to feel it before winging forward beneath the tunnel of flames. Hidden by the fire—and protected from it. The inferno should have singed her feathers, her hair. She only felt the cool night air.

The dragon shrieked, drew up. Irena slammed into its chest, shoving her spear into the pale green scales.

It was like lying against a stove; the scales burned with the dragon's inner heat. Her skin seared. Screaming, the dragon raked at her. Irena shoved her hand into the wound beside the shaft of her spear, called in her kukri knife. She tore open a three-foot gash in its chest. Her head filled with the heavy beat of an enormous heart.

The dragon's claws caught her left wing, tore it away. White-hot pain ripped across her back. Irena held in her scream, chan-neled it into rage. She hacked deeper, into a chest as hot as a furnace. Steaming blood poured over her face, her arms. Her knife hit a rib; she punched her fist between two bones, then ripped them apart—and hung with one hand as the dragon dove. She gripped her spear again, drove it toward the heart. Still not there. She rammed her shoulders against ribs until the crack of bone joined the dragon's roar. She cut deeper, digging her way in.

The heart glowed like an ember, so large she couldn't have circled it with her arms.

Irena didn't want to hug it, anyway. She stabbed her spear into the throbbing organ, shoving it deep. The dragon screamed, twisting. Clinging to a rib, she brought her legs up, pounded the heart with her feet. The chambered muscle split, spewing dark blood. Panicked, the dragon's claws raked its own belly. She lunged up into the chest cavity, hacked to pieces the quivering muscle.

When the dragon quieted, she dove out of its body, clinging to her knife and spear.

She couldn't see. The dragon's blood ran into her eyes. Agony dug razored claws into her back when she tried to fly. She couldn't vanish the wing she had left.

"Irena!" Selah's shout. "I have you!"

The beat of powerful wings drew close. Hands slid over her shoulders, then around her waist, gently pulling Irena out of her dive.

Irena almost forgot to wipe the dragon's blood from her mouth before parting her lips to speak. "Olek?"

"Burned, but alive and arguing. He won't let Jake take him away until he's seen you. Michael can't heal him."

Burned, but alive. *The stupid ox.* She didn't try to hold back her tears. They slipped beneath her closed lids, over her cheeks. "Michael is already here? What of the airplane?"

"Apparently, there was a miracle—and, apparently, Khavi thinks its fun to carry around a fleet of lifeboats in her cache."

Irena laughed, and felt Selah rub a cloth against her face, cleaning away the blood. When she opened her eyes, she saw her wing sticking out at an odd angle, mangled and the feathers coated with red. Gore covered her clothes and skin.

A hundred yards away, hovering above the water, a group of Guardians waited for them.

"You're still holding your weapons," Selah pointed out.

Weapons still heated from the furnace of the dragon's chest. "I can't vanish them." Or her wing.

"And I can't vanish this towel I just used on your face." Selah made a soft humming sound. "I also can't seem to 'port with you."

Irena nodded. She hadn't ingested the dragon's blood, but she was covered with it. If Michael, Selah or Jake could have teleported with a dragon as easily as they did another Guardian, this fight would have been much easier.

They approached the hovering Guardians. Irena's heart pitched to her stomach and heaved up into her throat when she saw Olek, held up by Jake. His skin charred, his clothes burned away—as was much of his flesh. She cried into the towel and didn't touch him, knowing that every movement must be agony.

But she felt the relief in his psychic scent, not his pain. And his eyes smiled at her before Jake teleported him away.

She searched the waters before glancing up at Michael. "Where is the dragon?"

"In my cache."

Irena frowned. "Could you have teleported with it?"

Michael gave her a look. "No. But a grigori can hold the pieces." His gaze slid over her body. The sticky heat of the dragon's blood disappeared.

With a grateful sigh, Irena vanished her wing. The sharp ripping pain in her back vanished with it. Though clean, her weapons retained their heat.

She reached out with her Gift and touched them.

CHAPTER 23

Taylor eyed the clock. Even before this prediction of Khavi's, even before the task force, she'd rarely ever left at the end of her shift. Tonight, she'd leave on the dot. *Technically,* she might still be working, since she and Preston were meeting with Wren to go over the security at the Stafford funeral—but Taylor wasn't ready to call the development of a plan to slay a demon congressman a cog in the wheel of justice.

Jorgenson wouldn't approve the overtime for it, anyway.

She glanced at the time again. The sun had set five minutes ago. She hadn't heard from Michael or anyone at SI—but even if their gathering had run late, he'd still be out there, waiting. If not, someone would have called her. Lilith . . . or someone. No news meant good news.

Of course, in her line of work, no news usually just meant the body hadn't been found yet.

She looked up at the ceiling, said quietly, "Michael, if you're here, Joe and I are ready to go."

But Joe wasn't, actually. He was staring wide-eyed at his computer screen, leaning forward in his desk chair like the

Giants were one pitch away from winning the World Series. "Andy, you've got to look at this."

She came around the desk. A live newsfeed ran in a small window; she couldn't hear the blond anchorwoman, but the inset showed a spotlight shining down on a cluster of boats tied together with gossamer strings. Taylor tilted her head, looked at the rings the boats made and the shimmering threads connecting them—the whole effect was almost like a spiderweb.

The headline stated that it had been an airline crash with no fatalities—and a freak electrical storm reported in the area was the probable cause. Great, that everyone survived, but she couldn't quite see what Joe was so worked up about. "Are we surprised it's not a goose this time?"

Joe shook his head, turned up the volume. "*—witnesses on a ferry are calling it a miracle. 'It just floated down into the water,' said one witness. Others are more skeptical, however.*"

They switched to video of a lanky, twenty-something kid with a backpack and an American accent, laughing and shaking his head. "*I saw a splash, that's what I saw. We saw it start to come down, but then the moon went behind a cloud or something. You couldn't see anything after that. Here—*" He held up a digital video camera, showed a dark screen. "*My dad paid fifteen hundred bucks for this before I came here, and I've got nothing. I should have been taking pictures of the naked blue lady who was strutting around the boat, instead.*"

At the mention of a naked lady, heads turned at the other desks. Joe turned the volume back down.

The anchorwoman appeared again. "*Reports indicate that fifty percent of the cameras on board recorded the same images.*" She tried to appear coyly amused. "*The other fifty show a nude blue woman—who, at this time, has not yet been identified.*"

"You see, Andy—our guys did that," Joe said.

She let the *our guys* slide without comment. A strange giddiness wouldn't stop shaking in her belly. Could they really have saved an *airplane*?

The camera panned over the crowd again. Taylor found her finger shooting out, pressing against the screen below the face of a woman wearing a black cloak, the hood thrown back to show her dark hair.

"That one! I saw her at Polidori's a couple of nights ago."

"I saw her at SI, but she had on this red dress . . ." He trailed off with a whistle and leaned even closer, his tongue almost hanging out. "God, it's a crime for a woman built like that to cover up her—"

"You said you were ready, detective."

Taylor straightened. The voice was as harmonious as Michael's, but definitely was not his.

Taylor turned to Khavi and gestured at the computer. "I guess he's a little busy?"

"Yes. I volunteered to come in his place while he got rid of the dragon."

A dragon? Speechless, she looked over at Joe, who'd gotten to his feet.

"You are going to Rael's house," Khavi said.

It wasn't a question—because, Taylor realized, the woman already knew. "We are unless you can see any reason why we shouldn't."

"No. We must."

"Well, let's head out then."

Taylor grabbed her coat, aware that half the bullpen was watching Khavi as if a pint-sized can of gorgeous had suddenly appeared in their midst, and she might start sharing it with all of them.

They weren't getting lucky today.

Joe opened both the stair door and the vehicle's rear passenger door for Khavi. Taylor rolled her eyes and shook her head as she slid into the driver's seat.

"Buckle up," Taylor told her when Khavi scooted to the middle and leaned forward, her elbows on the back of the front seat. Her braided hair was blocking the image in the rearview mirror.

"No, thank you. I have seen you arrive at Rael's house. The vehicle is not damaged, so we do not crash."

Taylor counted to ten, reminding herself they were planning to kill a congressman, so seat belts were officially low on the list. When she got to ten, she started the car.

"So were you there?" Joe turned to ask Khavi. "With the plane and the dragon?"

"Yes."

"How'd you do it? The plane, first."

"Michael carried the front, I carried the back, and Mariko supported the middle and made sure it would not break apart. Alice tied the boats together and readied them, and Radha took her clothes off and made humans imagine things."

"Yeah, I bet," Taylor said, giving Joe a pointed look. He raised his left hand, wagged his ringless finger. "And the dragon?"

"Irena tore its chest open and shoved her spear through its heart."

Taylor's brows rose. "Not Michael?"

"No. But he has the blood now, and that is what matters."

"Why?"

Khavi didn't answer. God, she hated this shit.

The grigori rested her chin on her arms. "I have told him that you will never love him."

Told who what? Taylor frowned and glanced at Joe. He shrugged.

"You lost us, lady," he said.

"Michael," Khavi said with the inflection of someone talking to a slow child. "I have told Michael that *she*"—Taylor felt a poke on her shoulder— "will never love *him*."

"Love *Michael*?" Could Khavi be serious? "As in, *love* love? Why would you tell him that? Why would it even cross your mind?"

It sure as hell had never crossed hers. For god's sake, she hadn't even gotten beyond thinking about rolling around on a bed with him—and when she did she pushed the image away as quickly as possible. He was the Doyen. It felt wrong, somehow, to think of rolling around on a bed with him, no matter how freaking gorgeous he was. Sure, he gave her a shiver now and then—but he wasn't exactly human.

And he wasn't in her league, anyway. When it came to romance, Taylor preferred reality.

Still, her stomach did a crazy little flip when Khavi said, "Because I saw that he will love you. But you will not love him, even though you will know him better than anyone—perhaps it is *because* you will know him. I do not know *why* you do not, only that you never return his feelings. So I told him, that he might guard his heart. And a door has shut. He will not love you now."

Taylor's throat tightened. Jesus, how fucking stupid was it that she felt as if she'd lost something that she never wanted or even thought about having? Something that, according to Khavi, she never *would* want.

Michael would have loved her?

But now he wouldn't.

"Do not feel sad," Khavi said, patting her shoulder. "You will no longer take his heart, but he will still take you to his bed. Many times."

"Wha—?" The word came up at the same time her breath went down the wrong way. She coughed and tried to convince herself that she hadn't heard that.

Joe made a choking noise. "Jesus, lady! That's just too far!" he exploded. "Where do you get off?"

Khavi frowned and looked out the window. "Here, I suppose. Continue on, detective. I will watch you."

She vanished.

Taylor couldn't stop coughing. Fuck vampires—the goddamn cigarettes and crazy Guardians were going to end up killing her. Joe offered her a bottled water. She took it, drank.

To his bed. Many times.

She'd bet he had a great big bed, covered in white linen. Not too soft, but the kind that was firm—so that when he got going, she wouldn't sink into the mattress beneath his heavy weight but feel the full force of every deep . . .

Jesus. Oh, Jesus. Lifting the bottle again, she gulped more water. She was *not* going there.

But the image got into her head.

It didn't go away.

❧

Irena woke up on the sofa in her forge. She sat up. Her heart filled.

Alejandro watched her from the bath, his eyes dark. She must have been unconscious for some time; his hair and eyebrows had already grown in, the beautiful structure of his face had reformed, and his flesh had healed. His fingers no longer resembled flippers. And though his skin was still shiny and pink, at least he *had* skin again.

She walked to him. Ice floated in the bathwater. She realized the shine of his skin came from some kind of gel, not the burn. Or not *all* from the burn.

She kneeled beside the tub. "You frightened me."

"If we are to compare levels of terror, I warn you now that you will not win. Nothing you have will trump watching you fight that dragon." He studied her for a long moment. "If you fear that a kiss will hurt me, please choose this time to remember that I enjoy the pain."

She'd never needed anything as much as she needed that kiss. With a shuddering laugh, she surged forward. She held her hands back, gripping the edge of the tub, but her mouth found his and explored, reclaimed. *Olek, my Olek.* He lifted his arms from the water, thrust his fingers into her hair to pull her closer. Icy water dripped down her nape.

A sigh came from behind her.

As Irena looked around, she contained her snarl—barely.

Michael stood in his linen tunic and pants, holding her spear and her kukri knife. The blades flamed with magical fire before he extinguished them. "You will want these."

She *did* want them. Everything in her leapt toward them, but she remained kneeling beside Alejandro. "Will they not be most useful in your hands?"

He shook his head. "No. They will be more useful in yours—

and if you should ever face another dragon, it will not be so difficult to defeat."

Yes. His sword could slice through stone like it was water. The dragon's scales would part beneath these blades, too.

She rose to her feet. "Will you show me how to make them burn?"

"I cannot. Unless you wish to drink the dragon blood first." A smile played around his mouth when she shook her head. "I thought not."

He passed them to her. Irena's fingers wrapped around the weapons; they looked no different than before, but she felt the heat within. She vanished them, and felt their presence in her cache like a gentle burn against her tongue.

When she returned to Olek's side, he sat up, as if he intended to stand. She placed her hand on his shoulder and held him there.

His gaze warred with hers. Finally, he relented and sat back into the water. "What of Anaria? When do we plan to return to Chaos?"

"Anaria has already left the realm."

Irena wondered if she only imagined that resigned tone in Michael's voice. But if so, she wasn't alone. Olek's face tightened.

"What has she done?" he asked.

"She killed a small dragon. Its blood, its heart—they are hers. I *have* closed the portal beneath the sea . . . but it does not matter so much now."

Irena's blood ran as cold as the bathwater. "What does that mean?"

"It means she used the dragon's blood to weave a spell that weakens the barrier between Chaos and Hell. She will return to Chaos and smash through it, and take her nephilim army into Hell—or Lucifer will see its weakness and break through to Chaos . . . and then to Earth, bringing with him more dragons."

Olek's hand gripped hers. "So either Anaria will take the throne, and the nephilim will gain the power to enslave human will—or Hell will soon find its way to Earth, with Chaos behind it."

"Yes."

Irena tasted the heat of her blade and spear. "How do we stop it?"

"Khavi has seen a way. Dragon blood can weaken the barrier—but it can also make the barrier as unbreakable as the will of the person who casts the spell."

Relief lightened Olek's grip. "You have dragon blood now."

"Yes." Michael's psychic scent darkened. Irena's hand began to shake in Olek's. "And I was born of it, when my father drank the blood so that I could be conceived."

And so was Khavi. Together, could they stop Anaria? "Is she preparing the spell?"

"We cannot prepare. It can only be done when it is to be done."

Irena's hands did not stop shaking. His every word had increased her dread.

Olek said, "Where is Khavi now?"

"With Detective Taylor." Michael paused. He bowed his head before looking up at them again. His eyes were obsidian. "You have done well, the both of you. And I—"

His head snapped back as if he'd been struck. "Irena," he said without emotion. "I need use of your knife."

She called in the kukri knife and threw it to him.

He caught the blade and vanished.

❦

Taylor knew it would go bad the second Wren opened the door. Lukacs—a vampire now—stood in the foyer behind her.

With her hand behind her back, Taylor signaled to Joe. He stepped casually to the side of the door, out of Lukacs's sight, and drew his gun.

Taylor hadn't seen Khavi since the car. Was she watching? Was she seeing this?

Why wasn't she down here kicking Lukacs's ass yet?

"Good evening, detective," Wren said, then mouthed, *Go.*

"Good evening, Miss Wren. I apologize for the lateness of our visit and for failing to notify you that we were coming, but an issue with the security arrangements for tomorrow's ceremony has arisen. If you can accompany us to the funeral home, I believe we can quickly sort it out and return you to your duties."

Sheer relief filled Wren's usually expressionless eyes. "Of course, detective." She stepped out of the house, onto the porch.

Taylor didn't see Lukacs move. One second, Joe stood beside the door. The next, Lukacs had ahold of his jacket and was dragging him past the foyer.

Joe fired up at the vampire, hit his gut. The vampire snatched the gun away, and hauled her partner up. His fangs gleamed.

Taylor burst through the door, gun in hand. She aimed for the forehead, fired.

The vampire reeled back, dropping her partner. A bullet in the head sometimes stopped a vampire. Not always. This was one of the 'not always' times—but he'd released Joe, and that was what mattered.

Taylor sprinted for him. Behind her, Wren fired into Lukacs's chest. *Should have told her to go for the head.* Lukacs didn't have the same problem. The vampire lifted his gun, aiming for Joe's face.

Not a chance in hell was that going to happen. Taylor threw herself over her partner.

Sharp bursts of gunfire rang in her ears. Her chest and stomach felt as if she were punched—once, twice. Fire burned in her gut, in her lungs. Bullets. Holy shit. She hadn't worn her vest. The vampire had shot her. Maybe killed her.

She'd thought it was going to be fangs.

Her head swam. She couldn't breathe. She heard Joe's hoarse voice, then his shout to help her, please help her.

Taylor opened her eyes. *Oh, look. Michael.* Not Khavi. Lukacs must have caught her when they were switching shifts. Bad luck. Just bad luck.

God, she didn't want to die.

She turned her head. The vampire's head lay on the floor next to her, staring. His body was somewhere else.

Pain shot through her like another bullet when Joe touched

her. His wrinkled face filled her vision. She hadn't seen him cry before. Not even at her dad's funeral.

"Let him save you, kid. Okay? For me."

She thought she said okay. Then looking down at her was Michael, who wasn't going to love her anymore. His hand touched her face. His eyes were *so* black. She couldn't even see herself in them.

His harmonious voice sang in her head, so beautiful. "You have sacrificed your life to save another, Andromeda Marie Taylor, and so I can offer to you a transformation. You will be a Guardian, you will be immortal, and you will serve."

"All right—but only if you never use my full name again." Her reply sounded stronger than she was. Maybe it was only in her mind.

If so, he must have heard it. "No conditions. A yes, or a no."

How could she say no? She'd already promised Joe. "Yes."

Taylor thought she felt his relief. She knew she saw a brief smile on his hard mouth. He sat back, his gaze still on her, and vanished his tunic. Thick muscle carved his broad chest.

And *there* was Khavi, with one of Irena's knives, which suddenly caught fire. With the burning point, she sliced symbols into Michael's bronze skin. Blood welled. His gaze never left Taylor's. Soon the symbols covered his torso, his arms—and when Khavi moved behind him, Taylor thought his back must now be bleeding, too. Khavi cut a final symbol into the side of his neck.

Then Michael leaned over her again, lifted her to his throat. "You must drink."

Taylor fought her revulsion. Savi had never told her about this part of the transformation. With vampires, yes. Not with Guardians.

But maybe they kept it secret, like they tried to do with everything else.

"Please, Andromeda," Michael said—then, "Taylor."

She put her mouth to his neck. Gagging, but she managed to swallow once, twice. Michael pulled away. She thought she saw regret in his expression as he looked down at her. Then he lowered his head, and his mouth opened over hers.

Oh, she thought. His lips weren't hard at all, but just firm—and so warm. His tongue stroked into her as if he wanted her to taste him, as if he needed her flavor in return. She gave herself over to the sensation.

Then a brilliant white light came and burned all sensation away.

§

Irena did not hold Olek down again. Five seconds after Michael left, he was out of the tub and dressed. They both paced the forge. Olek used his phone; no one knew what was happening.

A few minutes later, when Irena was ready to scream with not knowing, Khavi appeared with Irena's knife.

Irena could not believe she was glad to see the woman.

Khavi passed her the blade, and Irena scented the blood on it. Her breath stopped in her throat.

"Michael?"

"He is transforming Taylor. Come with me."

Taylor? Irena held out her hand, not hesitating, and let the sorrow and relief circle within her. The detective had not wanted to be a Guardian, would not want to lose her life, her home, and Irena was sorry for that. And yet she was fiercely glad the woman would live—was glad Taylor would fight beside them.

She glanced at Olek, saw the same mixture of emotion before the room spun, dissolved. She held onto his hand as her feet steadied. The heavy scent of flowers filled her lungs. Gunpowder, blood—Michael's, Taylor's, a vampire's. She looked around, recognized the room, the furnishings. Rael's home.

They'd been teleported into his large living area, near the window overlooking the bay. In the middle of the room, a brilliant light surrounded Michael and Taylor—too bright. Irena had to look away. Wren stood near the fireplace, her face expressionless, her emotions in a wild, terrified storm. Irena did not need to read Preston's psyche; grief and hope etched his lined face as he stood near the center of the room, staring at Michael and Taylor.

The brilliant light that surrounded them slowly faded, and Irena saw that their mouths were fused together in a deep kiss. She could not stop her laugh. In sixteen hundred years, she had never seen Michael kiss a woman—or a man, for that matter.

Olek glanced at her, amusement in his gaze. "He did not transform *me* in such a manner," he said, and set her laughing again.

"Me, either," she said, when she caught her breath. Wiping her eyes, she looked again . . . and her laughter died completely.

Symbols decorated Michael's skin. She turned, searching for Khavi, hoping the grigori would have an explanation. But Khavi had gone.

A frown settled between Olek's brows. He turned to Wren. "Where is Rael?" When confusion slipped into her psychic scent, he said, "Stafford."

She shook her head. "I only saw the vampire."

The light of transformation vanished. Michael rose, holding Taylor cradled in his arms. He looked to Olek. "Take her."

Preston stepped forward. "I can—"

"She is strong—she does not know how strong," Michael said. "When she regains consciousness, she might hurt you without meaning to."

The detective looked torn, but nodded. "All right," he agreed—yet still followed Michael as he gave her to Olek, and hovered as the transfer was made.

Irena frowned when Alejandro's face tightened. She glanced at Taylor. Blood collected at the corners of her lips. Her eyes were wide and staring.

Irena had *never* seen a transformation affect a new Guardian in such a way. Unconscious, yes. Not empty.

"This blood on her mouth is yours, Michael," Olek said. "What have you done?"

His back was to them. His bare shoulders were low, as if he bore a heavy weight. "I have given her part of myself and my power, and linked her to me. She will be the new Doyen. She will not lead you, but she will be the one who transforms and brings new Guardians to—"

"*Doyen*?" Irena started forward, her fists clenched. Rage ripped through her—rage and fear. "What does that mean? Where will *you* be?"

"I do not yet know." His terror and dread spiked before he covered it. "Do not fight this, Irena. Please."

She could not bear that plea. Tears springing to her eyes, she turned, sought out Olek. His horror echoed hers.

When she turned back, Michael had straightened and covered the symbols on his body with a black tunic. Khavi stood next to him, sword in hand. Kneeling beside her was Rael.

If the demon was afraid, he didn't show it. Despite the blade against his neck, his expression remained quiet, watchful.

Irena called in her spear. Her chest heaved. She wanted to kill something, anything, and now the demon was here like a sacrifice.

Michael caught Irena's gaze, shook his head.

It took all of her strength to lower her weapon. Behind her, she heard Olek ordering Wren and Preston back into the corner of the room. Carrying Taylor, Alejandro positioned himself in front of the humans. Irena joined him.

Whatever was happening here, their priority was to protect the people behind them.

Not a sign of Michael's earlier fear remained. His face had hardened to stone, his eyes to obsidian as he looked to Khavi. "You were to watch her."

"I watched her. And I did what I saw was best." Her mouth tightened, and she glanced down at Rael. "And then I saw this murdering dog who killed my brother."

"I killed no one," Rael said. "And I would not kill Zakril, who was my friend."

Khavi snarled. Her blade drew blood. "Demon liar."

"I tell the truth. Put me in front of your Hugh Castleford. You will see."

"We do not need to." Michael crossed his arms over his chest. "I will make you a bargain, Rael. You have only to speak the direct truth—always—and for as long as I live, I will vow to protect you from all harm."

Rael's head whipped around so that he could look up at Michael. The demon's shock was genuine.

His shock couldn't match Irena's. She clenched her fists on her spear, met Alejandro's gaze. Why would Michael possibly do such a thing? What could he *ever* gain from it? What did it matter if Rael spoke the truth? By tomorrow, they would have slain the demon—but if the demon accepted the bargain, Michael would be damned to the frozen field in Hell if anyone hurt him.

Or had she missed something—some slick wording that would enable Michael to claim an advantage?

The demon seemed to be wondering the same. His brows had lowered, as if he searched for a trap.

Michael said patiently, "You cannot lie, and you must speak plainly to answer questions you are given—no matter who asks them. In return, I will prevent anyone from harming you."

"Even her?" Rael jerked his head toward Khavi, who growled at him. "And yourself?"

"Yes. Anyone," Michael repeated. "The only exception would be self-inflicted harm. If you should ever choose to kill yourself, I will not stop you."

"There is little chance of that." The demon smiled. "I agree, then."

"Then it is done," Michael said.

By the gods. Shaking, Irena looked to Olek. Anger hardened his face, directed at Michael.

The demon would never suffer the consequences of the deaths—from Julia Stafford, to Zakril, to Eva and Petra, and surely countless others—for which he was directly or indirectly responsible. And if the demon attacked any of the Guardians, none could defend themselves or kill Rael without damning Michael . . . or being stopped by Michael.

"Why?" Irena could not stop her cry.

How could this be anything but a betrayal of everything they were? The demon would have free reign . . . or the Guardians would be forced to hurt someone they loved.

"So that we can see if someone will choose love—and kindness," Michael said quietly. With amber eyes, he looked toward the sliding doors and the balcony. "What say you, Anaria?"

Rael stiffened.

Olek turned, set Taylor on the floor beside Preston. He called in his swords.

The sliding doors opened. Anaria stepped in, her black hair twisted by the wind. Her gaze never strayed to Irena and Alejandro in the corner. Her dark eyes fixed on Michael, ignoring the demon who stared up at her. Pained adoration filled his features.

"You knew I was here?"

Khavi said, "I knew you would come." She pointed at Alejandro. "That one opened a door when he told you of Rael's betrayal. You stepped through."

Rael cast Alejandro a dangerous glance, as if marking him for death.

Anaria looked to Rael. "Did he speak true, friend? Did you kill Zakril?" Her voice wavered on the name.

Rael's lips drew back from his teeth in a grimace of agony. "Yes," he forced out.

She bent over as if stabbed, clutching her fist to her heart. "Why? For two thousand years, all that sustained me was the thought of seeing him again. All that kept me from madness was the hope that he would be waiting. I have never known agony as when my children said their father was dead—and you are the reason, my *friend*. So tell me, why?"

"Because I love you." Rael's face twisted, as if he suffered the tortures of Hell. "And I have only lived in the hope that you would be free and I would see you again—and that you would find me worthy."

She shook her head wildly. "You speak true, but that is not love."

"Anaria—" Rael reached for her.

She stepped back. "Your love is worth nothing to me. I will never want it."

It was as if the demon broke. His hand fell to his lap. He closed his eyes. Anaria called in her sword.

Michael stepped forward. "You heard the bargain."

She hesitated, then shook her head. "You made the bargain *knowing* he was a liar and a murderer. And if he lives, now he will kill without repercussion. *You* must pay the price for your foolishness."

"Do you not think I could prevent him from continuing as he has?"

Irena's fingers trembled. *Yes,* she thought. *He would.* Michael would have found a way out. Or he would have expected one of his friends—his fellow Guardians—to find a solution. The Guardians' faith in each other had to go both ways, or they would never trust anyone at their back.

If Irena knew that, then surely, *surely* his sister did, too.

"No," Anaria said.

Infinite sadness seemed to come over Michael. "You do not *want* to believe. You say you will choose love, kindness, forgiveness—yet you will choose vengeance over my soul."

As if his disbelief in *her* ripped off a layer of calm, Anaria spat, "I was not the one to make the bargain!"

"But you make a choice now."

The calm settled over her once more. "Yes. I do."

Anaria turned and walked away. For an instant, Irena believed that it was all she would do, and this would be over—and the only thing left would be to find a way to keep Rael safe while preventing him from hurting anyone.

Like putting him in a box with steel walls ten feet thick. Or a magically-sealed sarcophagus, just as Anaria had been trapped—

Rael's head slid from his neck onto the floor.

Irena stared, her mouth dropping open. She had not seen Anaria move. But she must have struck when she'd walked away. Now, she was only a small dot flying over the bay.

Michael's face became a bleak mask. He could have stopped his sister, Irena realized. But he hadn't—and because he hadn't, he'd broken his bargain. Now, as soon as he died, his soul would be trapped in Hell's frozen field . . . and eaten by dragons in Chaos.

"Holy Mother of God," Alejandro murmured. "The symbols on his body. The bargain. *Michael* is the spell, Irena."

She looked at Olek in disbelief. "The spell to strengthen the barrier?"

"Yes," Michael answered for him. "I am the only one strong enough."

She faced him. "You knew? You knew when you made that bargain?"

"Yes. But I hoped that Anaria would make different choices. I hoped she would show just a little . . . a little . . ." His throat worked; he could not finish it. He shook his head and turned to Khavi, embraced her. He pressed his lips to her forehead. "Be safe. And study well, my friend."

Khavi threw her arms around him, held him tight. When she withdrew, tears streaked her face.

Realization tore its way through her. By the gods. It was not enough that Michael broke his bargain—he would not be in the field until he *died*. Michael intended to kill himself now.

"No!" Her knees failed her. Alejandro's arms came around her, his face pressing to her hair. Irena's sob caught in her throat. "Why, Michael? Do you have no faith in *us*?"

"I can only face this because I *do* have faith in you. This is only to give us time, so that Khavi can find a spell to strengthen the barrier without me."

And to find a way to bring him from the frozen field? Back from death? Could Khavi do that? "How much time?"

"I hope not long." He stopped in front of them. His amber gaze locked with hers. "And you will lead them well."

No. But Irena could not deny that duty. She clenched her teeth, but the long, low cry building up within her still escaped. Michael's lips brushed her forehead.

"Do you swear that you can come back?"

"Yes. You will find a way."

If she could not, one of them would. "Do you lie?"

A brief smile touched his mouth. "Bring me back, and I will not be a liar." He glanced up over her head, and clasped Olek's forearm. "I could not have asked for better warriors at my side."

Olek's hand tightened, didn't let him go. His silky voice had roughened into coarse sand. "We will not fail you, Michael. We will not stop fighting."

"I know. I have faith in that, too."

He stepped past them, nodded at Wren, shook Preston's hand. He crouched in front of Taylor. His hand caressed her cheek. He looked at her for an endless span of time—a breath, a heartbeat. Irena had memorized Olek's face in less time.

Finally, he dropped his hand to his side. His voice deepened to a harmonious command. "Wake up now."

When she blinked, he stood and strode to Khavi. She lifted her sword. The grigori's beautiful face seemed to crumple—she tilted her head back and screamed. Before it had faded, before Irena realized what she intended, Khavi stabbed her blade through his chest, through his heart.

Michael fell.

Irena hadn't seen her move—but Khavi didn't try to avoid her when rage and instinct tore her out of Olek's arms. She caught the grigori, slammed her to the floor. Her spear came into her hand, and she shoved the point against Khavi's throat.

Irena's breath shuddered through her clenched teeth. She did not know which of them was crying harder. "You predicted that a demon spawn would fall beneath my spear. You were right."

"No." Even tears could not obscure the ancient light in Khavi's gaze. "That future has changed. *You* have changed."

"Irena," Olek said quietly. "We need her to bring him back."

Irena's hand shook. Blood welled around the tip of the spear. "No, we don't. We will do it without her."

Khavi closed her eyes. Her Gift swept out, drew in. "Yes," she said. "But it will take much, much longer."

Irena glanced at Michael's body. Her scream built. She swallowed it. Not yet.

She stood, drew away from Khavi. "After we have brought him back, I will kill you."

"We will be good friends by then." Khavi flipped to her feet. "Taylor! You must put his body into the in-between. You must do it quickly."

Sitting by the wall where Preston and Wren still waited,

the new Guardian blinked, as if confused. She'd woken, Irena realized—but she was not yet all there.

Alejandro's brows drew together. "What is the in-between?"

"The hoard." Khavi's hands flitted as if she searched for the word. "The . . . the cache!"

Was she mad? Irena stared at her. "A just-transformed novice cannot know how to do that."

Khavi growled in frustration, and despite protests from Preston, led Taylor to Michael's body. "She will not be a novice when it is in her cache!"

What did that mean? Irena feared she would soon find out when Khavi sent out a psychic thrust that *felt* the same as Irena pulling something into her cache. Khavi placed Taylor's hand on Michael's chest, over the wound her sword had made. A low hum began in her throat, swelling, adding to the psychic pulse.

Khavi stared earnestly into Taylor's face. The hum increased, and Irena had to fight the overwhelming compulsion to vanish her knife, the sofa, her clothes—every object around them.

For an instant, Taylor's gaze cleared, and Irena recognized the woman behind the blue eyes.

Then Michael's body disappeared.

The whole of Taylor's eyes turned obsidian. Her body went rigid, her head snapping back, her neck straining. She opened her mouth. A terrified, agonized scream shattered the air—in a harmonious voice that wasn't just her own.

Michael. Irena stepped forward. Khavi and Taylor vanished.

"What happened?" Preston rushed forward, his eyes wild. "Is she all right? Where is she?"

"Caelum," Alejandro said. "She is well. Some transformations are difficult, and she has taken on more than most new Guardians. She has to adjust."

Irena turned away. Olek had no idea if half of that was true—but there was little reassurance they could give the detective at this moment, so he'd done what he could.

"For how long?"

"A few days, perhaps weeks. You will be the first to know

how she is." Olek paused. "We will let you handle her affairs as you see fit. SI will back you up."

"You mean, declare her dead?" Swallowing hard, his expression lost, Preston shook his head. "I'm not ready to do that yet."

"Then we'll help you delay, as well." Olek clapped a hand to the man's back, and turned to Irena. "Are we ready for Lilith?"

Irena nodded. She picked up Lukacs's head, ripped out the fangs, and tossed it back to the floor. She vanished Rael's body—they couldn't let that be found.

Thomas Stafford was still alive.

She looked over at Wren. "Job well done. You've captured and killed Julia Stafford's murderer."

She felt the butler's disbelief. "By cutting off his head?"

Irena searched for a plausible explanation. She could not find one. Irena could lie, but not *that* well. She looked to Olek. "I finally understand why having Lilith at Special Investigations is a good idea."

Alejandro's smile didn't last. He held her gaze as he shifted into Thomas Stafford's form. His eyes changed color and shape, yet remained the same.

She walked to him, touched his hand. "You are still my Olek."

"Forever," he said.

❧

From his seat on the sofa, Alejandro watched Irena enter the forge in a swirl of ice, wind, and snow. She barreled through, vanishing her wings and white mantle. Clumps of snow had caught in her hair; she shook her head wildly, spraying that side of the forge. Then she spotted him.

Her smile broke him apart. For almost two days, he had not seen it. Two days in which he'd begun to try out the new role of Stafford, in which he'd stood over a funeral and accepted condolences for a woman who was not his wife—but he *had* grieved. For Michael, and for Irena, who had not waited for his role to let him go so that he could accompany her as she traveled to each Guardian and told them how their Doyen had been lost.

But she had not gone alone—she had taken Drifter, on crutches as he regenerated his leg, but still able to put anyone at ease; and Selah, a teleporter whom everyone trusted, who'd mentored many, and whose smile and softness could lighten the deepest grief. By asking them to accompany her, Alejandro thought, she'd made a first decision that showed what good hands Michael had left them in.

And he knew she wouldn't have let herself go in front of them. Never would she have before Michael had passed on leadership; now, she would consume a mountain of spiders in Hell before she did.

Here, though, she would.

She walked to him, and when he rose to his feet, she gestured him back down. She came over him, straddling his legs with her leather-clad knees pushing into the cushions, lay against him—her chest to his, her wet and cold cheek in his throat.

He did not mind the icy slide of water down his neck.

He held her. She did not scream this time, but wept—tears that rolled into a storm of sobs before quieting again. His throat ached when she lifted her head to look down at him.

She did not hide the vulnerability in her face. Her fingers stroked his neck; her smile wavered. "I hope I do not add to your list of regrets, Olek. I needed you before; now, there will be times I lean on you heavily, for advice or support—and my weight is no longer all my own."

"I will take it all, Irena." His hand found hers, caught and held. And he said what he'd always thought had been too obvious to say, "I love you, Irena. Do you know this?"

Her eyes filled. "Yes."

"Do you know you are not just my heart, but my life? One moment fighting with you is worth ten thousand years without you. I would die for you. I would kill for you. I would endure an eternity of torture so that you could laugh, and live." His fingers tightened. "You have me. You have all of me. And I will take all of you. Do you know this? If I died today, would you know this?"

She nodded, her tears spilling. "Yes."

"Then I have no regrets. Not even one. I would only have been sorry that I did not tell you before."

Her hands caressed his face, his cheeks. Her eyes glowed a fierce green. "Days will come when I will hate you, Olek. But there will never come a second that I do not love you."

It was her vow, he realized—her pledge. "You have said it better than me."

She laughed, and her mouth found his. She kissed him, again and again, her hands searching—he would always be there for her to find. Alejandro held her to him. And thought that never before had there lived a man as blessed.

Or as well kissed.

EPILOGUE

Jake was the one who found Michael, but it was Khavi who took them to the frozen field.

Lucifer's throne rose in the center of the field, an enormous black tower. With her knife and spear ready, Irena stood in a blanket of absolute silence, where the screams sliced deeper than in Chaos—she could hear nothing but the screams in her head. The cold was so fierce it burned. The faces of the damned formed the uneven ground beneath her feet. She only looked for one.

Olek touched her shoulder and signed that they had found him.

Irena followed him, her gut in a twisted knot. How had Jake found one face among so many? In the week that had passed since Michael's death, Jake must have spent every spare moment under the shadow of Lucifer's throne, in the silence and the screams, searching.

Reckless, stupid. And she would thank him when they reached home again.

She came closer, and realized one voice rose above the others. A familiar voice—a harmonious one. The pain and terror it carried almost brought Irena to her knees.

Alejandro sank down beside him. Michael stared up, his eyes frozen open—fixed and alive, *seeing*—his mouth stretched in his scream of agony and horror.

Irena felt the soft draw of Olek's Gift. He placed his hands on Michael's face, warmed him.

Khavi knelt beside him, her tears falling from her cheeks as drops of ice. *Michael,* she signed. *We have not much time. You must listen.*

Her heart aching, pounding, Irena scanned the horizon. Darkness moved at the edges.

You are linked to her, Michael. She screams, Khavi signed quickly. *She screams and screams. Caelum cannot hear her voice—it can only hear yours. Soon she will scream the realm apart. You have to hold them in, or she will die. Caelum will die.*

Raw pain filled his amber eyes. Slowly, slowly, his frozen mouth closed.

His scream was silenced. Others rushed in to fill it.

A shadow spread across the top of the throne. Irena adjusted her grip on her spear.

Khavi looked up. *Lucifer. We will not fight him. Not today.*

Irena nodded. She knelt, put her hand against Michael's face. Cold, but warmed by Alejandro's Gift, the ice did not burn. *We will return,* she swore, and saw Alejandro do the same.

Khavi bent over him again. *We will save you,* she signed, and smiled. *I have seen it.*

Irena caught a painful breath. Michael's amber eyes softened and laughter came into them. And here, in the midst of Hell, they looked utterly human.

She held on to that as they left.

ᴀʟᴍᴏꜱᴛ ᴛʜʀᴇᴇ ᴍᴏɴᴛʜꜱ ʟᴀᴛᴇʀ . . .

Alejandro looked up from his desk as Irena strode into his office. She closed the doors behind her, locked them. She turned and replaced her gray tailored suit with longstockings and her brief shirt.

And because *he* preferred to be in his own form with her, he changed, too.

Her eyes narrowed. "I don't think that Lynne believes I'm a federal agent."

"No, she does not," he agreed. The receptionist had never believed it—perhaps because Irena always left with her hair more mussed than when she'd arrived. "Her latest suspicion is that you are a whore who comes in to relieve my loneliness."

That amused her. "Truly?"

"Yes." He regarded her closely. "Are you here so that I can talk you out of killing Lilith again?"

She grinned. "No. Taylor woke up."

Relief slid through him. *Finally*. Though her screams had stopped after their visit to Michael—the first visit of many—she'd remained in a catatonic state. He knew Irena had feared Taylor would not come out of it. And Preston's face had taken on too many new lines; his new position at SI could not distract him from his worry.

As it should be, Alejandro thought.

"How is she?"

Her grin dimmed. "Confused. Scared." She came around his desk in front of him, picked up the bound papers he'd been reading through to make room, and sat back on the edge. "I cannot believe we are all not running and screaming."

He smiled and touched her hands. They were strong. The others' acceptance of her leadership had come easily. Not without bumps, but Irena had worked to smooth them all. "Michael was not a fool."

She nodded and looked down at the papers she held. "What are you working on?"

"A health care bill. Do you want me to read it to you?"

Her lips twitched. "I am a very busy woman now, so only a summary. How will you vote?"

"I haven't decided. It has good points. It also panders to lobbyists and partisan rhetoric rather than looking at what is right for the people it is supposed to help. So I must decide whether it is a step in the right direction despite the flaws, and work to make it better—or to toss it out and start over again."

He'd gone on so long just to amuse her, but now he froze as her expression changed from amusement to admiration. And, he thought with an ache in his throat, *pride*.

She placed her hand over his heart. "You stay loyal to this."

"Yes." He swallowed past the constriction in his throat, and added, "It will likely mean a short political career."

Her smile reappeared. "How long, do you think? This does not fit you as well as it should."

No, not perfectly. He enjoyed the challenge—but this was not where he would finish. "Only as long as we must keep Special Investigations going—and until we have enough resources to create something similar . . . and autonomous. No demons. No government. No outside interests. Only our purpose. Once we have that, it's where I will be."

"And for now, you work both sides of the fence." She looked at him again, not with censure, but with admiration. "I would not be capable—so I am glad it is you who does this part of our work."

He tried to imagine her in meetings, sorting through details, arguing minute points of conflict. Every scenario he came up with ended with shattered furniture or blood—and in her curses, no animal would be left unfucked.

"I am glad as well," he said.

She laughed and replaced the papers on his desk. "You are speaking in Washington on behalf of SI tomorrow, yes?"

"Yes. Are you certain you will not accompany me? Michael was at the first meeting."

"I will practice diplomacy for a few more decades first." The laughter faded from her eyes, and they darkened. "But remind the committee that we are all that stands between them and Hell."

"They might perceive that as a threat."

"So be it."

She rose from the desk. His hands slid up her thighs as she straddled him in his chair, then up the length of her bare back. Her arms wrapped his shoulders.

She did not yet kiss him. "I have from Lilith to you a report of a nosferatu in Tibet."

He felt her anticipation. "You'll go with me on this hunt?"

"Yes. And then an hour in the forge?"

"Two," he countered.

"Two," she agreed easily. With serious eyes, she regarded him. "I think we will do this, Olek. We will rebuild the Guardian corps. We will beat back the demons and the nephilim and Anaria—and every other threat that appears. We will bring Michael back."

"We will," he said.

"And us. We will work, too." Her throat moved, as if she was suddenly overcome with emotion. "It has been a good fight, hasn't it?"

The best fight he could imagine. Yet that was too obvious an answer.

"You say that as if you've already won," he said instead.

He watched the familiar, challenging fire light in her eyes. Her fingers tightened in his hair. "Haven't I?"

"No." Alejandro brought his lips to hers, and said against them, "We are not near to finished."

*Be sure to watch out for
Meljean Brook's next Guardian novel
coming in the summer of 2010
from Berkley Sensation.*

Kissing Midnight

THE FIRST BOOK IN THE FITZ CLARE CHRONICLES
BY *USA TODAY* BESTSELLING AUTHOR

EMMA HOLLY

Edmund Fitz Clare has been keeping secrets he can't afford to expose. Not to the orphans he's adopted. Not to the lovely young woman he's been yearning after for years, Estelle Berenger. He's an *upyr*—a shape-shifting vampire—desperate to redeem past misdeeds.

But deep in the heart of London a vampire war is brewing, a conflict that threatens to throw Edmund and Estelle together—and to turn his beloved human family against him…

penguin.com

M413T0209